SO-BBB-639

Single MOM

A NOVEL

Omar Tyree

SCRIBNER PAPERBACK FICTION
PUBLISHED BY SIMON & SCHUSTER

SCRIBNER PAPERBACK FICTION
Simon & Schuster, Inc.
Rockefeller Center
1230 Avenue of the Americas
New York, NY 10020

*This book is a work of fiction. Names, characters, places, and incidents
either are products of the author's imagination or are used fictitiously. Any resemblance
to actual events or locales or persons, living or dead, is entirely coincidental.*

Copyright © 1998 by Omar Tyree

All rights reserved, including the right of reproduction in whole or in part in any form.

First Scribner Paperback Fiction edition 1999
SCRIBNER PAPERBACK FICTION *and design are trademarks
of Macmillan Library Reference USA, Inc.,
used under license by Simon & Schuster, the publisher of this work.*

Designed by Karolina Harris

Manufactured in the United States of America

10

The Library of Congress has cataloged the Simon & Schuster edition as follows:
Tyree, Omar.
Single mom : a novel / Omar Tyree.
p.   cm.
1. Afro-Americans—Fiction. I. Title.
PS3570.Y59S5   1998
813'.54—dc21   98-35892
CIP

ISBN 0-684-85592-5
0-684-85593-3 (Pbk)

This book is for the struggles
of my grandmothers
Mercyle Tyree Simmons (RIP),
Betty Alston (RIP),
and Geraldine Briggs McLaurin;
my aunts
Sharisse Simmons Tolbert (RIP)
and Darlene Simmons Crawford;
my sisters
Deidre Adams,
Darlene Adams,
and Cydnee Randall;
my mother
Renee McLaurin Alston (RIP)
for having me;
and my father
Melvin Alston Sr.
for stepping in
and showing me the way to manhood.

When I first held my son
Time 4:33 p.m., Date May 31st, 1996
I knew I'd never let him go
simply because he was mine
and so was his mother
they belonged to me
and I belonged to them

. . .

THE NATURE OF THINGS
by Omar Tyree

to be continued

The Years Before

N E E C Y ' S a big woman in Chicago now. I'm proud of her! She sure
has come a long way from where we grew up in North Lawndale. Neither one of us grew up in high-rise projects, but things were still like the
show *Good Times*: getting out of one adventure, only to be involved in a
new one. Times still are hard for me, and I've been going from one job
to the next like "James Evans" to prove it. Hopefully, my next job will be
more stable, but I've been saying that now for years.

Neecy, on the other hand, was always good at keeping a job, *and* with
saving money. I remember I used to laugh at how cheap she was back in
high school. She became my one and only girl in our sophomore year at
West Side High. She used to show up in the stands at all of my basketball games with her girlfriends and holler, "Wes-side, Wes-side!" We had
big fun back then!

Neecy has moved out to the suburbs now. She lives in Oak Park with
my son, Little Jay, and her other little boy, Walter. She doesn't want me
calling her "Neecy" anymore either. She say it's ghetto. I guess that suburbanite shit went to her head. You're never supposed to forget where
you come from, no matter *how* successful you are.

I remember when I first broke her in after school one day. It was in
our junior year. Neecy hollered so much I thought I cracked a bone or
something. I didn't have much experience in the bedroom back then. I
didn't know how to be gentle with her. I had to *learn* to be gentle, you
know, because I loved Neecy. She was my girl. And after a while, she got

used to it. We would find a place to get into things every night before my games. She said it was for good luck. The next thing I knew, we were doing it damn near every day, wherever we had to go. I bet she don't want to remember that now either. But she can't forget about our son. Little Jay is the tie that binds us forever.

I *need* to get his damn name changed, too! She calls him a Jr., but she didn't even spell his name the same way as mine. We argued about that in the hospital. I don't care if most people spell it with a "y." Mine is spelled with an "i-e." How are you going to call somebody a Jr. with the wrong spelling? On top of that, he doesn't even have my *last* name! She gave her other son *his* father's last name; Walter Perry III. Sounds like some nerd shit. That's exactly how his father looks, too, like a black nerd scientist in need of a good barber. His name should have been Walter Peabody. I met him a couple of times, and we spoke for a minute, but I didn't have too many words for him. The only reason he got with Neecy in the first place was because I got sent to jail. I was locked up in the Indiana State Correctional Facility for two and a half years for armed robbery.

Shit just all went downhill for me in my senior year of high school. Things were looking good before that. I had Neecy, my basketball future, and everything else. My pop even let me drive his baby blue convertible. It wasn't brand new or nothing, but it was clean. Then we lost our last play-off game to Martin Luther King High School. I was messed up for a whole week after that. I was really looking forward to winning the championship that year. The whole neighborhood was. It was a big letdown. Then I messed around and screwed up my grades. Not to say that they were all that good to begin with, but at least I was passing. My pop died of a stroke that year, and Neecy ended up getting pregnant on me.

The school officials said I had to take a couple of classes in summer school to get my diploma, but that messed up my chances of going to a Division 1 college on scholarship. I would have to go to a junior college and transfer. But that would have taken forever. That's when I started hanging out with the Gangster Disciples. Since I was a star ballplayer, they never really pressed me to join before, but once I realized I wasn't going to college, I saw no reason *not* to join. All of my homeboys were already members, including my older brother, Marcus, and my younger brother, Juan.

I remember Marcus asked me, "What the hell are you doing? You take your stupid ass to college!" If he was so concerned about *me*, then why the hell was *he* in it? My little brother, Juan, was in before I was, so when I started hanging around, he was excited by the idea. Juan could never play basketball, so me being in a gang with him was like getting a brand-new brother to relate to. Since Marcus didn't want either one of us in the first place, we obviously couldn't hang with his crew, so we had our own. And I was the first knucklehead to go to jail. Fortunately, my jail time saved my life, but I can't say the same for my brothers, or for many of the other guys I hung out with. Most of them are dead now, including Marcus and Juan.

If I could do it all over again, I would never have gone near that gang shit. I would have listened to my older brother, buckled down, gotten my grades together, and gone wherever I had to go to play ball and make it to a good school. That's why I'm supporting my boy now. I want to make sure he gets his grades and his game together and goes to school on scholarship, like I never got the chance to do.

At six foot three and two hundred twenty pounds, I'm no small fry of a man, but Little Jay is already six foot five, and he's only fifteen! He's not as solid as I am, but he's still a kid right now. Little Jay may grow to six-nine or six-ten before it's over with. When kids get that kind of height, they can go pro right out of high school! Look at Kevin Garnett. He grew up in Chicago. And I don't hear anybody complaining about tennis players, young gymnasts, and ice skaters and shit going pro as teenagers, so why complain about these poor black high school boys going pro? Half of the damn kids that play tennis, gymnastics, and ice skate are already rich! I want to see my boy get the best out of life, too. And he can take his old man along with him. I had a hard way to go. Believe me! So my boy can score big now for both of us. Yeah, yeah!

J.D.

T H I N K I N G with the wrong head will never fail at getting an adventurous man into trouble. Now that I'm older and wiser, I honestly don't know *what* I was thinking when I got myself involved with a young mother and child! And even with her curvaceous, smoother than chocolate body, and the sex being as good as it was, how could I ever make the mistake of going unprotected and getting the woman pregnant *again?!*

I had no intention of ever marrying Denise. That's the simple and ugly truth of the matter. She just wasn't my type. That's not to say that Denise Stewart is a bad woman, or a bad mother, because she's not. In fact, she's been able to beat many of the odds associated with being a single mother. Nevertheless, I didn't find her to be sophisticated enough. Not to mention having to introduce her to my parents back home in Barrington. It made no sense to go through all of that. Marriage simply wouldn't have worked between us. We were two fish meant to swim in different streams.

With my monetary help and support, Denise has been able to do a commendable job as a single parent, and I have felt very proud of her accomplishments, as well as guilty about my role in her life's hardships. However, I *do believe,* at present, that it would be best for her to begin thinking ahead in regards to her children's growth and development and less on her need as a single mother to beat the odds.

Denise is a very strong-willed and determined woman, and she has been a hell of a mother, but statistics have shown that few women have been able to successfully raise young black boys in America alone. It's not a question of whether she *can* handle it, it's more a question of *should* she? The bottom line is this; I don't want to go into any long-winded, philosophical discussions about my decision, I just feel that it is time for Denise to pass the baton of parenting. I'm not trying to take her son, *our* son, away from her, I'm simply trying to do what I feel is right.

In fact, ever since attending the Million Man March with my son on October 16, 1995, in the nation's capital, I have thought long and hard about the responsibilities of fatherhood and to the African-American community. Denise is about to have two black male teenagers on her hands in another year, and I strongly believe that situations are about to become tougher than she could possibly be prepared for. I would like to step in and do my part now instead of later. Lord knows, I've already wasted enough valuable time being away from my son. It's time for me to step up with conviction and become the full-fledged father that I should have become twelve years ago.

Walter

DENNIS BROCKENBOROUGH

DENISE is a hell of a woman! In all of my years of chasing potential partners, I've never come across a woman like her. She's so damn confident and spunky! She could probably run for president and come in third, which would be damned good for a black woman in America! She's a hell of a catch, no doubt about it. I just didn't know *if* or how long I could expect to hold on to her.

I met Denise at the Black Women's Expo '96, inside of the huge McCormick Center along Lake Shore Drive. Me and a couple of the other drivers at Freeway Trucking Companies tossed on some sports jackets, slacks, and ties, and went down there just to see how fine those got-it-goin'-on sisters would be. I happened to stop and strike up a long conversation with Denise at her business booth—Present & Future Finance—about individual retirement accounts. She was a tall, deep brown sister with short-cut hair, and was full of zest for life, dressed in a charcoal gray suit. You could tell that she really cared about what she was doing, and she sure knew a lot about money, too. I thought the only thing women knew about money was how to spend it and how to hide it from their man. Denise sure taught *me* different! She knew how to make your money work for *you*.

I had a couple of lunch dates with her to discuss her business further, and the possibility of me becoming one of her clients. I really wanted to date her, but I would settle for doing business with her, especially if she could help me to invest my money, while giving me a little bit of her time. Then I offered to take her on a ride in my new tractor, a Volvo White. At first, she thought I was joking and laughed it off, but I was serious. I only offered a ride in my truck to sisters who I wanted to impress. You'd be surprised at how many women wanted to *at least* sit in my trucks over the years. My Volvo was only a year old at the time, and I didn't want to get into the habit of using it as a showpiece. Denise was only the third woman I allowed to sit in it, and the *only* woman who I asked along for a ride.

After a couple of weeks of reminding her about my offer, she finally found a weekend to take me up on it. The fellas on the job thought it was a long shot of me ever getting a chance to sleep with her. They thought she would turn her nose up, you know, like a white collar/blue collar thing. They had Denise painted all wrong. She wasn't even like that. I believed that she liked me from the start.

When we finally did indulge, in a nice hotel room near the Chicago Midway Airport, I let loose and did things I would never even *think* about telling the fellas. I made it my wild secret, and I planned on keeping it that way.

Denise asked me how often I took women to hotel rooms and got raunchy. She wanted an honest answer, too. She was born and raised on the West Side of Chicago, so I knew she wasn't one of those weak-minded sisters who couldn't take a man telling her the honest-to-God truth. That was another thing I liked about Denise, she had a strong stomach and was ready for the world.

I told her that I had done my share of women in my day, and that I had been married once to a whiner for two years, and had gotten a divorce before we had any kids. I told Denise that I had gotten an STD—chlamydia—only once, in my early years as a truck driver, and that I made sure to protect myself ever since. Then I told her that I had *never, ever* gotten as raunchy with *any* woman as I had been with her. I told her that if I never got the chance to sleep with her again, I wanted to give her a night she would never forget. She laughed real hard and said that she probably wouldn't.

The weird thing about my relationship with Denise was that she was reluctant to tell me much about her family situation. She had two sons from two different fathers, and no matter how hard I tried, she never went into detail about it, even after I met her two boys.

I figured I would do things with them that I would do with my own sons, if I had any. Truth is—I'm scared to find out—but I don't know if

I'm shooting blanks or real bullets. I tried plenty of times to set a bun in the oven with my ex-wife, but she never got pregnant. Maybe that's why she whined so much. Maybe she thought it was *her* fault.

Anyway, Denise introduced me to her two boys as a friend. I just recently got a chance to play miniature golf and basketball with them, as well as take them on a ride in my truck. I think they both realized that their mother and I were a little more than just friends, but since I've always had what the fellas call "boyish charm," I think they liked me anyway. I liked them too.

The older boy, Jimmy, was quieter and more easygoing than the younger one. Walter had that spoiled child thing going on. He pouted a little too much for his own good. He was one of those kids who needed extra attention. Jimmy was the total opposite; he seemed like he didn't need *any* attention. And boy could he play some ball! He had fast hands, fast feet, and the agility of a cat. That was especially good considering how tall he was at such a young age. I considered myself a tall, six foot one, rugged man, but Jimmy had me beat by a few inches when I first met him at fourteen. He looked like he grew another inch or two since then. The boy was a subtle giant with a baby face until he got on a basketball court. Then he turned into an athletic monster, slammin' and jammin' everywhere! Jimmy was a good kid, too, with no behavior or attitude problems from what I could see. The only blemish against him was that he had failed a grade. Denise told me that the Chicago school system had actually passed him to the fourth grade, but she wanted him to repeat the third grade at a more challenging school, because she felt he didn't know what a nine-year-old should.

Walter, on the other hand, had excellent grades, and was obviously bright and creative. I could tell just from the things that he said and noticed. Nevertheless, I think he was jealous of his big brother's athletic ability, and the fact that Jimmy had more friends than he did.

Denise told me that they had just recently moved into the Oak Park suburbs, and that Jimmy left a lot of friends behind in Chicago. He didn't seem too attached to his buddies in the Big Windy to me. I think Walter took it worse than Jimmy did. In fact, I was sure of it. Maybe Walter wanted to associate more with kids from the West Side in order to feel that he was connected to the toughness of the city. Walter needed a father figure *badly*. Both of them did. And if their fathers weren't serious about playing a more committed role in their lives, then I was seriously thinking about picking up their slack.

I liked both of Denise's sons, and I figured it would be a noble decision to be a father to two boys who could use one, as well as a good man to a hell of a sister. All Denise Stewart had to do was say that she would have me.

Brock

F I R S T of all, I don't blame the white man, the black man, my parents, the Chicago streets, or anyone else for the crazy decisions that *I* made in my youth. I was young, naive, and hasty, like many of these other girls out here today, running around believing that some little boy loves them. And I don't blame a lot of these little boys out here for wanting to get inside of a girl's pants either, because that's how God made them. But I *do* know that we *all* need to start teaching children how to be more responsible about sex, *and* to be prepared to deal with the consequences of their actions.

Now, just because I feel that way, and just because I've started to go to church every Sunday, that does not mean that I think I'm perfect. Nor do I *abstain* from sex and going out with men, because I am *not* a nun. I'm just saying that we *all* need to reevaluate what's going on with teenage pregnancy and this single-parent household thing.

I don't have delusions that every mother and father are just *supposed* to be together, but society does need to address some of the issues that don't make any damn sense to me. Like, for instance: welfare recipients aren't allowed to have their children's fathers around. Then if the mother goes out and gets a job, she ends up getting stripped from most of the housing and health care benefits that she still needs. These damn fast-food chains don't pay women the kind of salaries, nor afford them the kind of benefits, they need to raise a healthy family. And this whole child support thing, with deadbeat dads, just pisses me off! I mean, if a man has a child, and he *knows* that it's his child, does he think that this infant is just going to feed itself, clothe itself, take care of itself, and pay for its own diapers and medical needs? Some of these men out here are just plain trifling! And now, all of a sudden, my oldest son's father wants to be Daddy again because the boy can play basketball. Yeah, no thanks to him! J.D. hasn't even bought his son a pair of sneakers in *eight* years! And them damn things cost money, because the cheap ones won't stay on his big-behind feet!

I really don't mean to sound all harsh and mean-spirited or whatever, because I'm usually a nice person, but no one has given me a *thing*, and it's probably made me a lot less sympathetic to all the hypocrisy that's going on in society today. I have to mention that to Walter Jr., every once in a while, because he figures he did me some kind of favor by supporting *his* son. That money wasn't going to *me*. I wouldn't even think about using my kids like that, but some women do, and that's what makes these child support cases a lot more difficult than they need to be.

Walter wants to be a father now, too, especially after taking his son to the Million Man March a couple of years ago. Then the boy got in trouble for shoplifting last year, and Walter kicked his commitment to fatherhood plan into fifth gear, as if *he's* going to be around to supervise his son's behavior every second of the day. Kids are *all* going to do some things that they'll need reprimanding for, but since Walter thinks he has all of the answers, he doesn't know any better. He actually thinks that our son is turning into a thug, which is the furthest from the truth. I delivered the boy, and I've been around him his entire life, so I *know* better than that, nor would I *allow* him to become a thug! However, he does burn more of my energy than my first son *ever* did!

Another recent development in my life has been my younger sister, Nikita. She has one daughter from a jailbird, just like my first love, and now, she's moving on to more confused, sex-driven men, who are scared to death of any kind of responsibility. She is really taking me to the test. She's looking to jump into the same ugly bed that I'm climbing out of every morning. After telling her over and over again to think about the decisions she makes, the only other thing I can do is grab ahold of her panties and hold them up against her will. And I can't do that. Nikita's a grown damn woman!

I would have to say that the bright spots in my life, that keep me going, are my faith in God, my love for my two sons and family, my single mothers' support group, and my career. Oh, and I do have a new companion in my life who keeps things bearable for me when times get hard. The man can really hold a good conversation. Dennis is older, mature, divorced with no kids, and definitely my style; over six feet tall and all man. J.D. was my style, and my first love, but he was never mature. And Walter was none of the above. He was short, insecure, skeptical, and another damn story altogether. But I really don't know how far things are going to go with Dennis either. I honestly don't expect much in relationships anymore. Dennis could be here today and gone tomorrow like so many other men in our lives. I'm not sure if it would work out in the long run anyway, so I just take things one day at a time. I mean, if we stay together, then fine, but if not, then that's fine too. Like my best friend and troubleshooter, Camellia Jenkins, told me when we first met, "Girl, a man can make your day, but only *God* can make the universe!"

Who said that men could make the universe anyway?

Denise

July 1997

Basketball

WHAAAAAHH . . . ! Whaaaaahh . . . ! Whaaaaahh . . . !"

"Neecy, what the hell is wrong with him?" I had my son in my arms, cradling his head, rocking him back and forth, and trying my best to calm him down and stop him from crying, but it wasn't working. He was six months old. I was nineteen, and that crying shit was driving me crazy! I wasn't ready for no damn kids! But Neecy was taking it in stride.

She said, "He's teething."

"Well, how come he only does this shit at night?"

"That's when his teeth grow the most."

"Oh, well, that's just great. So when are we supposed to get some damn sleep?"

I didn't know the first thing about kids. And I was terrible at changing diapers.

Neecy looked at me like it was no big deal. She took a deep breath and said, "I'll hold him."

I gave him to her and climbed back in bed. We were staying in my small room at my mom's place at the time. Marcus had already moved out. It was 1982. We planned to get married that next year when we could afford our own place and a decent wedding.

Neecy took Little Jay out into the living room that night where she and my mom finally got him to stop crying. I felt relieved that he was quiet again, but I felt kind of useless too. It didn't seem like anything I did was right. Little Jay never stopped crying for me. I was thinking that maybe my son didn't like me, and he just wanted his mom and his grandmother, you know, that motherhood bonding thing.

When Neecy got back in bed, I asked her, "How come he don't stop crying for me?"

She took another deep breath and sighed. I could tell she was getting tired of my whining. But what the hell, I was going out of my mind! I just wasn't prepared for a kid.

Neecy said, "You just have to be more patient with him. He would stop crying for you. You just have to stop getting so excited about everything."

That was easier said than done. Getting excited was how I lived. I was always hyper. It was in my genes, I guess. So how the hell was I supposed to be calm and deal with a kid? That shit seemed impossible. I started thinking that maybe I would be more useful once the boy got older and started walking and talking.

That night was the beginning of the end for me. My concentration was already shot from not getting a chance to go to a Division 1 college and run ball. Then I had a baby to deal with. I started smoking weed and hanging out with the GDs to get away from all of the stress. Then I just stopped coming home altogether, afraid of my own family, like a big punk.

My little brother, Juan, said, "I wouldn't even worry about it. It's not like Mom ain't there to help out. So don't even sweat it, man. Mom ain't gon' let nothing happen to him."

What the hell was I doing listening to him? It was a good thing Juan never had any kids, but many brothers who thought just like him were. And we grew up in the same household, with our father. The saddest thing about it was that the comment made sense to me at the time. Let Neecy and my mom raise the boy. They knew more about babies anyway. They were mothers.

That was fifteen years ago. So of course, I haven't always been around my son, and I couldn't really argue if Neecy decided to bitch about me wanting to spend a day or two with him after so many years of not being there for him. But he was still my son, so she couldn't really *stop* me from seeing him either. It wasn't as if I was an abusive father to him or anything.

I remember she used to complain all the time when I did get him. She said I was taking Little Jay to all of the wrong places. It wasn't like I was trying to, I just knew all the wrong people everywhere I went. Being a part of a gang family and spending time in prison will do that for you. But now it's different, since she moved him out to Oak Park. Little Jay is old enough not to be influenced by my gang affiliation anyway. Or at least I *hope* he is. He doesn't need to be involved in that shit no more than I needed to be. Just to be on the safe side, though, Neecy made me promise to stay in her neighborhood with him. Ain't that some shit? I felt like I was on probation again.

Not only did I promise to stay in Oak Park, I also agreed to meet my son at the playground instead of at their house. I hope Neecy didn't think that I would rob her or something stupid like that. I stopped that dumb stuff a long time ago. I didn't want to get into an argument about it though, so I just told her that I'd meet him at the playground.

I got to the playground at quarter to eleven. It was still nice and cool outside before the summertime heat kicked in. I was supposed to meet my son closer to ten, but I got off to a late start. He was already there at the playground when I arrived, and he was shooting foul shots.

I watched him make four consecutive shots from the foul line before I let him know I was there. It was just him and the basket, and some smaller kids at the other end of the court. Since it was Oak Park, most of them were white kids.

"I guess you can coach Shaq, now," I said to my son. "You want me to call up the Lakers for you?"

He turned, noticed me, and smiled. Little Jay never talked much. He was more of a watcher, one of those kids who takes everything in. He definitely had my size, but he looked more like his mother in the face. I always had a serious, rugged look about me. Little Jay looked more like a black man's model for tall men in elegant suits. The advertisers would love him!

I grabbed the ball from him and shot around. I was so out of shape, it felt like I was playing in water. I looked like Mr. Universe when I first got out of jail, but that was over eleven years ago.

I hit the ground after a layup and felt like a giant sack of Jell-O. "Shit!"

Little Jay just laughed at me. Then I went ahead and challenged him like a fool.

"What, you think you got something for me, partner? Come on and show me then."

My son looked at me, embarrassed. He didn't have to say it, it was obvious. He was thinking, *Go on home, old man. Go on home.* That only made me more persistent.

"Check me the ball at the line," I told him and walked to the foul line. I tossed off the Chicago Bulls baseball cap I was wearing.

Little Jay shook his head and started to laugh again.

I said, "Come on now, give me the damn ball."

By that time, the youngsters at the other end of the court had stopped shooting to pay attention to us. They had all seen my son play before, but I know they didn't know who *I* was. They probably thought I was some crazy old man about to get his ankles and his pride broken. And they were right.

My son finally checked me the ball, and I took off with my old high school moves. It must have looked like I was in slow motion. Little Jay smacked the ball out of my hand before I could even get the shot above my head. Those youngsters broke out laughing. That should have been enough to make me quit, but I convinced myself to keep going, like a kamikaze pilot.

"All right. Good one. Now check me again," I told him. "It ain't over wit' yet. We just gettin' started."

When he checked me the ball at the line again, I backed up and tried a jump shot. Little Jay got just enough of it to turn the shot into an air ball. Then he grabbed it before it bounced out of bounds and casually reverse dunked it.

"Whooo-weee! Do that one again, man!" Those youngsters were enjoying that early morning show like it was the Harlem Globetrotters. I liked my son's reverse dunk myself.

"Okay, let's see what kind of moves you got," I said with a grin. It was pretty clear that I wouldn't have anything for him. At least not before I spent a couple of months working on my game and endurance. So I figured I might as well play my role in the clown show.

I checked my son the ball, and Little Jay took a quick step to the basket, put on the brakes, and shot the ball in my face, while I stumbled backwards over my own feet. If I didn't have any basketball skills of my own, I would have fallen flat on my ass.

"Good one," I told him.

One of our little spectators shook his head and said, "You better quit while you're ahead."

I said, "I ain't ahead *yet*," and kept on playing.

After a while, I tried to use my weight advantage and experience to back my son down under the basket. It worked a couple of times, but then he started to back off and wait for me to shoot. I gave him a couple of head fakes, but that didn't work either. He ended swatting my shots around like we were playing volleyball.

"That's enough, man," he told me. "I got a game to play later on." He held the ball away from me as if I were a child.

I gave up trying to get it from him and asked, "Oh yeah? Where is this game at?"

"At the rec. center out here," he answered.

I was already drenched with sweat, and we had only played for about ten minutes. I should have brought an extra pair of shorts and a T-shirt with me, especially since I knew we'd be meeting at the playground that morning. It was an easy guess that we'd end up running some ball. I had already fantasized about it after seeing Little Jay play a couple of his junior high school games. Those younger kids in junior high couldn't stop him from scoring. He told me that he averaged 33 points a game, and I believed him! He scored 38 and 32 points in the two games that I saw. Little Jay was *more* than ready for high school. And I mean *varsity!* He would be enrolling in his freshman year of high school in September.

My son continued to hold the ball and began to walk off the court. "Where are you going?" I asked him.

He said, "I'm going home to change. And I'm thirsty."

I didn't know what to say at first. I was wondering if he knew about his mother not wanting me over at the house. I figured we'd sit down on the benches and shoot the breeze, father and son. I didn't know exactly what to talk about with him, but girls would have been a pretty good start. Whenever a young man plays any kind of sport well, he's going to attract the attention of big butts in tight skirts, especially with Little Jay's choirboy looks. He was the kind of quiet, good boy that girls could take home to their fathers.

Fathers never liked me. I don't know if Neecy's father, Antonio, would have liked me either. Her father died in a car accident before I met her in high school. It was a case of drunk driving, so Neecy made sure that I never mixed the two. She showed me plenty of pictures of her father. Come to think of it, that's exactly who Little Jay looked like. It's sad, but my son hadn't gotten a chance to meet either one of his grandfathers. By the time he was born, my dad was dead too. It must be some kind of epidemic going on with black fatherhood in this country. A lot of us are just not making it, and for a lot of different reasons. You have death, jail, no jobs, scared brothers who run away like I did, and then you have some mothers who don't even want the fathers involved. I knew of a couple of guys like that myself. It was a good thing Denise wasn't like that.

I started daydreaming about the good old days of hanging out with my old man. I used to love seeing his rugged brown face up in the stands at my games, even when he wasn't all that healthy sometimes. He was my father, and I respected him. I loved him. Little Jay snapped me out of my daydream by passing me the ball. I guess it was time for me to develop some good old days with my own son.

"Hey, Jimmy, is that your father, man?" one of those youngsters asked him. The kid was speaking kind of low, but young, rowdy kids have never been good at whispering.

I felt kind of awkward about Little Jay's answer. My heart skipped a beat. I was actually nervous about it. What would Little Jay say, and how did he really feel about me? I hadn't been around him as much as I should have been. I don't think I would have responded that great if my father had been in and out for years.

Little Jay smiled that easy smile of his and said, "Yeah."

I was relieved. Big time! I got myself together and followed my son off the court. His good answer got me new respect from those youngsters who had been laughing at me. All of a sudden, they were looking at me in awe, as if they wanted autographs or something. I looked back at them and spun the basketball on my index finger. I said, "I used to be good, too, when I was *his* age." Those youngsters even looked like they believed me.

Neecy lived just three blocks from the playground. I didn't say much on the way, I was just checking out the sights. Little Jay had it good, and I'm damn sure certain that he knew it! Oak Park had the green grass and the healthy trees that *all* neighborhoods should have. Black families had just started moving out there not too long ago. That's when the whites usually begin to move out. I was wondering if the white neighbors were ready to call the police and report us as two suspicious-looking black men in shorts with a basketball. I still had a guilty conscience to deal with over my previous lifestyle. That guilty conscience was something I had been working on. It's harder to get out of a mental jail than it ever will be to get out physically. That's why so many guys go right back in once they're released. They've been conditioned to feeling guilty, and a guilty conscience will lead to guilty actions every time.

I said, "So what do you think about your new neighborhood?"

Little Jay smiled and said, "I like it."

"What about your little brother? I bet he likes it, too," I assumed. *His* father didn't come from the West Side like Neecy and I did, so Walter III was probably used to seeing the good life. I heard his daddy grew up in North Illinois somewhere. People have plenty of money and land up on that northern end, or at least from what I've heard, because I've never been there to see it for myself. I even wondered if Neecy had ever been up that way.

Little Jay shook his head and smiled again. "Sometimes he do, sometimes he don't."

I was surprised. "What don't he like about it?" I asked.

"He just don't like living in the suburbs."

I burst out laughing. "He don't like living in the suburbs? What he think, he's a city slicker?"

"I guess so."

We got to the front door, and Little Jay pulled out a key that hung on a metal chain, under his T-shirt. I hesitated at the door. "I'll just wait for you out here," I told him, sitting on the front steps.

He looked back at me and asked, "You want me to get you a T-shirt and some shorts? I got some that can fit you."

I looked at him and grinned. Baggy clothes was the style of the day with young folks. "You know, we wore extra-large clothes with no belts in jail, because that's what they gave us. Now you young guys are running around, wearing extra-large clothes and no belts because it's trendy." I laughed and said, "All right then, hook me up, and I'll wash them and give them back to you next time."

I was still hesitant to go inside, but Little Jay was waiting for me. I guess he didn't want me sitting outside on the steps, sweating and whatnot.

"You not coming in?" he finally asked me.

I was acting ridiculous, and so was Neecy. Little Jay was the only one making any sense. I wasn't going to rob their house! What kind of a father would I be if I did that?

I got up and said, "Yeah, I'm coming in. What the hell?"

Neecy had bright blue carpet throughout the house, with nice furniture that I didn't want to sit on until I got out of those sweaty clothes.

"Damn! It looks like your mom put a lot into this place," I said. The house's two stories didn't look that elaborate, it was just extra clean, and a long way from where Neecy and I had grown up.

Little Jay smiled and led me to his room. He had a bunch of basketball posters on his walls; Anfernee Hardaway, Shawn Kemp, Barkley, Pippen, Jordan.

"Which one is your favorite?" I asked him.

"Hardaway."

I nodded. "You wanna play guard?"

He hunched his shoulders. "I don't know yet. If I keep growing, maybe I'll play the three position, like Pippen and Grant Hill."

I nodded again. "Yeah, that's what I thought about it. I played the two and the three when *I* was in high school. As you can see, I wasn't as tall as you, though. I would have had to play the two in college. And I had a chance to go to a couple of junior colleges, but I didn't."

I was hoping my son would ask me why, so I could give him an early pep talk about staying focused in school, but he didn't, so I figured I would save it for later. I didn't want to push anything on him, especially so soon. He hadn't even started high school yet.

My son gave me a change of clothes, and I put them on in the bathroom. That place was spotlessly clean, just like the rest of the house, and it smelled like incense.

Shit, this woman is serious! I guess I should stop calling her "Neecy," I told myself.

I walked out of the bathroom in my son's clothes, and he tossed me some sport deodorant.

"I stink, too, hunh?" I asked him with a chuckle.

He reached out his hand and said, "If you don't want to use it . . ."

I said, "Naw, I'll use it. And thanks."

I was feeling good about my son. Our relationship was just fine. I was sure glad he wasn't one of those disrespectful punks that talk shit about their fathers. I mean, I *did* realize that I was far from perfect, but I never put a hand on his mother, and I did come and get him whenever I could. I *know* I could have done a lot more, but that was all in the past.

I said, "You know, I start this new night job next week. Hopefully, if I'm able to keep this one, I'll be able to see a lot of your games this year." My son was actually the main reason why I even applied for a nighttime position. I would have rather had a daytime gig, but once I thought about Little Jay in his freshman year of high school, I figured it might have been a blessing in disguise for me to have a nighttime job. I could go to more of my son's games than my father could make to mine.

He looked at me and asked, "What kind of hours do you work?"

"From twelve to eight," I told him.

He said, "Man, I hope you don't fall asleep in the stands."

I laughed and said, "Naw, your games wouldn't be until later on, right? And I don't need that much sleep. I ain't raisin' no baby or nothing." Then I smiled and said, "I remember when you used to sleep all day and cry all night. So this'll be just like old times with me staying up late on account of you."

We shared a laugh. Then I asked him, "So where's this rec. center? Is it big, with fiberglass backboards and whatnot?"

"Yeah, it's pretty big, but they don't have fiberglass backboards."

Nevertheless, I couldn't wait to see the place. I hadn't been inside of a good-looking gym in a *long* while. I hung out that entire day with my son, watching several summer league basketball games. He was one of the youngest and tallest guys on his team, and the coach had him playing small forward, just like I thought he would. Jay played the position well, too. He scored 19 points, had four blocked shots, and plenty of rebounds. His team won 68–54.

Jay told me their record was 7–1. The only game they lost, he had fouled out of. The play-offs for the championship started in another week. Then Jay told me he would be joining another league. It was early July, and he had already played in a spring league. I used to play basketball all year long when I was his age, too.

Before I got ready to leave him, I told my son to tell his mother I said thanks for her cooperation. I saw a recent photo of her in the living room that I was thinking about for the rest of that day.

"Is your mother, ah, talking to somebody?" I ended up asking my son. I really didn't feel right asking him that, nevertheless, I wanted to know. I *had* to know! I was feeling lonesome. I mean, I had a few women I was seeing off and on, but they weren't like Neecy. Neecy was prime, barbecued rib. The other women I had were cold hot dogs, with no mustard. *Why couldn't I have done things right?* I asked myself. *I could have had a beautiful family with Neecy.*

Jay looked shocked by the question. "Hunh?"

I know he didn't want to answer me, but I pressed him anyway. I had already asked, and it made no sense to turn back.

"Who is your mother seeing? You heard me."

I tried to make it sound as lighthearted as I could, but I still wanted to know.

Jay laughed and looked away a few times.

"I'm not gonna cause any trouble, man, I just wanna know," I told him.

"She's talking to some truck driver." He still couldn't look me in the face when he said it.

I was shocked as hell! "A *truck driver?* You bullshittin' me?" There was no way in hell I was going to believe that! *A truck driver! Ms. Denise "Big Shot" Stewart that didn't want to be called "Neecy" anymore! No-fuckin'-way!*

Jay looked at me and said, "She calls him her friend."

I was staring at him, still in disbelief. "I don't *believe* this shit!" I shouted. "A truck driver?!" Then I calmed down and asked, "Does he own the company or something, and he just drives trucks for a hobby?" I figured it *had* to be a catch to it.

Jay lightened up and started to laugh. "Naw, he's just a driver."

It wasn't that funny to me. "So, I guess he's been over to the house and all that, right?" I asked. I stopped my son before he answered me and said, "Matter of fact, I don't even want to know any more. I never should have asked you that in the first place. You just tell your mom that I said thanks."

I rode the blue line train back to the West Side and was more pissed than a motherfucker! A damned truck driver! And she didn't even want *me* inside of her house! Ain't that some *shit!* But I guess I brought it all on myself.

Full Custody

M Y wife Beverly and I sat at the dining room table in our spacious, two-bedroom townhouse in Lincoln Park, on the lower North Side of Chicago. At the moment, we were in silence. I had just shared my thoughts with her

WALTER about gaining custody of my adolescent son, and Beverly just stared at me. I realized it would be a tough situation for her to handle. There was no way to break such life-altering news to my new wife without expecting a few waves to smash up against the shore. Nevertheless, I had to get the idea out in the open to at least see what the reaction would be. I figured we needed to have a pros-and-cons discussion on it.

We had just finished eating juicy steaks for dinner that she had excellently prepared. My wife should have been a young gourmet chef in an upscale restaurant, instead of a young college administrator at Loyola. She worked wonders with food. Maybe I could invest in a restaurant called Beverly's for her in a few years.

"How long have you been thinking about this?" she asked me. She was easing into the process and getting all the facts. Beverly has always been a rational woman; tall, stately, attractive, and reserved. That's why I felt so comfortable with my decision to marry her.

"Actually, for a few years now," I answered. "I began to feel more strongly about it after I saw how close you were with your nieces and nephews. They really love you," I told her.

Beverly had been around my son on a few occasions before we were married. He even went to a picnic with us at Union Park and met her extended family. Beverly had two married sisters and one unmarried, with five nieces and three nephews. Her oldest niece was thirteen. I thought they all got along with Walter quite well.

"And how does *he* feel about it?" she asked me.

"Well, I honestly think that it would have to grow on him." I leveled with her. "But it's for his own good, sweetheart. He's a very intelligent boy, and I just don't want to sit back and watch him become another ugly statistic, if I can do something about it."

Beverly began to show her first signs of disagreement with a noticeable grimace. "Well, they *do* live in Oak Park, Walter. I mean, that's not exactly the ghetto. It's far from it."

I nodded to her. "Honey, I know that, but in case you haven't noticed, my son is what you would call—for lack of a better word—a wannabe. He looks up to his older brother; he lived in the West Side of Chicago for a number of years, and I think he wants to be, you know, what they call *hard core*. He was even picked up for shoplifting in a mall last year.

"I mean, those are the kind of things that a good role model could stop before they get out of hand," I suggested. "And I just want to make sure I don't make any mistakes by procrastinating, while trying to convince myself that things are going to be all right."

Beverly sat quietly again. I had told her enough about my relationship with Denise for her not to be in the dark about things, but I knew that we were ready to have another discussion about it. It was only logical; Walter Perry III was Denise's son.

"And how does Denise feel about this?" my wife asked, right on cue. We had been married for a mere six months, but we dated for nearly three years.

I took a deep breath. "That's going to be the biggest problem," I answered. "I had mentioned the idea of a son spending more time with his father for those crucial teenage years, and she all but ignored me."

"I can imagine," Beverly commented.

We were planning on having kids of our own, and I could hear her motherly instincts kicking in. Beverly was twenty-seven and I was thirty-two. Our biological clocks were good and ready for children.

"You never thought about marrying her?"

She had never asked me that before. I figured that before we were married, maybe she just didn't want to know. My answer was quick and decisive. "Never."

Beverly peered at me. "I'm just curious as to why not."

"She just wasn't my type."

She was still staring. "Explain that to me."

I sighed. It's always tiresome, tedious, and definitely challenging to explain the mistakes of your youth. "We talked about this before," I said. "I told you. I was a young college student with an interest for a local Chicago girl, who had a lifestyle that was totally alien to my own.

"It was a doomed relationship from the start. And in a more perfect world, it never would have happened."

Beverly shook her head and stood up from the table. "You know, it really irks me that men continue to have these *flings* with women they don't care two cents about. These women are human beings, Walter. They're not pieces of flesh."

I listened to her words and wondered if she felt ashamed of marrying me. What if women were just as willing to factor out men who had children, like men often did to them?

"Honey, we've already agreed that it was a poor decision on my part. Now, at this point, there is nothing that either of us can do to change that, but we *can* make a difference in my son's life by accepting an imperfect situation and dealing with it on very real terms."

Beverly seemed to be in so much turmoil that I was impelled to stand up and hold her.

"Have you ever stopped to think about how *I* would feel about this?" she asked me.

"That's what I'm doing now, by sharing my thoughts with you," I commented.

She leaned away from me and looked me in the eyes. "Walter, you made it seem more like your future intentions, rather than just some thoughts that you were having. I mean, sure, your son is nice to have around *sometimes*, but what if I like the closeness and the space that *we* have together before we have our *own* kids? And maybe, I would be more accepting of this kind of thing after I had a chance to discover motherhood on my own. I want to go through each stage of it, instead of being tossed right in the middle of parenthood. I mean, I'm sorry, but I just don't know if I'm ready for this," she told me, before breaking away.

I had no idea she would react so strongly. "I thought that you loved kids, after seeing how you dealt with your sisters' children," I responded to her.

"Walter, that's because I know they're not my constant responsibility. I can say no to them, and have time to myself whenever I want. And at least, while you're pregnant, you can go through nine months of getting ready for that loss of freedom. You're asking me to give up that freedom immediately."

"Beverly, it's not like he's an infant. If anything, he would be able to help out, more than get in the way."

"Okay, well, if *that's* the case, then why are you so concerned about his future? I mean, it's obvious that you want to take him on as some kind of project, and if he's really not intending on being here and enjoying what we have to offer, then how is that going to be helpful to us? You already said it yourself; he wants to run the streets, and I don't know if I'm ready to deal with that right now."

"Look, we're not talking about some at-risk youth from a foster home, we're talking about my son here."

"Yes, *your* son! *Denise's* son! And I don't want to be in the middle of this any more than I already am," my wife blurted out to me. Then she marched off to the bedroom.

I sat back down at the table and thought about taking a couple of Advil. I rarely had headaches before the night Denise Stewart announced that she was pregnant with my child. I thought of her as an exciting and seductive adventure while finishing my undergraduate studies in business at the University of Illinois at Chicago. However, she quickly became a long-lasting headache, and a constant reminder of my stupidity. It took me four years to even admit the mistake to my parents. I thought they may have disowned me. Fortunately, it never got to that point. In many ways, I was still a nervous kid back then, getting all worked up and exaggerating things.

I met Denise at a club in Greektown during those early eighties, where I had an off-campus apartment nearby. After growing up in Barrington, so far away from the action of a big city, I was eager to mingle with brothers and sisters from Chicago. Denise was two years my senior, and at the time, she had a Jheri curl that hid most of her attractive brown face. But it was her body that *I* was crazy about, and she knew how to use it. Whenever we were intimate, I felt like an explorer in an ancient, lost city of treasure, especially when we visited one of her Chicago locations. I think that added to my fantasy, the mission of traveling through a rough city to sleep with a woman who had been there. A native.

I was so strung out for Denise's pleasures that I practically flunked out of school at one time, for absenteeism, tardiness, and incomplete assignments. Then she told me that she was pregnant, and everything changed. Not only *was* she pregnant, but she was four months pregnant, past the first trimester. She said she was confused about whether to tell me or not. Therefore, she procrastinated.

I was a blind idiot who didn't even notice that she was picking up weight. I hung up the phone with her and broke down and cried. After that dreadful night, all I thought about was my schoolwork, my career in banking, and getting back on track with my life, as if my liaisons with Denise had all been a bad dream that would somehow go away. However, I had to face reality.

I wasn't there for her every day, but I made sure I gave her the money she needed to raise a child. Outside of a marriage proposal, I gave her whatever she asked of me. And Denise had never asked for marriage. I don't believe she ever thought too strongly about it. It was pretty obvious to both of us that she was still in love with her first son's father. He was doing time in jail for armed robbery, so I became Denise's temporary adventure as well. We were trading places, so to speak. Or more like sharing places in our universal lust. So when she got pregnant, it was understood that we wouldn't become a family, we would simply deal with it.

Since Denise was nearly halfway through the pregnancy, abortion was out of the question. She told me she didn't believe in abortions anyway. She said that it was for selfish people who had no heart. And she was right, because I was scared to death, and all I could think about from that night on was how much I wanted to be by myself, while focusing on my schoolwork and my future.

A Hardworking Woman

B

DENISE

U T see, your situation is unusual for a single mother. Most of us are struggling just to put food on the table. You don't have that problem. The only thing *you* need a man for is your social life, really," an angry mother snapped at me. She had brought her two kids along with her to our monthly meeting place at the Harold Washington Library Center in downtown Chicago. Nikita was there with my niece Cheron, and my sister definitely didn't need to hear comments concerning my healthy income. She already had enough excuses not to straighten out her life.

A lot of the women in our group looked at me as some kind of Cinderella story, and I got so tired of being in the middle of things that I didn't know how to respond to it anymore. On one hand, I sympathized with single mothers because I *was* one, but on the other hand, I wanted to tell many of the mothers there to stop whining so much and get on with their lives. I wasn't going to *apologize* to them for having my own money! I worked damned hard for it! Yet, a lot of them wanted to view my success as unrealistic. I'm not saying that every woman had to own her own business, but to provide for your kids, you *at least* had to be motivated to do all that you could.

Sometimes it felt as if I were being punished for my success. I was being punished for being a single mother, never being married, making a living, staying positive about my future, and for being able to live through hell and actually come out on top!

Camellia stepped in with all of her large frame and came to my rescue. "Look, it doesn't matter what kind of job you have or how much money you make, if you're a single mother, there's gonna be some common issues that we *all* face. This organization isn't just for *poor* mothers, it's for *all* mothers."

When Camellia said that, the two white women in our midst looked relieved. It wasn't as if they were that wealthy, it was just good for them to hear Camellia's inclusive position. They had only been to two of our previous meetings, and every time the sisters got a little emotional, they looked as if they were ready to haul ass out of the room. Sometimes, I felt as alienated as they did, and Camellia and I were the ones who had *started* the group.

"Well, we don't all have *everything* in common in here, that's all I'm saying," the spiteful sister responded.

Women like her were exactly why I need strength to keep going. Somebody had to be strong enough to show them that they weren't helpless, and spitting out envious venom wasn't going to help anyone.

Camellia went on and said, "I think it's important for us to reestablish what the Single Mothers' Organization is all about, in order to stop us from getting off track.

"We are organizing for the common goals of day care, health care, affordable housing, personal health, and just having someone to talk to about the everyday hurdles of being a single mom. And no one issue will be handled as more important than the others because they are *all* important and interchangeable at different times in our lives.

"One mother's struggle for food and shelter is another mother's struggle for health care and day care. The need for medicine and a kid's emotional and educational development are just as important as food and clothing in the overall scheme of things."

The SMO was approaching forty members, most of whom were black women. There were some long faces and mumbling about Camellia's comments, but no one stepped up and said anything. Camellia was no doubt our leader, and she ran a tight ship. In another society, she could have easily been a queen. However, in Chicago, in 1997, she was a single woman with kids, like all the rest of us in that room.

By the end of the meeting, I was worn out, from my headache to my throbbing feet. Honestly, I was getting tired of coming. Misery loves company, and there were too many women in the group who wanted to be miserable instead of empowered. They didn't want to hear my story of self-determination, hard work, and triumph; they wanted to hear my little sister's story of how some no-good man, and the rest of the world, had done her wrong and messed up her life.

They didn't want to hear how Camellia and I, both single mothers with two children, had worked out the struggles of parenthood. We had alternated work schedules, watched each other's kids, and shared a crappy two-bedroom apartment on the South Side before eventually running out of room. That was eight years ago, and we had done a lot of growing up and soul-searching since then.

I was the one who kept all of our finances in order while Camellia, as Jesse Jackson loves to say, kept hope alive by convincing me that we could make it. I wasn't always a confident and driven woman, but Camellia kept reminding me that confidence can be built by simply believing in yourself and doing things successfully.

Math was always one of my favorite subjects in high school, especially applying how it relates to real life. Somebody had to account for the total cost of diapers, baby clothes, blankets, milk, groceries, educational toys, visits to the pediatrician, and medicine and ointment for the many infant ailments and rashes. If you factor in the cost of day care, things *really* start to add up. That's not including your *personal* monetary needs. Needless to say, I did a hell of a job at keeping us afloat economically, and Camellia kept us looking on the bright side of things emotionally.

Before I knew it, she was pushing me toward a career where I could utilize my financial talents. I didn't take her challenge seriously at first, but then she started calling around to financial institutions and asking them how "a talented friend" could break into the business of being a financial analyst of some sort. I actually received a few callbacks, and ended up participating in plenty of seminars around Chicago, sponsored mostly by life insurance companies.

It amazed me just how much more I knew about money than people who had college degrees and earned salaries in the high five digits or more. A college degree didn't mean that any of those people had to stretch a dollar as far as I had. When I learned about money markets, mutual funds, compounding interest, and various types of credit, loans, and low interest rates, I formed an entirely different outlook on my economic future.

I figured that if people who knew less about money than I did could maintain wealthy lifestyles and have nice homes and drive expensive cars, then I *knew* that I could turn my life around and get with the program. All I needed was an opportunity.

Despite how many of those financial analysts and consultants told me that I really didn't need a degree, just a few courses in finance and on-the-job training and experience, I still wanted validation; a college degree. Being a single black mother, born and raised in the West Side of a huge city like Chicago, I knew that I would not be taken seriously unless I had that piece of paper in hand. And I knew that a college degree would give me a much stronger voice.

To make a long story short, some of the financial people I met, who were impressed with me, were able to pull some strings and get me a sizable grant to attend Chicago State University, to study business administration. If I got anything above a 3.0 GPA, I was told that I could qualify for a full scholarship. I ended up graduating in three years, magna cum laude, with a 3.65 GPA and had job interviews lined up at several insurance companies. But I wanted to take things even further than that. So what I did was accept the job offer from the highest bidder, and worked for a few years to get my feet wet while saving money and establishing credit. Then I went and got my insurance license from the state of Illinois to become an independent broker and got a low-interest business loan to open up my own office. My plan was to go after as many single mothers in the community that I could, and reeducate them on money and opportunity. In the meantime, I talked Camellia into enrolling at Northeastern University Center for Inner-City Studies for a degree in social work.

Camellia always had bright ideas. It was her idea to work together as parents, to use my talents professionally, *and* to start an organization to help other single mothers. It took Camellia a little longer than it took me to get a degree, but she did finish, and was immediately hired to work for the city government. The year of her graduation, 1993, we began planning the SMO. And that was our story: two Cinderellas. Then again, I can't really relate Camellia and myself to Cinderella, because no Prince Charming did a damn thing for us!

"So, I guess the meeting didn't go how you thought it would tonight, hunh?" my sister Nikita asked me. I was driving her and my niece back to my mother's house on the West Side. Mom simply refused to move. She said she didn't want to be a burden to me since I was doing so well. I gave her money whenever I could though, and a lot of that ended up going to Nikita and Cheron.

"I guess not," I mumbled. I didn't have too many words for my sister that night. She was itching to ask me for some money, but I didn't give her the chance. I was tired of giving her handouts. She was still living at home and barely working; twenty-seven years old, and *turning* twenty-eight. I didn't even get out of the car to go in the house and say Hi to my mother. I didn't have time to stop. I had to get back home to my sons. I was so glad they were old enough to stay at home that I didn't know what to do with myself. I couldn't overdo it though, so I was anxious to get home.

"Tell Mom I said Hi, and I'll call her when I get a chance," I told my sister.

Nikita looked at me and didn't even say good-bye. She slammed my car door with Cheron in her arms, disappointed that she didn't get a chance to ask me for money. That was typical of her attitude, and I was getting tired of trying to tell her about herself, so I let her go ahead and have her tantrum.

On the way home, I called Camellia from my car phone. We made sure to always talk after our monthly meetings to discuss our progress. I said, "You know what? We've survived through so much together, and with this support group, it just feels like we're starting all over again."

"Well, Denise, you have to understand that everybody's not on the same level that we're on."

"I *do* understand that," I argued before thinking.

"No, I don't believe you do," Camellia responded. "The truth is, we've been able to do more on our own than some people are able to do in your ideal *two-parent* families. And that's not saying that it was *fair* for us to have to go through all the trifling things we've been through, and are *still* going through, but you have to understand that there is no game plan to this thing. I mean, I would honestly say that we've had a lot of the Lord on our side."

It was also Camellia's idea that we start attending church regularly. She had a girl and a boy, Monica and Levonne, who were around the same ages as my kids. They were practically cousins. They had all been around one another since they were toddlers. But at least Camellia's two kids had the same deadbeat dad. She continued, telling me how good a job we had done:

"And like I keep telling people, Denise, you don't become a parent for a few years and then it's all over with. Once you have children, that's it. You're going to be a parent for the rest of your life, and you're gonna have to go through a million different changes."

Camellia was going through some recent changes herself. Monica, her sixteen-year-old daughter, had recently started dating seriously. Two condoms fell out of her purse while Camellia was carrying it from the living room couch back to Monica's room. That led to an all-night, on-the-spot discussion about the responsibilities of sex, which reminded me to do the same with my son, Jimmy.

"So, did Jimmy like hanging out with his father yesterday?" Camellia asked me. She always managed to do more of the talking between us. You would think that she had called me. We always talked about our kids and their fathers. That was how we met and became such good friends years ago.

"Jimmy's never really had a problem with his father," I responded. "He's been around him enough for it not to be some new experience. If it becomes a regular occurrence, *then* I'll have to see how he responds. But the whole thing with *Walter's* father hinting about wanting custody all of a sudden is *really* bothering me."

"You really think he wants custody?"

"Why else would he start talking about 'what's best for *our* son'?" I asked. It seemed obvious to me. Walter had always been a calculating man, with what I considered a major Napoleon complex. He had a master's degree in business, and worked for Chicago Federal Savings, one of the largest banks in the city. He didn't make idle chatter either. Two plus two *always* equaled four in *his* book. "I think he took that *Boyz N the Hood* movie a little too seriously," I said lightheartedly.

Camellia didn't catch my humor. She realized full well that it was my ego talking. Deep down inside, I was terrified of losing a grip on my family. Making life better for my two sons was my number one force of motivation.

"Well, I'm pulling up at the house now, Camellia. Let me run on in here and square away these boys of mine, and I'll call you later on or sometime tomorrow," I said, as I parked my black Honda Civic. I didn't need any fancy car to get around in, just something that would be reliable. I did, however, want to allow my sons a chance to grow up outside of the tough streets of the West Side. So moving out to the Oak Park suburbs was a necessity.

"Break a leg," Camellia joked with me.

"Girl, please," I told her. "That's all I would need right now to put me in the nuthouse for good." When you're a single parent, you don't have time to get sick. And that's the honest-to-God truth!

I walked into my house and found my sons in the family room watching them damn music videos again! They had taped several of those rap shows, and would watch them over and over, or play video games. It was better than having them run around in the streets, so I couldn't complain too much.

"Anybody hungry?" I asked them.

"Yeah," they both answered. Usually, if there were no leftovers to microwave, they made themselves peanut butter and jelly sandwiches, hot dogs and beans, or just ate cold cereal while I was out. I didn't expect them to try and cook anything. You know how most boys are, they look at cooking as being girlish, but sometimes it's necessary. I realized that soon they would have to learn how to cook, whether they liked it or not, I just hadn't gotten around to teaching them yet.

"Okay, well, let's order some pizza," I told them. But first I turned them damn videos off.

I was so exhausted that I couldn't even sit down and eat with them when the pizzas arrived. I changed into some comfortable clothes and was ready for bed by ten-thirty, past Walter's bedtime.

He pouted. "Aw, Mom, how 'bout eleven o'clock? I'll be thirteen next year."

Jimmy laughed at him, and I quickly gave him a look to leave his brother alone.

"Okay, well, *next year* we'll sit and talk about it. However, *this year*, you're still twelve. Now go on to bed."

Jimmy would be next, shortly after his brother. I liked Jimmy to be able to watch the nightly news, to see what was going on in Chicago and around the world. I wanted him to see how black men were being portrayed every night, so that he could learn to be *unlike* what America seemed to expect from him. I wanted to counteract the negativity by making my son sick of seeing and hearing about black men and black boys doing wrong.

I never let him watch those silly late shows unless they had someone with a good message to send to young people, which seemed to be hard to find. Too many black celebrities only talked about making more money or how much fun they were having while hanging out in Hollywood. I didn't want my son overexposed to all of that. He was already leaning toward stardom with basketball. But I didn't want to take the sport away from him, especially since he loved to play the game, and was so good at it. I just wanted to make sure he balanced it out with a good education and strong political views on the world.

Excuse me for treason, but I didn't want my son turning into another Michael Jordan. For all the years that the people in Chicago treated the man like a god, I have yet to hear him say anything of value, specifically to black boys in Chicago—or to black boys around the country for that matter—who were killing themselves over his hundred dollar sneakers! I wanted my son to have responsibility and a duty to any community that loved and supported him as a successful black man, which entailed more than just dunking basketballs and winning championships.

If any black man could be treated like a god in America, in the 1990s, with all the hell that black people are going through, that man should have strength and dignity enough to carry a torch for his people and make them proud of being black, while giving them inspiration to carry on, which few *celebrities* seem to want to do. So often I had to ask myself, *Lord, where are the Muhammad Alis and Jackie Robinsons of the '90s?* and hope that my own son could fill the void one day.

Peer Pressure

H E Y Brock, I know you've slept with that *corporate* sista' by now. The way you've been acting lately, I'd say you've done her a couple of times. Either that, or you've been having a lot of wet dreams about her," Larry said with a laugh. "Shit, you've known her long enough to get some, and you *surely* haven't been chasing any other women lately. This sista's corporate shit is *that* good, hunh, Brock?"

We were standing near my truck at the shipping dock in Cicero, Freeway Trucking Companies' Midwest headquarters, right outside of Chicago. Larry was built like an Olympic wrestler with broad shoulders, and was full of bravado. I used to have the same physique and ramrod attitude five or six years ago, but then I stopped working out, and more importantly, I stopped *hanging* out. I got plain old tired of all the bullshit. Truck drivers were not all beer-drinking, foul-mouthed sex maniacs, but enough of them were to support the stereotype. On the other hand, a lot of the guys were dedicated family men who just happened to drive eighteen-wheelers. I was trapped somewhere in the middle when I met Denise a year ago. Since then, I was leaning toward the latter, the family man image. I had recently turned thirty-seven years old, and my days of kissing and telling were over.

"I doubt if you'll ever know, brother, especially not from me," I responded to Larry.

Larry was often my co-driver on long runs. He was nearly ten years younger than me, partying hard and playing the field of women like *I* used to do. He was one of the guys who was with me at the Black Women's Expo when I met Denise.

"So, you mean you still ain't gon' tell me nothin', playa'?" he asked, pressing me.

"That's *exactly* what I mean, young blood. This ain't no damn high school locker room."

Larry frowned and said, "It never was, but that didn't stop you from tellin' me everything before."

I moved away from him, heading for the driver's side of my truck. "Yeah, well, I've changed. And this one is important to me," I told him.

We were both wearing blue cotton T-shirts of fine, sand-knit quality. When it got cold in the wintertime, I broke out with the rugged Carhartt jackets and overalls that construction men liked to wear. There were no plaid shirts for me. I liked to travel in my own style. Whenever I needed a haircut and a shave—which, before I met Denise, was often—I usually wore a Chicago White Sox, Cubs, Bears, or Bulls hat to represent my proud city. It made for good conversation while out on the road at the truck stops. Guys were always willing to talk sports. And although Larry would joke about my being old, he broke his neck to copy everything I bought, right on down to my deodorant and socks. It was a wonder that he never asked me what kind of drawers I wore. That's a typical young blood for you, always yapping, and rarely trying to figure out how to do their own thing. Most of them fail at something once, then they immediately start copying everybody else.

Larry climbed into the passenger side, still planning on bugging me about my personal life. "You really think . . . Naw, I'm not even gon' get into it with you," he said, stopping himself short.

I knew what he was thinking. He was thinking that Denise would never be as serious about me as I was becoming about her. I thought of our relationship as temporary for a while myself, but since we continued to enjoy each other's company, I decided that I had to stop thinking so short termed.

Why *wasn't* I worthy of a Denise? She wasn't born with a silver spoon in her mouth. She came from modest roots just like I had, and just like Larry. On the job, the only thing the guys knew about Denise and I was that she was a kick-ass Chicago businesswoman, and I was a truck driver from Chicago's South Side. They had no idea how affectionate we had become, or how vulnerable Denise could be sometimes. Her independence didn't mean that she didn't *want* or *need* a man. She wanted a steady man just like I wanted a steady woman in my life again. And despite her career stature, she never made me feel any *less* of a man. The guys at the job were assuming that Denise and I were oil and water, and that we couldn't go the distance. It was an assumption that I was out to change.

I looked over at Larry and asked him, "What are you thinking, Larry, that I can't hold my own up against this woman? Is that it? Because if that's the case, then I got news for you, young blood. I'm not going anywhere, and she ain't either," I told him.

He smiled. "Are you sure about that?"

I revved up my engine and got ready for our three-day, two-night run to Florida, Arkansas, and back up to Illinois. "You damn right I'm sure," I told him. "It's just like you said; I've been with her long enough to know, right?"

He nodded to me, still grinning.

"Well, there you have it then," I said, blowing my horn to clear out our path. The shipping and receiving docks in Cicero were always busy with truck traffic.

Larry chuckled and stared out the window as we began to pull off. He just wouldn't wipe that damn smile off his face. He made it seem as if he knew something that I didn't. I got so concerned about Larry's opinions on the class issue that I refused to let the conversation die.

I said, "Hey, man, what the hell is wrong with you young bloods and sisters who make their own money anyway? Don't you realize that the more money *they* make, the less you have to break *your* neck? I mean, does that make any kind of sense to you guys?"

"It *would* make sense if it worked that way, but it don't," Larry responded.

"What do you mean, '*it don't*'?" I had an idea of what he meant, I just wanted to hear him explain it for himself.

He said, "It seems like the more money *they* make, the more you *have* to make."

I nodded my head and smiled. Larry was telling me exactly what I knew already: the young bloods were scared to death of the challenge. "Larry, you know how much you can make as a truck driver?"

"A lot more than what some of these so-called *corporate* sisters make. Just because they work in a tall building and wear a damn suit and stockings don't mean that they make all that much."

"Exactly. So why are you so concerned about how much money you're *supposed* to be making, when you already *know* that you can make more than they do."

"I *do* make more than they do. Most of them, at least."

I shook my head and pitied him. I couldn't imagine anymore that I was once so young and petrified by successful women myself. I said, "Larry, it's all in the mind. The more secure you feel about yourself, the less you worry about competing with a woman's income."

"I'm just saying though, Brock. I mean, I meet a lot of women nowadays, and the first thing that comes out their mouth is, 'Oh, I got my MCA from this university, and my Ph.D. from that university, and I studied with so and so and worked for such and such company' and on and on. You know what I mean, man? Nobody wants to hear all of that shit!"

"And nor do *they* want to hear, 'Baby, my dick is a size nine, I can screw for three straight hours, and I can lift a woman over my shoulders thirty times.' "

Larry broke out laughing. "Are you *sure* they don't want to hear that, brother?"

I smiled and thought about it. "Actually, a few of them might," I added with a chuckle. "But what I'm trying to say here, Larry, is that you can't let these women scare you away when they start talking about their degrees and whatnot. That's just their way of telling you who they are, so you don't go in there thinking that they're gonna put up with no bullshit. And the proper term, *I believe*, is M-B-A."

Larry calmed down for a minute. He knew that I was right.

He looked over and said, "They still treat you like shit when they find out that you don't have any of them damn degrees that they got. You ever been to college?" he asked me.

I nodded. "I went to DePaul for a few years and dropped out. It wasn't my kind of ball game."

"Well, it wasn't mine either. I dropped out before I even went," Larry said with a chuckle. He seemed to be proud of it.

"And that's exactly why you feel inferior to them," I told him.

"Why, because I didn't go to college? That don't mean everything, man. I shouldn't have to walk around braggin' about degrees and shit. Just let me be me, plain old Larry Nicholson."

I smiled at him again and said, "Exactly. And that's why 'plain old Larry Nicholson' needs to stay away from 'Corporate Susie,' because he can't handle her. And it's *not* because he *doesn't* have a college education, but because he doesn't feel *comfortable* with not having one."

Larry frowned at me. "Yeah, whatever, man. Fuck 'em anyway. They got the same thing every other woman got."

"And you want some of it, too. Don't you?" I asked, teasing him. "You just don't know how to go about getting it. Therefore, it's driving you crazy. And it would drive you *crazier* if you saw one of these sisters walking around with a white man on her arm."

Larry looked at me with his eyes blazing. "You damned right I'd be mad!" he yelled at me. "They don't have to necessarily talk to me, but it's plenty of other brothers that they could talk to. They need to at least keep it in the family."

"Well, that means that more of you young brothers need to get busy working on your confidence, education, and everything else. Because I'm gonna tell you something, young blood, these women ain't looking for no 'plain old Larry.' In this day and time, they're looking for a Superman. And I'm not talking about just the money, either. I'm talking about a man who feels *good* about himself *and* who takes care of his business. You hear me, Larry?"

"Yeah, I hear you. And I'm a Superman right here," he said, pounding his chest with a smile.

I shook my head and pitied him some more. Larry didn't have a clue. It was going to take him another ten years to find out what I already knew. Maybe longer than that. Some brothers never learn; a woman can never be more than an equal match for a confident man, no matter how many degrees she has *or* how much money she makes. A confident man can always rise to the occasion. I firmly believed that. That's just the way the Lord made it. One confident man and one confident woman make for plenty of confident children.

Before I knew it, Larry was falling to sleep in his chair. I told him to climb in the sleeper and get some rest so he could take over the wheel that night. Then I got to thinking about Denise. Thinking about her made my trips seem a hell of a lot shorter, and my return a lot more meaningful. There was a time, back in my early years of truck driving, where I looked forward to getting away and seeing new places. Even while I was married, I looked forward to getting away. Every trip was like a mini vacation to me. But after twelve years on the job, I've seen just about all I want to see, and the thrill of going away is gone. Denise gave me the thrill of returning home.

I reminisced on the first time she agreed to go out with me on a real date. It was after the Fourth of July weekend. Both of her boys had gone away to summer camp, and Denise had a full week to herself, which was a blessing in disguise; and a big opportunity for me.

I bought some Giorgio Armani cologne because of its mellow, nonaggressive appeal. Although I had stopped working out, at six foot one and two hundred pounds, I was still no cream puff, and I didn't want to overwhelm Denise with my physical presence. I wanted that first date to be a meeting of our minds.

I hopped out of my Maxima, fresh from the car wash, and knocked on her door. It was the first time I had ever worn a suit on a first date in my life. Denise opened her door, wearing a midnight blue, curve-hugging, knee-length dress.

I smiled and said, "Hello, gorgeous," before handing her the two red roses I had bought for the occasion. I was trying to make the best impression I could. I told her one rose represented her and the other represented me, two hearts and souls coming together.

"Aww, isn't that the sweetest thing," she gushed at me, with a peck on the cheek. As I walked her to the car with the roses in hand, she added, "Mmm, you smell good, too. What kind of cologne are you wearing?"

I answered her like a king. "Armani." Then I opened the passenger-side door for her and helped her to slide her sexy brown legs in. When I first went to lunch with Denise, I asked her if she worked out, because her body was in such great shape. She said, "Yes, every day from six-thirty A.M. until eleven-thirty P.M." I broke out laughing. The woman was so darn busy that her body remained skin tight naturally.

"So, where are we going?" she asked me.

"You ever heard of The Retreat, on the far South Side?" I asked her.

Denise's face lit up. "That's the place where they turned a mansion into a restaurant, isn't it?"

I smiled. I figured she had heard of it. I said, "Yeah, that's the one." I was proud of my good choice of a first date.

"Have you ever been there before?" she asked me.

"I sure haven't, but I always *wanted* to go there. Now I get the chance to do it with you."

"Dennis, you really didn't have to do all this." She seemed embarrassed by my hospitality.

"But I wanted to," I insisted. "Now get ready to enjoy yourself, because I put a lot of thought into this." I damn sure wasn't going to take her to some low-budget place to eat. I wanted the best, and I figured that The Retreat would represent success in black business.

We got there and enjoyed the place and sucked in all of its elegance, but Denise seemed to be missing something. I could just feel it. She became too silent not to have things on her mind. The wisdom that age and experience gives you was beginning to kick in for me. You get a certain calmness that makes you feel you can tell what's going on in a woman's mind.

I asked her, "So, what are you striving for now?" I wanted her to tell me that she needed something, or someone. Someone like me.

"I'm just trying to maintain what I have, basically. I mean, we're only human. All we can really do is strive to be better people."

"What if we never quite reach our goals, whatever they may be?" I asked for the hell of it. I just wanted to keep her talking to find out who she was and how she felt about things.

"Well, in that case, I would ask, 'How hard did you try?' And if you gave it your all and still didn't succeed, I'd tell you to come up with another game plan."

I smiled at her. I thought she was going to say that your all is the best you can do.

Denise chuckled and proceeded to read my mind. "I get tired of people telling me they've done all that they can do. The truth is, many of us haven't done *half* of what we can do. Everybody needs to push a little harder to accomplish their goals. That's a major problem in society today; too many people are half-steppin'.

"Like you, for instance," she said to me. "Dennis, you could have taken me any place, worn whatever you wanted to wear, and spent a lot less energy on me, but you chose to do more, and I really do appreciate it. However, that still doesn't mean that you're gonna get under my dress anytime soon," she told me with a grin.

I laughed out loud. She was as honest as I was. "And that *is* the truth," I admitted. What else could I say?

She reached out and held my hand. "You know, it's amazing how when people don't get what they want the first time around, a lot of them just get sour and never put their hearts back into it. Because the bottom line is that we're not gonna get everything we want *when* we want it. The world just doesn't work that way. At least not for most of us. Only a few of us are lucky that way," she said.

I nodded to her. "Yeah, and those are usually the type of people who are never satisfied with anything."

"Because they never had to struggle," she responded. "They take things for granted. Struggle makes us all a lot stronger, and those who are afraid of struggle are the ones who are just plain immature. They're like little children, needing somebody to lead them through every step of the way. Then they want to get tired all of a sudden. 'Oh, I'm so tired.' "

I found that Denise could go on for a while, talking about the shortcomings of society, motivation, positive thinking, and the general lack of progression. She was just a dynamic woman. By the time our food came, I hardly had an appetite. I just wanted to listen to her. I kept wondering why she wasn't married, or *at least* taken.

"So how did you wind up getting into the finance business?" I asked her. Before that night, I had only asked her about the business, and not how she got into it.

"It was just something that I found I could do well," she answered, eating a tender salmon dish. I ordered steak, cooked well.

"Most of us never fully utilize our talents," I told her. "I took piano lessons for about eight years, and just decided to give it up after high school. It just didn't seem like a manly thing to do, you know. But sometimes I find myself daydreaming about continuing on with it, like Thelonious Monk or Herbie Hancock or somebody."

"Oh," Denise perked. "I *thought* your hands felt kind of soft for a *truck driver*. So, you're a Mr. Piano, incognito."

"Now, wait a minute, I didn't say I was a pro," I told her.

"You don't have to be. Can you *play* the doggone thing?"

"Oh yeah, I can play. I just didn't wanna get to lying on myself, having you think that I can *jam* on the thing. Because I'm not that good."

"You're better than me. I never played the piano a day in my life," she told me. "We never owned one."

"Well, in that case, I'm sure I can show you a thing or two, just to get you started with a little something."

She gave me this long, mischievous grin that made me think of us together, naked. It was one of the many small hints I observed that told me Denise was definitely interested in me.

"I would like that," she said.

I was certain that she would, but like she said before, we don't always get what we want the first time around. I would have to go over what I knew before I even *thought* about showing her anything! I knew I would have been rusty.

I didn't expect a kiss on the lips that night, but to my surprise, Denise gave me a wet one at her doorstep anyway.

"That's for your effort," she told me with a smile.

"All I ask is that we can do it again," I responded.

She held my hand again and said, "Don't worry. We will. I promise. It just might not be when you want, or when *I* want. It may be sometime in between."

"Well, that's what they say, 'Real relationships are about compromise,' " I told her. "Okay then. I can agree to those terms."

I went home alone that night and remembered it being the most pleasing closure of a first date that I ever had. It was maturity. I thought of Denise as a worthwhile mission, and I had my heart all the way into it. I had committed myself to going that extra mile for something, *someone*, I should say, who was definitely worth it.

Back on the road, my ten legal hours of driving were up. Larry and I had stopped at a truck station in Kentucky, ate some fattening fast food, and were ready to get back on our way to Orlando, Florida. It was close to nine o'clock at night, and time for Larry to do his part at the wheel.

"You ready, man?" I asked him.

He stretched and answered, "Yeah, I'm ready."

I traded places with him and we got back on our way. Larry would get in these moods where he wouldn't talk while driving, and that was fine with me, because sometimes I got tired of his yapping. He never made much sense half of the time anyway. He wasn't too much trouble either. That's why I didn't mind him being a part of my run team. A guy could easily drive you crazy on a three-day run, and the older I got, the less I wanted to chance driving with guys whom I may have had problems with.

After Larry was at the wheel for a while, I got tired and went inside the sleeper to crash myself. When I woke back up, abruptly, to the sound of a police siren, it was after three in the morning, eastern standard time, and Larry had gotten us pulled over for speeding.

"Shit, Larry! How fast were you driving?"

"Ninety. What are you worried about? It's *my* ticket, right?"

I said, "You got that right. What state are we in anyway?"

"Georgia."

I nodded and waited to get back on the road.

The Georgia state trooper asked Larry how long he had been driving, our destination, and asked him for his medical card. Then he asked Larry if he was by himself, and I was forced to show my face and IDs.

"Shit, man!" I snapped at Larry afterward. "If this was *your* damn ticket, then why did *I* have to get up?"

"Man, fuck that honky. He wouldn't have done all that shit to no white drivers. All he had to do was check the logbook."

I shook my head and went back inside the sleeper. "Just get back on the damn road. Okay?"

Larry looked me in the eye and said, "You watch how you talk to me, motherfucker. I'll *crash* this damn thing."

"Yeah, well, you better make sure that I die if you do, because if I live, I'm gonna cut off your arms, and then your legs, and then your dick, and watch you bleed to death on the side of the road."

Larry broke out laughing and said, "You're a sick motherfucker, man."

I told him, "That's right. Don't ever fuck with an old man, young blood. It's dangerous."

"You ain't *that* damn old."

"Yeah, but I am old enough. Now just shut up and keep driving."

Larry was quiet for a few minutes, then he said, "Man, I gotta get to the next rest station *fast*. I gotta take me a *log* of a shit."

I smiled. Good thing the next rest station was only two miles away. Sometimes, you get caught in between exits and have to drive ten, twenty miles before you reach the next rest room. I thought about Larry having to take a shit in the dark woods and a deer running out to kick him in the ass, and I broke out laughing.

"What's so funny?"

"Your momma's buck teeth," I told him.

I caught him off guard. All Larry could do was laugh with me. You get silly sometimes after being on sixty-hour-*plus* runs with a guy. Every kind of emotion you can imagine will likely pass through you. That's why it was so important to team up with someone you could get along with.

When we pulled over to the rest station so Larry could use the toilet, I got out and stretched. Then I found myself with an urge to call Denise and ask her if she had received the roses I sent to her earlier. I knew she had. It was simply an excuse to talk to her.

Denise answered her phone on the first ring, just like I knew she would. She was a light sleeper, and she was always concerned about her image with her sons. Late-night phone calls weren't something she condoned. Nevertheless, she had begun to bend the rules, just a little bit, for me. I guess she understood just how much it meant to me. You get lonely on the road a lot.

"Yes, Dennis, I got the roses," she said, before I could ask.

All I could do was smile. She knew me better than I thought she did. Sisters are more perceptive than most guys give them credit for anyway.

"Did you have a rocky trip or a smooth one?" she asked me, loud and clear. She sounded as if she was *expecting* my late-night call. Maybe she did expect it. We had been going strong for a full year, and I had driven thousands of miles away from her and always managed to call her with expressions of love.

"It was the smoothest ride that I could hope for. The only thing that would have made it better would have been Denise Stewart in the passenger seat instead of this rock-headed Larry."

"Hmm, maybe next time," she told me.

"And how did *your* day go?" I asked her.

"It was very trying as usual. The roses made it a little better though."

"Well, you know there's plenty more where those came from."

"I would hope so. I would hope that there was a whole package of sweet, chocolate muscles where they came from, too."

I broke up laughing. I loved it when Denise talked that talk. "It's more chocolate where those roses came from than you could ever hope for," I responded.

She chuckled. "I hope this doesn't turn into one of those nasty all-nighters. I have to get up early and take care of my usual business. Call me back with part two tomorrow. TGIF."

"No problem, baby. No problem at all. It'll be the same time and same place, after the crickets start creepin'. I wouldn't want Larry to hear our conversation anyway. He's too young to hear it."

Denise laughed again and said, "Okay. I'll look forward to the call."

As soon as I hung up the phone, Larry climbed back into the driver's seat and smiled at me.

"You just finished talking to that *corporate* sister, didn't you?"

"First of all, the woman's name is Denise. Denise Stewart. And secondly, it's none of your damn business who I was talking to."

Larry grinned. Then he tried to look serious. He said, "Old man, you better climb back inside of that sleeper and get yourself some rest. 'Cause if you keep talking that shit like you talkin' you gon' *need* every minute of it."

I said, "You ain't *that* tough, young blood," and climbed back into the sleeper.

"Yeah, but I see you did what I *told* you to do," he responded to me.

I ignored him and got comfortable for the ride. I smiled to myself and hollered, "Wake me up when we get there!"

Larry didn't know anything of what Denise and I had together. My relationship with her was total peace and tranquillity. What I felt for her was exactly why lovestruck men think of women as mommies, no matter how old they get. She fulfilled all of my needs, from the little boy in my ticklish toes, all the way up to the scattered graying hairs on my aging head.

Another Sunday

I DENISE don't know what the problem is with black men and church, but I have to fight every Sunday morning to get these two boys of mine dressed and ready to go. It's as if the Bible was only talking about Eve in Genesis, and there was no Adam. The funny thing is, the Muslim brothers don't seem to have that problem at all. You see hundreds of brothers attending Louis Farrakhan's mosque on the South Side.

"I can't find my socks!" Walter hollered from his room.

Every Sunday it was the same thing, either his socks, his tie, his suit jacket, or his dress pants were missing. I guess he thought he could actually get out of going to church by deliberately misplacing his things, but I had news for him.

I pulled out a pair of brand-new dress socks I bought just for the occasion. I had a few extra ties in my closet just in case he misplaced them, too. I was planning on buying a couple of extra suits for him and keeping them in my closet as well.

"Wear these," I told him, tossing the socks on his unmade bed.

Jimmy walked by and laughed. He was dressed and ready to go, with his hair brushed, and he was smelling like cologne. I turned and stared at him as he headed through the hallway toward the stairs.

"Ah, Jimmy, is something going on at church that I don't know about today?" I asked him.

Walter started to laugh. "He thinks this girl likes him," he said, dropping a dime.

Jimmy looked shocked for a minute, then he just shook his head and went on about his business. I immediately thought again about having that conversation concerning sex, responsibility, and condoms with him.

I really didn't want to bother Jimmy about it that morning, nor did I have the time, but I was curious. I walked down the stairs and into the kitchen where my giant of a son was having a quick glass of orange juice. He tried his best to avoid eye contact with me.

"So, ah, which girl is it?" I asked him. The boy was only fifteen, and I had been looking up to talk to him for three years already. I wasn't exactly short myself, especially with heels on.

Jimmy sighed and shook his head again. "Come on, Mom. He don't know what he's talkin' about. Why you listenin' to him?"

I thought about that question for a minute. "Well, first of all, I never remember you being so *eager* to go to church on Sunday. You got your hair greased and brushed this morning, you're all ready to go, and ah, is that some kind of cologne that you're wearing?" It was obvious that *something* was going on inside that teenage mind of his.

He set his glass on the counter and said, "I'm just trying to help you out, Mom. Since you want us to go to church every week, I figure I might as well stop fighting it."

I smiled, and that quickly turned into a laugh. "Is that right? You're trying to help *me* out? Well, I don't know if you know it or not, but the Lord don't ask for you to wear cologne," I told him.

"He don't ask for us to wear suits and ties either," Jimmy countered with his own smile.

He had a point, but I wasn't through with my interrogation yet, so I pressed him for answers. "So, you're telling me that you're absolutely sure there's no girl in this church who you would like to see today?"

His smile got even wider. "It's a lot of girls in there that I would like to see. But that don't mean nothin'. I'm going because you *wanted* us to go."

"So, in other words, if I said that we're going to a different church today, that wouldn't bother you at all? Is that what you're telling me? Because you're going to church *for me*, right?"

He hesitated and started to laugh. "But why would you want to go to a different church? All of your friends go to this one."

I grinned. The boy must have thought that I was born yesterday. "Mmm hmm, that's just what I thought," I told him. It was *definitely* time for our talk. I stepped close to my giant son and asked, "Jimmy, have you, ah, *done the do* with any girls yet?"

Walter must have snuck up on us and heard my question, because the boy laughed so hard I thought he would break his rib cage.

"What is your problem?" I turned and asked him. He was plenty immature to want to get in trouble in the streets. It was a godsend to have *Walter* out in the suburbs! The West Side of Chicago would have chewed him up and spit him back out.

"Nothin'," he answered.

I decided I would talk to Jimmy again later on that evening, while Walter was over his father's house. I had agreed that his father could pick him up after church and drop him off at summer camp that Monday. I had Walter pack two extra sets of clothes and underwear with him to take to church.

When we arrived at church that morning, back on Chicago's far West Side on Augusta Boulevard, I watched to see who was watching my oldest son. It looked like every girl over twelve and under nineteen was eying Jimmy, and my mind was *not* playing tricks on me.

Walter noticed it himself and got to laughing again. I was getting tired of his silliness, so I quickly grabbed his left arm and pinched him through his suit jacket.

"Cut it out."

"Oww, Mom!"

Jimmy looked at his younger brother and grimaced. "Sound like a little girl," he commented.

"What?" Walter protested loudly.

I stopped walking down the aisle and grabbed both of them right there and whispered to them very sternly, "Look, I don't need this from *either* of you. Okay?"

Jimmy started to smile, but Walter was still pissed at being called a girl. I couldn't argue with it myself. I was used to seeing much more physical and tough-minded boys, but that's not the kind of thing a mother could tell her son. I just hoped that he would pass through his many developmental stages and turn out all right. One thing was for sure, Walter would not last one minute in Chicago. I was almost certain of that. I sheltered him as much as I could and he didn't have the street smarts that most city kids have. Jimmy, on the other hand, knew how to conduct himself in the streets, and since the skill of playing basketball was so well respected in Chicago, so was he.

We sat in our usual seats on the left side of church, next to Camellia, Monica, and Levonne. I wondered if Jimmy ever thought of Monica as a girlfriend. She was only a year older than him, and most young guys considered her attractive. She was already wearing the fancy hats and matching gloves to church, and getting the extra attention that it afforded her. However, I realized that Monica and Jimmy were too close to being cousins to seriously think about dating each other.

Anyway, Jimmy sat down right next to Monica, and they immediately started acting giddy and secretive. I didn't hear a word Reverend Gray said that morning. He was usually pretty loud, but I was busy eavesdropping on Monica and my son.

I was planning to ask Camellia all the details about the chat she had with her daughter. Usually, I stayed out of their business, but after I saw how Jimmy and Monica were carrying on, I was dying to know what they *thought* they knew. Fortunately, we attended the early, shorter service. Otherwise, we could have been in church for three hours or more.

"You know, you two were really carrying on today," I told them after church.

"Mmm hmm, and the church ain't the place for gossiping," Camellia grunted with a frown.

I gave her a look. She knew better than that. It was more gossiping going on in church than at your average high school. The bigger the church, the more the gossip. But that would never stop us from going.

When we walked out, Walter's father was double parked out in front, and on time as usual.

"What do you think about his wife?" Camellia whispered to me.

I gave the tall, thin sister a nod while she sat in the passenger's side of Walter's silver Lincoln. The car was too big for the man if you asked me, but it was perfect for a Napoleon complex. "I have nothing against her," I answered Camellia. I couldn't lie to myself and say that I wasn't at all jealous of her, because I was. Nevertheless, my jealousy had more to do with the fact that she was married than anything regarding *Junior*. She would have her hands full with him. I didn't envy that liaison at all.

Then my son started with his usual pouting. "I hate going over his house," he mumbled with his overnight bag in hand. "It's always *boring* over there."

"Yeah, well, that's just what you need, some quiet time to calm your behind down and think," I told him. "Now give me back my car keys."

"How was church?" his father asked me as he walked over. He and his wife were dressed for church, too. I never bothered to ask, but they probably went to some white Catholic church on the North Side that let out after only an hour of service.

"It was fine," I told him. I'm not saying that it was right, but I rarely had many words for the man. I just didn't know what to say to him half the time.

He spoke to Camellia, her two kids, and then to Jimmy.

"How's basketball coming, Jimmy? I know you can dunk by now, right?"

Jimmy nodded to him and smiled. "Yeah, I can dunk."

Too bad you can't, I was too mature to comment to Walter. I *did* think it though, and that was bad enough. At only five foot nine, he was easily the shortest brother I ever dated. Everything about him was unusual for me. I had always been attracted to tall, rugged men. Walter Perry Jr. was short, well-groomed, and extremely pretentious. I hated to think it, but his son was following right in his footsteps, no matter how hard he tried to rebel. Maybe Walter III knew that better than anyone, which made his rebelliousness more meaningful to him.

"I'll see you tomorrow, Mom," he said to me as he climbed into the backseat of his father's car. It was his little joke to always let his father know that he would be coming back to me.

I smiled at my son and watched the silver Lincoln as it pulled off, heading east on Augusta.

"You're thinking about the custody thing, aren't you?" Camellia asked me. She knew me too damn well.

I nodded to her and said, "Yeah. I'm just wondering how he would turn out."

"Probably just like his father," Jimmy said with a chuckle. "He already act like him now. Look like him, too."

"Yup. He does," Camellia's son Levonne agreed.

Camellia said, "Yeah, and you don't act or look *anything* like your father, Jimmy. The only thing you got from him is his height," she responded to my son.

I said, "His father played basketball, too. He almost made it to the state championship during our senior year," I told Camellia. I don't believe I ever mentioned it to her before. It wasn't one of my priorities.

Camellia gave me a devilish grin. "Don't tell me you're reminiscing."

I shook my head and said, "Not hardly." Then I looked to my son. "No offense, Jimmy, but I loved your father a *lonnng* time ago. It almost seems like another lifetime."

Camellia laughed and rumbled all over. "Erykah Badu," she responded. "That's my *girl!*"

"Mmm hmm," Monica hummed with an eager nod. "I like her songs, too."

Levonne was ready to go home. He hadn't said much all day. He was thirteen and a frail boy who had been suffering from sickle-cell anemia, so I guess I was always concerned about his health.

"Are you all right, Levonne?" I asked him.

He nodded and said, "Yeah, I'm just tired."

"That's because he was up late last night, watching videos," Camellia snapped. "He knew he had to go to church in the morning. He'll know next time."

Levonne didn't want to go to church in the first place, just like my sons and millions of other sons around the country. Church was no thing to his sister Monica, though. In fact, I think *she* enjoyed church-going more than Camellia and I did.

I thought about Jimmy and Monica growing up so fast. I looked to Camellia and I said, "I'll *definitely* be calling you tonight, because we have to talk. You know what I mean?"

She looked at her daughter and my son and nodded. "I know *exactly* what you mean."

Jimmy looked away, embarrassed.

Monica said, "What did I do now?"

Her mother answered, "Whatever you *did* or ever *do*, I'm gonna find out."

Monica sighed, shook her head, and walked off.

"And I'm not joking about that either," Camellia said behind her.

I said my good-byes and started walking in the opposite direction, toward my Honda. I couldn't wait to get one-on-one with Jimmy. He sat inside the car and looked out the passenger-side window. Before I even started the engine, I asked him, "Do you have anything to tell me, son? I want you to know that I love you very much."

I didn't want to be too hard on him, I only wanted to know if he needed to begin protecting himself.

He sunk his face into his hands and began to shake his head. "What do you want me to tell you, Mom?"

"I want you to tell me if you've been doing something."

He shook his head inside of his hands again. "Not yet."

"*Not yet?*" It was the wrong answer! "Look at me when you talk to me, Jimmy. Now you're about to start high school this year, and you need to stop dropping your head so much. You're too damn tall for that! If it's one thing I *hate* it's big, tall basketball players hanging their heads low and not knowing how to talk to people."

I couldn't help it. I was beginning to get hyper. But I knew that Jimmy could take it. It wasn't right, but I had been very hard on him before I learned how to be a more sensitive mother.

Jimmy's response to my yelling at him as a child was probably why he acted so reserved half the time. He just wasn't going to let anything get to him. I read a book before called *Cool Pose* that talked about the reserved behavior of young black men, and Jimmy fit the book to a tee.

He raised his head and looked into my face. He had such a delicate face to be so damn tall. And he looked just like my father, chocolate brown and extra handsome. "I mean, I'm not gay, Mom, so of course I'm gonna start being attracted to girls. What do you want me to do?"

I started up my engine and said, "First of all, I want you to respect the rights of women. And just because you *think* that you're ready to begin having sex, that doesn't mean that you have *the right* to force yourself on *anyone*."

"Mom, I wouldn't—"

"I'm not finished yet," I said, cutting him off. "I want you to protect yourself from these little *hot* girls out here, running around with no common sense, getting diseases and pregnant and everything else. And I want you to be *honest* with yourself about whether you really *like* a girl, or whether you just want to sleep with her because *she* likes *you*. I'm *not* gonna stand for that! You hear me? If you don't like her, then just be friends with her or leave her alone completely.

"That's why so many of these basketball and football players are having so many problems with these women out here now. They think they can just sleep with anybody who says they like them and do whatever they want to with them," I ranted. I was really going overboard. After I gave my oldest son another look, I could see that I was scaring him to death, and that he would probably not tell me anything again in his life. I needed to calm myself down, get a grip, and even apologize for blowing up at him if I needed to. I just didn't go about things the right way.

Jimmy shut his mouth and began to stare out the window again.

After a few long minutes of silence, I decided to pull over and apologize.

I touched my son's left arm, slid my hand down to his, and squeezed it as tightly as I could. "Jimmy, I am so sorry for that, honey. I didn't mean to go off on you like that, it's just that . . . a lot of things have been on my mind lately, and this conversation just really caught me off guard, so I didn't get a chance to prepare myself for it and control my emotions a little better.

"Actually, we really should have had this talk a long time ago, but it's my fault because I wasn't even thinking about it," I told him. I smiled and said, "I guess that, since you spend so much time playing basketball, I forgot all about the social aspect of your life. Of course, girls would start noticing you. You're handsome with your height. A lot of tall guys are goofy and uncoordinated at your age."

Jimmy immediately lightened up with a smile that turned into an easy laugh. It wasn't fair, but his personality allowed me to get away with a lot more than I should have been able to. That same easygoing nature of his could make a girl believe that he liked her more than he really did. Jimmy was most likely going to be a Chicago "playa" whether I liked it or not. And if I pushed him too hard, he would only learn to ignore me. Even so, I planned to do all that I could to stir him away from using women as scoring boards and as trophies.

"Baby, I just ask you to do me one favor, okay? When you start to go out and date and all, I just want to meet the girl," I said to him. "And I promise not to blow up again. Can we agree on that?"

Jimmy hesitated. "I mean, what are you gonna say to her?"

"Just regular talk. You know, 'How do you do,' 'I like your shoes,' that kind of thing."

He started to laugh again. "What if you don't like her shoes?"

I shook my head and smiled. "That was just an example. Maybe I might like her hairstyle instead," I told him. "Or maybe she may play basketball, or run track, or something, and I can ask her about that. You know, just normal stuff."

He thought about it.

Then I said, "The bottom line is that you really shouldn't go out with a girl who you're going to be afraid to bring home to your mother. That should be one of your rules of selection. And that includes white girls, too," I added with a look.

Jimmy shook his head. "Nah, it won't be no white girls coming home with me."

"Well, you know there's gonna be plenty of them at this high school you're going to in September."

"Yeah, but that don't mean I have to talk to 'em."

"So it's a deal?" I asked him again.

He grinned and slowly nodded. "Yeah, it's a deal."

"And if I make you feel uncomfortable about it, then I want us to be able to talk about that, too. Okay?"

"Yeah, okay."

I leaned over and kissed my son on the cheek and said, "I love you," like a young girl in love. And I was in love, with both of my boys, and I wanted them to always do the right things.

Walter III

I cannot understand how children Walter's age can actually believe that they are old enough to make important decisions about their lives. My son thinks he knows plenty, and he's not even a teenager yet. Times have really changed from when I was young. When I was twelve years old, back in the seventies, I had to ask my parents if I could even take my bike outside. I spent most of my time at that age collecting comic books and baseball cards. Of course, I wasn't raised in the West Side of Chicago either.

WALTER

"Are you interested in comic books or trading cards at all?" I asked my son. Walter, Beverly, and I sat at a table for four at the International House of Pancakes, because that was where my son said he would like to eat.

He devoured his mouthful of pancakes before he answered me. "*Spawn* is my favorite comic book. I just started collecting basketball cards last year," he said with a nod, while wiping strawberry syrup from his mouth. "They have a movie coming out next month. They had a TV show that was on HBO, too, but my mom wouldn't let me watch it."

Beverly grimaced and asked, "Wasn't that the cartoon that came on at midnight? I heard that it was pretty gory, and it had some rather strong language in it. I don't think that show was for kids. I heard a few college students talking about it."

Walter frowned at her. "What about *Batman* then?"

"Well, *Batman* is violent, too, but at least they don't show blood flying around or use foul language," she responded to him. "Do they use that same language inside of the *Spawn* comic book?"

"No," Walter answered snidely.

I could see that my wife was getting off on the wrong foot with him, so I quickly intervened and changed the subject.

"How about the WNBA? Have you been watching any of that?" I asked him.

He sucked his teeth and said, "No, man. They can't even dunk. I saw Lisa Leslie try to dunk on the first game against New York, and she missed it. That was stupid! My brother, Jimmy, can beat all of them. They can't even beat high school guys. I don't even know why they're getting paid for that."

"Because they're professionals, and they've worked very hard on their skills just like the men have," Beverly responded. She was obviously pissed at my son's comments, and she was trying her best to keep her poise.

"Well, you know, that league is just starting out, son. I'm sure that in a few more years you'll see more women developing their calf muscles so that they can jump just as high as the men. Some things take time," I said, intervening again. If I wanted to spend more time with my son, I definitely had to try and make him feel comfortable and at home around me.

"I gotta go to the bathroom," he said, excusing himself from our table.

My wife looked at me and said, "He sounds very chauvinistic, and I *do not* like it."

"Beverly, he's still a young boy. You have to learn those things as you develop maturity."

"When did *you* learn?" she asked me.

"It was a lot later than you would think."

"Yes, and sometimes it definitely shows," she snapped at me. "I think boys need to be taught a lot younger about how to act in the presence of women, *and* how to treat women. We are not some kind of second-class citizens just because we're less physical than guys are."

"You see that my *nephews* know how to act," she commented.

I didn't want to go into the discussion any further, so I took a sip of my coffee and proceeded to daydream. I hadn't been a so-called "roughneck" in my adolescent years, but I wasn't as "soft" as Beverly's nephews were either. I tried to play ball with those guys at a family picnic once, and they were so busy trying not to get dirty that it wasn't even fun. It's rather hard not to let the boys be boys in America, or in any other society for that matter. It's in a boy's nature to be unruly. When they don't have enough opportunities to roam on the wild side, their natural desire to take risks will only manifest itself somehow later on in life, like with my infatuation with Denise.

When Walter walked back out from the bathroom, I made sure to look and see if his hands had been washed. Fortunately, they had been. Beverly always checked her nieces and nephews for clean hands at the table, and I was sure that she would have commented on that as well. In fact, she seemed to be three times more alert about my son's habits ever since our conversation about custody.

"So, what are some of your hobbies, Walter?" she asked him as soon as he sat back down. "Can you swim, play the piano, or do you just like football and basketball?"

She had been around him enough to know that he liked football and basketball, but she had never explored his other likes and dislikes. To be honest about it, I hadn't explored his likes and dislikes either. Beverly had asked a good question.

"Umm, I like to swim. We learn different swimming strokes at camp."

"What about golf or tennis? Have you ever thought about those sports?"

"Yeah, we have a tennis court at the playground that's near my house. At first, I didn't know how to play. Those white kids were beating me all the time, but now I'm better at it. Next year, I might get my own racket and join this tennis team they have."

I was surprised. Beverly had enlivened him. Usually my son was either smart-mouthed or closed-mouthed with us.

Beverly looked at me and said, "We could buy him a tennis racket and a can of tennis balls, Walter. What do you think about that idea?"

I couldn't believe my ears. I guess Beverly was warming up to the idea of getting to know my son a little better, and that meant the good *and* the bad. I had always thought that she would be a great partner in the child-rearing department, and I was right.

"Sure, we could buy him *that* today," I answered her. "And then we could go out somewhere and play miniature golf."

My son was all smiles. "I like miniature golf," he said. "My mom's friend, Brock, took us to play miniature golf a couple of times."

Walter caught us off guard with that comment. My wife and I looked at each other.

"His name is Brock?" I asked him instinctively.

"No, that's his last name, Brockenborough. His first name is Dennis, and he drives an eighteen-wheeler truck. He let us ride in it a couple of times, too."

Beverly and I were speechless. Walter didn't get it at all. Kids are like that, they just say different things without realizing the impact that they have.

"So, ah, how long have you guys all been friends?" I asked him. I couldn't help to be curious. If there was another man spending quality time with my son, through an association with Denise, then I thought it was only fair that I know about it. It wasn't as if I were a lost-and-found dad who hadn't been around his son. I didn't like being kept in the dark about that kind of thing. I would rather have Walter's good or bad male habits coming from me than from some other man. Or at least, I would like to have the opportunity to know that someone else was stirring the pot.

"Since last year," Walter answered. "But me and Jimmy just started hanging out with him a couple of months ago."

It was a good thing that we had all finished our food. Had my son told me about "Brock" half an hour earlier, it could have spoiled my appetite. It wasn't as if I were concerned about Denise's social life, it was just that it was spilling over to my son without me knowing about it.

"Ah, excuse me, we'll have the check now," I said to our waitress.

Beverly still had not said a word.

"Well, I guess we need to go home and get changed," she finally commented as we all stood. I guess she was going to try and ignore the issue, but I sure wasn't. I made a mental note to give Denise a phone call the first thing that evening.

When we walked out to the car, I asked my son, "Is Brock your mother's boyfriend, or just a guy that she knows from somewhere?" I knew better than that, but I couldn't stop myself from thinking about it. If Denise had the man around the kids, then he was *definitely* more than just a friend. She rarely mixed her personal life with her sons. Even when I dated her, I wasn't around her son, Jimmy, much.

"Well, they go out and stuff, sometimes," Walter answered.

Beverly gave me the evil eye. She let my son inside the car and shut the door in order to have a word with me before I continued with my interrogation.

"Walter, please, let it go," she said. "Let's just have a good time with him today."

"*Let it go?*" I asked her, a little too excitedly. "How can I let this kind of thing go? I didn't even know about this man. I told *her* about *you.*"

Beverly sighed and said, "Look, we'll talk about this later on. Okay? It's not fair for you to keep asking *him* questions about it. He doesn't know what's going on."

I childishly said, "If he thinks he knows everything else, how come he doesn't know what's going on here?"

On that note, Beverly shook her head and climbed in the car. I got in after her, planning on holding my tongue for the rest of the ride. My wife was right; it was no sense in taking anything out on my son. He didn't have any control over anything. I still wished that he had told me about "Brock" a lot earlier, though. A year seemed *far* too long to be left in the dark.

We bought a pair of quality tennis rackets and two tubes of tennis balls from a sporting-goods store before going out to play miniature golf. I had gotten over the initial shock about Denise's friend, but I still planned on calling her before I went to bed that evening.

Once we got Walter on that miniature golf course, he turned into your average twelve-year-old kid, competing against us on strokes, while maintaining an overconfident and youthful swagger.

"*I'm* Tiger Woods!" he joked, like in the popular Nike commercial. I had to laugh at that one. He was beating us both; me by four strokes and Beverly by six, as we neared the eighteenth hole.

"Well, then, loan me a million dollars, Tiger. You can afford it," I joked back to him.

Walter looked at me and frowned. "No way, partner. No freeloaders allowed."

"*Freeloader?* I said *loan* me a million dollars, not can I *have* a million dollars."

"All right, but you have to pay fifteen percent interest on every year that it takes you to pay me back," he told me.

I looked at Beverly and she broke out laughing.

"You mean to tell me that you would make money off your old man?" I asked with a smile.

He looked at me and said, "Business is business, Dad. I can't break the rules for nobody."

Beverly laughed again. My son knew that I worked as a corporate ac-counts executive at Chicago Federal Savings, but I never realized that he understood banking so well. I was actually proud of him. Unfortunately, on my part, I was forever underestimating him. I guess that's what can happen when you're not around a child as much as you could have been. You can easily underestimate, or even overestimate, their potential because you're not that familiar with their normal levels of acceleration and retention. I think his mother's career in financial consulting, however, accounted for a lot of his knowledge on money. That was one of the many reasons why I could never tell her I was the son of a millionaire. I kept thinking that she would eventually try and take me to the bank.

I said, "Okay, what if, ah, Moesha wanted to borrow a million dollars? Would you charge *her* fifteen percent interest?"

"Who, *Brandy?*" he asked me.

"Yeah, Brandy," I said. Her television sitcom about black adolescence and family was so popular that I had forgotten the young singer's real name.

"Oh, man, I would charge her *twenty-five* percent interest!" he answered excitedly. "She has her own TV show, *and* she got a record deal. She's *paid!*"

I looked at my wife and said, "The boy sounds like a money mogul." *And maybe it's even in the genes,* I pondered to myself. My son was beginning to remind me of his grandfather, *my* father, Walter Perry Senior. My father had made a killing in suburban real estate over thirty years ago during the mass American migration from the big cities, mainly white migration. My father was one of the few black men to capitalize on suburban property by using white partners to do most of the meeting and greeting with home buyers and developers, while he masterminded the game plan and bought up more property. Of course, his white partners eventually caught on and started their own companies, but by that time my father had already become a multimillionaire. In fact, I was surprised that not that many people knew about it. My father had done an excellent job of remaining behind the scenes with his wealth, and I had done an equally good job of keeping my inheritance under wraps from Denise. Nevertheless, I had to admit that sometimes I had nightmares of her finding out and taking me to court for millions. Therefore, I made sure that I was never late or short with giving her money for my son. I also had to make sure not to give her too much extra, because I didn't want her getting too curious about my wealth.

• • •

When we got back home that evening, Denise's phone call was at the top of my list of things to do.

"Where are you going?" Beverly asked me.

I didn't want to make the phone call from our bedroom and have my wife listening in, so I planned on making the call from the den.

"I'll be back up in a few minutes, honey. Go ahead and go to bed."

Beverly gave me an inquisitive look. "You're not planning on calling Denise tonight, are you? I mean, it *is* kind of late, and we *all* have to work tomorrow."

It was close to eleven o'clock, and my son was well on his way to dreamland. I was beginning to wish that my wife was too, because I needed to make that call to Denise while the questions were still burning. It was eating me alive!

"Look, I'll just be up in a few minutes," I repeated. I knew that an argument about it would only waste more time.

Beverly sighed and said, "Walter, you need to calm down and think this thing through. Now just sleep on it and call her tomorrow. Okay, honey? I mean, we all had a good time today and I don't think that you should ruin it with this late phone call. She *does* have a right to go on with her life, and I'm sure that she wouldn't have her kids around anyone who would have a bad influence on them. Now just stop overreacting to this thing and come back to bed."

Beverly was being quite persistent. I stood there frozen for a moment. My wife did have a point, but I still wanted to make that phone call. The next thing I knew, Beverly had pulled me back to the edge of the bed and was rubbing my weak spot through my pajamas.

"Is this phone call more important than *us?*" she asked me. "Because I want my husband in bed with me, *right now.*"

Before I knew it, I had a hard-on. That's a damn good sign in any marriage! As long as your partner can get you aroused in two seconds flat, every problem in the world has the ability to fade into oblivion without extensive headaches or the need for psychological therapy.

I smiled and asked, "Do I need to close the door then?"

Beverly smiled back at me. "I don't think it would be good for *us* to be a bad influence on little Walter, either. So I think it would only be right to close the door," she told me with an extra little squeeze on my tool.

I forgot all about that phone call to Denise. I went and checked to see if my son was asleep in the guest bedroom. Once I saw that he was asleep, I crept back to my bedroom, softly shut the door, and happily climbed into bed with my wife.

"So, what do you think about my son now?" I asked her as I kissed her bare stomach and worked my way up.

"I think he's very bright, as I always did, but he's also a little rough around the edges, just like you're being with my nipples," she answered with a smile.

I chuckled and softened up my foreplay. "Sometimes it's good to be a little rough," I told her.

"Yeah, but don't overdo it. Okay?" she said with a hint, as I worked my way back down. "In some places it's good to be gentle and polite."

I chuckled again and went on about my business of enjoying my wife.

The Night Shift

J.D.

D., what's happenin', partner?! I ain't seen you around here for a long while, dawg! What'cha been into? I see your old lady's been doing fine. She got her own office down on Halsted Street in Greektown. I saw her down there just last week."

I shook Barry's chubby hand and smiled at him. I was on the near West Side, close to ten o'clock on Monday night. I was planning to visit an old girl I used to see before reporting to my new job by eleven-thirty. The night-shift position I was starting was at a paper company in that same area.

Barry lived on the near West Side all of his life, shooting the breeze on the street corners and selling good weed. I met him years ago, around the same time I started seeing this girl, Kim. I used to hang out all over Chicago. Since I played basketball in high school, and I had gang affiliates from the Disciples spread out all over the city, I could go any-damn-where I pleased!

I said, "I've been doing a little bit of this and a little bit of that, man, just trying to keep these ends meeting."

Barry nodded. "Yeah, we all gotta do that." He looked as out of shape as he used to, with his fat, meaty head and bowlegs.

"You still selling that good weed you used to sell?" I asked him. I was just curious. I wasn't thinking about buying any.

He looked at me and frowned. "Shit, dawg, I'm still livin' ain't I? And if I'm *livin'*, I'm sellin' it. Why, you want a dime bag?" he asked me.

I shook off the temptation. "Naw, man, I gotta get ready for this new night job in a few hours. I'm gon' try out this midnight shift down at this paper company on Roosevelt."

Barry started laughing. His teeth looked like they needed some serious cleaning. Maybe he'd been smoking too much of that weed of his and not brushing his teeth much. I'd had to start taking better care of my body and hygiene once I rededicated myself to keeping a job. Then I started noticing all of the poor habits of the other guys. I don't think I paid it much attention before.

"The night shift, hunh?" Barry asked me. "Man, I've been working this night shift out here for twenty years," he said, referring to selling weed on the streets. I don't think he ever got arrested for it either. He always kept his money low-key. I don't even think Barry ever owned a car. He just borrowed them when he needed to.

"Yeah, well, maybe I'll check you out some other time," I told him. "I'm on my way to Kim's spot before I make it to this job."

He started smiling again. "You still knockin' Kim, hunh?"

"Naw, not really. I just looked her back up recently."

Barry nodded. "Yeah, well, it do sound convenient and all, especially if you're gonna be working the night shift on Roosevelt. You can just pop on past Kim's spot, get yourself some food and ass, and roll back out for work."

He made it sound like I was a damn swamp leech, but that's exactly what I was planning on doing, establishing a convenient association with an old girl I used to screw.

I said my good-byes to Barry and headed to Kim's apartment. First I had to buzz her on the intercom to get into her aged-looking, four-story building.

"Who is it?" she asked through the rusty, fake silver box. It shocked me. I didn't realize how loud the thing was.

"It's J.D."

"Okay," she answered, buzzing me in.

I made my way up the musty, narrow staircase to her apartment on the third floor and stopped before I knocked on her door. She had a son, too, a six-year-old. I was wondering if he was there, and if he was asleep. I didn't feel like staring into the curious eyes of her kid. He always made me feel guilty about sleeping with his mother. And he always wanted to play with me as if I was his father. That just made me think about spending more time with my own son.

"Long time no see," Kim said when she opened the door. She was wearing a one-piece blue dress that stopped at her smooth, muscular thighs. It was the kind of dress that you could easily slide right off whenever you decided to get busy. I tried not to stare when I first walked in, but I couldn't help it. Kim had run track all her life and she had the best body, except for Neecy, that I had ever wrestled buck naked with. Kim wasn't that bad looking in the face either. In fact, she was pretty, she just had an ugly attitude that could scare guys away from her. She always liked *me*, though, and I wasn't afraid of her.

"So, you got a new job in this area, do you?" She was leading me into her living room area with her ass jingling in front of me. I knew she didn't have anything on underneath her dress. I guess she had the same idea that I had, sex for old times' sake.

As soon as I took a seat on her green couch, she pulled out this fat joint with a lighter and offered it to me.

I looked at her like she was crazy. I didn't want to get high, I just wanted some of that body. "I got a new job to go to in a couple of hours, girl. What's wrong with you?" I asked her.

She smiled and lit it up for herself. "That just makes more for me then."

We used to get high and go at it every time I hung out with Kim. I guess that some things never change for some people.

"Did you buy that from Barry?" I asked her.

"Naw, I got my own shit now," she said.

I looked over at her twenty-seven-inch TV and her Aiwa stereo system. Outside of the building she lived in, Kim was doing all right for herself. "You still work at that restaurant?" From what I remembered, she worked in a restaurant close to downtown on the near South Side. Chicago was basically broken into three sections, North, South, and West. Near or lower meant that you were close to the downtown area, and far meant that you were not. Blacks lived on the South Side and West Side. Whites lived on the North Side and Southwest. The East Side of Chicago was basically the waterfront of Lake Michigan. I grew up in North Lawndale, located on the far West Side, but like I said, I *went* anywhere that I pleased.

Kim shook her head and exhaled the smoke. "Naw, not at that same one. I work at a new restaurant now, down on Adams Street."

Adams Street was even closer to downtown. That meant that she was probably making more money, which would explain her upscale-looking apartment, or at least from the inside.

Her weed was pretty strong, but I still didn't get tempted. I didn't want to go to work *smelling* like I was high either, so I clicked on her floor fan and moved it right in front of me.

Kim started to laugh. "This job must be real important to you." She had these sexy, Chinese-type eyes, and you could never tell when she was high. Kim's eyes always looked small.

"You damn right this job is important to me!" I snapped at her. "They're paying eight-fifty an hour!" Kim had never been to jail like I had. It took me nearly two years to get a job after I came out, and most of them were temporary positions where I had to start all over again after a couple of months. I was looking for something permanent that paid me something, because minimum wage was a damn joke! So I wasn't planning on screwing up my new job opportunity. Good ones didn't come along too often.

All of a sudden, Kim turned sour on me. "Maybe you shouldn't be here at all then. Because I don't want to be the cause of you losing your good job and all. So, um, why don't you come back when you're not working?"

She started walking toward her door as if I was leaving. I looked at the clock and it was only ten-thirty. I had at least another forty-five minutes to blow, and Kim was still looking good to me. I figured I could talk to her and calm her down for fifteen minutes, dig in to her for twenty-five, and wind things down before it was time for me to go.

"Hey, Kim, come on back in here, sis'. I didn't mean to get like that on you."

She slowly walked back into the living room. I patted my lap for her to sit down, but she ignored me.

"You know, you're blowing my high with all this job shit, man. I mean, you make it sound like you're all *greater-than-thou* all of a sudden," she said to me. "You gon' just come up in here expecting to get all up in between my legs, and then won't even get *high* with me! And then you gon' turn on my damn fan so you won't *smell* like you on, for some damn job! I mean, if you feel like that, Jay, why did you even come here tonight? You knew you had to go to work. Because see, *I'm off* tonight, and I *do* enjoy myself when I'm off!"

She was getting pretty loud with me. I looked around and said, "Calm down, girl, you might wake up your son."

"My son is over his grandmother's."

"Oh, I didn't know that," I said.

We were both quiet for a couple of minutes.

"Shit!" Kim snapped again. She even put the weed out. I couldn't believe I had pissed her off that much. "And I went and took *a shower*, for this shit!" she said.

When she said that, I started to laugh, and my pants began to tighten up on me. Maybe it wouldn't take fifteen minutes to talk her into it after all.

"You're telling me you're all showered up and whatnot, hunh?" I asked her with a grin. "Come here, Kim."

She came just close enough for me to grab her onto my knee. Then I slid my hands under her dress, up her thighs, and to the treasure palace.

"I shouldn't even give you none," she teased me. She pushed my hands away. "You don't want to go to work smelling like pussy either."

I started to laugh. "Wait a minute. You said you took a shower, right? And if *I* smell bad, then we can take another one."

"Whatever, Jay. I don't even feel like it no more, man. How's Denise doing?"

I looked up at her and frowned. "Yo, why you always asking me about her when you get mad and shit?"

"Okay, well, how's your son doin'?"

I tried not to let it get to me. "He's tall," I said. "That boy's six-five already, and can play ball better than me; better than I *ever* could. He's gonna be something else to watch. I can't wait to see him play high school ball."

Kim thought she was slick. Asking me about my son was the same as asking about Denise. Kim wanted to get serious a long time ago when I first started seeing her. I didn't know how to break everything to her in one setting, so I told her that I was still seeing my old lady, Neecy. It was a lie at the time, because I felt guilty about not telling Kim about my son. The truth came out in the end though. Kim caught me shopping in a shoe store downtown when Little Jay was around seven. Kim was pissed off at me, but she never really let me go, either. Then she ended up getting pregnant by some knucklehead who was scared to death of me. I think she did that shit just to get back at me, which was sad. I still felt guilty about that. That probably added to my discomfort whenever I was around her son. Kim should have just found some other guy and gone on with her life. She was attractive enough to find someone nice. I never could understand why she was so weak for me. Denise damn sure wasn't. Or at least not anymore.

Kim looked down into my face and asked, "Do you ever miss being with her?"

I couldn't believe she was asking me that. She still had not gotten over her jealousy. Neecy and I had not even touched each other in thirteen years. I started to ask myself why I had even come back to see Kim. She was picking up from where we left off years ago.

"You know what," I asked her, "why do we even do this shit to each other?" I was throwing up my hands with the whole thing.

"I don't know," she answered. She stood up and walked away from me. "You need to ask yourself that question."

I didn't have anything to say. I had no answer for myself. Did I want some sex that bad? I wasn't so sure about my reason for being there. Maybe I just wanted to see how she was doing.

"You know, I wanted to marry you at one time, Jay," Kim said to me. "Even though I knew you had been to jail and you couldn't really provide for me, I just loved being around you. I felt like I was somebody important when I was with you." She looked at me and started laughing, as if the shit was an old joke that *used* to be funny.

"Yeah, that's just because of what I was a part of back then," I told her. My fifteen minutes were up, and it didn't look like I would be getting any skin that night. Maybe that was my problem with Kim, I never took her seriously. All I really wanted from her was good sex. It was *real* good when we were both high. Outside of being physical, we had never communicated any real feelings to each other. I think Kim understood that, and without us being in that special sensitive state that marijuana gives you, we were both scared of the truth.

"So what are we doing now?" she asked me. "Because I don't really understand this. Are we just fucking each other? Are we friends? I mean, what the hell are we?"

I was stuck again, and my time was running out. Why was I thinking so much about the time? I guess I was still taking Kim for granted, and I was still not communicating with her.

"I don't know," I finally answered. What else could I say? I wasn't going to tell her that she was my fuck partner, even though it would have been the truth. It didn't seem right to say that. Or maybe it *was* right, to just tell the truth like it was. But how many guys in their right mind would do that? In fact, maybe we were *all* out of our minds. Maybe relationships just didn't work for men. It seemed like the only time you were happy with a woman was while you were chasing her or having sex with her. Everything else was like being in prison again, where you can't do all that you would like to do. I think love and all that emotional stuff is at its purest form when you're young and don't know anything about life yet. Because once you get older and you know more, that love shit can really get complicated on you and drive you out of your damn mind! That's why men try their best to stay away from that shit. Because when it hits you, there's nothing you can do about it. You end up strung out like a man about to be hanged, waiting to die or to be given mercy.

By the time I left Kim's apartment, I hadn't gotten any sex, but I was glad I was gone! I felt like I was on death row in that place. The room was getting smaller and smaller with every question she asked me. I think that was the best thing to happen to me on my first night of work. I felt energized, like walking out of jail again. If I had gotten some sex, I would have been at least a little tired, and I probably would have wanted to call it a night by the middle of my shift.

I ended up getting to work twenty minutes early and met Roger Collinski, the Polish manager who hired me, at the employee entrance. When I applied for the job, he interviewed me, and we got to talking about our sons and sports. Roger had four sons, and all of them played various sports. He started working the night shift so he could be around during the daytime to see more of their games and practices. I told him I wanted to be able to do the same with my son, and that he was starting high school in September. I think that conversation was what got me the job. Even though I had a record, Roger could relate to how I felt about watching Little Jay run ball. It was like I was getting another chance at being a kid again, and he understood that. I was so happy that he gave me a chance to prove myself that I didn't want anything to go wrong.

"Hey, you're early," he said to me. His manager's office was right next to the employee locker room, so I guess he could keep an eye on any stealing. Or maybe that was my guilty conscience working overtime again.

I said, "Yeah, I know I'm early, but as far as I'm concerned, this job might as well start at eleven. That way, I'll never be late."

Roger looked at his watch and said, "In that case, you're late right now."

I looked him straight in the eyes and said, "It won't happen again, boss. And you can count on that."

Roger laughed and offered me some coffee. He looked like an old-time football player himself. He wasn't as tall as I was, but he *was* as thick as me, *and* he looked as physical in his stance. He had thick gray-ing hair and a bushy mustache to go with it.

"Yeah, I'll take some, with plenty of sugar and cream," I said to him, with a big Uncle Tom grin. I learned how to butter up my employers over the years. It gave me a good reference list for when they couldn't use me anymore. It didn't work too well on brothers though. The broth-ers always thought I was trying to get over on them with some bullshit. I hated working for brothers! A lot of them were the most skeptical bosses in the world. Not all of them, though, because plenty of them were cool. I don't want people thinking that brothers never tried to help me out, it was just more of a strained relationship most of the time because they knew more about me. Some of those white bosses, on the other hand, were some closet racists who couldn't even talk to you with a straight face.

Anyway, Roger gave me a locker number and a dark blue work shirt that had a PPI patch in red and white on the left. The company name was Paper Plus Incorporated. On that first night, I was basically shown the ropes. PPI had three main departments: sales, manufacturing, and shipping and handling. I worked in shipping and handling, which was mostly warehouse work. What we did was stack all of the paper to be ready for shipping, and this paper could get as high as twenty-fucking-feet in the air! If a big enough stack of it happened to fall off from the top, it could put a lump on your head the size of Quasimodo's hunch-back! Other than that, it was a pretty simple job. The hardest part of it would be to just stay up and finish. I would even get a chance to ride forklifts to load up the trucks at the loading docks. When I learned that, I thought of Neecy and her truck-driving boyfriend. I still couldn't be-lieve it. If that was the case, then she could have had *me* back in her life.

"So, what do you think?" Roger asked me at quitting time. It was seven forty-five in the morning. We were lounging in the locker room area. It wasn't that many brothers working at that place, so I guess I could say I was lucky to be there.

"I think that this coffee is gonna be my new best friend," I joked with my new boss. I had my eighth cup of the night in my hand. Roger let the guys get as much coffee as we wanted from the machine in his office.

He smiled and said, "Yeah, you'll get used to it. Usually, it takes your body a good week and a half, and then you won't need as much coffee."

"How much coffee do you drink?" I asked him.

He laughed and answered, "Too much. Actually, I'm down to four cups a night now. When I can get it down to two, then I've *really* done something."

"How many did you start off with?"

"How many did you have last night?" he asked me.

"I'm closing in on ten."

He laughed again and said, "Yeah, I started off with about that much. But we have a five-cup minimum around here. Anything after that, you have to cough up a quarter."

I dug in my pocket for some change, and Roger held up a hand to stop me.

"Jesus, Jay, I was just kidding ya'."

I said, "Yeah, well, that quarter thing is a good idea. I'd get down to two cups in a month with that."

I liked my new job, *and* my new boss. Roger was a straight-up kind of guy. Things were looking good for me so far, but I had to remind myself that it was only my first day. Once I got to know more of the guys on the job, that's when I figured things would really begin to shake themselves out. Hopefully, it would be for the best.

When I got home from work that first morning, or rather to my mother's house in North Lawndale, I was beat. I damn near missed my stop on the train *and* on the bus. I was hoping that I would get enough sleep that morning to get up in time for Little Jay's summer league championship game at four o'clock that afternoon.

I don't remember what time it was, because I never bothered to look, but my mother woke me up that morning to tell me that Kim had called to apologize to me. I had forgotten that we had the same damn phone number for so many years. Kim hadn't called me in a long while! I had always called her more because I was on the go most of the time.

"*Apologize?*" I mumbled to my mother. "Apologize for what?"

She had this look of confusion on her face. She was dressed and on her way out for work. My mom had been working at nickel-and-dime jobs to pay the bills forever. She could have made the Workers Hall of Fame. A lot of black women could. I couldn't deny that. They were some hardworking somebodies!

"She didn't say what for. I told her you were sleeping and she said to tell you that she apologizes for last night, when you wake up. Now I don't know what she's talking about. You would know before I would," my mom fussed at me. She could have made the hall of fame for that, too. Sometimes I wished that she could just ignore me instead of fussing so much.

She stood in the doorway as if I had an answer for her. "I don't know what she's talking about, Mom," I mumbled again.

"Well, I'm goin' in to work," she told me. "You got some leftover chicken and potatoes inside the refrigerator. And if you want anything else, you gotta make it yourself."

I figured I'd call Kim later on and find out what she was talking about, but then I got curious. I couldn't sleep anymore. I just knew she wasn't calling to apologize for not screwing me. She didn't owe me anything. What the hell was wrong with that girl?! I had no idea that my loving was *that* strong to her. She was losing her damn mind!

I stumbled over to the phone in the hallway, pulled it into my room by the cord, and called Kim back.

"Yeah, this J.D. Did you just call my mother, talking about you wanted to apologize to me or something?" I cut straight through the chase.

"Oh, yeah, I did," she said. "Hold on for a minute." She clicked whoever it was off her other line and came back.

"You apologize for what?" I asked her.

"Well, when you told me that you had that new job, and I saw how serious you were about it, I felt bad about myself, and I was sort of jealous. I mean, it all came as a shock to me, that's all."

"*Jealous?* Jealous of what? *You* got a job, and it looks like you're doing *well* to me. I don't even have my own damn place. I mean, what do *you* have to feel bad about? *I* should be the one feeling bad. I'm thirty-four years old and still living with my mom."

Kim didn't make any damn sense, and she was starting to irritate me! You would think that she was the ugliest woman on the planet with the way she *acted* sometimes.

"Yeah, but I was the one with the reefer, and I got all mad because you didn't want to smoke it with me. You just wanted to be presentable on your first day of work, and I realized that I had a lot of respect for what you were trying to do with yourself. And when you talked about your son, you seemed really proud of him, and it just all took me by surprise. You looked real good last night, too."

I guess she was thinking that everything was going to be all fucked in my life when I came over there. Like they say, misery loves company. I just didn't realize that Kim was still that damn miserable.

"Hey Kim, can you answer me a question?"

"Yeah, what?"

"Are you enjoying your life? Because it damn sure don't seem like it."

Kim paused for a long time. I was sorry I even asked her that. What the hell was I thinking?!

"I guess you can tell, hunh?" she asked me back. She sounded real sad about it.

"Naw, you told me last night that you knew how to enjoy yourself," I said.

"Jay, that's just because I was fuckin' mad at you last night, that's all."

I think they call it manic-depressive when people go from happy to sad to angry so quickly. But what was Kim so sad and angry about?

I asked her, "So, you mean to tell me that after all this time, you still haven't found somebody that you could be with?" I had to hear it from her mouth instead of just assuming it.

"I wasn't looking for nobody."

"Why not?" I asked her.

"Were *you* looking for somebody else?" she snapped at me. She had a good point. I wasn't. After Neecy, I was just happy to be screwing different women.

"Why do you like me so much then, Kim? Can you answer me that question?"

"No, I can't."

I didn't know what else to say to her, but I knew that she wanted me to do her again. Real good! I could just tell. Kim was strung out on me like a stray cat for food.

"You still want my company?" I asked her.

"You know I do."

I started to smile and couldn't help myself. There are so many things that people take for granted in life that it doesn't even make any sense. For whatever reason, true love, I guess, Kim still wasn't gonna let me go.

"All right then," I told her. "I'll come back over after my son's basketball game tonight."

"I'm working tonight," she said. She wasn't *that* crazy. She still had her bills to pay. She said, "Why don't you come over after you get off in the morning and rest over here."

That's a good idea! I thought. It was better than catching a train and a bus all the way back to my mother's in the morning.

"Are you sure?" I asked her. I didn't want to do it if it was going to be a forced situation.

"Look, is my name Kimberly Booker?"

"I don't really know. I never saw your birth certificate," I joked with her.

She sucked her teeth and said, "Just be here in the morning. Okay?"

I chuckled and said, "Yeah, okay."

When I hung up the phone with Kim that morning it felt like I had started something I wouldn't be able to control. The whole thing was her idea. I didn't like that too much, but I figured I had to stop running away from shit. I was a grown fucking man, still afraid of everything I had no control over! So I told myself that no matter what happened, I wasn't gonna run away like a punk anymore.

Time and Space

JIMMY was having a championship basketball game, but Denise and I were not going. She said that her son's father would be there and that it was their time and space to spend together. It made perfect sense to me, of course, but I was wondering how long it would take for that kind of thing to play itself out in our relationship. Because eventually, we could all end up at the same place at the same time. There was no way of getting around it.

I took a seat on Denise's living room sofa and wondered if she had even told her sons' fathers about our relationship. Since she was running around making phone calls and cooking dinner, I had to wait awhile before I got a chance to ask her.

It amazes me how much energy women seem to have. They cook, clean, work eight and nine hours a day, and still have time for their kids, their girlfriends, and the men in their lives.

I sat back and relaxed, reading the Chicago news before Walter came up and took a seat beside me.

"Have you ever driven your truck to L.A.?" he asked me. He was always asking me where I had been.

I said, "Yeah, I've been to Los Angeles a few times."

"What does it look like out there?"

"It's real spread out," I told him. "A helicopter would come in handy trying to get around out there. And the highway traffic is ridiculous. It's too many cars out there."

"What do the neighborhoods look like?"

"Flat," I said with a laugh. "They have mountains and stuff out there, but most of your inner-city neighborhoods are on level ground. They don't really have high-rises like Chicago has. It's a whole lot of Mexicans, Koreans, Filipinos, and everything else out there, too. More than what we have."

"You ever see anybody get shot?" Walter asked me.

I looked at him and frowned. "Why are you always asking about crime and stuff? That ain't the only thing going on out there. Why don't you ask me if they have a lot of swimming pools or something? The weather is always warm, that's for sure. Or at least compared to what we get over here. Their idea of cold weather in Los Angeles is fifty-five degrees."

"So why do they wear long shirts and baggy jeans and stuff out there then?"

I said, "You know what? I think you've been watching too many of those rap videos. They don't all wear long shirts and baggy jeans out there. That's just some of them."

"You ever get in any big accidents in your truck?" he asked me with a grin.

The boy just wouldn't quit. He loved talking about drama, more than any other kid I had been around.

"Do you ever think about directing movies?" I joked with him. He was definitely the type. His imagination was out there. Walter had the small body and big mind that plenty of directors seemed to have. I started to smile, thinking about Spike Lee and the kind of questions that he probably asked as a kid.

"Yeah, I could do that," Walter answered with a smile.

"What kind of movies would you make?" I asked him.

"Umm, how 'bout a movie about a truck driver who's like a hero, who drives from town to town and fights off the bad guys?"

I started laughing. "That sounds more like a TV series than a movie. I do like it though."

"All right, all right, movies," he said. He was getting excited by the idea. "How 'bout this then, a movie about a black gang that gets sent out in space to a deserted planet, and then they end up fighting aliens and saving the world."

I laughed even harder. "That idea has already been done a million different times."

"Not with all black people," he argued.

"How 'bout a black horror movie? I haven't seen too many of them," I suggested to him.

"Yeah, I could have a boy who gets killed come back from the dead to get his payback."

I started to frown at him again.

Walter changed his mind and said, "No, they did that already, too, in that *Tales from the Hood* movie. This guy got killed by the cops and then he came back from the grave to get them."

"You saw that?" I asked him. I remembered when the movie was being advertised, but that was a couple of years ago. Walter would have been ten years old, or younger.

"Yeah, we rented it from the video store. That movie was funny."

"Did your mother let you watch that? They had cuss words in that movie, right?"

Walter looked toward the kitchen and grinned. "They got cuss words in a lot of movies. That don't mean *I'm* gonna do it though," he said.

"Good," I told him. "And you remember that you said that."

Denise finally walked out from the kitchen and told us that dinner was ready. We both stood up and joined her in the dining room to eat. Denise made sure that we washed our hands first.

"I already washed my hands," Walter told her.

I hadn't, so I went inside the bathroom to take care of business. When I got back out to the dining room table, Walter was talking about playing tennis.

"Do you have any rackets?" I asked him.

"Yeah, my father bought me some rackets on Sunday," he told me.

I nodded. That reminded me to ask Denise if she had spread the word about us. I planned on remaining cordial and biding my time until I got a chance to ask her in private, but Walter just kept on running his mouth.

"Hey, Brock, I shot a forty-nine in miniature golf on Sunday. I'm getting closer to your forty-two record. My father got a fifty-four."

"That's *Mr.* Brock," Denise corrected him.

I really didn't mind it myself. It didn't make a difference to me. In fact, just plain *Brock* sounded more personal. The boy would probably never call me "Dad," that was for sure.

Walter had me tempted to ask a few questions about his father, but I felt it was inappropriate. Denise was definitely going to have to level with me that night. I wanted to know everything.

After dinner, we were finally alone. Denise said, "Brock, I'm getting ready to go and pick up Jimmy. I'll call you later on tonight."

"What does that mean? You want me to leave?" I hadn't even asked her any of my questions yet.

"Well, I figured it would be nice to have you over for dinner since you're just getting back in from out of town, but I have other things to do."

I was just about to heat things up when I saw Walter getting himself ready for their car ride by tying up his sneakers. I calmed myself down and said, "I have a few things I want to talk to you about tonight. I don't like how things seem to be between us."

Denise brushed it off and responded, "All right." She seemed to be in a rush all of a sudden.

"Are you gonna see him out there tonight?" I asked her, referring to Jimmy's father.

"Of course I will," she said to me. "But I don't have time to talk about it right now, I'm already running late."

"All right, well, I'll talk to you later on then," I told her on my way out the door. A younger man may have gotten pissed by the brush-off.

Denise nodded and said, "Okay," and headed to her car.

"See you, Mr. Brock," Walter said to me, waving.

I waved back to him. "All right, Walter. And you come up with some more original movies, okay? I like the truck driver thing."

He smiled and slid into the car. Then I waved to Denise through her front windshield before she took off. I felt terribly empty when I climbed into my Maxima. Denise was making me feel like the outsider that I was. I actually thought that we were a lot closer than that. Maybe I had it all wrong.

I got back to my place on the South Side and had a sudden urge to look at old pictures of my ex-wife. I was thinking that maybe it would have been more practical for me to have worked things out with Teresa than to get involved with a mother of two. However, Teresa never made me feel the way I did with Denise. I never had any feelings of urgency around my ex-wife. It didn't seem like I cared about too many things when I was with her. Whenever I was with Denise, I considered everything. Maybe that was because my whole relationship with her was more of a long shot.

It's funny how people love to gamble. Gambling causes a rush of excitement, getting something for nothing, or getting more than what you *thought* you could get. Maybe my luck was running out with Denise and I was finally being shown a closed door. I hated to admit that, because that would have meant Larry Nicholson knew something after all.

"Shit!" I cursed. I couldn't believe I had let myself get so close to someone with such a complicated lifestyle, but I wanted to at least talk to Denise about it before I jumped to any conclusions. If I was gonna go out, then I was gonna go out fighting.

Right when I began to sit down and think up a game plan, I got a call from my sister, Debra, out in Tucson, Arizona. Debra was thirty-four, the same age as Denise. She went to DePaul three years after I attended. She studied in political science, graduated in the top tenth percentile of her class, and received scholarship and grant monies to attend graduate school at Arizona State. Talk about a power sister on the move, Debra was one of them. Since she had relocated to the land of the sun, I kept forgetting to think about her and *her* war stories concerning love. Debra was not married, had no kids, and was not even concerned about starting a family. Every time I talked to her, I wondered if any of that had changed. She was so entrenched in the black politics game in Tucson that she even called herself D. Brockenborough to throw people off from her gender. That gave her opportunities to move up the ladder pretty swiftly while working on plenty of political campaigns in that area. It even got to the point where political competitors would fight over who received her services, and Debra made no bones about switching teams if better opportunities presented themselves to her, including working with white politicians. I often joked with her and called her a trader, but she paid me no mind at all.

"How have things been going lately, big brother? I talked to Mom and Dad, and they seem to be doing fine. How are things with you?"

I used to hate when Debra called me "big brother" years ago. It made it seem as if she was rubbing her success in my face, just like Larry would have assumed. I wasn't *always* so sure of myself, especially concerning my little sister. She had made our parents proud, while I made them scratch their heads and ponder. Maybe something really was wrong with black men, myself included. Many of us just didn't seem to be able to take the heat of competition.

I joked with her and said, "Teresa's moving back in with me." Debra never liked her. She considered my ex-wife a whiner long before I could see it. I just thought that Teresa was a little sensitive.

Debra responded, "I know you wouldn't do that, Dennis. So what's *really* going on in your life?"

"What's going on in *your* life would be a better question," I told her. I didn't feel like talking about myself to Debra that night. She would start figuring out solutions when sometimes I didn't want any. When you get to a certain age, you can call it senile if you want, but you like to figure out your *own* damn problems.

"Don't wanna talk about it, hunh? Same old big brother," she said with a chuckle. "It's good to see that you're healthy."

"What about you? Have you been doing anything healthy lately?" I could picture my sister calling me from one of the tallest buildings in Tucson, as she paced in front of her office desk where she was working overtime. Since it was after eight in Chicago, it was only after six in Tucson. Debra would work up until nine at night sometimes, a workaholic just like Denise. I guess I was already used to dealing with her type of woman from being so close to my sister. Of course, I never *dated* my sister. Her body wasn't as fine as Denise's anyway. Debra had a blackboard butt like a white girl. Not *all* black women were gifted. I used to wonder if that had something to do with my sister's reluctance to flaunt her sexuality, but I excused that as plain ridiculous thinking on my part. White girls didn't stop flaunting what they had.

"Well, I've been playing a lot of golf lately," Debra answered.

"Golf?" Despite the popularity of Tiger Woods, I could picture her being one of three black faces out there, all of which were newcomers who couldn't play a lick. "What kind of scores are you getting?"

"Well, I just started breaking a hundred recently."

"And what kind of campaign are you working on this year, white or black?"

"Power has no color," she answered.

I took that to mean a white campaign. "So you're trading on us again."

"No, I'm simply trying to learn how to get us what we need."

"By sleeping with the enemy?"

"Whatever it takes."

I didn't mean that "sleeping with the enemy" term literally, and I was terrified to ask if *she* meant it that way. If my little sister was out there, literally, sleeping with white men in the politics game, then I didn't even want to know about it.

I said, "So, how hot is the weather out there, the same as usual?"

"Well, does Chicago have wind?"

We laughed, and were off the subject that quickly. Debra didn't want to go into her personal life either. Good idea.

I looked at my watch, wondering how long it would take for Denise to get back in from picking up her son.

"When's the next time you might make your way on home?" I asked my sister.

"Oh, I'll pop up when I'm least expected. You know how hectic my schedules can be."

"Yeah, well, get in touch with me when you do," I told her.

"All right, big brother. I'll talk to you next time."

I hung up with Debra and thought about how quickly she could size up an unconfident man. If America kept producing women like Denise, Debra, and plenty others, a lot of these young men could end up wearing skirts in the next millennium. That was the prevailing thought line for my game plan with Denise. I figured it may have been time to show her a little bit more of my backbone.

Denise didn't call me until after eleven. I forced myself not to call her because I didn't want to seem pressed about it, and I wanted to see if she would stand by her word.

"Brock, this has turned into a very long night for me, and now I'm extremely tired. So if it's at all possible, how about we do lunch tomorrow instead?"

I paused for a moment. "It doesn't sound like I have a choice," I told her. I had been waiting for nearly four hours to talk to her. It really seemed like she was trying to avoid the issue.

"Don't take it like that," she pleaded.

"How am I supposed to take it then?"

"Just meet me for lunch tomorrow."

It sounded real simple to *her.*

I asked, "What if I *can't* meet you for lunch tomorrow?"

She sighed and said, "Okay, you win. Let's talk now."

I didn't like how that sounded either. I said, "Denise, what do you and I mean to each other?"

She didn't answer me right away. I guess she had to think real hard about it. Then she said, "I need time to evaluate that kind of question."

"*I* don't," I told her.

"Okay then. What do *I* mean to *you?*"

"You mean *a lot* to me," I told her.

"And what exactly does 'a lot' mean, Brock? I mean, where do you expect us to go with this?"

"Oh, so I guess now it's all coming out. You never meant for us to be much," I said. I swear, if I was ten years younger, I would have started cursing her out, full of immaturity and ego. Fortunately, I was getting too old for that kind of irrational behavior. I believed that Denise realized my maturity and was using it to her advantage to keep me at arm's length.

"Brock, it's not as if we've made some kind of commitment to each other. We've been having a good time and everything, but you have your private life and I have mine."

"Oh, so *that's* how you see it? I thought I *was* part of your private life. I don't have a private life outside of you. I thought I made that clear when we first started sleepin' together."

I didn't mean to go there. I hadn't felt that passionate with a woman for a long time. Like the saying goes, *It's a thin line between love and hate,* and Denise was really bringing that thin line out of me.

"I think you need to calm down before we finish this conversation. Okay? Because I'm not going to get into this."

She said earlier that I had won, but in reality, she had. Denise had effectively turned me into a whiner. I felt ashamed of myself. I had to get a better grip on the situation. What would a young man like Larry think if I didn't? I had to lead by example.

I said, "I understand that you've had a very hard time to get to where you are, Denise, but life isn't easy for any of us. And when you find yourself with an opportunity to make life more meaningful by including another loving and giving person in it, I don't find anything wrong with that. Now, I'm not the most religious man, but *you've* been going to church every Sunday for years, and I still don't think that you've learned how to open yourself up to sharing the gift of love that God gave to all of us.

"So, with that, I'm sorry for wasting your time, and I'm sorry for caring so much and wanting to be a part of you and your family."

Denise gave me another long sigh. "Can I call you tomorrow?" she asked me.

I said, "I don't want you to feel obligated. You've made it perfectly clear to me tonight that you don't need me in your life. I'm just window dressing."

"I didn't say that I didn't want you in my life."

"Nor did I, but it seems that you only *want me* on *your* terms. I'm a human being, Denise. I'm not some damn vibrator that you can turn off and on. I got feelings over here."

"I understand that."

"Do you? I mean, do you really? Because it just seems to me that you've gotten so used to showing your own strength and pushing your way through everything that you've forgotten how easy it is to step on people in the process."

"Brock, I'm sorry. Okay? But like you've already said, things have not been easy for me, and I just don't count on too much from people anymore."

I said, "Look, you told me when I first started going out with you that we all need to push a little harder to attain our goals in life, but now you're turning your back on all of that. Or maybe *I'm* not a part of your goals.

"I'm not asking you to count on me, Denise, I'm just asking you to be real with me," I told her. "And if we're really gonna be together, then I think that you should *also* let everyone involved *know* about it. Because it's not like we just met each other yesterday. We've been doing this for a year now, slippin', slidin', and hidin'. And frankly, baby, I'm tired of that shit."

"Well, you're just gonna have to give me time. I'm not gonna tell you anything right now that I really haven't thought about yet," she told me.

That was a bunch of bullshit, but I was going to let it slide. Denise had plenty of time to think about where things were headed between us. Even Debra would have *thought about it* after seeing the same man for a damn year! Or would she? Had relationships become so fruitless to women that they didn't expect *anything* out of them? Then again, since Denise and I both had hectic work schedules, the most we got to see of each other in that year was an average of once or twice a week. Maybe we did need more time together before I could realistically expect progress.

I calmed myself down again and said, "All right. That's fair. We'll do it that way then." I was planning on playing my cards slowly and taking things as they presented themselves, one step at a time.

"Thank you," Denise told me.

"Okay. Well, have a nice sleep."

"I sure will."

I hung up with her and felt honestly confused. Was Denise all talk and no action? I was itching to find out. I knew one thing though, no matter how rich or powerful women got, men still have to handle things like men, and that means explaining your territory: how you feel, what you expect, what you're *not* gonna take, and how you need to be respected.

I had a lot of respect for Denise. There was no question about it. However, if I ever expected to take things further with her than just being a sneak-around friend, then she had to have some respect for me as well.

Strength and Angels

AFTER taking lunch, I walked into my small office, near downtown Chicago on Halsted Street, and prepared my desk for a two-thirty appointment. Elmira, my Latina secretary, gave me the message that Walter Jr. had called while I was out.

"He didn't leave a message?" I asked her. That was unusual for Walter, but I figured whatever it was, it had to be dealing with our son. If he was calling during work hours, then it was urgent. Or at least from *his* point of view. I was just hoping that he wouldn't be bothering me concerning a custody battle unless he was seriously ready to go to court. In all honesty, I didn't believe he had an *inch* of a case! Nevertheless, that didn't mean that I wasn't at least nervous about it.

"He just said that he'd call you later on tonight at home," Elmira told me.

I told myself not to worry about it. I had a job to do.

"Any other messages?" I asked my secretary. She would have told me on her own if there were; I wanted to move on to a new subject as quickly as I could by forcing the issue.

"No, it was just that one call," Elmira answered, with her beautiful, dimple-faced smile. She was a really attractive young woman, who received plenty of invitations to dates, from every kind of man under the sun. But Elmira was smart enough to know what true love was, and she wasn't going to sell herself short by being overwhelmed with the offers.

I felt guilty when I first thought about hiring her because I realized there were many sisters in Chicago in need of a good job. However, after I thought about how black men and women had been ignored by whites, hiring *their* own people, I decided that my Latina sister, a minority herself, was just as needful for a fair opportunity. Besides, she was the best applicant for the position. Then she was able to get me plenty of clients from Chicago's Latino community, which I did not expect at the time I hired her, but I damn sure accepted after the fact. So it all worked out for the best.

At precisely 2:36, Sylvia Livingston, a thirty-nine-year-old mother of three, and a lifetime resident of Chicago's South Side, walked into my office. It had just stopped raining earlier, and the sun was back out in full force, creating a muggy heat. Sylvia had walked right through the middle of it, wearing a burnt orange suit, an off-white blouse, and a matching wide-brimmed church hat. Fresh sweat was pouring down her face as she furiously wiped herself with a handkerchief.

"Oh, I'm *so* sorry I'm late, Sister Stewart, but those buses never seem to act right when you're in a hurry. Those bus drivers get ta' socializin' and singin', and all the while, you got some place ta' get to," she said as she took a seat in front of my desk.

Sylvia was one of my most progressive clients. I had called her down to my office to discuss different programs to shell money away for her youngest son to go to college in ten years. She was one of the few welfare recipients that I could convince to start some kind of savings. She understood the type of determination it would take to turn her finances around. She found herself a steady job, got off welfare in less than three months, and had been working hard, steadily, and more important, saving her money ever since. I was so proud of her commitment and progress that I made an oath to myself to sing her praises as much as I could to other clients who needed an extra push to believe that they could make it.

After she had explained her tardiness and sweat to me, I smiled and offered Sylvia some bottled water out of my mini refrigerator.

"Oh, thank you *so much*, Sister Stewart, I *really* appreciate this," she responded. She took the bottled water and gulped it down without using the plastic cup that I had given her. "Whew, that's some *good* water! Praise the Lord! He is so *great!* Only *he* can make water this good, sister. What's the name of it?" she asked, inspecting the label. "Clear Lakes, like in cleanliness."

Sylvia was definitely a character. She had been through more men

than I care to think of, but she did love her children. I couldn't hold her
jones for love against her. I guess "The Good Lord" was her new
boyfriend.

"So, how much did you say you had saved away for David again?" I
asked her. If I hadn't cut her off, we could have spent a half hour talking
about nothing.

"Oh," she said, digging through the papers in her purse. She pulled
out an account statement and read, "Four hundred sixty-two dollars and
twelve cents."

"And you still have that in the money market?"

"Just like you told me."

"Okay now, to get even more interest out of his savings, I've been
looking at some aggressive growth accounts that are yielding as high as
thirteen to sixteen percent."

"Mmm," Sylvia grunted. "The money market is only four point five
percent."

"That's right. So you see how much of a difference it would make in
the long run," I told her.

"Three and four *times* the difference," she said, with wide eyes.

I smiled and nodded my head, right before the phone buzzed.

"Hello," I answered.

Elmira said, "It's Walter, calling you back. He said it would only take
a second."

"And that's about all I have," I told her.

Walter came on the line and said, "I just wanted to ask when would
be the best time to call you tonight. I know how busy you are, and I really need to talk to you."

About what? I wanted to ask. But I held my tongue.

"Tonight may be a bad night altogether," I told him. "I have a lot of
runs to make. How about I just call you tomorrow night?"

"What time?"

Sylvia was all up in my face. I had to get off that phone, and in a
hurry, especially with "Sister Livingston" in my office. She could read
conversations like a detective. In particular if they were with men. She
could smell a man in the air like a chef could smell food.

"I'll let you know around this time tomorrow."

"Thank you," Walter responded.

I looked at the big grin on Sylvia's face and realized I had gone past
my second.

She said, "These men believe they can just barge into your life anytime they good and well please. Don't they, Sister Stewart?"

I shook my head, smiled, and set out to ignore it. "Ah, getting back to business, Sylvia."

"*Oh*, I'm sorry, Sister Stewart. I didn't mean to get into your personal associations. *Please* forgive me! I had no right to do that. No right at all!" Her apology only prolonged the issue.

I tried to ignore it again by passing her the information I had gathered.

"Do you forgive me, sister?" she persisted.

I looked up and said, "Of course, I forgive you. We're only human. Only a few of us can live without talking about men, and believe it or not, the men are even worse than we are sometimes."

"Yeah, but they talk about us so *nasty*, Sister Stewart. Do you listen to some of these rap songs they have about us today? These young rappers are talkin' 'bout doin' it this way, and doin' it that way, two at a time and all kinds of nasty, godforsaken stuff. They even got the young women gettin' just as nasty now. Foxy Momma and carryin' on."

"Foxy Brown," I corrected her. I only knew because my sons were fans of hers. I had mistakenly fallen right into Sylvia's favorite subject: nastiness.

"That's her! And do you see some of these videos that they're in?" she asked me.

Of course I had. I had been the one to turn them off whenever I caught either of my sons watching them instead of doing more constructive things, like flipping through the World Book encyclopedias I invested in, or learning how to better use the computer I had bought. In fact, because of computers and the use of the Internet, I had heard it said a few times that encyclopedias were on their deathbed.

"Ah, Sylvia, we are really getting off on a tangent here, and I want to get us back on track. Okay?" I said with a lighthearted chuckle.

She looked stunned for a second, as if I had snatched away her Thanksgiving Day chitlins and called her a sinner. "Ah, you're right, sister. You're *absolutely* right! I need to get this filth from my mind."

I couldn't help but smile at Sylvia. She just couldn't help herself. Before we could get back to business though, I got another phone call.

"Is this one *really* important?" I asked Elmira. My patience was beginning to wear thin.

"Ah, it's your son, Jimmy," Elmira bashfully responded. It wasn't her fault that I wasn't getting much done.

"Okay," I told her with a pause. I prepared myself for anything. Sometimes I just wished that my sons would call every once in a while and say, "Mom, I love you." But that was only wishful thinking.

Jimmy was *telling me*, not *asking me*, that he was going to the movies.

"I don't think that's a good idea. Your brother will be getting home from camp before you get back," I calmly responded to him. "Why don't you wait and take him with you?"

"Mom, I got friends going? I get tired of taking him with me."

"So, what are you gonna do, leave him at home?"

"Yeah, he can watch TV or play the video games until *you* get home?"

Wrong answer! "Ah, I don't think so. Okay? Now if you don't want to take him with you, then you wait until I get home. As a matter of fact, you wait until I get home to discuss this anyway, because I don't want to hear his mouth about you not wanting to take him."

Jimmy said, "Aw'ight." He hung up a little too quickly. I didn't have time to respond to his attitude. I would deal with it when I got home.

When I hung up the phone again, Sylvia lightly touched my hand.

She said, "Before I met you and Sister Jenkins at SMO, I didn't have a *clue* how to handle my boys. But you two have taught me so much, and have given so much of your time to so many others, that I really do believe you all were sent from the Lord. May God bless you, sister. And may he give you the strength to keep doin' what you're doin'."

I smiled and said, "Thank you very much, Sylvia. Sometimes, you just don't know how much I need a healthy pat on my back for my efforts."

She said, "I *know* you do. We *all* need a pat on the back. And sometimes we all are called on by the Lord to be his angels."

I nodded. "Well, you've surely been *my* angel, Sylvia," I told her.

"And you've been mine right back, Sister Stewart."

I said, "Okay, now let's get back to what we were doing."

Sylvia straightened up in her chair and responded, "Aggressive growth accounts for my son to get to college."

I smiled, shook my head, and got back to my work. Sylvia may have been a character, but she was nobody's fool; at least not anymore. And I was good and proud of her.

Every time I even thought about giving up on helping people, I found new strength to keep going. Maybe Sylvia was right, and my gift from God was being helped along by words of encouragement and faith from plenty of human angels spread out all around me. I *needed* every single one of them, too!

I got home, had a talk with my two sons about family togetherness, cooked dinner, and ended up having yet another conversation with my younger sister. I talked to her about her responsibilities as a mother and how bad habits with men can make her life a lot harder than what it needed to be.

"Nikita, Mom said that you were out all last night and left her to watch Cheron." I really didn't want to be the disciplinarian in my sister's life, but *somebody* had to do it.

She sighed and said, "You know what? I don't even know why she told you that. She knew I was going out. She *said* I could leave Cheron with her!"

"Yeah, well, she didn't know that you were gonna be out *all night*. She probably thought that you were just going to a movie or something. And knowing you, I can imagine you didn't give her any specifics," I argued.

Nikita and my two-year-old niece, Cheron, had just moved back in with my mother a couple of months ago to a two-flat house on the West Side that I was helping to pay the mortgage on. I hated to tell Nikita to shape up or ship out, but we both knew that I could if I had to. She had been trying to save up to find a new place of her own, and that was the only reason my mother and I decided to let her stay, rent-free. I had given my sister plenty of money before, but she would blow it on I don't know what, so I wanted to see how responsible she could be when saving her own money. To hell if *I* was gonna help her get an apartment and then have *my* money go down the drain over *her* stupidity!

Nikita had a serious problem of being suckered out of her pocket change by these corner-hanging men she likes so much. She reminded me of a younger version of Sylvia Livingston, but at least Sylvia had come to her senses and realized that her children were her priority. I don't know what it was going to take for my sister to get that message, but she needed to get it fast, because she was nowhere near being a teenager who didn't know any better.

"So, does this mean that I have a *curfew* while I'm living here? Because I'm too old for this shit," she snapped.

"Exactly. And you're also too *old* to be hanging out in the streets like you do," I responded.

"Neecy, I wasn't *in* the damn streets! Okay? I'm not out there like that!"

"First of all, I'd like for you to call me *Denise*—"

"What?!" she shouted at me again. "You know what? I don't even need this shit! So if you and Mom want me to move out, just say the word. Because y'all not gon' treat me like some damn kid!

"I go out for *one* night, and then I have to deal with all of *this?!* And it ain't even fair!"

I was ready to tell her that nothing in life was fair, and that if she thought she could use that as an excuse to fuck up, she was dead wrong! However, before I got a chance to, she walked away from the phone and slammed the door to the second bedroom that she and her daughter were sharing. I had already learned *my* lesson, but like I kept telling my mother, I could not live *Nikita's life* for *her.*

My mother picked up the phone and said, "You see how hardheaded she is? She's just like you were, but at least you knew how to take care of your own kids."

I didn't know whether to take my mother's comments as a compliment or as a reminder of how irresponsible *I* had been. I was a lot younger than my sister when I got into trouble, though. Sometimes it seemed as if she was playing a destructive game of catch-up. Nevertheless, dealing with her problems, and everything else that was going on in my life, only added to my daily headaches.

I hung up with my mother after she made several more comparisons and contrasts between my sister and me, and decided to call Camellia.

I sighed and said, "Camellia, I've been getting my tail kicked from every which way, and I need you as my good friend right now, because I can't take much more of this."

"Take much more of what?" she asked me.

"Of everything; my sister, my mother, my sons' fathers, Brock, work. I just need a damn vacation somewhere!"

"Well, go ahead and take one. I've been telling you that for a while. When you have your own business, you can take as many vacations as you want."

"Yeah, and then you won't *have* any business," I told her. "Besides, that would be irresponsible to the people who count on me."

"Mmm hmm," Camellia grumbled, "that's exactly why you're so burned out now, Denise, you won't allow yourself a chance to rest. Everybody deserves a vacation, especially single mothers. But we seem like the last to get one. And *you* can afford it.

"But anyway, ah, what's the problem with Brock?" she asked me, changing the subject. "I thought that he was your knight in shining armor."

I tried to refer to Dennis by his first name as often as I could, but since he was used to being called "Brock," the two names became interchangeable. I was one of the few people who actually called him "Dennis." I guess I was name sensitive because of my own resentment at being called "Neecy" and wanting to reestablish myself as "Denise." It was just an issue of respect for people's proper names. Then again, I loved to refer to Walter as *Junior*, in an attempt at slander. However, he *was* a Jr.

Anyway, I answered Camellia's question and said, "He's getting serious, and he wants to announce us to the world."

"Mmm," Camellia grunted. Then she started to laugh. "I knew *that* was coming. But I bet he ain't talking about no wedding bells yet, is he?"

"And I'm glad he's not. That would just make my life *more* complicated. I haven't even told either of my sons' fathers about him. I just didn't think it was any of their business."

Camellia paused for a moment. "You know, I just had a good discussion about that. And I came to the conclusion that the best thing to do in that situation is to be up-front with your children's father, or *fathers*, as quickly as you can. That way you don't feel guilt-ridden when you're in a new relationship."

"Yeah, but are you gonna do that every time you go out with a new man? That sounds ridiculous. 'Oh, by the way, I'm going out with John tonight.' That doesn't make any sense to me," I argued.

"I thought about that too, and the conclusion was that we simply can't date as many men as we would like to," she told me. "Most of us should have been more picky about our men in the first place, but now we're *forced* to be. Because you can't have all those different men around your kids."

Camellia was always thinking of single mothers as a whole, including white, Latina, *and* Asian mothers.

"Well, I'm not talking about having every man around your kids. I would *never* do that," I responded to her.

"But you *do* have Brock around them," she reminded me.

I said, "Dennis is a good brother, though."

"And that's the *only* kind of brothers we should be dealing with," Camellia said. "I had the same discussion with Monica; 'If you can't bring them home for me to meet, then you need to leave them out there in the street. And I *don't* expect to meet a new one every other month either!' "

I burst out laughing and immediately thought about the talk I had that Sunday with my son. "You're right about that," I told her.

"You *know* I'm right. We talked about this *several* times. But see, that's why you need to keep your faith in our meetings," she advised me. "Whether these evil sisters are jealous of you or not, they still need to hear your story of success. They need to have a concrete example to emulate. They need a monthly dose of you like taking nasty medicine," she said with a laugh.

"Yeah, and that's exactly how I feel sometimes, like nasty medicine," I responded. I felt better already. Camellia Jenkins was my *girl!* The biggest angel I knew!

"So, are you still recruiting white women?" I joked with her. Camellia wanted to reach out to everyone. The SMO had become her mission in life.

"As a matter of fact, I am," she answered.

Chicago wasn't known for its racial harmony. White women did their thing and we did ours. White women always seemed to act as if their problems were so different from ours, except of course when they needed us to beef up their number of feminists on certain political issues. Camellia was out to change that.

I chuckled and said, "They wouldn't let us in *their* organizations unless we were Oprah Winfrey and friends, and only then as their 'special guests.' "

"Yeah, well, we've never been exclusive like them, and we never will be," she insisted.

I had some thoughts about that, but I didn't mention them. I had been around a few groups of upper-class sisters who *were* exclusive. But they were definitely a minority in the African-American community. Most sisters were hardworking, underpaid, blue-collar women.

"I'm bringing Nikita with me to the next meeting, too," I told Camellia.

"Mmm, how's she doing?" she asked me.

"I just finished talking to her, as a matter of fact. She's doing about the same, still denying everything," I answered. "She told me off and dropped the phone because I had a few words about her hanging out all night and leaving Cheron at home with my mother."

"Well, bring her on," Camellia said. "But you need to drag her behind into church, too."

I chuckled and said, "One step at a time, girl. One step at a time."

After hanging up the phone with Camellia, I thought hard about calling Dennis. It had only been a few days since we last talked about the extent of our relationship, and I hadn't called either of my sons' fathers to break the news. I didn't know if I really wanted to. I still considered Dennis to be my privacy issue. However, I *had* allowed him around my sons, Camellia was right about that. And deep down inside I guess I really wanted to bring him closer to me through his interaction with the boys.

I looked at the clock and it was close to ten. The boys were still up watching television down in the family room. I had smoothed everything out with them, and promised Jimmy that he could go to the movies with his friends that weekend. As it turned out, his friends had changed their minds at the last minute and decided to go on Saturday after their basketball game. I guess I had more angels working for me than I thought.

Anyway, I walked in the family room to join them, to see what they thought about Brock. I knew they got along with him, but I still hadn't told them that we were anything more than friends, although I realized they could have easily assumed as much.

I turned the TV down a notch. They knew they didn't need it up so loud. It seems like everything boys do is in excess. Then they keep the same habits when they become men.

"Can I talk to you two about something?" I asked them. I knew it wouldn't be their kind of discussion, so I was being polite.

Jimmy looked at Walter and said, "Oh boy, here we go."

I got pissed off before I even started. "And what is that supposed to mean?"

Jimmy smiled and shook his head. "Nothin', Mom."

"It meant *something*. You said it, didn't you? Anyway," I said, getting back on track with what I wanted to talk about. "How do you two feel about Brock?"

They looked at each other and started to smile.

"What about him?" Walter asked me.

"Well, you know, what do you think about him? Is he cool?" By asking them that, I was attempting to be a "cool mom" myself.

Jimmy grinned and responded, "Yeah, he's aw'ight."

"Why, you like him?" Walter asked me.

Jimmy was paying strict attention to that answer.

"Okay, what if I did like him?" I responded.

Then Jimmy started to laugh.

"What's so funny?" I asked him.

He shook his head again, still smiling. "Nothin'."

"My dad was asking me about him this weekend," Walter told me.

I looked at him and questioned, "He was *asking* about him? What do you mean he was *asking* about him?" It seemed that the cat was out of the bag anyway. I don't know what made me think it wouldn't be, especially with *Walter's* big mouth.

"He asked me if y'all were more than friends and stuff, and I didn't know. But now you're saying that you like him," he answered with a grin. I guess that was a good thing. I'd rather see a grin than a frown.

"Well, how did your father even know about him?"

"I told him that he took us to play miniature golf, and that he was your friend."

I just started to smile. I decided right then and there to call both of their fathers and tell them about Dennis the next evening.

"And what about you, Mr. Giggles? Does *your* father know anything?" I asked Jimmy.

He said, "Yeah, he knows."

"When did you tell him?" I asked him.

"A couple weeks ago," he answered with another chuckle. My oldest son was getting a big kick out of the whole thing.

"Did he ask, or did you just come out and tell him?"

"He, ah, asked me if you were seeing anybody."

"And you told him what?"

Jimmy just couldn't stop smiling and laughing. He was making *me* feel silly.

"I'm serious about this, Jimmy. What did you tell him?" I asked him again.

"I told him that you had a truck-driver friend, that's all."

I was shocked. "You told him that Brock was a truck driver? What did that have to do with anything?" It wasn't funny anymore. I knew exactly how J.D. thought, and me going out with a truck driver was not his idea of where I should be as a black businesswoman. Something like that would encourage him to continue regarding me as some ghetto girl. He already found it hard to refer to me as Denise instead of Neecy.

I shook my head and let out an "Oh my God! I don't believe you told him that," I said.

Jimmy, seeing how surprised I was, began to curb his laughter. "My bad, Mom. But he was gonna keep asking me about it until I told him something."

"So what did he say about it?" I could just imagine.

Jimmy started again with the laughing. "Well, he says stuff like, you know, 'How's your mom and her truck driver doin'?' "

Walter started to crack up, too, after that. I felt crushed, but to hell with J.D.! Who was *he* to talk?! Brock was a decent man, and he was just as tough or intelligent as anyone. Plus, *he* knew how to treat a lady!

"And what about you? Did you tell *your* father that Brock was a truck driver, too?" I asked my youngest. Walter's father would have expected as much. He always considered himself to be of a higher class anyway. He acted just like a white man sometimes. I guess I was the plantation mistress who bore him a mulatto child. The self-righteous asshole! That was exactly why I didn't tell either of them about my relationship with Dennis. It wasn't any of their damn business!

"I didn't tell him that he was a truck driver," Walter said. He sounded as if he was proud of himself. Then he added, "I just told him that he *drives* a truck."

Jimmy looked at him and said, "Aw, man, that's the same thing."

I chuckled and shook my head. "Well, *I'll* be telling *both* of your fathers what I need to tell them tomorrow, because I *definitely* don't need *you two* spreading my business."

After my sons had gone to bed, I thought again about calling Brock. It was after eleven by then. I didn't know if he would be in or not, but I called anyway and got no answer. Then his answering machine came on.

"Hello, this is Dennis Brockenborough. As you can see, I'm not in right now, but kindly leave a message, and I'll get back to you as quickly as I can."

For a minute, I didn't know what kind of a message to leave or if I even wanted to leave a message. I simply told him that I had called and that he could get back to me at his earliest convenience. After I thought about it, I came to the conclusion that maybe it would have been best to talk to Dennis only after I had spoken to J.D. and Walter. I was sure that he would eventually ask me about them again, so I was hoping he wouldn't call me back for a day or two.

Lord give me strength *indeed!* I prayed as I went to bed. *And thank you for all of your angels!*

Know Thyself

B WALTER EVERLY handed me the phone shortly after I got in from work. "It's Denise," she said, before leaving the room. She always gave me privacy when I spoke to Denise. Beverly did not want to be involved in any issue that she didn't need to be concerning my son's mother.

I had tried to contact Denise at work about her truck-driving boyfriend spending time with my son. After calming down for a few days, it slipped my mind. Her phone call reminded me.

She said, "So, I guess you know that I've been spending time with someone—not that it's any of your business—but I thought it would be best that you hear it from me before you start jumping to conclusions about what you heard from your son."

"Actually, my only concern about it was not *knowing* that this man had been spending time with my son," I responded to her.

"That's only been recently," she said.

"Nevertheless, that *was* my concern. So, how many times has he been out with my son, and where were you during these outings?"

Denise paused and responded, "Walter, I am *not* calling you to discuss times and dates, I was simply letting you know where I stood with things, so that you wouldn't accuse me of something ridiculous."

"And what would I be accusing you of?" I asked, just to humor myself. Denise swore that she knew my every thought, and that always bothered me because she really didn't.

"Of having my son around *so-called* bad influences," she snapped.

She was right about that, I had to admit it. I especially didn't like my son being around her oldest son's father, J.D. No young, impressionable boy should be around him.

"Well, I'm sure that your choice of men is highly respectable," I shot back at Denise. I really didn't need to say that, it just happened. I believe I was a little peeved that she had read me right. However, her track record with men was *far* from perfect.

She responded, "See, that's the kind of shit that makes me hate even having to speak to you. You're *not* a saint, okay? I just want you to know that. And I'm sure that your wife knows it, too. She just puts up with your ass because she feels dedicated to being a good wife. She would leave your *phony ass* in a heartbeat if she wasn't!" she yelled, before hanging up the phone in my ear.

I considered her actions to be rather childish. I was even tempted to call her back and tell her about it, but I decided against it.

It was very quiet as Beverly and I ate tuna casserole that evening. We seemed lifeless for some reason. Kids running around can make a household lively at all times, but we didn't have any yet. In the silence, I thought more of Denise's phone call. I kept thinking about her comments concerning my wife staying with me out of dedication. What was so wrong with that? Dedication was what *all* marriages should be about, but since Denise had never been married, I guess that she wouldn't know. Nevertheless, I needed some reassurance from my wife.

I said, "Beverly, I want to ask you something."

She lifted her head toward me with her fork in hand. "Yes." I got lost for a second, staring at her perfect face. She had so much simple beauty, composure, and class. My parents loved her as much as I did.

"Do you, ah, consider me a hard man to love?"

She immediately started to grin. "What would make you ask me that?"

"I don't know," I lied. "I just figured that I'd ask you."

She stopped grinning and nodded her head. "What's your own opinion on that?"

"To tell you the truth, I really haven't given it much thought," I told her.

Beverly began to frown. That didn't look like a good sign. "Sometimes, it doesn't seem that you consider a lot of things," she responded.

I said, "So, that sounds like I *can* be difficult."

"You just fail to think about others a lot of times. The world and everything in it revolves around you," she responded. "But, you know, I expected that being that you're an only child."

I began to wonder how long Beverly had thought that way about me. "And how long have you had *this* opinion?" I asked.

"Walter, you've *always* been that way." She said it as if it was as constant as gravity.

"So, how come you never told me that?"

"In so many words, I have," she said. "You just never seemed to hear me."

She started grinning again, as if it were some kind of joke to her, and that began to piss me off. "Beverly, if you did something I didn't particularly like, I'd tell *you* about it," I snapped at her.

"Yeah, you always do," she said back.

That got me even hotter! "I don't believe this," I said. "You've felt this way about me the whole time, and you've never said a word about it."

"Yes, I have," she shot back at me. "I've already told you that I have."

"Yeah, but you didn't tell me straight, you beat around the bush about it. God, I hate that!" I shouted at her. "If you have something to say to me, Beverly, then I would appreciate it if you said it like you mean it!" I didn't mean to keep raising my voice at her, yet whenever I got excited about something I couldn't seem to help it.

Beverly stared at me with evil intentions. She said, "There are a lot of things that you do that I don't like."

"Oh yeah? Well, let's get them all out in the open, now that we're finally being *honest* with each other." I was filled with plenty of venom that night. My wife was really pushing my buttons.

She stopped eating her food and asked me, "What has gotten into you? Was it something that *Denise* said?"

"No, it was what *you* said!"

Beverly stood up from the table. "You know what, I don't think I want to have this discussion anymore." I knew that she was pissed then, but I was pissed, too!

I don't know what got into me, but I reached out and grabbed her arm. "Why do you insist on running away from everything? Why can't you just sit here and discuss this with me, man to woman?"

She angrily pulled away from me. "How dare you accuse *me* of running away from things! You're the one with a twelve-year-old son from a college fling, not me. So *who* ran away?!"

"Okay, here you go with that again," I responded. She could never get over the fact that I had a past. I'm sure that her past wasn't as rosy as she made it seem, yet I never dwelled on it. "I never bring up your past," I told her. "Why do you keep bringing up mine?"

"Because you think that you're Mr. Frigging Perfect! And frankly, Walter, I don't think you *care* enough about *my* past to even bring it up. Everything is about you; what *you're* doing; what *you* want."

"Well, Beverly, if I'm just so into myself, then why would you even marry me? Why would you marry a man who doesn't care about you; a man who only thinks about himself?"

I knew that I had gone overboard, but once the question left my tongue and hit the air, I wanted an answer for it.

Beverly just stared at me in silence again. Then she turned her head and mumbled, "Maybe I shouldn't have. Maybe it was a mistake."

I was knocked off my feet! I don't know what kind of answer I expected, but I sure wasn't expecting that one. I began to twiddle my fingers with nervousness and looked away. Suddenly, I had a strong urge to leave, and I went with it.

"Where are you going?"

"I'm just going out to think," I told her.

I could feel Beverly's eyes burning a hole through my back as I made for the door. But like she said, I only thought about myself, and I wanted to get out of there, so I ignored her. I even heard her footsteps following me. I made it out the door and let it hit me in the back before she could get in another word.

I walked down into the garage, quickly slid into the car, and pulled off for a drive. I thought I was free until my cell phone rang. I let it ring four times before I finally answered it. "Yes."

"You know, Walter, I just think that it's funny how you were just telling me how *I* like to run away from things," Beverly said over the line.

"Yeah, well, maybe you're right," I responded. "And maybe I *do* have a problem."

"I never said you had a problem. You asked me a simple question and I answered it. I don't know what you wanted me to say, but I thought that our love for each other was based on honesty."

"Beverly, you make it real hard to be honest with you when you throw everything I've been honest *about* right back in my face every time we have an argument."

"Well, how do you think *I* feel when you accuse me of not telling you things when I *know* that you weren't listening?"

I said, "I never doubted our marriage though, Beverly. Never have I done that."

My wife was silent. I was still wondering why she decided to say "I do," if she didn't really feel for me. My emotions had been shattered. I guess I had taken her love for me for granted, and I was finding out that maybe she didn't love me at all. Maybe it was my economic security that made her say "I do." I hated when I thought that way. It always made my family's wealth seem as if it was a curse.

"Walter, you have to learn to trust people," Beverly suggested when she spoke to me again. "Everyone doesn't think the same way that you do, and that blocks you from understanding other points of view. I don't see everything the way you see it, nor do others. But that's the way *all* people are. We are all a bit eccentric in our own little ways."

I was speechless, so Beverly went on:

"I love you as much as you love me, but I'm open enough to understand how your mind works, where you don't stop to evaluate how mine, or anyone else's, works, for that matter," she said. "You just want to force your way through everything. And if someone doesn't understand you, then you say, 'Screw them,' and you can't have that attitude, Walter. It's time for you to face the music."

I still wasn't planning on going back home until I got good and ready to. "Yeah, well, I'll face the music when I get back in tonight. Right now, I still have to clear my mind," I explained to my wife. If I went back home too early, it would only lead to more tension in our house. I figured it was good for me to clear my head.

"How late are you planning on staying out?" Beverly asked me.

Until the cows come home, I thought of responding. However, that would have been childish on my part. "In a little while," I told her.

She said, "Walter, I wanted to marry you because I love you, I still love you, and I'm gonna love you until I can't love you anymore. But I'm human, and sometimes you can really get under my skin with your selfishness. So, I'll be home in bed when you get back. Okay? And I'm not running away."

I calmed down a bit after that. Reassurance was all that I wanted in the first place. "Okay, I'll see you later on then."

"Don't make it *too* late. Or I'll be asleep when you get in," she warned me.

"I won't," I assured her.

I hung up the phone and began to shake my head. I was thirty-two years old, but some of my actions made me feel more like a troubled adolescent, just like my son. How was I going to be a role model to him when *my act* wasn't together yet? I guess I had only been thinking about myself again, believing that I had the only solution. And I had the nerve to think of *Denise* as being childish.

I never thought of myself much as a "Junior," but whenever I reflected on some of my actions, it was rather hard to deny. I was a spoiled and selfish child, living in the shadow of a successful and overbearing father.

I remember when Denise first decided to name our child Walter Perry III, upon learning that it would be a boy. I was so pleased that we had come to peaceful terms on how to handle the situation that I was hesitant to comment on it, but of course, I had to. However, it seemed that the more I spoke against it, the more she persisted in doing it. I told her that she should at least name him Walter Stewart, using her last name like she did with her first son, Jimmy. Denise then explained that she had planned to rename her first son "Daniels," after *his* father, once they had gotten married, which, of course, never happened. That's when I first began to have nightmares about her discovering my family's wealth. I had always thought about it, but I didn't have those all-so-real bad dreams until the naming process was official, Walter Perry III. And when I finally told my parents face-to-face, four years after the fact, my father simply shook his head and walked away. To this day, I've been afraid to ask if he had limited or even cut off my inheritance in his will. So I was indeed a "Junior" whether I referred to myself as being one or not.

I began to wonder how long I could continue to keep Denise in the dark about my wealth. Sometimes, because of the power of my dreams, I believed that she already knew about it. After all, I had never lied to her about where my parents lived. Since she had never been to Barrington, however, maybe she could not make any correlation about the extent of the wealth that was there. Or, then again, maybe she did know and didn't care. Since she had become a successful woman in her own right, and had moved out to Oak Park, maybe she was saying she didn't *need* any of my family's money. Yet, after my attendance with my son at the Million Man March two years ago, an event that my father felt I should have stayed away from, I had been thinking that the righteous, "atoning" thing to do would be to come clean to Denise and my son about *everything*. I just had to bring myself to find the courage to do it.

I drove downtown along Lake Shore Drive while listening to Joshua Redman's soothing jazz album *Wish*. It was a very peaceful night out, and couples were walking hand in hand. Once I had thought everything over concerning my life and my conflicts, I realized that I just had a silly argument with my wife, and that she was only being honest with me. I was a selfish and shallow man who had been hiding from the truth. And as I continued to suck in the peace of those couples walking in Grant Park and along Lake Michigan, I began to feel romantic myself. I even thought of Beverly and me having our own child. We talked about it a few times, but we never went into detail. I guess we both looked at it as a project in progress. My parents didn't have *me* until they were both in their thirties. Nevertheless, *I* already had a twelve-year-old son.

I bought a pint of strawberry ice cream from a mini market on the way home and made it back in before eleven. I grabbed two spoons and took the entire bag straight up to our bedroom to share with my lovely wife as part of my apology to her.

Beverly smiled when I walked into the room with the ice cream and spoons in hand. She was propped up against two pillows and reading a book. She was wearing the black silk negligee that I had bought her for her birthday a few months ago.

"Aww, isn't this sweet," she said, reaching for her spoon. "How did you know that I had a sweet tooth?" she asked me.

I smiled back at her and said, "I'm just trying to get into the habit of thinking of others."

She took her spoon and kissed me on the lips. Then I got a closer look at the book she was reading, *Men Are from Mars, Women Are from Venus*. I didn't even know that she had that book. I didn't say anything about it though. I had other things on my mind.

"So, where'd you drive to—if you don't mind my asking?" Beverly asked me.

"Just along Lake Michigan."

She took a scoop of ice cream and said, "I love how the water seems higher than ground level at night. It's almost as if it could spill over and submerge the city of Chicago."

I chuckled and responded, "Yeah, it does seem like that. It makes you feel like running in the opposite direction."

With her book lying across her lap, I was tempted again to comment on it, but I forced myself not to. Instead I asked, "Beverly, when do you suppose that we'll be ready to have kids of our own?"

She was the only one of her kin who was not yet a mother.

She grinned and said, "Wow, you're catching on to this thinking-about-others thing pretty fast. Now you're reading my mind. I was thinking about kids tonight myself."

After she told me that, it made the situation seem awkward. I didn't want to say anything else, I just wanted to hold her in my arms.

"I'm sorry about what I said tonight, Walter. I don't want you to think that I didn't want to marry you, because if I didn't, I wouldn't have."

"And I'm sorry for being Mr. Inconsiderate all this time."

"You couldn't help yourself," she teased me.

I didn't want to ask her if she wanted to begin the baby-making process, but it was definitely on my mind. I was hoping Beverly could read my mind like she claimed I was doing with hers.

Once we finished our ice cream, I asked her if she wanted me to turn the lights off and click the news on.

"You can turn the lights off, but we don't need the television on," she told me with a grin.

I grinned back at her. "It looks like you have something else in mind," I said.

"Maybe I do."

I clicked off the light and felt a hard-on coming. Then I stripped down to my underwear and climbed back into bed. Beverly moved to my side of the bed to snuggle.

"Are you getting chills like I'm getting?" she asked me.

"Yeah," I told her, kissing her shoulders. Neither one of us went as far as to announce it, but I do believe that we were officially ready to begin the baby-making process.

As Beverly slid her hands under my shirt and kissed my chest, I thought how fortunate I was to have her. I made a note to try as best as I could never to take her feelings for granted again, especially if she was to be the mother of my children. I heard that pregnancy can be really emotional for some women. During Denise's term with Walter, I didn't take the time to find out. I wasn't planning on having the same thing happen with my wife. I planned to participate every single step of the way.

Broken Dreams

I was just about to leave the house and head for Kim's place before going to work, when my mom called me.

"The telephone is for you!" she hollered. It seems like my mom was always hollering about something. Maybe it was because she had been ignored by three hardheaded sons for so many years. It was all our fault, and she had learned to cope with it the only way she knew how, fussing and hollering at us. What else could a small brown woman do with three big black boys in the house and an ailing husband?

I walked back to the phone asking her, "Who is it?"

My mother looked at me and said, "It's Denise." Then she asked, "Is everything all right with Little Jay? Nothing happened to him, did it?"

She couldn't imagine Neecy calling me for anything else. Neecy and I had stopped civil communication years ago.

"Oh, okay. Well, here's Jimmie," my mother said, handing me the phone.

"Hello."

"I just wanted to let you know that I *am* seeing someone and that he *has* been around Jimmy from time to time," Neecy said to me. It sounded like she was in a rush.

"Yeah, I've heard," I told her. "You got yourself a little truck driver," I said with a laugh.

She said, "He's *far* from little."

"Yeah, I guess he would have to be big enough to handle the wheel," I cracked.

"And handle his business, too," she told me.

I stopped laughing after that. It sounded like she was trying to rub things in my face. Yet, I was trying to do the same damn thing to her. It was a sad situation for both of us.

I asked, "Is that all you called me for?" I think my feelings were hurt.

"What else would I be calling you for?"

Obviously, she still had some bad feelings left. I tried to simmer the conversation down a bit.

"I thought you were calling to tell me that you missed me," I said, fantasizing.

"Don't flatter yourself, Jay. I haven't missed you in a long time."

That *definitely* hurt! Neecy had sure gotten meaner over the years. I remember when I could make her laugh and enjoy my company at the drop of a dime. I guess all of the things I put her through had finally caught up with me. She was deciding to give the bullshit back to me.

I said, "You really do hate me now, hunh? I remember when you used to love me." I walked away from my mother when I said that. I didn't want her getting too much into the conversation.

"And I remember when you used to do the right thing," Neecy responded to me.

I got pissed off and said, "Look, Neecy, I'm on my way to a new night job right now. I've been hanging out with my son, and I *haven't* been arrested for shit. I *am* doing the right damn thing! Don't call me up talking that shit to me! Who do you think you are?" I was having a tantrum, a grown-ass man.

"I'm a mature parent who has provided for *your* son for fifteen years without all of a sudden jumping on some *bandwagon* about playing some damn basketball!"

I was so fucking mad that I didn't know what else to say! My mother stood in my face just waiting for me to go off. Instead, I just handed the phone back to her and headed for the front door.

"Where are you going?" she asked me.

She knew where I was going. "I'm going to work," I told her again.

"Neecy, what did you say to him?" I heard my mother ask as I walked out. Mom sounded as pissed as I was, and she was calling Denise "Neecy." Maybe she was on my side for a change.

I walked to the sidewalk and got curious as hell. I wondered what my mother was about to say. I turned around and went back inside like I forgot something. Mom was letting Neecy have it!

"He's been trying real hard to better himself and all he talks about is his son. And I don't care if it's just about basketball right now. They'll start to talk about other things eventually. That's just how men are. *All* of 'em are sports crazy! My late husband was a big basketball fan, too."

I walked into my room and noticed that I *had* forgotten something, my cigarettes. I grabbed them and walked back out to listen in on my mom again.

"I understand how you feel, Denise. And nobody knows my Jimmie better than I do, so I know what he hasn't done. But I *also* know what he's *trying* to do! And it doesn't do him a bit of good for you to call over here and get him all upset right when he's about to go to work! I'll have you know that Jimmie works all night long now!"

I looked over at Mom and got concerned about her health. She was getting a little too excited. It looked like the steam was about to blow her head off.

I walked over and tried to hold her. "Calm down, Mom. I'm not that upset." I wasn't, after seeing how pissed off *she* was. I was getting a kick out of it! Neecy was getting some of her own damn medicine! My mom was a strong black woman too, and she had been through enough problems of her own in this hard black world.

She shook me off and said, "I don't need you to tell me what to do. I know how to handle myself. You just go on to work."

I shook my head and smiled, but I didn't go anywhere. I wanted to see what Neecy's response would be.

Mom calmed down and said, "You don't have to apologize to me. But I do believe that you owe *Jimmie* an apology."

I was ready to break out laughing like the kid that Neecy thought I already was. My mom had put her back in her place. Quick!

"Now I'm not telling you what to do, Denise, I'm just saying how I feel about this, because I see Jimmie every day, and you don't. So I know what he's been doing and what he's *not* been doing.

"Mmm hmm," Mom mumbled. "Well, he's standing right here now, about to head out the door for work. You want to talk to him?"

I looked at Mom. She stopped, listened, and handed me the phone.

"Hello," I said, expecting an apology.

"Jimmie, I think we need to talk, face-to-face, about our son."

"What about him?"

"We'll discuss it when we discuss it," she answered.

I knew better than that. Neecy just didn't want to say anything around my mother. She didn't really want to talk about Jimmy, she wanted to talk about me. And she wasn't apologizing either. I didn't think that she would. She had too much damn pride, just like I had.

"Aw'ight, you name the time and place, and I'll be there," I told her.

She said to meet her at her office that next afternoon and gave me the address on Halsted Street. I agreed to it without thinking. It was a simple manhood thing to prove that I wasn't the least bit afraid of her ass! She wasn't really no high-class sister, she was just a wannabe.

When I hung up the phone with her, my mom looked at me and said, "You should have married that girl when you had the chance, Jimmie."

I couldn't believe she said that. I just stared at her. I knew it was the truth, though. Deep down inside, I envied Neecy so much I didn't know what to do with myself.

Mom went on and said, "She's very protective, and she speaks from the heart. She's just real confused right now. And I know exactly how she feels. Sometimes, as a black woman, you just sit down and pray to God and ask him why he made you love black men so much."

I looked at my mom and she had tears welling up in her eyes. She had lost three black men, my father and both of my brothers. We didn't even talk about it much. Both of my brothers were killed in gang-related shoot-outs. Knowing that the people who did it were still alive, and that I hadn't tried to do anything about it, wasn't too healthy for me. But I'd only end up back in jail or dead my damn self if I tried to get revenge. That's why I kept thinking about my son going pro in ball. I needed a big dream to hold on to. I had to feel that one day I could escape all of the shit the world kept feeding me. Or all of the shit that I kept making for myself. Either way, whether it was my fault or the world's fault, I was just tired of dealing with it.

"Go on to work, Jimmie, before you end up being late. You don't need no more excuses. You hear me? So go on," my mother warned me. She took a seat on the living room couch and wiped her eyes. I stood there daydreaming about my brothers and my father, three more victims of Chicago's impoverished West Side.

I walked out the house feeling as if I was carrying boulders on both of my legs. I didn't feel like going to work anymore. I was in good shape before Neecy's phone call. I was looking forward to work. But after all of the drama, it seemed as if the energy had been drained out of me. By the time I made it to the bus stop, I was thinking about getting high and spending the night with Kim. She wanted me to stop by and see her again in the morning anyway.

"Yo, Jay, I hear you workin' the night shift, man! They still hiring?"

I turned around and spotted my man Calvin sitting on a milk crate across the street from the bus stop. He was a sophomore when I was a senior at West Side High. He was the only sophomore who made varsity that year on the basketball team. The boy had skills back in the day! But he was looking ragged that night.

"What's been up, Cal!" I yelled at him. I rushed over there to give him a pound before my bus came. Calvin smelled like he pissed on himself. I shook his hand anyway.

"Bring me an application when you come back," he told me.

I looked over into the corner of the abandoned storefront he sat in front of and noticed fresh piss running down the cracks in the sidewalk. I was relieved that Calvin had taken a leak, instead of going on himself, but he still looked terrible. His twisted face made him look fifty. He was only thirty-two.

All of a sudden, I was glad to see my bus coming. "Aw'ight, I'll see what I can do," I lied to him. I ran back across the street to my bus.

"Aw'ight, dawg!" he hollered at me.

I took a seat next to the window and watched Calvin being approached by some young hustler offering him a small package.

An older black woman sitting in front of me grunted, "Mmmph," and shook her head.

Calvin didn't want any damn job. He wanted to be high. High forever. Because when you're high, you don't have to punch in, wear no uniform, listen to no bosses, or wait on no hot, funky bus. When you're high, you're not going anywhere, and your only track of time is how long it took you to get from one high to the next.

I sat there on the bus, philosophizing about getting high for the entire ride to the train station. Then I thought about it some more while on the train. By the time I got off at my stop, I knew that I wanted to be at work, because I liked being able to go places. Getting high always made me lazy, especially when I was still running ball every day. That's when I first started sitting around thinking about doing stupid shit, like robbing people. In fact, I was high the night I got arrested.

I got to work at ten of twelve. My boss, Roger Collinski, looked at his watch and said, "You're late," with a smile on his face.

I grinned at him and said, "Yeah, I knew I should have taken that taxi. You just can't count on these buses sometimes."

We laughed about it. Then he asked me about my son's basketball game.

"My boy did all right. He had twelve points, eight rebounds, and a couple of blocked shots, but he was in foul trouble most of the time," I told him. "They ended up losing sixty-eight to fifty-seven. It was the other guys on the team that lost it for 'em. They were playing like they didn't expect to be there, all nervous and whatnot. My boy was the only one playing defense, that's how he ended up getting in foul trouble."

Roger nodded and said, "I know just what you mean. My oldest son, Johnny, had a great arm in high school, but he didn't have any guys who could get down the field and catch the deep ball. My second son, David, used to work out and catch the ball with him, but he was a freshman when Johnny was a senior.

"Now David has some great hands in his junior year, but the quarterback sucks; a damn candy arm. I even thought hard about transferring my boys to a school where they could really use their talents, but I decided not to. Because although I love the game of football, I understand that an education is the only guarantee to success. Now *that* ain't even good enough. Nowadays, you gotta get yourself a master's degree, kick ass, and take names!"

"Yeah, that's the same predicament my son'll be in this year. He'll be going to Belmont Creek," I told him. "I don't know if they'll win much, but at least he'll be the star of the team in a few years."

Roger looked at me and said, "Belmont Creek? That's in Oak Park, isn't it?"

I said, "Yeah, he lives out there with his mother. She went and got herself a degree in business, kicked ass, and took names," I added with a chuckle.

"You see that?" Roger told me, smiling. "Now your boy's in good shape. Belmont Creek will definitely get him ready for college."

Whitney Young High School would, too, I thought to myself. Whitney Young had a reputation for academics, a magnet program, and they were on the rise in basketball, too. But you had to kick ass and take names to even get in there. Many Chicago kids couldn't get in.

Anyway, I thought about Little Jay's future that whole night at work. Before I knew it, it was checkout time again.

"Man, you were working like a maniac tonight. You took some speed before you came to work, some No-Doz or something?" my co-worker Orlando asked me.

"Naw, man, I just had a lot on my mind," I answered him.

"Lando" was one of the few brothers there who worked with me. There were two Mexicans there, too; Eduardo and Jesus, pronounced "Hey-Zeus" in Spanish. Once I got to know him better, I would joke with him every now and then, about giving me the power of Hercules. I don't think he got the joke at first, but after a while he caught on. The rest of the guys were Polish, Irish, and Italian. Chicago was a very ethnic city, like most big ones are.

When I was walking out that morning, Roger pulled me aside and said, "Remember what we were talking about last night?" He was speaking in low tones.

I looked at him confused.

"You know, about teamwork and talent with our sons?"

I said, "Oh, yeah. What about it?"

"Well, sometimes you have to make sure that *you're* always prepared, regardless of what everyone else is doing. You know what I mean?"

At the time, I was just thinking about getting over to Kim's house and getting some rest. I said, "Yeah, I know what you mean. And the cream rises to the top." I was bullshitting again, just staying in good with my boss.

He said, "Yeah, but sometimes the cream has to learn how to keep a good team together by making crucial decisions and sacrifices."

"Unh hunh," I mumbled with a nod. I was just ready to get out of there.

Roger gave up on what he was trying to tell me and smiled. He saw that I was itching to go. "I'll see you again tonight, Jimmie," he said to me. "Get yourself some rest."

"Definitely," I told him. On my way to the train, Orlando stopped me on the street and asked me what the boss had talked to me about.

"Nothin'. Just sports, education, and leadership and stuff," I told him. I didn't think much of it.

Lando looked at me and asked, "You like that guy, man?"

I *did* like Roger. "Yeah, he's all right," I said. "He don't give *me* any problems."

Lando was a short, secretive-looking brother. He was the kind of man who always had some undercover news. He said, "I don't trust that white boy, man. I wouldn't get too close to him if I was you. You know how these white boys with a manager position are. They're laughing and joking with you one week, and firing you the next."

I looked into Lando's small, frowning face, and all of a sudden, Roger's advice made perfect sense to me. He was telling me not to get mixed up into the crowd. He was telling me to always make my own decisions. So I did just the opposite of what Orlando was telling me. I didn't get close to him and the other guys. Roger was the one who had given me the job, so I considered him the *first* man to trust.

Sure enough, after a few more weeks, people were getting fired, and Lando was one of the first on the list. I had been through that same shit countless times before, but not this time. Lando had complained, but he was always disappearing on the job. He was forever taking extra-long breaks and getting out of doing shit. I would have fired his ass if I was the manager, too! That's what Roger meant when he talked about keeping a good team together by making crucial decisions and sacrifices.

I appreciated Roger for taking a liking to me and looking out for me like he did. White, black, green, or yellow, if a man looks out for me, then I have to respect him for that. There are too few real friends in this world to turn down a sincere handshake just because of the color of the hand. It took me thirty-four years to realize that. A lot of brothers would never trust a white man; we have too much baggage in our history of their wrongdoings. But I was glad that I trusted Roger. He turned out to be a real friend.

Anyway, I got over to Kim's place that morning, and her son, Jamal, was staring me in the face as soon as I walked in.

"Hi," I said to him. What else could I say?

"Hi," he said back. He smiled with a bunch of energy and jumped on my legs.

I reached down and lifted him up into the air. He felt heavier than I thought he would be. I was a little drained in the strength department from working all night. I damn near dropped the boy.

"Watch that!" his mom yelled at me.

I laughed it off and put him back down. "Shouldn't he be in summer camp somewhere?" Neecy had always sent Little Jay and Walter to camp.

"These camps cost too much," Kim told me. As soon as she finished saying it, she realized that she was wrong. She started acting shaky, just like a guilty person. I was very familiar with the nervous energy that guilt could cause. I mean, how much of a financial burden would it be to send your only kid to summer camp? I never had any stable money to do it with. If I did, I would have been able to move out of my mother's place a long-ass time ago! Kim *had* stable money, she just wasn't looking out for her son's best interest. I was beginning to think more like a responsible parent before I even knew it. I knew right from wrong when it came to kids. I just had to begin applying myself.

"Maybe I'll send him next year," Kim told me.

I was tempted to ask her how much the summer camps cost, but I decided not to. It wasn't my decision to make. But I did care about it. Jamal should have been with other kids somewhere, enjoying the summer and his youth. You're only young *once*. I wish that I could have been young again. I would have done a lot of things differently.

"You play basketball?" Jamal looked up and asked me. As a black man in America, once you reach a certain height, that question will always be in the back of people's minds, especially with the popularity of the NBA and the connection to urban playgrounds in the '90s. Hell, in five more years, with the start-up of the WNBA, people might start to think of tall black women as ballers too. Maybe Neecy had a point about overemphasizing basketball. That's not all that we do.

I said, "Who told you that?"

Jamal smiled and said, "My mom."

I figured that. I guess she was going to try and use her son to get closer to me with the whole basketball thing. That wasn't right either, but I was too tired to think about it. I just wanted to lay down. "Well, not anymore. I just watch the game now," I told him. Then I asked Kim if I could lay down. She led me to her room.

Jamal followed us in.

"No, Jamal, he can't play with you right now. He's been working all night and he needs his rest," she said, closing the door and pushing her son out. She made it sound as if we were going to play when I woke up. I wasn't planning on it.

Kim stuck her head back in the door a minute later and asked me if I wanted some breakfast.

"If I'm still up when you finish, I'll eat it," I told her. "But if I'm not . . ."

She smiled, all happy-looking, and said, "I told you my son likes you."

I shook my head and stretched out on her king-size bed. She actually had a *king-size bed* and was complaining about the cost of sending her son to summer camp! I couldn't believe that! I had heard about single mothers who spent more money on themselves, but to actually be that close to it was ridiculous.

I ate a little bit of Kim's scrambled eggs, sausage, and pancakes and fell asleep. When I woke up, it was two-thirty in the afternoon. The only reason I was up was because Kim had to go to work. She was making a bunch of noise in the room while she got dressed.

"Where's your son?" I asked her. I just knew she wasn't going to try and leave him there with me.

"He's going over to his grandmother's. Why, you thought that I would try and get you to baby-sit?" she asked with a grin.

I smiled back at her. "I was just making sure that you wasn't, because I got somewhere to go." I didn't really feel up to making it down to Neecy's office, but at least it was the truth.

Kim asked me, "When are you leaving?"

Actually, I didn't feel that tired anymore. I said, "I might as well leave now."

"You don't have to leave right this minute if you don't want to. I can give you the extra key, and you can give it back to me when you come back," Kim told me. She was really coming on strong!

I said, "Naw, I'm late already. I need to get going."

"Well, I can give you the extra key anyway, in case you wanna come back and get some more rest."

I started to feel like a turkey being fattened up for the kill. I jumped up out of that bed and got myself together. "When are you getting off work?" I asked her.

"Eleven o'clock."

"Damn. Well, I won't see you again until tomorrow," I told her.

She started smiling and said, "Or, you could stop past my job."

I looked her over. Kim was wearing this tight black uniform that hugged all of her curves, with a skirt that stopped well above the knees. I started wondering what the rest of the women at her job looked like, just out of curiosity. "Where is it at again?"

Kim wrote down the address, got me something to drink, and we all left without me getting that extra key she kept pushing.

"Tell Mr. Jay bye," she told her son.

Jamal smiled at me and said it.

I told him, "Bye, little man," and headed on my way. Kim wasn't even trying to hide anything. She was being outright *bold* about wanting me in their life. I just wasn't trying to commit to the idea.

I jumped on a bus heading to Halsted Street and found myself getting nervous. I really didn't feel up to arguing with Neecy. I was already two hours late. Maybe she would have some other things to do by the time I got there. I tried to convince myself not to go, but my manhood wouldn't let me back down. I used to *rule* this girl, and I didn't care how successful she was, I couldn't allow her to turn around and *rule* me! So I planned to march into Neecy's office like a man and set her ass straight!

This tall Hispanic babe was her secretary. I said, "I'm Jimmie Daniels. I had an appointment to see, ah, Denise Stewart, at one o'clock. Is she still in, or is she busy?" I was dying to call her Neecy, but I was willing to bet that if I said it, her secretary wouldn't know who the hell I was talking about.

"Ah, yeah, she's still in. Hold on one minute." She buzzed Neecy on an office phone. "A Jimmie Daniels is out here to see you. He says he had a one o'clock appointment . . . Mmm hmm. Okay." She hung up the line and said, "She'll be with you in five minutes."

Shit! The last thing I wanted to do was sit out there and think about what I wanted to say to her. I just wanted to be raw and spontaneous. Sometimes, when you think too much, you end up ruling out a lot of things. Then again, sometimes you get a chance to think of some better things to say, and that's exactly what I did. So by the time Neecy and I were sitting face-to-face in her office, I was totally at ease.

"How long have you had this night job?" she asked me.

"Not even a week," I told her.

Neecy was wearing a navy blue business suit, an off-white blouse, and a colorful scarf around her neck. I had on the same pair of blue jeans, blue shirt, and brown shoes that I had gone to work in the night before. But so what?

"First of all, you're late."

"And I still made it here," I told her.

"Is that all you have to do, just make it there, not on time or anything?"

"Am I checking in at a clock down here? I make it to my job on time."

"Is it stable?" she asked me.

"I hope it is."

"And what if it's not?"

"Then it's back to the drawing board."

She nodded her head. "I see. Well, your mother seems pretty excited about it," she said to me.

I got slick on her and said, "Look at it this way, if Little Jay got an A on his first math test, that wouldn't mean that he's gonna get an A in the class, but he would be off to a good start, right? Now wouldn't *you* be happy with that?"

Neecy was trying her hardest not to smile. I was glad that I got a chance to wait before I talked to her. I was going to show her ass that I was still intelligent, and that I could sit there and beat her at her own damn psychological games.

She started to shake her head and said, "You know, I just don't know what to think about you. I just keep thinking that I'm gonna get burned again. Or, rather, that your *son* is gonna get burned," she said, correcting herself.

"I know you want to see me do well, Denise. I want to do well, too," I told her. "You think I liked being a fuck-up for so long? You think any man likes that shit? Hell no! But you can only play the cards that you're given until you get a better hand. So that's what I'm trying to do now. I'm trying to establish some type of longevity, and something to look forward to in the future."

I could tell that Neecy wanted to care about me. It may not have been a romantic thing anymore, but she still cared about me as her son's father and as a black man struggling to survive. I could see it in her eyes, no matter how tough she tried to be with me.

"And you think that your son's playing basketball is gonna be that future for you? What if he gets his feelings hurt like you did, and he finds out that he's not as good as we all *think* he is? Then what?"

It was a good question. I was stuck for a second. Then I said, "What if after you got your degree in business, nobody wanted to hire you? What would you have done?"

She shook her head in denial. "There was no way it was gonna happen. I knew what I was capable of before I even went after the degree. The degree was just icing on the cake."

"So, you were that confident, and here you are," I said, looking around at her office.

"Yeah, but I wasn't going up against one-in-a-million odds either," she argued.

"You wasn't? A single mom with *two* sons, going to college and becoming a successful businesswoman with her own office and payroll? Oh, yeah, I read about that every day," I told her sarcastically.

Neecy finally broke a smile, but she still wouldn't soften her toughness. "You may not read about it every day, but us single mothers are out here getting the job done however we have to, and *that's* a fact. But young black boys playing professional basketball is still a long shot, no matter *how* you try and slice the cake. I just don't want my son to go through the same things that his father has."

"He won't," I told her.

"And what makes you so sure?"

"Because you're his mother. And I'm damn sure that you're gonna tell him how I went downhill, if you haven't already told him. I'll make sure that I tell him too, but only when the time is right."

"And when is that?"

"When he needs some inspiration, some moral support, or just plain old empathy," I told her. I was poised and logical. I said, "Don't take the boy's dream away, just because *you're* afraid of it not happening. You should never do that to a kid. That's what's wrong with so many black kids out here now, they have scared parents snatching their dreams away."

"It sounds more like it's *your* dream to me," she responded.

"Yeah, well, maybe it is. Maybe *I* need some inspiration. Is anything wrong with that?"

"It is when you use people."

"Oh, so is that what you think I'm doing, *using* my son?"

"You tell me."

By that point, I was just plain disgusted. I didn't even feel like talking anymore.

Neecy said, "Let's say that he couldn't play basketball, and he was just an average kid with average height. Would you still be this interested in him? You weren't when he was younger."

"Aw, now, see, that's a bunch of bullshit!" I cursed at her. "You know damn well I've been a part of his life! Money ain't every-fucking-thing, Denise! Okay? Now you go home and ask Jay if he loves his father. And he'll *tell* you! Okay? So don't run that shit on me!"

I got so excited that I didn't realize how loud I was getting, *or* that I was standing, until I finished my statements.

Neecy looked embarrassed. "I didn't say that you were *never* there—"

I cut her off and snapped, "Yeah, whatever. You just save that shit." I headed for the door and left it open when I walked out, because if I would have closed it, she wouldn't have had a damn door!

Neecy had lost all of her love for me. I couldn't see how she could get so cold. She was an Ice Lady! I felt sorry for her in a way. It was like she had floated off to her own island somewhere. And as far as the whole thing with me "using" my son, I wasn't going to pay that shit no mind. I planned to keep supporting him and going to all the games that I could. *Neecy* had the problem, not me. I was doing the right thing. Just because she was angry about how I had been in the past, it didn't make her right to *predict* how things were going to be with my son and me in the future.

I walked out of her office building and onto Halsted Street and looked at the piece of paper that Kim wrote the address of her job on. I was hungry as hell, and I wondered what they had on their menu. I wanted to get Neecy off my mind as quickly as I could. I figured if I could fill up my aching stomach and my sore eyes with the sight of Kim in her work uniform again, it would do the trick for me. One thing was for sure, I would take Kim's down-to-earth sexiness over Neecy's high society beef any day of the week.

Slow Down

I didn't want to call Denise back until I had a chance to go over things in my head. Once I did have a chance to think, I invited her out to a Friday night dinner at an Indian restaurant called the Eastern Spice. I had another three-day trip coming up and I wouldn't see her for a while. If we didn't talk before then, I had no idea when we'd be able to sit down and discuss things. I wanted to get it out of the way beforehand, to have a clear head while out on the road.

"So, what movies did your boys get from the video store?" I asked her. I was just making small talk. We were so hesitant with each other that it was like starting over again on a first date. I knew that our conversation would get serious sooner or later. There was no sense in rushing into it.

"They, ah, had the Tupac Shakur fever. So they got *Gridlock'd* and *Poetic Justice*."

I nodded. "Yeah, this rapper stuff is getting to be a sad situation."

Denise sighed and responded, "If you live by the sword, you die by the sword."

"I hear his estate is worth millions of dollars now."

"I bet it would be. The young man had a lot going for him. He just took a fast turn in the wrong direction. I hope that my boys will be able to learn something from it. That's the only reason why I let them watch it. I don't believe that shielding kids away from all of the things that are going on will necessarily be successful. Sometimes they need to be able to see these things so that they can be strong enough to make their own decisions about what's right."

I nodded, while wondering in what direction *we* had turned, and what decisions *we* had made about what seemed right for *us*. "What do you think about our direction?" I couldn't help asking.

"What about it?"

I don't know what Denise was thinking about, but her mind didn't seem to be into things that night. Maybe she was thinking about an issue concerning her sons, her younger sister, her job, her mother . . . There were so many things that she juggled around in her life that I didn't know where to begin with her sometimes.

I said, "Are we headed up the road, down the road, or do we have a flat tire that needs fixin'?"

She smiled at that one. "I'd say we were on cruise control, just trying to figure out where we'd like to go. Unless you know already."

She raised a brow at me, throwing the ball back on my side of the court. *Did* I know where I wanted to go with things? I don't think I did. I knew that I loved Denise's company, and I felt comfortable being around her and her sons, but there were many obstacles in the way of us becoming a committed couple. Denise had only recently told her sons' fathers about me. Then again, maybe that meant that she *was* ready to be serious about us.

Our food began to arrive before I could comment. We had various small dishes to share from with some very different tastes.

"Mmm, have you eaten here before?" Denise asked me after trying an appetizer she seemed pleased with.

I smiled. I was always trying different things with her. "No. I just figured we'd do something different," I told her. She had taken me to a few different places as well.

"You know, I'll be honest with you, Dennis, I just don't know what to think about relationships anymore," Denise told me out of the blue. "It just seems that the more you expect, the less you get. Then when you don't expect anything, everything just falls into your lap. And I don't know how to respond anymore.

"Sometimes I feel like a bumper car," she explained. "You turn on your engine and start moving ahead, and then you get knocked sideways. So then you say, 'What the hell?' and you start bumping right back. But frankly, the shit hurts, so you tell yourself, 'Let me see if I can make it around this track without getting hit anymore.' And you get to rolling around, feeling good about it, then all of a sudden, *boom!* Somebody hits you out of nowhere. And as soon as you get rolling again, that's when your damn car cuts the hell off."

I broke out laughing. You couldn't get any more clarity with any other analogy, unless you've never been on bumper cars before. Denise didn't find it humorous though.

"I'm serious," she said with a straight face. "You know why I've never been married?" she asked me. We had never spoken about it before. We had only talked about *my* previous marriage.

"Why?" I asked her.

"Well, number one; I didn't want to force anything, and number two; I didn't need anybody's pity. And a lot of brothers would run that same game, acting as if my life was ruined because I had kids out of wedlock. 'Aw, baby, you got two kids? What happened to their fathers?' At the same time, they're busy trying to screw you, right? Then if you say anything even *halfway* serious, they get to acting like assholes—'Oh, I just don't know if I'm ready to handle them two kids you got.'

"It was just pitiful. It was the worst kind of dating you could ever imagine."

"Is that why you have this hot and cold approach with me?" I asked her.

"How else am I supposed to feel? I mean, it's hard enough to deal with a man nowadays, when you *don't* have kids. We could have everything clicking between us, and then at the end of the day, the question pops up, 'What do we do about your kids?' And I'm like, 'Well, you know, they're not going anywhere, at least not until it's time for college.' Because, see, I'm not some crazy white girl who's gonna drown her kids in a car, and blame it on a carjacking, just to keep some damn man. Hell no! I'm not that kind of crazy!"

"Yeah, that was kind of sick," I agreed with her.

Denise snapped. "That girl was out of her damn mind! I may get horny sometimes, but I ain't crazy."

I smiled. We calmed down and dug into our food after that. I wasn't sure what else to say. I still hadn't answered Denise's question about my intentions toward her. You can think about a lot of different things in life, but then when it comes to making a split-second decision, it can rattle your brains. I didn't want to say the wrong thing at such a critical time. I still wanted to be patient and think everything through.

"To tell you the truth, Dennis, I really think that we need to slow down," Denise finally decided for me. "I mean, I usually didn't allow too many men around my kids, but after we talked about them a few times, I just wanted to see how you would respond to them. I guess I just wanted to see what the chemistry would be like. And once I saw that they liked you, I pretty much let things get out of hand without really talking about it.

"Honestly, I was a little afraid to talk about them, because I didn't want to hear that same old lame excuse from you," she told me. "I mean, you brothers have to understand that when you're dealing with a woman who has kids, that there's gonna be complications involved. Some brothers act like your kids are fine when things are going well, but all of a sudden, they're a burden when you start talking about more than sleeping around."

"Well, that's because it's the truth," I leveled with her. "Especially when the kids are extra young. I mean, tonight is a perfect example. Your kids are old enough to stay at home and watch videos while we go out, but what if they weren't? Then we'd have to get baby-sitters, take them with us, or we wouldn't be able to go out at all."

"Speaking of which, let me call these boys up right now," she responded with a smile, excusing herself from our wide, circular table.

I sat there and thought about things. It's normal for a man to not want a ready-made family. Fatherhood is something you grow into, just like motherhood, and it makes things a lot easier when it's *your* seed you're watching grow. I thought about it a few times, but I never asked Denise if she was finished having kids yet. With her career ambitions and all, I just took it for granted that she was. That was another complication I had to think about. A lot of questions I simply had to ask her about. How could I effectively come to any conclusions about where *I* wanted to go, without even knowing what Denise's boundaries would be?

When she returned, I was tempted to ask her a bunch of things. I said, "What do you think about having more kids?"

"I thought about it. Plenty of times," she answered. "But I wasn't gonna do it alone again. And since I didn't have any stable relations with men, time just passed by."

My next question got stuck in my throat. Denise jumped the gun on it anyway.

"What about now?" she asked. "Honestly, I don't know. I mean, of course, I'm in a better situation now than I was years ago, with my sons being older and me being economically secure and all, but it would really have to be something I felt strongly about doing."

"Yeah, I would imagine so," I responded with a grin. Having children was no easy business, and I had never been through it before, so it would be a whole new experience for me.

"Actually, I was surprised that you didn't have any kids of your own," she told me. "Once you cross that big three-o, you can't look forward to dating too many men your age who don't have children. I've been around a lot of different situations, especially being a founding member of the Single Mothers' Organization with Camellia. We've heard all kinds of stories. Some men went as far as to even lie about their children. I wondered if *my* sons' fathers ever did that."

I asked, "Remember that first night we spent together in that hotel room near the airport?"

She grinned and answered, "Mmm hmm. What about it?"

"Did I sound like a man who would lie to you that night, with all the things that I told you in that room about my past sex life?"

She thought about it. "Yeah, you have a point. You went from A to Z with me. I wasn't expecting all of that," she said.

"That took a lot of courage for me to do. And I appreciate the fact that you didn't up and run away from me after that," I told her.

"You didn't say anything that was *that* outrageous."

"Nevertheless, I put myself on the line for you."

"And I've done the same with you by letting you into my sons' lives and telling their fathers about you," she responded.

I nodded with a smile. "It took you a while."

She smiled back at me. "It was only a matter of time. But even with everything being out in the open now, I still think that we should slow down a bit and get our bearings. I don't want either one of us rushing."

I said, "I agree," right before the waiter asked us if everything was all right. "Yeah, it was a splendid dinner. Everything was perfect. Now we'd like to have the check."

We did some small talk on the way back to Oak Park, then I walked Denise back to her front door, where we were hesitant again.

"Well, ah, I had a beautiful dinner tonight, how 'bout you?" I asked her.

"Like you said, it was perfect."

I was speechless, wondering if it was okay to ask for a kiss. I felt ridiculous. Then Denise started to laugh.

"You can kiss me if you want," she told me.

I smiled. "Was I wet around the lips for one? How'd you know what I was thinking?"

"I'm thirty-four years old, Brock. Give me credit for learning *something* in this lifetime."

"Momma knows best," I told her, moving in for the kill.

We had one of those slow, tender kisses that men and women give each other when they've been together for a while. It wasn't long enough for lust, and it wasn't short enough for a peck. It was somewhere in between.

I backed up and Denise said, "Have a safe trip home. Okay?"

I nodded and smiled at her, taking in all of her beauty, poise, strength, dignity, intelligence, and everything else. I walked back to my car with a bounce to my step, feeling relaxed and secure again. A good slow-down date was just what we needed, especially with me heading out of town. I could have a peaceful trip without thinking too much or too little. It was perfect. So I turned my radio up loud on V103, and jammed with the DJ as I cruised on back to my apartment on the South Side.

September 1997

Severe Growing Pains

I T was only the second week of school, and already I was about to have a heart attack! Ms. Walker, one of Walter's seventh-grade schoolteachers, was calling to inform me that he had been involved in a stabbing incident at school, and that he was being taken to the hospital for minor stab wounds.

DENISE

"Which hospital?" I asked her. "Forest Park?" I was already packing up my things to leave, and I had a full schedule that Tuesday.

"Ah, yes," Ms. Walker responded. She sounded rushed and paranoid. I bet she never imagined having to call a parent regarding a stabbing incident of one of *her* students. Stabbings in junior high school she had probably only heard about on the news. I was embarrassed by it myself, but at the moment, I was too concerned about my son's welfare to show it. I had just met Ms. Walker and plenty of concerned parents at a PTA meeting at the school that previous Friday.

"Okay, I'm on my way," I told her.

She wasn't finished with me yet. "Ah, Ms. Stewart, I think they have a few questions they want to ask you."

"Well, they'll have to wait," I responded, quickly hanging up the phone. I was in a rush to get down to that hospital. I didn't have time to dispute who *"they"* were, or what *"they"* would want from *me*. I just wanted to see my son.

Fortunately, I had gotten the call concerning my son shortly before my lunch hour. I told Elmira to reschedule all of my appointments for the day.

Elmira looked at me and said, "All of them?" with a pained expression on her face.

I didn't want to tell her too much of my personal business, but I knew I had to tell her something.

"Walter was involved in an incident at school that I need to take care of, ASAP!"

Elmira immediately read the panic in my eyes, and the seriousness of my tone. "Okay. I'll get on it right away," she said.

"Thank you," I told her. I was out the door in a heartbeat!

After rushing through lunchtime traffic, I arrived at the hospital, gave the receptionist my name, and asked to see my son.

"Oh, yeah, he's in room two-fourteen," the receptionist informed me.

It appeared as if my son's stabbing was the hot gossip of the day. I noticed the other patients and family members all eying me from the waiting room as I rushed up the hallway and to the stairs. I damn sure was not going to wait for an elevator!

Three police officers were waiting outside Walter's room; two white men and one black man.

"Are you the mother?" one of the white officers asked me.

"Yes, I am," I responded, stepping by him and into the room. I didn't have time for any of their questions at the moment. The only thing on my mind was seeing my son alive, and examining how badly he had been cut.

Once Walter saw me, he dropped his head and was ashamed of himself. I think he was a bit nervous, too, about what I was going to say or do to him.

I forcibly calmed myself and asked him, "Are you okay?"

He nodded. He had white bandages wrapped around both of his hands.

I looked down at them and held them up. "What happened?"

A dark-haired Indian doctor addressed me. "Ah, Mrs. Perry, I'm Dr. Houran," she said with her hand extended.

I took her hand and said, "I'm *Ms.* Stewart."

"Oh, I'm sorry." She humbled herself. "Okay, now, Walter *is* your son, right?" she asked, to make sure.

"Yes, he is," I told her.

"Okay," she said, relieved. I knew exactly how she felt. Women, of all nationalities, had it extra tough as professionals. We could not afford to make *any* mistakes.

"Walter has minor cut wounds on both of his hands," she informed me. "They're not deep enough for stitches, but they are deep enough to need cleaning and rewrapping with antibiotics at least three times a day. You'll need to wrap them in gauze, preferably in the morning, in the afternoon, and before he goes to bed. His hands may take up to a week to heal, but they'll still be sore for a while. So I wouldn't have him doing anything too strenuous with them for at least a couple of weeks.

"I'll set up an appointment for him to come back in next week, to check up on his progress," she added.

I looked at my son's wrapped hands again, and then back to the woman doctor. "So that means he won't be able to do his schoolwork."

She shook her head with a grimace. "Well, he won't be able to take any notes for a while, unless he can write with his left hand. He has a cut on his right thumb, and that's going to be awfully sore for at least a week. In fact, sometimes the shallow cuts are a lot more irritating and painful than much deeper wounds."

"Tell me about it," I agreed. "I've had plenty of paper cuts to attest to that."

The doctor and I shared a short, controlled laugh. Walter wasn't laughing though. He fully realized that he would be the one in pain.

Once I knew that my son would live, I was ready to get to the bottom of things.

"Okay, now, what happened?"

All of a sudden, the three police officers decided to inch their way into the room, invading my privacy.

"Ah, if you don't mind, I'd like to talk to my son *alone*, please. And my lawyer is on the way," I lied.

"Ah, ma'am, we just want to ask a few basic questions."

"And you can ask them when my lawyer gets here," I told them.

Dr. Houran smiled at me. She said, "Are there any other questions you'd like to ask me?"

"Not yet, but give me a minute to think," I told her with half a smile.

"Okay, well, I'll leave you two alone. I'll have the nurse give you plenty of gauze and antibiotic ointment before Walter checks out today."

"Okay. Thank you very much," I told her.

The doctor left the room and closed the door behind her. The three police officers were still waiting outside to harass me, as if my son were a full-fledged criminal.

"Okay, now tell me what happened," I asked him again.

Walter took a deep breath and said, "These guys came up to the school at lunchtime, looking for my friend. And then we all got into an argument."

"What friend is this?" I asked him.

"Mikey."

"*Mikey?*" I snapped. "What's the boy's full name, Walter? Is he in your classroom?"

"No, he's in the eighth grade."

"*The eighth grade?!* Well, what are you—" I stopped myself before I got too excited and backed up a bit. "What is the boy's full name, Walter?"

He was hesitant to tell me.

"WHAT'S HIS DAMN NAME?!" I said, raising my voice. I was ready to grab my son's hands and squeeze the hell out of them, I was so angry! I was in no mood to deal with that code of the street shit!

"His name is Michael Riley."

"Michael Riley? Is he black?" I was making the same assumption that most Americans had been trained to make; the black kids were always the ones causing trouble.

"No, he's white," Walter told me. He looked up into my eyes for a re-action. I guess he was proud to say that the boy was white. As young and as immature as Walter was, he understood, as fully as I did, what race meant in America, even on his minor level.

"So what happened? You and Michael Riley had a beef with some other boy?"

"No. I wasn't even in it."

"You weren't in it? So what were you trying to do, protect this boy? Is that it?"

Walter's head dropped again.

"Look at me when I'm talking to you, boy! Were you trying to protect him?"

Walter said, "I wasn't really trying to protect him. It just happened."

I had a picture of the entire incident in my head already. Walter's lit-tle white friend, "Mikey," wanted to play a "roughneck," and when some *real* danger arrived, he punked out, and my son, Mr. Hero from Chicago, jumps in there and gets himself stabbed!

"Boy, you don't make no damn sense!" I yelled at him. "How come he wanted to be *your* friend? Because you're black? And he wanted to be *down?* And how come you can't be friends with the smart boys? You're smart, aren't you? Or are you trying to be the school tough guy now?

"You *need* to be with boys your own damn age!"

I was pissed, and all of my own prejudices were leaping out of me. My son was making his know-it-all father seem as if he was right. And that only added to my disappointment.

Walter was shaking his head. "Naw, Mom, it wasn't even like that."

"No, Mom, that's not the way it was," I corrected him. I wanted to correct everything that was slipping, including my son's *English,* if I had to!

He looked down once again, then flipped his head up before I was ready to reach out and smack him! I didn't move out to Oak Park so my son could become the black tough guy at school and get himself stabbed. I could just imagine what the administrators, teachers, and parents were all thinking at his school.

"And what did the principal say to you about this?"

Walter looked really nervous when I asked him that. "Umm, I think they wanted to talk to you."

"You *think* they wanted to talk to me?!" I snapped. "Did they talk about suspending you, Walter?" I asked him. I knew that would be next; either that or kicking him out of school altogether.

Down went his head again. I knew the answer before he raised it back up.

"They were talking about kicking me out of school," he mumbled.

My hands raised up to my temples, and I had to restrain myself from turning into a lunatic inside of that hospital room!

"Okay, just calm down, and we'll sit and talk about this tomorrow," I told myself out loud.

Walter looked at me and said, "I'm sorry, Mom," and started to cry.

I wished that I could cry with him and tell him that everything would be all right, but I had been through too much to cry. I leaned closer to his hospital bed and held his head to my shoulder.

"We're going to go back to your school tomorrow morning and straighten everything out," I told my son. Out of curiosity, I asked him, "So what happened to your friend? Did he get suspended too? Are they talking about expelling *him?*"

Walter shook his head. "No. All they did was talk to him."

I leaned back to look into his tearstained face. "All they did was *talk* to him?! Were you all in the same room?" I couldn't believe it! That damn white boy was getting off scot-free, when he had been the one to start off the drama in the first place. It looked like I was going to need a lawyer after all. And I knew *more* than a few good ones!

"Mmm hmm," I mumbled to my son. "I see *exactly* how this is going. And I'm going to have a surprise for their ass!" I said. "Now Walter, everything that you're telling me is the truth, right? Because, boy, if I find out that you're lying, about *anything*—" I was so incensed by the whole ordeal that I couldn't even finish my sentence. My son got the point though, and he answered my question.

"I'm telling you the truth, Mom," he whined through his tears.

I said, "Yeah, well, you better be. And now I have to call your father and tell him everything."

My son looked up at me in silence. I didn't know what part was worse, him getting stabbed, the school talking about expulsion, or having to call up his father and tell him that he was right about Walter going bad on me, as small and as silly as the boy was!

I was so upset that I didn't know what to think. Raising kids in the nineties was pure hell! Even when you try and move out to the suburbs, they *still* find a way to test your damn nerves!

I looked down at my son and said, "Boy, you have *really* done it now!" I didn't know what else to say to him. I just felt so helpless, which was the worst feeling in the world for me. I absolutely *hated* feeling helpless! I had worked too damn hard to regain my life to feel helpless about protecting my son from the evils of the street.

Walter began to cry even harder at seeing how angry I was. He said, "I didn't mean for this to happen, Mom." His voice had turned into a squeal.

My natural mother instincts kicked in, and I hugged the boy like he was dying. I said, "I know, Walter. I know. Now just calm down." But in my mind, I couldn't help thinking that half of the black boys in prison had said the same damn thing, "*I didn't mean for it to happen.*" That excuse only made it seem worse to me, because it sounded like they were saying they couldn't control themselves. And I just *knew* that I wasn't raising a child who had *no* self-control! I just *knew* it, like a thousand other mothers *thought* they knew! *Damn* he had me mad!

Boys Will Be Boys

WALTER

W H I L E on the phone with Denise, I looked at Beverly and couldn't believe my ears.

"What's wrong?" my wife asked me. We had just finished eating dinner.

I help up my index finger so that I could get all of the details first. It sounded as if Denise had everything mapped out already.

"So what time should I be there?" I asked her.

"Nine A.M. sharp," she told me.

I nodded my head and said, "I'll see you tomorrow then." I hung up the phone in near shock.

Beverly was still awaiting a report. "So, what's going on?" she asked me again.

"Walter was involved in a stabbing incident at school today. The school officials are now thinking about expelling him. Denise wants me to meet her up at the school tomorrow morning with her lawyer," I answered. I didn't know exactly how to feel yet. I had a mixture of guilt, anger, pity, disappointment, fear, and anxiety all wrapped up in one, which left me immobile, as if paralyzed.

"Oh my God!" Beverly gasped. "Did he stab someone?"

I shook my head, still numbed by the news. "No, he didn't stab anyone," I was proud to say. "He had both of his hands cut while grabbing the knife of the alleged attacker."

Beverly frowned and asked, "So why is *he* being expelled? Did they expel the other student? Did Walter start it? Even if he did start it, he wasn't the one with the knife, right?"

"The kid with the knife was not even a student at the school," I informed her. "The attack occurred inside of the schoolyard during their lunch hour. Apparently, there was a white student involved, who's attempting to let Walter take the fall for it."

I shook my head and said, "There's just a lot more to this story that I don't have all of the details to. Denise doesn't have them all either, so she asked me to meet her at the school tomorrow with her lawyer."

"Mm mm mmm," Beverly grunted. "And this is *junior* high school! What's next, kindergarten?" she asked rhetorically. "I hear they're already bringing weapons to grade school. This is just getting out of hand!" she snapped. At least she had an immediate response to things.

In fact, I had never witnessed Beverly so animated before. Her motherly instincts were kicking in early. We had just recently found out that she was expecting. The due date was May 13, 1998.

I sat there at the table still daydreaming about what had gone on at school with my son. "I just can't *believe* this!" I finally ranted. "Damn it!" I yelled, standing up from the table. I had all of these different emotions boiling up inside of me with nowhere to go. I just had so many questions to ask, and so many to answer. Whose fault was it? Was it mine, for not being there for my son? Was it Denise's, for being a workaholic? Was Walter simply a bad kid who couldn't help himself? Or was it a sign of the times of growing up in America?

Beverly rushed over to calm me down. "Do you want me to take off from work tomorrow and go down there with you?"

She was being really supportive. I loved my wife. But Walter III was an issue between Denise and me. Beverly being there would have been a second left shoe. Then again, if I did take Beverly with me, the school officials could attest that a solid, two-parent household was waiting in the wings for my son as a safe haven against the problems he could find himself mixed with in the future. Maybe the stabbing incident was a direct message for me to stop shuffling my feet and gain custody of my son before something more drastic occurred. Suddenly, I began to think about calling my own lawyer.

I leaned away from my wife to look into her face. I asked, "Beverly, would you support me if I wanted to gain custody of my son now? I mean, you see how crucial a time this is for him. The next time he may be involved in a shooting."

I knew that I was wrong before my wife even answered me. We would have to sit down and discuss it when we were both in a sane state of mind, and not with a stabbing incident and expulsion from school on the table.

Beverly looked into my eyes and answered, "Yes. Yes I will."

I had already decided that I would disavow her answer. It wasn't a fair time for me to ask her. However, I *was* pleased to find that she would support me if push came to shove. I figured that her recent pregnancy had something to do with her change of attitude. Nevertheless, I was forcing myself to be more considerate than I had been in the past. It was all a part of maturity and respect for others. And that respect for others was the reason why my final decision was to observe how Denise would handle things before I jumped to any wrong conclusions.

"Not yet, honey," I told my wife, with a desperate hug. "But I'll let you know when. I just hope that it won't be too late."

When I showed up at Walter's junior high school in Oak Park, I met my son, Denise, and her lawyer inside the principal's office. Denise was worked up and ready for a battle. Not that we were best friends or anything, but she barely spoke to me. She talked more to her lawyer, attorney Melvin Fields, a lean and rather calm brother in his early forties.

While we waited for all the included school officials to join us inside the office, I looked over and said Hello to my son. He had both of his hands wrapped in gauze.

"How are you feeling?" I asked him.

"I'm all right," he mumbled, lacking the energy that I was used to seeing from him.

Denise said, "His hands are going to take up to two weeks to heal."

"That means he won't be able to do his homework for a while," I commented.

Before Denise could respond to me, the principal walked in with the vice principal, the disciplinarian, and one of Walter's seventh-grade teachers. None of them were black, and all of them looked nervous and apprehensive.

The principal, a stately man in wire-framed glasses, addressed us: "Ah, Mr. Perry and Ms. Stewart, after going over the details of the case, we've all decided that we will *not* be expelling your son from the school, and that he can rejoin his classes as early as tomorrow. Ms. Walker has told us that Walter is a good student, and we've had no other disparaging complaints about him, so we apologize for the mishap."

Denise looked around at everyone inside the room. "Wait a minute," she said, "I didn't come down here to have this thing just brushed under the rug. My son was *attacked* on *school premises*, suspended, and told that he would be expelled, then police officers asked *us* who, what, when, and where, and now I take off a second day from work for you to tell me that everything was a *mishap!* Oh, no, you're *not* getting off that easy!" she ranted.

Denise wasn't going to be denied her battle that morning. I wasn't planning on leaving so early myself. We both wanted an explanation for their actions. Denise and I were actually in agreement with each other!

"First of all, where are *Michael Riley* and *his* parents?" she asked them.

The principal looked to the disciplinarian. The disciplinarian looked like a high school football coach in a dark suit. He could have used a tailor to make his suit fit his broad shoulders a little better.

He said, "I spoke to Michael Riley, and he informed us that he witnessed the attack, and that it was unprovoked on Walter's behalf."

"Did he *also* tell you that he was involved in it?" Denise asked him.

The disciplinarian looked to the vice principal, a tall woman in a gray business suit. "We were planning on having him back in our offices to answer more questions about the incident today," she told us.

"And will there be any police officers around when you're asking *him* questions?" Denise jarred them. I began to wonder what her lawyer was there for. I guess he was the silent voice, carrying the long, legal stick of the law to crack heads when the opportunity presented itself. I was curious to see the guy in action just in case I would need the experience for future reference in a possible custody battle.

The principal decided to speak up again. "Ah, Ms. Stewart, if you will, you have to understand that this was something we've never had to deal with before, and we didn't know exactly how to handle the situation."

"Yes, you did," Denise calmly responded. "You knew how to handle it. You said, 'Let's get rid of this black troublemaker and make him an example for everyone at our school.'"

It was a beautiful setup on her part. All of a sudden, it felt awfully stuffy in the room. We could all use some fresh air and some bottled spring water.

Then her attorney decided to join in with the discussion. "Will any of this show up on Walter's permanent record?" he asked the principal.

"Ah, no it will not," the principal answered eagerly.

"It shouldn't show up on *any* record," Denise snapped.

"It won't," the vice principal informed us.

"And do you have any security at the school that would extend to the students while inside of the schoolyard?" Mr. Fields asked.

The principal looked to the disciplinarian, who quickly turned red. I guess security was part of his responsibility.

"Ah, yes we do," the broad-shouldered disciplinarian answered.

"Have the police found the other party involved in the stabbing yet?"

"Hopefully, they'll have him in custody by later on today."

Mr. Fields then questioned the vice principal. "And you say that you'll be talking again to the other student involved?"

"Michael Riley," Denise added. It seemed as if she had memorized the name, and she was making sure that she wouldn't forget it.

"That's correct," the vice principal answered.

"And is he a white student?" Mr. Fields asked.

At that point, the principal started to turn red. "I see exactly where you're trying to go with this case, ah—"

"Attorney Melvin Fields," Denise's lawyer filled in for him, with a quick extension of his card.

The principal took it in hand and continued with his response: "Mr. Fields, we don't look at this as a racial incident. We see this as a freak occurrence at our school that will *definitely* not happen again," he assured us. "There were just a lot of mistakes that were made in handling it."

Mr. Fields nodded as he rose from his seat. "I understand. I understand that perfectly. These kinds of mistakes are always made."

"Especially when it comes to dealing with black people," Denise interjected. "Black *boys* in particular."

It was obvious that the school officials hadn't had sufficient time to get their stories together. I was quite sure that they didn't expect for Denise to come at them with a lawyer so fast. Had they known, I believe they would have been forced to counter with a lawyer or two of their own that morning.

Mr. Fields headed for the door and addressed the principal before we left. "By the way," he said. "We'll be back in touch."

I was wondering what would have happened had Denise been a poor single mother with no lawyer, and her son's father happened to be a jobless black man who was nowhere to be found. In fact, had that been the case, Walter would have never been allowed to enroll at the Oak Park Junior High School. Education and economics were definitely power in America, no matter *what* color you were!

Before we all made it out the door, Walter's teacher, a twenty-something recent college grad, apologized for everything. "You really are a good kid, Walter, and I hope to see you back in school soon," she said to my son.

Denise turned and shook the teacher's hand. "Ms. Walker, I want to thank you for your support on this, because my son is *not* some street thug, and I want *everyone* to know that. He's a good kid with a good head on his shoulders, and I will *never* let someone try and wipe their hands with him and label him a bad kid. We have to be supportive of our youth and let them know that they are loved, and that they can make it in this world."

Ms. Walker nodded. "I couldn't agree with you more," she responded as we walked out.

When my son, Denise, her attorney, and I all made it back outside to the school's parking lot area, I asked Walter again if he would be okay.

He nodded and mumbled again, "Yeah, I'll be all right." I never remember seeing him so glum before.

Attorney Melvin Fields reached to shake my hand before heading to his car, a brown Lexus coupe. "It's good to finally meet you, Mr. Perry," he said to me with a smile.

I shook his hand and nodded to him, full of concern. *It's good to finally meet you,* I thought to myself, repeating his comment to me. *Had Denise been talking to her attorney about me? And to what extent?*

I thought again about calling my own attorney.

Denise turned to me and said, "I'll keep you updated on everything."

"Please do," I responded.

We all made it to our separate cars and pulled off. I then wasted no time at all getting on my cell phone and calling my lawyer, only to get his answering machine.

"John, this is Walter. I need you to call me ASAP at my office. Something's come up with my son and we need to go over some things. I'll fill you in on everything when you call me."

I made it back to my downtown office on the seventeenth floor of Chicago Federal Savings Bank by eleven-thirty, and I felt exhausted. I had three afternoon meetings to attend that day, two with clients, and a late-afternoon meeting with the chief executive of accounts regarding new bank policies.

Half of those damn internal meetings were not even necessary. We could all read the memos on our own. Meetings were just used as a reason to show off the boardrooms and order food, if you asked me. It was a big waste of time and money to fool the staff into believing that they were really involved in something of importance. However, by your third meeting, you pretty much know the name of the game as a "bullshit your workforce" policy. Over my three years of working at CFS, I had been in nearly two hundred meetings and was simply tired of all the pep talks and evaluations.

I was one of the few black executives, not only at *my* bank, but at many of the larger banks in Chicago. Unfortunately, I had been around plenty of black men and women who did not have the emotional toughness or stamina to make it through the many games of corporate structure. It wasn't only *what* you knew, but how you *used* what you knew to get ahead. You had to be confident and secure with your ideas, know the language, and be able to explain yourself under tremendous pressure.

Many black men, more so than the women, it seemed, could not stomach the racism. However, I was able to push ahead despite it. The old boys' club stood on the grounds of no mercy, no retreat, which would immediately factor out anyone who could not stomach being tough-minded for at least ten hours per day. I had been well schooled, and therefore, I was hard to intimidate. After being raised by my father, going head-to-head with him for the majority of my life, I could virtually run CFS and go toe-to-toe with anyone! However, that didn't necessarily mean that I enjoyed my work. Most of the time, I found myself being rather bored with it.

From my office window, I had a perfect view of the famous Sears Tower. Whenever I got bored, I loved to stare out at that tall, black building and think about my place in the world. Maybe I really needed to become an entrepreneur and run my own ship like my father, or even Denise. Sometimes I actually envied her. She was more a people person than I was, yet she had the drive and self-determination of an owner.

I thought about her comments concerning our son that morning, and I had to admit that she was a hell of a mother. She and her lawyer had successfully played a game of left jab, right cross, as in a boxing match. Denise jabbed the school officials and kept them off guard with her emotion, and her attorney was the big legal knock-out punch.

I was impressed. I was also apprehensive about going up against them.

Denise truly loved her son, and she had a long-term invested interest in his success. I don't think I realized that before. Raising kids took much more than just rules and regulations; it took a lot of heart, persistence, and adaptability. Suddenly, I longed to have that challenge, and to raise my son.

My wife called me and broke me from my daydream. I had called her from my car phone after contacting my attorney, and left her a message as well. Beverly immediately wanted to know how things had gone at my son's school that morning.

"Well, I must say that I gained a lot of respect for Denise. She really knows how to handle herself," I admitted to my wife.

To my surprise, Beverly responded, "I figured that. Denise is a very strong woman."

"And *who* told you this?" I asked lightheartedly. Beverly had never had a full conversation with Denise.

"Well, to successfully raise two black sons in America, during the *nineties*, a woman would *have* to be strong," she answered. "I know that my older sister Elaine is strong, raising my niece, Karla, by herself."

Elaine was indeed the strongest of Beverly's kin. *And* the oldest. I was cornered again by a heavy feeling of guilt. What had absentee fathers done to help single mothers in raising their children? Money was hardly everything. What about the importance of moral support and physical presence? And what about the importance of fatherly love?

I said, "So, you believe that she's been successful?" I would agree with it, I just wanted to know what made Beverly so sure.

My wife thought about it before she answered. She said, "Elaine told me once that life isn't so much about what happens to you, because things are going to happen to us that we can't really control from the time that we're born. Life is more about how you *respond* to the things that happen to you, or how you go about accomplishing what you want to do in this short time that we have in the world. So yes, I believe that Denise Stewart has done a heck of a job with what she's had to live with.

"Some of the strongest people in the world have had to fight through hell, so that they can make it to their heaven," Beverly told me. "And that idea of heaven is different for every one of us."

Right as she finished her statement, I got a call on my other line. "Hold on for a minute, Beverly. This may be John Ford. I left a message with him before I called you this morning."

"Okay, well, we'll talk later," she said.

"Well, let me see if it's him first. Because if it's not, then I'd rather talk to you."

She chuckled and said, "Okay, I'll hold."

"Thank you." I clicked to my other line.

"Hey, man, I got your message. What's going on with your son?"

"John! Okay, hold on for a second," I told him.

"Beverly, it's him, and I have a busy afternoon today, so I'll see you at home tonight."

"Bye, Walter," she told me.

"I love you," I responded.

"I love you, too."

I hung up with my wife and clicked back over to my attorney. "Walter was involved in a stabbing incident at school . . ." I went on to tell him all that I knew and asked about our chances in a custody battle.

"Well, we can make a case out of anything, but this sounds like a normal parental concern, and she's already on it," he advised. "It's not as if it's neglect or abuse. And the fact that she's already taking care of it makes it even less of a case for us. Your son is what, twelve, thirteen now?"

"Twelve."

John thought about it. He was a young, aggressive guy from Detroit. He graduated from the University of Michigan in Ann Arbor. He came to Chicago about seven years ago with his family, to get away from the economic despair of Detroit and to practice his trade in a stronger metropolitan area.

He came to a conclusion and said, "Look, man, I'm not into breaking up families, because I have a wife and three kids of my own, but do you think your son would want to live with you instead of with his mother? Because if he's almost thirteen years old, the judge could appoint a guardian ad litem, and your son could *almost* choose who he wanted to be with."

I had to think about that myself. "So, he could actually make a choice?" It seemed too easy.

"Well, it's not exactly that simple, because most judges are going to naturally lean toward the mother. However, the older he gets, and the more he understands what's going on, the more the judge is likely to weigh his opinion. But it's still not a guarantee."

I immediately thought about showing my son how much he had to gain and got energized. "Okay, well, let me work on that," I responded.

"Are you really sure you want to do this?" John asked me. "Why don't you just ask to spend more time with him?"

I stopped and thought again. "I'm still not absolutely sure, but I do know that I love my son, and I just don't want to stand by and watch him become another ugly statistic or a failure if I can do something about it. I believe he has a lot of potential, but I need more than just weekends to help him grow. I mean, at least her other son, Jimmy, has basketball to concentrate on."

John said, "I see. Well, hey, man, if you believe you can make a difference, then do what you have to do, and I'll represent you in court."

I hung up the phone and was ready for anything Denise had to throw at me. If I gained custody of my son, I wouldn't have to worry about hiding my family's wealth so much. Denise could never really say that my son had been cheated of anything anyway. And even if she did, I could make sure that any monies gained would be set aside for my son in a trust account. I didn't mind him sharing with his mother and brother later on down the road, I just worried about his mother taking me to court on her own accord. Nevertheless, I wanted to show my son how much he had to gain by becoming a full-fledged Perry. It was just the kind of news that I needed to brighten up my day.

Fatherhood

"Y O U like your high school so far?" I asked my son. Wearing a blue cotton vest over a white tennis shirt, Little Jay even looked like a suburban schoolboy. We were shooting the breeze at the playground after school.

He nodded to me. "Yeah, it's all right."

Having to meet him at odd places made me feel like I was an outsider. I was still happy to see him though, and I couldn't wait for basketball season to get started. Then we would really do some bonding. But we weren't running ball that day. I just wanted to talk to him, father to son.

"Are there a bunch of white kids in Belmont?" I asked him. I knew the answer to that, I was just making small talk.

Little Jay smiled and said, "Yeah."

"You think that's good for you, being around more white kids?"

"You don't get in as much trouble," he told me with a grin.

"Yeah, you got that right. Unless you're into taking PCP and bungee jumpin'," I joked.

Little Jay shook his head. "People who take that stuff are crazy. And bungee jumping? You *know* that's crazy."

I said, "Good. Because anything that can ruin your health or crack your skull wide open ain't good for you."

We shared a laugh and watched these white kids trying hard to dunk a basketball on the courts.

"Hey, Jay, man, come over here and show us how to do it!" one of them yelled. They looked tall enough to dunk, they just weren't able to explode off the ground. It didn't look like they were trying hard enough to me. Dunking basketballs doesn't naturally come with height. You have to work at it. White folks always assume that athletics comes natural for black people, and that's bullshit! I know that for a fact. Because whenever I stopped working on my game, all of a sudden other guys were able to handle me.

Little Jay yelled back, "Naw, man, not today! Ricky can dunk! Ask him to show you!"

Ricky was a lanky white kid in a baseball cap. He had an unlit cigarette hanging from his pink lips, a suburbanite trying to be urban hip.

"Naw, man, my ankle is messed up today! I'm not dunking!" he yelled back.

I looked at my son and shook my head. "Them white boys are always gonna be asking you for demonstrations. You wait till you get to college. Then these same white folks got a nerve to complain about how much money you can make in the pros.

"Hell, if they didn't love the black athlete so much, these ball clubs wouldn't pay them millions of dollars to shoot a basketball in the first place.

"What do you think about that?" I asked my son.

He hunched his shoulders and said, "Sometimes it seems like they get a little greedy."

I looked and frowned at him. "Greedy? Shit! You know how much these ball clubs and sporting goods companies make off these black athletes?" I snapped at him. "Even these colleges are getting paid; coaches, scouts, and everybody involved. I think it's only right that these boys get their millions. Jordan *deserves* thirty million a year!"

My son nodded. "Yeah, I would say *Jordan* deserves it, but not a lot of these other guys. Jordan sells out arenas everywhere he goes, Jordan and Shaq."

I smiled. It sounded like my boy had been doing his basketball business homework. But I wanted to talk about more than just basketball with him. I wanted to know what else was going on in his life.

"So, what have you been doing with yourself, you know, with your free time and whatnot?" I asked him.

He said, "Nothing really. I'm just chillin', going to school, and doing my homework."

I knew he was probably working on his game whenever he got a chance to, but I had to force myself not to ask about it.

"What about your little brother, Walter? What has he been up to?" I asked.

Little Jay shook his head and smiled. "My mom is thinking about suing his school," he told me.

"*Suing the school?* For what?"

"Walter got stabbed in the hand at the schoolyard by another kid that didn't even go there."

I frowned. That damn Walter kid was dying to be a roughneck. He had always been asking Little Jay about my gang affiliations. Jay didn't have much to tell him though, because I never talked about it with him. The only reason his little brother even knew was because Neecy had run *her* mouth.

"What was Walter doing, talking trash?" I asked my son.

"Naw, it was some white boy who was talking trash, and Walter was taking up for him," he answered. "And then the school suspended Walter and not the white boy. My mom was pissed off about that. That's when she called up her lawyer."

I started laughing, imagining Neecy up at her son's school with a lawyer, telling them white folks off. "So Neecy lookin' to get paid now, hunh?" I joked.

My son looked hesitant to laugh with me. Maybe it was because I had called his mom "Neecy" again. She had probably drummed the name "Denise" in his head like she was doing with everyone else.

"I mean, Denise," I said to him.

He smiled. "She just wants people to use her proper name," he said to me. "Ain't nothin' wrong with that, is it?"

"Naw. I guess not," I responded. "I hear that actor Laurence Fishburne don't want people calling him Larry anymore either. But, you know, that's just something I'll have to get used to."

He said, "I know. You're used to calling her that."

I started to laugh again. Little Jay wouldn't even say the word "Neecy."

"You think your mom is like a drill sergeant sometimes?" I asked him. My son just laughed it off. I couldn't even imagine living with his mother anymore. She had gotten used to being a mother for too long. I even wondered how she treated her truck-driver friend. I had to admit, that single mother job could really harden a woman. Either that or make her desperate for a daddy. I started thinking about my relationship with Kim and *her* son. I was spending more time with them than I ever planned to.

I said, "Jay, ah . . . you ever feel angry at me for not being around?" I had a lump in my throat, but I felt it was only right to ask him. I had to get it out in the open.

My son nodded and looked away from me. "Sometimes, yeah. Like, when my friends had their fathers there to watch our games and stuff."

I asked, "So it feels good to have me in the stands, then?" I knew the answer to that, too. I just wanted to hear it from my son's mouth.

He grinned and said, "Of course. It feels good when anybody's in the stands for you, because Mom was busy most of the time, doing other stuff."

"She never came to any of your games? She used to come to all of mine."

He smiled and said, "Yeah, she told me. But, naw, she's been to some of my games. She said I'm a lot more coordinated than you were. She said you used to get fouled and knocked around a lot."

I broke out laughing. "That was my strategy, to get their big men in foul trouble. I used to take the ball right at them like a crazy man. That doesn't work against *you* though," I told him.

We sat and watched those white boys trying to dunk again.

"They gon' need to work out with some ankle weights or something," Little Jay commented, shaking his head and grinning.

"Yeah, or *something*," I agreed with him.

I looked at my watch. It was after four. "You, ah, got your homework to do, right?" I didn't want my son sitting around too long at the playground. I just wanted to see him. I had some things to do that day myself.

"Yeah, plus my brother is home by now anyway," he answered. "Mom'll be calling any minute now to check up on us."

I stood up from the bleachers and said, "If she ain't called already."

Little Jay stood up after me. "I'll just tell her I was out here talking with you," he said.

I stopped in my tracks. "You gon' tell her what?" I shook my head and said, "Naw, naw, man, don't blame this on me. You knew where you had to be." I didn't want Little Jay picking up any bad habits on my part. No way was I going to allow that. Making convenient excuses was how I got myself off track years ago.

I said, "Jay, I love you, man, and I love being around you, but never make excuses for what you *know* you're supposed to be doing. It took me *years* to learn that lesson, and I *damn sure* don't want you following in *my* footsteps. I don't care if you *were* hanging out here and talking to me.

You listen to your mother, 'cause she's done a damn good job of raising you."

For a second there, I couldn't believe what I was saying, but it was true. If my son was going to have a chance at playing professional basketball, then he was going to have to stay focused on taking care of business and staying out of trouble, even if it meant he couldn't shoot the breeze with me.

I waited for him to respond to me.

He dropped his head a little. "Yeah, I know," he mumbled.

He looked like a big kid who had just been told that he couldn't go to the circus. I felt guilty. I guess Little Jay really did like his old man being around him. I felt good about that part.

"Come on, man, let me walk you home," I told him, tossing my arm around his shoulder.

He got his books together and started walking with me.

I looked into my son's choirboy face and said it again, "I love you, man." I was proud to be his dad.

Little Jay looked back at me and responded, "I love you too, Dad."

Shit, I can't lie! After my son said those five words to me, I felt like a kid my-damn-self! What the hell was I thinking all of those years when I was away from him? I thought about fatherhood for the rest of that night. I also thought about Kim's boy, Jamal. I didn't want to admit it, but I was forced to. I was in a position to be a father figure for him. I was being given an opportunity to start from scratch, without all of the late-night diaper changing and feelings of uselessness. I knew that Kim could use my help with Jamal. It was no doubt in my mind.

After making a few runs, I got back to my mother's that night and started getting ready for work. I couldn't find any of my clothes.

"What are you looking for?" my mother asked me. "You know you took most of your clothes over to that woman's house. And everything you left over here is dirty."

I had finally taken Kim's spare key, but I still didn't consider myself to be officially living with her. I guess I was having my cake and eating it too.

My mother said, "You know what, Jimmie, you're doing the same damn thing that gets a lot of these young couples in trouble today. Now, I've tried my best not to say anything about it, but either you're gonna commit yourself to being a part of this woman's life, or you're not. You can't have it both ways and live in both places. It just ain't fair, Jimmie. It's not!"

I didn't have the time nor the energy to argue with my mother that night. Besides, she was telling the truth again. I was getting nothing but the truth from every angle, just like I had been getting for the majority of my life. However, I had always chosen to accept some of those truths and act on them, while ignoring the others. That's the way it is with a lot of people.

I broke down and admitted it to my mother. "I know, Mom. It's already been on my mind. Trust me."

"So what are you gonna do about it then?" she asked me.

I wasn't prepared to answer that question yet. *Knowing* the right thing and actually *doing* the right thing were *miles* apart.

"I guess I'm gonna find out sooner or later. Ain't that right?" I asked my mother with a grin.

She didn't see the humor in it. She started to shake her head and walk away to her room. "You should have known that when you first started going over there. I knew it from the first phone call she made!" my mother hollered from the narrow hallway. I was sure she did know. I knew it myself. Kim was a needful woman. It was another truth that I had ignored.

I got over to Kim's house an hour before work, to get my missing clothing together. Kim didn't have too many words for me when I walked in. The silent treatment usually meant bad news. She was watching television on the couch with Jamal, and he was on his way to dreamland. He got reenergized when he saw me though.

"Hey, J.D.," he said to me. He was so tired that he tripped over his feet trying to get up and run to me. I told him to call me J.D. because that "Mr. Jay" stuff reminded me too much of "Bentley" on *The Jeffersons.*

I scooped him off his feet and said, "Time for bed, little man."

He turned it into a game and tried to wrestle his way back to the ground, but by then I was halfway to his room. It's amazing just how playful kids can be. I never remember Little Jay having so much energy. He seemed more reserved than the average kid. Jamal and Walter were high-energy boys. Young kids seemed to be getting more energy as we got closer to the year two thousand.

I got Jamal ready for bed and asked him if he had done his home-work. I had never asked him that before. Obviously, the conversation with my son was still fresh on my mind.

Jamal said, "I wrote my name in cursive today."

"Oh yeah? Well, how do you spell it?" I asked him.

"J-A-M-A-L."

"Okay, now what about your last name?"

Jamal smiled and said, "L-E-V-O-R-E."

I was surprised. I thought he was about to spell B-O-O-K-E-R.

Kim walked in on us and tucked her son into bed and kissed him good night on his forehead.

"Good night, little man," I told him as his mother clicked off the light.

"Good night," he mumbled to me.

As soon as we walked out of his room, I asked Kim about her son's name. "His last name is Levore?"

"Yeah, that's his father's last name," she told me.

The next thing I knew, I was feeling jealous. Kim had given Jamal *his* father's last name, and my only son didn't carry mine.

"What's wrong with you?" I asked her. She was still moping around like she had an attitude problem.

"Nothin'. I'm all right," she grumbled. "I just expected a phone call from you, that's all."

I shook my head. I had to get ready for work. I didn't even want to go into that conversation. I had been on the move too much to stop and call Kim that day.

I looked into the hallway closet and found my blue work shirt. It was the only one that was still clean. I had some serious washing to do.

"You need to buy your own clothes hamper instead of throwing every-thing in trash bags," Kim fussed at me.

"All right. I'll buy one tomorrow," I said. I still wasn't looking forward to any discussion on phone calls. I got dressed in a hurry and ended up with another ten minutes to burn before leaving for work. I was itching to ask Kim more about her son's last name.

I looked over at her sitting on the green couch and noticed that she was rolling up a fat joint.

I asked, "Why you gotta do that tonight?" Her smoking was really starting to bother me. Kim seemed to smoke whenever she had a few hours to herself. It was a good thing they didn't test urine at her job, be-

cause she would have been fired on the spot. Employers had been testing my urine for years. If *I* wanted to keep a job, I couldn't even *think*
about smoking weed anymore.

She said, "Because I'm stressed out right now."

"Because of a damn phone call?" I snapped at her. I couldn't believe
that shit! Women can be so fucking petty sometimes!

Kim stared at me. "Don't raise your voice while my son is asleep. In
fact, don't raise your voice at me, period."

"Well, what about you smoking while your son is asleep?"

"What about it? You see I got the fan on?" she answered me.

"What if he woke up in the middle of the night or something, and
caught you out here with a joint in your mouth?"

Kim shook her head. "That boy sleeps like a brick, just like his father
used to. You see how hard it is getting him out of bed in the morning."

I shook my head back. "You just don't care about him, do you?"

"What?!" she shouted. "Don't tell me I don't fuckin' care about my
son! Who do you think been raising him for six years?"

"Why did you give him his father's name then?" I asked her. It was a
sneaky way to slip that question in there.

Kim calmed down a bit. She said, "So I wouldn't forget who did it." It
was just that simple to her.

I asked, "Have you had that many men?" She made it sound like she
was some kind of whore. I didn't like how that sounded at all.

She said, "No, but I usually try and forget about the sorry-ass men I
did have. That's why I keep changing my phone books, to get rid of old
numbers and fucked-up memories." She smiled at me and took her first
drag of the joint.

I knew it was time for me to get out of there then. Kim was showing
her true ghetto-bitch colors. I didn't want to go to work smelling like
weed anyway, but something stopped me from leaving. I walked over
and grabbed the joint out of her hand and put it out in the ashtray.

"What the hell are you doin'?!" she yelled at me.

"Don't raise your voice while your son is asleep," I reminded her.
Then I said, "Look, if you got something you want to say to me, then
you settle that shit with me. Don't sit in here smoking weed and getting
attitudes if you're not gonna express what you're feeling about shit, because being high ain't gon' change a damn thing."

Out of the blue, Kim started laughing. I knew the weed couldn't have
gotten to her that fast. She said, "Oh, check you out. Mr. Righteous. As
if *you're* perfect."

"Yeah, but at least I'm trying," I told her. "I thought that you wanted to try, too. That's the only reason why I keep coming over here."

Kim dropped her head and got quiet on me. I guess she realized that she was wrong. She looked back up at me and said, "I'm doing the best that one person can do. Okay?" She looked at me real hard, as if I should feel guilty about something. And I did feel guilty. My son didn't have my last name because I hadn't been there for him. I guess I didn't deserve it.

I looked into Kim's face and asked, "Are you giving up on me already?" It sure seemed like she was. It had been only a few months since we started seeing each other again.

She answered, "I don't know. Should I?"

I thought about it. "Why would you?" I asked her.

"Because I'm tired of the damn letdowns."

I nodded. I understood exactly how she felt. I was tired of being denied a job or being the first man laid off because of my jail record. "I didn't give up on trying to find a stable job after getting out of prison," I told her. "Just imagine how that shit felt, having to tell all these employers that I went to jail for armed robbery thirteen years ago."

Kim nodded to me. "Yeah, you're right. That is tough."

"But what I'm trying to tell you, though, is that you can't sweat the past, you just gotta keep pushing for your future. That's how I was able to get back on the right track," I told her.

She said, "Well, answer this question for me then, Jay. Am I on that right track for you, or am I just a quick stop in the bushes?"

Damn! I thought. She blew my mind with that question. I tried to answer it the best that I could. I said, "I would like for us to be on that same track, but you gotta be willing to work with me."

"Yeah, yeah, I heard all that shit before," she responded. "See, that's exactly what I'm talking about, I don't need any more letdowns."

Then she stood up and started rushing me. "Go ahead to work, Jay. I don't want you to be late on account of me. Just go ahead and do what you gotta do."

I didn't like her rushing me out of the door like that, but she did have a point. I was nowhere near making a decision about where she and her son fit in my chaotic life. But I *was* starting to care about them, I just didn't know how involved I wanted to be.

The issues of family and fatherhood lingered on my mind for that entire night at work. I even decided to ask my boss, Roger, about it. He had been married to the same woman for twenty-five years. He was bragging that night about his son catching two touchdown passes and returning a punt for a touchdown in his third high school football game of the season.

"How 'bout that, Jimmy? My boy's making a name for himself even with that candy-armed quarterback throwing him the ball this year."

I smiled and said, "Yeah, I can't wait for my son to start basketball season."

"You think he's ready for varsity this year?"

"Yeah, he's ready. I'm just wondering if *Chicago* is ready," I bragged.

"My boy has six touchdowns in three games already. If he keeps that up, he'll end up with more than twenty for the season," Roger responded.

He was too energized about sports to talk about family affairs at the beginning of our night shift, so I waited until later on when things were winding down.

I caught him in his office after six in the morning. "Hey, Roger. Can I talk to you about family for a minute?"

He looked at me surprised for a second. Outside of our sons and sports, we never even mentioned family. "Yeah, why not?" he answered me. "What kind of problems are you having?"

I didn't want to go right into talking about *my* situation, I just wanted to talk about families in general. I asked, "Well, what do you think about the American family in general? Is it strong, weak, or what?"

He looked at me and said, "Actually, it stinks. I think America has too many people more concerned about themselves. We spend too much time talking about raises, overtime, advanced degrees, better neighborhoods, and all that other hoopla for the sake of the children, but we're actually spending less and less time as a family unit. That's the reason why I took this night-shift position three years ago, so that I could see my boys play in the prime time of their lives, high school. Because once they go off to college, they're gonna start becoming their own persons, and everything they do in sports then will be recorded on tape anyway."

I thought about Neecy not being able to make it to many of our son's basketball games, and about the two of us as a couple.

"What do you think about couples today, you know, just men and women?" I asked him.

"Well, it's all the same thing to me. If you grow up in a household where overtime and five degrees were a priority, they end up being a priority with you. So we have a bunch of kids today who get married and never have any time to really enjoy each other's company. That's what love and marriage should be all about, enjoying each other's company, not income, stocks and bonds, and what preschool Junior's gonna go to. You know what I mean?"

There was no way I could see myself climbing back into the picture with Neecy, so I thought about Kim and my situation with her. "And what do you think about single mothers?" I asked.

Roger looked at me and paused for a second. "Well, Jimmie, I don't know what your situation is with your son's mother, but there shouldn't be any single mothers if you ask me. I had a great uncle right here in Chicago who married a woman with four children. And my father told me that he thought to himself, *Why in the world would Uncle John do something crazy like that?* But you know what, my father told me that all of those kids loved Uncle John like he was the only father they ever had. And at the end of the day, Uncle John was a very proud man who could stand tall as an example of what a good man *should* be. He didn't get all into the ego of having kids of his own, as long as he was able to contribute a piece of his soul and goodness to developing decent human beings. And now he has a truckload of decent, God-fearing grandchildren. And they are *all* my good cousins."

I figured there was nothing in the world I could say to rationalize my situation to Roger. I decided to keep my mouth shut. I was tempted to ask him what kind of woman his uncle had married. I doubt if she was as heart-worn as Neecy and Kim were. I hate to stereotype, but it seemed like white women took things a lot easier than black women did. Maybe they were less opinionated, and they didn't have the baggage of society repeating how strong they were supposed to be. It was as if America was telling black women that they didn't *need* a black man because they were so damn strong on their own! My mother wasn't strong enough to keep her three, hardheaded boys from getting into all kinds of trouble in the streets, nor were many other black mothers. Most of the guys I did time in jail with never even mentioned having a father in their lives. I never thought of it that way before, but it looked like a setup to keep black men and women apart while weakening their families.

I kept debating whether Kimberly Booker was worth being with, considering her smoking and attitude problems, while there I was, a one-time convict, who was getting a second chance on his *own* life. Who was *I* to be so picky? I was a straight-up hypocrite, getting myself a second chance while denying one to Kim.

I thought, *Yeah, maybe Roger is right, the American family stinks!* And I could smell the stench all around me.

True Companionship

D E N I S E called me over to her house after midnight, so I knew that whatever it was, it was important. I didn't have to work the next day, so I rushed right on over to Oak Park, planning on staying up with her all night if I
B R O C K   had to.

When I pulled up to her door, Denise was waiting for me on the front steps with the lights out.

"Is everything okay?" I whispered to her. She obviously didn't want to draw any attention to herself.

"I just needed to talk to you in person tonight," she told me as we stepped inside and quietly closed the door. I followed her to the family room where a very dim lamp was left on.

"Is Walter doing all right?" I asked her. Denise had told me about her son's incident at school. I figured that had a lot to do with her distress.

"Yeah, he's okay. They let him back in school and apologized to him. I'm just concerned about whether I should take the school to court or not?"

I wanted to get all of the facts before I agreed or disagreed with her. I asked, "How much are we talking?" We took a seat on the sofa.

"Between two and eight million," she answered.

I nodded. That was all the facts I needed to hear. If her boys weren't asleep, I would have even whistled. Two to eight million dollars was a considerable amount of money!

"What's stopping you from suing?" I asked her.

"You know you rarely ever get as much as you ask for in these court cases," she responded. "We would probably end up being awarded *less* than two million."

"That's still a million and change more than nothing," I told her. "*I* would take it."

Denise chuckled. She was wearing short gray one-piece pajamas and black socks with her slippers. She slid the slippers off and tossed her feet into my lap. "I'm just debating whether or not I want to go through with all of this. I mean, we're talking about a major change in Walter's life here."

"Yeah, a change that could set him up for life," I responded, rubbing her soft feet. I didn't see what the problem was. From what I had been told, she had a definite case against the school.

"Do you realize how much of a big deal this would be if I go through with it? We're talking about a lot of media attention."

I thought about that and nodded my head again. "Yeah, you're right. Good-bye private life." That changed the entire thing for me. How, indeed, would everything come together? Would I be pushed aside as an outsider again? What role would I play?

"Or, I could settle this out of court with the school for a lot less money, but without all of the extra drama involved," Denise added.

I couldn't think about my selfish insecurities, I had to think about the greater good of the case. "Then again, Denise, this could set a precedent for all of the other black kids in America who are stereotyped as troublemakers. The school systems from coast to coast would be forced to watch how they treat black children from now on."

"Yeah, and it could also give them another excuse to be afraid of enrolling us. Then the media would come in and dissect my life and my family, and start talking about the shoplifting incident Walter was involved in last year, and me having two sons from two fathers and never being married, and then get into my sister's life, and I just—" She stopped and shook her head, exhausted from thinking about all of the intangibles involved.

The case was a lot more difficult than it seemed, and it appeared that Denise had already considered things from every angle.

She started to chuckle and said, "On the other hand, I've been trying to think of it as a payback for all of the shit I've had to go through as a single mother. Maybe if we had enough cases like this one, we could share the money between single black mothers all over the country. But that's just the ghetto girl in me taking over. Nobody owes us anything; nobody but these sad fathers."

I thought about commenting on that, but I quickly decided to leave it alone. Instead I asked, "Have you thought about the reaction from the women in your Single Mothers' Organization?"

"Mmm hmm," she mumbled, stretching out in my lap. "We would probably end up sharing every dime with them. They already look at me and my sons as a Cinderella story. Winning a multimillion-dollar court case is all they need. This would just give them *more* of a reason to hate me. And it would give my little sister a million more reasons to call me up for money."

I shook my head and grinned while rubbing her back and shoulders. "It sounds like you're between a rock and a hard place," I told her.

"Tell me about it. That's why I had to have your company tonight. I can't even sleep over this thing," she responded. "And the thing is, the average mother wouldn't think twice about it. They would just take the money and deal with whatever. But I mean, it's not as if we're poor anymore, you know. So it's just not that simple for me to decide."

I decided to look at it from a totally different angle. "Okay, Denise, let's say for a minute that you were married to the father of both of your sons. Would this decision be as hard for you to make then?"

She sighed and said, "Brock, there's no sense in even answering that question. I mean, the reality is that I'm *not* a married woman with one father for both of my sons."

"But what I'm trying to get at is to have you think about what the main issue is here. I mean, are you ashamed of who you are, and you don't want everybody to know? Because if you are, then that's an honest fear, and I just want you to be able to face up to that."

Instead of answering my question, Denise readjusted herself in my lap and leaned up to kiss me. The kiss was as if it were the last of a lifetime. It was very passionate and meaningful, as if I would be going over to war in the Persian Gulf tomorrow.

I looked into her eyes and asked, "What was all of that for?"

She ran her fingers to the back of my neck and answered, "For your company."

I could tell that she didn't want to talk anymore. She would have plenty of nights to think about the incident with her son and what to do about it. But for that night, and for that moment, she simply wanted an understanding man. So I fell into Denise's arms and kissed her back, holding her like a newborn baby, until her passion became too strong to deny.

She whispered, "I don't want to use you," as I slowly undid her night-clothes.

I said, "You're not. And I'm glad to be here for you, whenever you need me."

"Just make sure that you protect us," she reminded me with a grin and a peck on my lips.

"Always," I told her.

Then we went on to make slow and quiet love on the family room floor, conscious of being subtle enough not to wake her sleeping sons.

I got back in after five in the morning and thought long and hard about being Denise's lifetime partner. The passion we shared that evening was definitely too much for me to bear. It was like a curse, pulling me back into sickness again.

"Shit!" I mumbled to myself. "What happened to taking things slowly and thinking things through?"

I tried to laugh it off, knowing that I wouldn't sleep again without en-visioning myself at Denise's side in a full family setting. That night we spent together was a curse indeed; a curse of how sweet it could be. True companionship.

Fathers and Sons

"WE'LL be back around seven tomorrow evening," I told Beverly at the front door. It was a sunny Saturday morning, and I was taking my son with me to Barrington, Illinois, for a short stay with my parents to let him realize what he was connected to.

"It's no rush. Take your time," Beverly responded to me. It was her idea that Walter and I make the trip alone for father-and-son bonding, as if we were going fishing.

I smiled and said, "Actually, I wanted to get back home in time to devour more of that splendid cooking of yours. You have my mother beat by a mile. You've spoiled me."

She asked, "Your mother's going to cook?"

I laughed. "Yeah, I wish that she wouldn't, but you know how she likes to show off sometimes."

My wife smiled back at me and said, "I'll see what I can do then."

Walter was already heading toward the garage with his bags in hand for the car. His hands had healed enough not to need any new bandages. That was a good thing, because my parents would have flipped if my son still had his hands wrapped during our visit. They would have had a thousand *more* questions for me, on top of the thousand that I already knew they would ask.

"Bye, Walter. Have a nice time," Beverly told him.

"I hope so," he whined. Unfortunately, I don't think he looked forward to seeing my parents again. We had visited only twice before, once when he was five, and again when he was nine. Both times were torture for him. My parents didn't have the kind of house that young and curious visitors would enjoy. They had a "don't-touch house" of expensive furniture, sculpture, paintings, and knickknacks of memorabilia on every counter- and tabletop. It was a kid's nightmare. I didn't like spending too much time at my parents' house myself. I remember counting down the days before I was finally off for college.

However, since Walter was older, I didn't think it would be as bad on him. I was hoping that he would begin to assess the extent of the wealth that he was surrounded by, and be inspired to feel more connected to it.

When Walter and I started out on our one-hour journey to Barrington, I let him listen to the cassette tape he had brought along with him. He seemed hesitant to play every song. He kept fast-forwarding and rewinding.

I said, "You know, if you're only interested in a few songs, then you need to buy singles instead of the entire tape. Because you're only going to break my stereo system with all of this back-and-forth button pressing."

"Oh, my bad," he told me. He ejected his tape and decided to listen to the radio instead.

"You can play your tape, Walter. I just don't want you skipping past everything."

He was still hesitant. "No, we can listen to the radio," he responded. I had it on WGCI just for him. WGCI was one of the young, urban contemporary stations. Nevertheless, I could not help wondering whether my son wanted me to hear the kind of music he listened to. I was hoping it wasn't full of profanity and degradation to women. But if it was, I knew that he wasn't playing it around his mother. I knew Denise would not allow that. However, I didn't want to start off on such an authoritarian foot with him, so I decided to let it slide until we made our way back to Chicago that Sunday afternoon. Then I planned to bring the subject up again.

"So, you say that things have pretty much been back to normal at school?" I asked him.

"Yeah, once I got my bandages off. At first, everybody was just staring at me."

I nodded. "Yeah, I can imagine. How's your writing going?"

He exercised the fingers on his right hand. "Oh, I can write now. It was hurting when I first tried on Monday. But it's all right now."

"Did you miss much homework?"

"No."

"So, you'll still be able to get straight A's then?" I asked him with a smile. It was no harm in aiming for the moon. I already knew that my son was *capable* of getting straight A's.

"So far I can," he answered.

"Are you going to try out for any sports teams this year?" I figured that basketball would have been a natural choice for him, since Walter looked up to his older brother so much. Yet, my son was much shorter than his brother was at the same age, and Walter had never participated in team sports. I wondered how much genetics had to do with that. I wasn't much of a sports fanatic as a kid myself. At five foot nine, I was a lot shorter than Jimmy's father.

"I might try out for track this year," my son told me.

At that point, I came right out and asked him, "What about basketball?" I figured he could at least play point guard if he made it close to six foot. Since Denise was tall herself, with a father who was well over six foot, there was a strong possibility of my son getting a growth spurt. *My* father, on the other hand, was only an inch taller than I was.

Walter hunched his shoulders. "I'm not that good at it," he said.

My son's simple answer caused me to frown. I couldn't imagine such a confident kid taking such an easy way out. "Are you saying that in comparison to your brother? Because you shouldn't judge yourself up against him. He's been playing basketball a lot longer than you have."

"I know, but I'm just not good at it. I mean, I tried it and all."

I asked, "Well, what are you good at?"

"Schoolwork."

I smiled. I liked that answer, but it didn't appear that Walter felt as proud as I did about it. He said it like a grudge.

"Do you *wish* that you were good in basketball?" I asked him.

He nodded. "Yeah. I wish I was good in football, too. But my mom wouldn't let me play that."

With his small size, I could see where Denise would have some worries about him playing football, but not basketball.

"Have you tried out for track before?" I asked him.

"No."

"So what makes you think you'll like that?"

He hunched his shoulders again. "I don't know. All you have to do is run."

I laughed. "Son, I think it's a lot more to it than that. You're going to be running a whole lot of laps if you go out for the track team. They run at least three or four miles a day."

"I can run a mile," Walter stated. "I used to jog in the mornings with my brother. I could even keep up with him."

I was tempted to say, "That's because you were jogging," but I left it alone. I think participating in sports would be good for Walter. At least it would keep him occupied from thinking about the streets. And I seriously doubted his school grades would suffer.

I said, "Yeah, well, maybe you *should* go out for the track team. What do you usually do with your free time?"

"Play computer games."

I grinned at him. "Yeah, that figures," I said. "All the time I spent *outside* riding my bike, your generation spends *inside* with joysticks in their hands."

Walter smiled back at me. In my opinion, that computer game, joystick mentality definitely added to turning out plenty of antisocial kids. The more I thought about it, the more convinced I was that Walter should participate in some kind of school sport.

"Are you sure you want to go out for the track team?" I asked him again. "We can buy you the best track shoes out there."

He looked at me and answered, "Yeah, I don't care."

I said, "All right then. I'll talk to your mother about it when I take you back home tomorrow night."

He yawned and said, "Okay."

In the next five minutes, Walter was sound asleep with his seat leaned back. I looked over at him and thought about my son's potential for the rest of the ride. With the right guidance, he could be anything he wanted to be, except for maybe a basketball or football player. Those two sports were overrated for black men anyway. There were so many other professions that young black men were ignoring. Maybe my son could even become a sports agent and represent his brother's interest for a professional basketball team one day. Walter would definitely need a passion toward sports to do that.

Maybe he could even run for some type of political office. He had plenty of drive and opinions. With that profession in mind, however, he would need to clean up his social preference for being "a roughneck" and join debating teams. He could do that. Walter would make a very strong politician. Then again, maybe he wouldn't want to bullshit the people like many politicians are forced to do. Maybe Walter could be a bank executive like his old man. He already understood the workings of capital gains, interest, and loans. Then again, maybe he could become an entrepreneur like his mother and grandfather. I didn't like my job all that much anyway, and Walter seemed more ambitious than I was at his age, so maybe he would need to control his own destiny.

Walter's potential was unlimited! I was excited just thinking about it. It turned an hour drive into what seemed more like twenty minutes. My son was far from being a street thug of any sort, he just needed me there to remind him of that.

I woke Walter up as we drove through the private property entrance and up to the familiar four-bedroom stone-built house of my upbringing. My parents were already sitting out on the front lawn, awaiting our arrival. They seemed eager to be meeting with my son again. The first visit was a shocker, and the second was spent just feeling the situation out. Of course, they asked to see him a lot more in between, but I didn't feel the moral support from them at that time to continue bringing him. Maybe things had changed, and their hard-line attitudes had softened a bit. Especially after I had married Beverly and announced her recent pregnancy to them. Nevertheless, I had my own intentions anyway. After all, Walter wouldn't be staying with my parents in Barrington, he would be staying with Beverly and me in a brand-new house of our own. I just wanted him to feel the power of my family's wealth.

Walter woke up, stretched out, and immediately spotted the new live-in maid my parents had hired. She was a Dominican woman in her late thirties. She looked a lot younger though, and she was browner than all of us; a deep, shiny brown with long black hair and matching black eyes in a cream-colored uniform and soft shoes.

"That's the maid?" my son asked me, watching the attractive helper pour tea. When he was nine, my parents had a much older black woman who worked there at the house. They usually allowed the maids to return to their families on the weekends unless they were having company, which was the case with us.

I smiled, reading my son's young mind. "She's the new one," I told him.

Judging from his gleeful expression, I don't believe he was unhappy to be visiting any longer.

"Is she gonna tuck me in bed?" he asked me with a healthy laugh.

I shook my head and told him to calm down. I couldn't help but smile at it. Walter had a normal boy's attraction to the opposite sex, that's for sure.

"Well, how are you?" my mother, Dolores Perry, greeted us with a hug. Her hair was turning a brighter gray by the year, yet my mother did not have one wrinkle on her smooth brown face. She was turning sixty-four in November. My father, Walter Perry Senior, at sixty-six, had already done most of the graying that he could do. I guess that came from all of his worries and anxieties. I hoped the same wouldn't happen to me, but I figured it probably would.

My father stood up from the white lawn chairs and shook our hands with a nod. He was never the excitable type. He was the kind of successful man whom you had to prove everything to. At first, he even asked me to have a blood test on Walter, but I turned his ridiculous suggestion down. I *knew* that Walter was my son. My father even complained about Walter carrying on our name, but I ignored that as well. What was done was done.

"Well, we're both healthy and well rested," I told my parents, alluding to Walter's nap inside the car.

My son looked at me and grinned.

"Are you sure that Beverly couldn't have made it?" my mother asked me.

Beverly and I had just visited three weeks ago to announce the news of her pregnancy. It was obvious my mother was still apprehensive around my son. Maybe I should have visited with him more often, so that my parents could get used to seeing me with him. However, I had just recently increased my own activity with my son.

"Not on this trip, Mom. She needs her rest," I answered.

My mother nodded. "Okay, I understand," she said. "She's going to need all of the rest and energy that she can get. It took me eleven hours to deliver you." She took a quick look at my son, and I proceeded to read her mind. She wanted to ask how long it took for Denise to deliver him, but she held her tongue instead.

"Five hours," I filled in for her. Denise made sure that I knew, yet I declined to participate in Walter's birth because of all the emotions that would have been involved.

"Well, the guest room is all ready for you," she told my son, blowing off my answer. I was sure she had heard me. "Lucy, could you get my grandson's things and take them to his room, please," she addressed the maid.

The word "grandson" lingered in my head for a second. I was shocked and caught off guard by it. Usually, my parents called Walter "the boy." Maybe they really were coming to grips with my son. It was definitely not an overnight process.

When Lucy, short for Lucienda, gently took my son's bags, he began to smile.

My father caught his stare and grunted, "Young man, that's exactly what got your *father* in trouble. You mind your manners." It had a lot of bite to it, yet my father tried to camouflage the deep flesh wound with a sheepish grin.

My mother turned and looked at him with horror. She got sour and snapped, "They're no different from *you*. Neither one of them."

I thought of retrieving Walter's things and getting the hell out of there already! I didn't bring him there for that. My father's comment was highly disrespectful to all parties involved; my son, his mother, myself, *and* Lucienda, whether Walter understood the slander or not.

I said, "Thanks a lot. Thanks for starting us off on such a good foot. I really appreciate that," and walked away from him. How could I have regularly brought my son around such lethal venom? My father had just reminded me, in light speed, why my son had only been to Barrington twice.

I decided to lead him into the house while my parents got to arguing with each other out on the front lawn.

Once we made it inside, Walter looked up and asked me, "Was my mom a maid?"

Evidently, he *did* understand the slander. "No, she was not," I told him.

"So why did he say that to me then?" Walter had tears in his eyes. I knew I couldn't stay there after that.

I shook my head and responded, "Let's go get your things. We'll have a talk about it tonight. Just me and you."

"We're leaving?" he asked me. He seemed surprised by my suddenness. He was attempting to hold back his tears, but they were rolling down his face already, while he tried to wipe them away. I could feel my son's shock and anger in my gut, and I decided there was no other decision to be made about it.

"You don't want to stay here, do you?" I asked him, just to make sure. My mind was already made, even if he said yes. We were leaving. Pronto!

"No," he told me with a sniff. That settled it. We marched up to the guest room and picked up his bags.

My mother stopped us on our way back down the stairs. "What are you doing?" she asked me. My father was standing at her side. He had apology written all over his face, but it was too late for that.

"Your father has something to say to you; to both of you," my mother informed us.

"Yeah, well, he can save it for another time. If there *is* another time," I told her. I didn't even want to look at the man. He had ruined everything.

"Well, you're not driving back to Chicago right now, are you? Junior, you just got off the road. You should at least give your legs a rest."

"I will," I said, as my son and I made our way to the front door. "At the Titan Hotel."

"Well, maybe we could all have dinner over there," she suggested. She was trying her best to keep things from falling completely apart.

I wasn't so optimistic. "Or, maybe not," I responded to her. We were quickly back out the door.

My parents argued some more while we reloaded the car.

"Junior, we'll be over there for dinner this evening. You hear me?" my mother yelled toward my son and I.

I climbed inside and started the ignition. When I looked up again, my mother was at my driver's side window. "I love you, honey." Then she looked inside at my son and added, "I love you both."

I said, "Yeah, I just wish that *he* would learn how to," and drove off. I didn't mean to be so short and disrespectful to my mother, but if I stayed there a second longer, I might have said and done some vicious things to my father, things my son did not need to hear or see.

The Titan Hotel in northern Illinois was one of the most elaborate and expensive hotels around. The average room there costs no less than two hundred seventy-five dollars a night, and it was only eighteen miles from my parents' house, off Northwest Highway. I tried to use every excuse I could to stay there, and had managed to do so on four separate occasions, including a stay after the prom with an ancient-history girlfriend.

When we pulled up to the heavy, gold-trimmed doors, Walter asked, "Is this where we're staying?" I imagined he would have sounded a lot more excited about it had he been in better spirits.

"May I take your bags, sir?"

I popped the trunk and the bellboy hauled our bags inside for us. Then I gave the car keys to the valet parking attendant.

"Enjoy your stay at the Titan," he told us.

"Oh, we plan to," I responded.

I had already made reservations from the car phone for a room on the twenty-third floor with my platinum Visa card. The twenty-third floor was one level down from the penthouse, where there was a dance floor, a restaurant and bar, and a large outdoor swimming pool. There was an indoor swimming pool and a sauna on the fourth floor. The Titan Hotel was a visitor's dream!

By the time Walter had taken a good look at our bedroom, he was already in better spirits. The color television set was thirty-five inches with surround sound, cable, and pay-per-view movies.

"Man, this place is *tight!*" he told me. He took a seat on the La-Z-Boy chair and leaned it back as far as he could.

" 'Tight' means good, right?" I asked him with a grin.

"Yeah," he answered, clicking on the television.

"Are you hungry?" I asked him. "How about we start off with some seafood. You like shrimp, don't you?"

He nodded like a madman. "Yeah, I like shrimp. And crab cakes."

"Coming right up," I told him. I got on the phone to order room service. I planned on going all out for my son, no matter how much it cost me.

We watched college football on cable while we ate our seafood. We planned on buying trunks and going swimming once our meals settled. The Titan Hotel had a gift shop that sold swim trunks and beach towels. Then we could shower, re-dress, and shoot some pool and play video games on the penthouse level.

After we had done all that we could do in one day, I sat with my son inside of the penthouse restaurant, while he enjoyed an ice cream float of vanilla and Sprite.

"What do you think?" I asked him. "Did you enjoy yourself today?" By then it was after ten at night. I wasn't planning on giving Walter a curfew that evening. If he could hang, I was willing to let him stay up until the sun rose.

He said, "Yeah, I could stay here *every* weekend!"

I chuckled and asked him, "Would you like to?"

"How much does it cost?" he asked me.

"Let's put it this way," I answered, "if we planned to stay here every weekend, then we're talking Tiger Woods money. Can you handle that?"

He nodded and said, "Yeah, I can handle it. Just give me ten years."

I smiled. "Oh yeah? And would you bring *your* son out here?" I asked him.

He licked his lips of ice cream and responded, "Yup. I would bring my *whole* family."

"My father brought me here when I was young, too," I said. My father had taken my mother and me to stay at the Titan twice. I'd been in love with the place ever since. Every few years or so they added something new to keep up with the times, like the computer room on the twelfth floor.

Walter looked up at me for a second and asked, "How come . . . he's so mean?"

He didn't even know how to refer to my father, and I couldn't blame him. I had ignored my parents' messages all that night, and had only called home to talk to Beverly briefly. She knew how important bonding with my son had become to me. I was going to allow no one to get in the way of that.

I said, "Sometimes, son, people get ideas about what they would like to have for themselves and for their children, and they kind of lose their way in the chase. I think that's what happened to my father."

Walter frowned with his lips still covering his straw. "He looks successful to me. You do too. So what is he mad about?"

My son had a good point. However, he did not see the struggles that I had along the way, including my dealings with him and his mother. Nor could he imagine the struggles and drive that his grandfather had.

"I wasn't always successful, son. And there were a lot of *wrong* decisions that I made along the way."

Walter took it all in and asked, "Did you ever want to marry my mother?"

The power of innocence can conquer mountains sometimes. I made sure that I used the right words, or the politically correct words, so to speak, so that my son would not hate me.

"You know, you're going to find out in life that everything doesn't work as planned, and your mother and me were one of those things that was not going to work."

Walter put two and two together. "He doesn't like my mother, does he?"

I took a deep breath, wishing that I could avoid the question. "Unfortunately, not," I answered.

"Why? Because she wasn't successful enough? She is now. What about now? You think he'd like her now?"

I said, "With some people it just doesn't matter. They form an opinion of someone else, and they try their hardest to go to the grave with it."

My son nodded and said, "Like white people. They always think that we're doing something wrong."

I didn't want to admit it, especially while we were smack in the middle of being served by them, but again, my son had a valid point. "Not all of them," I told him. "Some of them *have* made changes concerning their feelings toward African-Americans."

"Yeah, as long as you make a lot of money," he snapped. Maybe he could be a politician after all. He surely knew the name of the game; money, power, and race.

My son was throwing out his full deck of cards at me, and I wasn't sure how long I would be able to match him.

I said, "Well, you can't worry about how others feel about you, you just have to go ahead and be the best person that *you* can be. That means that you have to stop worrying about the streets so much. Because there's nothing wrong with being a good student and getting ahead in life."

He nodded. "I know," he said. "My mom talked to me about that after I got stabbed at school." Then he asked, "You think that . . . my grandfather's a good person?" He was forcing himself to think as a family. I considered that to be progress, but his question was another tough one.

Damn! I thought to myself. I needed some fresh air. I said, "Sometimes people can be very selfish, and in their selfishness, they don't see that they're actually hurting others with their words and actions."

As soon as I finished my sentence, I thought about myself. Was *I* a good person? Hadn't *I* made assumptions about Denise's character and discarded her because she wasn't "successful enough" for *me? Like father like son,* I thought. Suddenly I felt nauseous, as if I had too many drinks that evening with not enough food to hold it down.

I said, "Let me ask *you* a question, Walter. Do you, ah, think that *I'm* mean, like my father?"

My son looked at me and slowly nodded his head. "You used to be," he leveled with me. "That's why I never liked being with you. But now, you know, since this summertime, it's been fun."

I had to take a long sip of my drink to calm my nerves at the table. I hadn't felt such strong emotions since Denise first told me she was pregnant with Walter, thirteen years ago. I didn't even feel as emotional when my wife told me that she was pregnant, because we were both expecting it. To hear my son tell me that he was finally beginning to have a good time with me was the best news in a long time, and all the love that I should have felt for him years ago wanted to pour out of me all at once.

Before I could gather my composure, I told my son that I was sorry and that I would never be mean to him or his mother again, and basically went on to promise him the world. When I realized it, Walter was holding my hands and telling me that it was okay, while he looked around the room at who might have been watching us. My son was actually embarrassed at my overflow of emotions. It was funny how quickly the tables had turned.

The next thing I knew, I broke out laughing and wiped my face off as if I had been crying. It wasn't *me* who had cried. It was some other guy. It was some deep spirit inside of me that jumped out and was taking over. It was love.

My son said, "Do you want to play some pool now? Those other guys just left the pool table."

I nodded. Walter wanted to get me back to being a normal dad as quickly as possible. I told him, "Yeah. Why not?" I asked our waitress for the bill, while Walter scrambled to grab the pool table.

My son and I went to bed after one o'clock in the morning that night. Afterward, I woke up to use the bathroom. When I came back out, I stood at the side of the bed staring at my son in the dark. He was curled up under the sheets like a human snail. I sat down on the long, pine-wood dresser and thought about him. He was a hell of a kid! And it didn't seem to take much for him to love me. All I had to do was love him, spend time with him, and respect him as a young, maturing human being with dreams, aspirations, and emotions of his own.

Before I knew it, that sobbing, tear-running spirit called love had jumped up and taken control of my body again. The second time, however, there was no one there to be embarrassed about it, so I let it take control of me as I cried in the dark.

Walter Perry III was my first, and so far only, son, and I loved him. It was just sad that it had taken me so many long years to come to the point of accepting it, and wanting to be a real part of his life instead of just a monthly paycheck.

Dealing with the Truth

A F T E R the incident at Walter's school, I had the boy on academic lockdown. He was not allowed to watch videos, nor play any video games. I wanted him at home, doing his homework and reading good books, **D E N I S E** period, end of story. Jimmy needed to be concerned about tightening up his grades, too, if he wanted to play basketball his freshman year of high school. So he drew some of the heat as well. And I didn't want to hear a damn thing about being unfair! He was in school to learn what he needed *first*, and if he was doing what he was supposed to do in the books, then I had no problem with him playing basketball.

Before wrapping up my things at work, I gave my attorney, Melvin Fields, a call for an update on the possible lawsuit with Walter's junior high school. I was leaning strongly toward telling him to drop the lawsuit and settle with the school out of court for Walter's medical bills, personal damages, my loss of pay, and his attorney's fees. But to my surprise, Melvin had some other news for me.

"Remember you were asking me about the possibility of a custody battle for your son?" he asked me. He sounded overexcited for some reason, and that was unusual for him. Melvin was one of those show-me-the-money lawyers who only got excited for major cases. I guess he wanted to be the next Johnnie Cochran. He was only working for me because he respected my career and dedication to the community. I really thought that he liked me in another way, but I wasn't trying to go there with him. The man had enough women in tow already, and I was far from being a groupie.

Anyway, I said, "He still doesn't have a case, right?" I was a little concerned. I wondered why Melvin was bringing it back up. It was already settled that we would win the case in court, hands down.

He said, "Well, I was going over everything with the lawsuit and all, and a friend of mine brought it to my attention that Walter Perry *Senior* was a major realtor during the sixties and seventies. And we're talking about *major* major! But he's pretty much kept things under wraps. Did you know anything about that?"

I thought about Walter being from Barrington, Illinois. "I didn't know exactly what his father did, but I knew that he had some money," I answered.

"Yeah, well, you just don't know how *much* money," he informed me. "We're talking multimillions here! How much was Walter giving you a month again?"

I could see where Melvin was going with the case already, and I didn't like it. As much as I would have *loved* to stick it to Walter and his family, I just wasn't that kind of woman. I didn't need their damn money anyway! That was why I never bothered to pursue finding out more about his family in the first place. If I *really* cared, I could have asked around, or even taken a drive up to Barrington to find out for myself.

Melvin had been digging himself up a high-profile case, but I was *not* the one to give it to him. He had just helped me to make up my mind; I wanted to settle with the school out of court. I just didn't need the extra stress or attention of a court case of any kind. I had enough things going on in my life as it was, and more money was *not* the solution.

Melvin went on and said, "I have to look into things a little further, but this is *definitely* something that we need to look into. Inheritance is serious business!"

I said, "Okay, well, I hate to cut you off, but I'll need to talk to you about this a little later, because I have some runs to make." I didn't even want to think like Melvin. That was exactly why I wouldn't date him. He wanted to go after Walter and his family's money, and all the while, he was just like them, pretentious and very much into classism.

"Well, I'll be back in touch, sister. I'll be working out all of the particulars for you."

I hung up the phone with Melvin and immediately called my sons at the house to check up on them. I was going to my monthly SMO meeting, and I told them I would be back home around nine. Leftovers were in the refrigerator from the night before, and they knew my pager number. I basically wiped the entire conversation with Melvin from my mind. He was starting to remind me of a snake, which was exactly why I had so many problems respecting Walter Jr.

I packed up my things, said good-bye to Elmira, locked up my office, and headed for my car in a parking lot around the corner. I had to pick up Nikita for the SMO meeting. Our October meeting was actually being held in the last week of September. For the first week of October, Camellia informed us that she would be going out of town for a few days to help organize a family wedding in Memphis, Tennessee. So we decided to have our October meeting a week in advance, rather than a week after. We were going to discuss the issue of education, testing, college grants, and scholarships for our children. Since the new school year had already begun, no one wanted to wait to have that important a conversation.

When I arrived at my mother's, Nikita was just starting to get herself together.

"I thought you said you were going to be ready?" I asked her.

Her hair was still undone, and she was just beginning to brush her teeth and put on her clothes.

My mother looked up at me from the couch and shook her head. My niece Cheron had fallen asleep in her lap. "She was born late, and I guess she's always gonna be late, Denise," my mother commented.

I looked over and felt sorry for her. I always felt sorry for my mother. She had put on a lot of weight over the years while dealing with my sister and me without our father. My mother knew a few nice older men, but she never got too involved with any of them. It just seemed that she had gotten satisfied with life just above the poverty line and having no partner to share her experiences with. I guess my success was too little and too late for her to regain her exuberance for life. My mother just seemed to sag down low and take it all, like a helpless mule.

I calmed my nerves for a second and took a seat next to her on the couch. "Are you okay, Mom?" I asked her with a hug.

As usual, she nudged me away. "Would you stop worrying about me. I'm fine," she fussed.

I came up with anything I could to try and cheer her up anyway. "Would you like to fly to Florida for Christmas, Mom?" I asked her. I wasn't planning on taking another no for her answer.

Nikita stuck her nappy head out the hallway bathroom and said, "I wanna go to Florida."

"I wasn't talking to you," I told her. I was tired of her damn freeloading! Knowing my mother, she would have tried to take Nikita and Cheron to Florida with her. Nikita didn't deserve a vacation. She needed to *earn* a vacation first! But my mother treated them as if they were the last family she had in her life. It was almost as if *I* wasn't related anymore. She made me feel like I was some damn wealthy cousin or something, and that bothered me.

"Why would I want to go to Florida during Christmas?" my mother asked me. "Do you know how much overtime I get during the end of the year?"

"Look, Mom, I'll pay you the overtime money back. Okay? Now you need a vacation."

By that time, Nikita was practically staring down my throat. "Take it, Mom," she advised.

I knew where that was heading. Nikita was scheming on using Mom to get herself a ticket to Florida. After all, our mother couldn't enjoy Florida by herself.

I cut my sister's plan short with a suggestion of my own. "I'll tell you what, Mom. I'll pay for a ticket for you and your good friend, Ms. Regina, to go down there and spend a week together. Okay? Ms. Regina would really like that. And you two could just go down there and enjoy yourselves."

Nikita's mouth dropped open like a hungry kid denied a slice of pie. Then she had the nerve to ask, "What about me and Cheron?"

"Look, you just get ready to go so we can make this damn meeting on time," I snapped at her. Nikita really knew how to work my nerves! You would think that she was sixteen sometimes!

"You hear how she talks to me, Mom? Now all that is uncalled for."

I was about two seconds away from kicking my sister's immature, non-working, always complaining *ass!* Instead, I took a deep breath and ignored her. I used to wear my sister out as if *I* were her mother when we were younger. I figured she would mature on her own and learn from *my* mistakes, but I guess I was wrong. *Dead* wrong!

"I'm gonna buy those tickets for you, Mom," I insisted. "And I'm gonna call Ms. Regina myself and tell her."

Nikita marched back into the bathroom to finish her hair.

My mother finally responded to my suggestions. "Well, I guess it would be different. But what am I gonna wear?"

My mother was definitely a woman from the old school. It was a challenge just getting her to do the simplest things. I said, "Mom, don't worry about that. That kind of thing isn't even important. You can wear anything you want."

She looked at me and responded, "Well, it's important to *me*. Aren't *you* concerned about how *you* look when *you're* out in public?"

I just couldn't win with her. I said, "Okay, when the time comes, we'll go out and get you some warm-weather outfits."

"Are we gonna wait until the last minute?"

At that point, I believe my mother was simply overwhelmed with the acceptance of the idea. She was just talking to be talking.

"Okay, so it's all done then, Mom. You hear me? You're going to Florida with Ms. Regina," I said, cutting off her idle chatter. Then I stood up to get ready to leave. "Nikita. Let's go!"

My sister finally got her jacket and hat and headed out the door. If I had known she was going to wear a hat, we would have left a lot earlier with her nappy head.

"We'll be back around eight-thirty, Mom," I said, as we walked out the door.

"Okay," she answered with a nod. I think the idea of flying to Florida had succeeded in cheering her up. She was already reaching for the telephone to talk about it.

Nikita asked, "What are we gonna talk about tonight? Don't y'all run out of subjects or something? How many years have you been in this thing again?"

I took a deep breath as I opened the car door to let her in. Nikita had two abortions and one miscarriage before finally having Cheron. I thought my sister needed some psychiatric help myself, but imagine trying to convince my mother of that. Too many African-Americans falsely believed that counseling was something only for rich white people. However, the country's poor people needed professional counseling the most! My sister was a perfect example of that.

I planned on ignoring Nikita until we made it to the library center downtown. She was going to have to answer her own questions. But she wouldn't let me ignore her.

"Denise, I don't know why you think you're better than me. You didn't start doing good until late in your life either," she said to me.

There was no way in the world I could ignore that. I responded, "So is that your excuse to keep screwing up, because you think you can turn it all around whenever you get good and ready to? Because it ain't that damn easy."

"*You* did it."

I looked at my sister and asked, "So what are you saying?" She made it sound as if I were as crazy and confused as she was.

"We came from the same house and the same parents."

She said it like it was the most important observation in the world. Like she had gotten a perfect score on her test paper. I was damn-near ready to pull the car over.

"But we damn-sure haven't come from the same mind!" I told her. I got frustrated and yelled, "Girl, you are really starting to . . . dammit, something is really wrong with you! Do you understand that? You really have problems!" I couldn't even get all of my words out.

"*You* have *two* kids, *I* only have *one!* Remember that, okay! Before you jump on your *high* horse!"

I swerved the car from the road, hit my brakes, and threw it in park. I grabbed my sister by her jacket and screamed, "You gotta fuckin' problem with me living my life?! You need to *grow up*, live your *own* damn life, and stop *worrying* Mom to death! And you *need* some damn mental help, because you're *crazy!*" I knew I shouldn't have said that, but I did. All of the frustration I had pent up from everything else going on in my life was all coming out on my sister.

"Bitch, I'm not crazy!" Nikita hollered back at me. She was never a good fighter. I realized that as soon as she threw the first punch, missed, and broke my damn rearview mirror. I could have worn her ass out right there inside of that Honda! But suddenly, I came to grips with myself, and just grabbed her by the arms.

"Nikita!" I yelled at her.

She was going ballistic, like a junkie having a withdrawal.

"Nikita, cut it out!" I yelled again.

Bystanders were minding our business from the sidewalk, but I paid them no mind. Then my sister yelled at the top of her lungs, "GET THE FUCK OFF ME, YOU BITCH! GET OFF ME!"

After that, I figured I had to smack her before things *really* got out of hand. I coiled back my arm and hit my sister so awkwardly with my left hand that it felt like I had snapped my wrist.

"SHIT!" I hollered. I immediately grabbed my wrist and looked to see if I had broken anything. Nikita pulled away from me and brought her knees up into her chest, curling up into a ball. Then she started breathing heavy and mumbling, "I can't stand your ass! Bitch! I hate you! Think you're better than somebody! You ain't shit! You ain't *shit!*"

Once I realized my wrist wasn't broken, I made sure the doors were locked, turned the ignition back on, and drove off. I had no idea where I was going. It was no way we were going to make the meeting that night. And I wasn't gonna let Nikita out of my car until we had a good long talk. I didn't care if it took all night.

"Take me the fuck home!" she shouted at me.

I shook my head and said, "Not tonight. You're not going home. We're going to Florida." I was going to try out my own psychology on her.

"Look, bitch, just take me home," she mumbled again.

I said, "Nikita, I'm not gonna be another one of your bitches. Okay? So don't call me that again. And I mean it!"

I was becoming my sister's mother again. Then she gave me the silent treatment. I didn't mind that so much. At least I could concentrate on what I was going to do with her.

I jumped on the Eisenhower Expressway and headed west toward my home in Oak Park. Then I started to think. I thought about how I had gotten pregnant with my first son, Jimmy. His father and I were having safe sex at first. Then when things started going downhill in J.D.'s life, sex became more of a crutch for him, and my naive behind went along with it. I thought that by having sex with him as much as possible, all of his hurt would go away. I should have put on the brakes and given J.D. someone to talk to. I should have used more of my mind to reach him, and less of my body. But the sad truth in America is that, when situations of distress and a lack of guidance surface in young lives, young boys end up in jail, while young girls end up with babies. That was exactly what happened to J.D. and me.

The next thing I knew, I began to talk out loud so that my sister could hear my thoughts and possibly learn something:

"With Walter Perry, I got caught up in a fantasy that I could actually go away somewhere and live happily-ever-after with him, knowing damn well that we were just using each other. He wanted a ghetto girl to screw, and I wanted a college man to have dreams about," I said.

Then I chuckled and added, "Walter wasn't even my damn type. He looked lost whenever he came to visit me, like somebody had just dropped his ass off in a business suit on a dirt, country road somewhere.

"And when I messed up and got pregnant by him, I actually fantasized that he would ask me to marry him. Did I ever ask him about it? Hell no!

I knew. He never talked about his family to me. He never talked about his career. He never talked about anything but how exciting it was to be with me, like it was all a visit to a damn amusement park or something."

I looked over at my sister still balled up in her seat and agreed with her. "Yup. You're right, Nikita. I'm no better than you. But I *refused* to let my life go by without getting something out of it. And I'm gonna make sure that my sons get something out of their lives, too. But you have to *work* for what you want. Hard! Because *nobody's* gonna give you anything for free!

"Free shit is for people who can't get it on their own. So as long as I can work, I'm gonna *earn* my damn keep! You hear me?"

Nikita didn't say a word, so I went on:

"Now I have both of these fools coming back into their sons' lives, one because of basketball, and the other because of a recent spark of self-righteousness."

My sister cut me off and mumbled, "Look who's fuckin' talking?! You don't hit me! Who do you think *you* are? Ms. Perfect? I should get your ass arrested for this! Look at my damn face!"

The whole right side of her jaw was swollen. But it was nothing that an ice pack couldn't fix. I don't think it was broken. I didn't hit her *that* hard, just awkwardly. Nevertheless, my sister had a point, negative actions do not make for a positive response.

"I'm sorry that I hit you, Nikita. I was wrong," I told her.

"I *know* your ass was wrong!" she snapped.

I was speechless for a moment. Maybe *I* needed some counseling as well.

"If you're so perfect, how come you're not fuckin' married to somebody?" Nikita mumbled. She wasn't looking at me when she asked, and I don't think she expected an answer either. She was using her statement as a return smack in the face. And it worked, because I didn't have an answer.

I finally nodded to her and said, "Okay? If I'm no better than you or anybody else, then you do better than me. You find a stable family home for yourself and Cheron, and do all of the things that I haven't been able to do, like getting married. Okay? And you find out how to be happy with yourself, because I sure haven't found out how. Every day is a new struggle for me. And I'm getting tired of it. So maybe you'll have more energy and better luck than what I've had."

Nikita didn't respond to me. Instead, she asked, "Can you take me the hell home, please?"

I sighed. I didn't see where I was making any ground with her. I said,

"Don't you know that I love you. You're the only sister that I have, and I just don't want to see you in my same situation. I mean, sure, you only have one child *now*, but what about three, four years from now. How many kids or—" I cut myself short before I said "abortion." I don't believe that would have enhanced the discussion.

"Well, I like your way of showing me that you love me," my sister responded sarcastically. "Do you show my nephews that you love them the same way? Maybe I need to call the cops for them, too."

I found the first exit I could and made a U-turn so I could take my sister back home before I kicked her out of my moving car. I had refrained from hitting my sons, but discipline was discipline, and when it was needed, it was needed.

"You've never hit Cheron, right?" I questioned Nikita.

"Yeah, but I don't try and act like I'm *right* about everything."

"So you've hit her when you were wrong?" I asked.

"You hit me when *you* were wrong," she countered.

"Oh, so maybe you need to call *the cops* on yourself, too, then."

She said, "Whatever. Just take me home."

I tried to ignore her again, but Nikita didn't know how to be ignored.

"Can you *please* turn the radio on or something?" she huffed, while staring out the window. She was a complete, irritating, and self-absorbed child in charge of raising a child of her own. After a while, I couldn't wait to get her out of my sight. But unseen did not mean unthought of.

When I got Nikita back to my mother's, she slammed my passenger door as if it was me. I sighed, shook my head, and drove off. I didn't want to face my mother after hitting Nikita in the face like I did. My mother had always taken the baby's side of the story. That was a big reason why Nikita was still acting like one.

I drove home thinking about my sons. Had I been unfair, or wrong with them? Since the discussion didn't go well with Nikita, and I was still in the mode of truth telling and understanding, I figured I could pick up where I left off with them.

When I got home and walked into the family room, they were both playing video games. Walter tried to play slick like he was really reading a book, but Jimmy started to laugh and couldn't control himself. Poor Walter was so petrified that he didn't know what to do. They had no idea that I was going to be home so soon, and neither did I.

I said, "Walter, you're *not* slick, and Jimmy, *you* should *know* better," and that was all I planned to say about it. I had other things on my mind.

Jimmy asked, "Was the meeting canceled? Grandmom called and said for you to call her back. She sounded upset, too."

"Yeah, I know she called," I responded. I had expected as much. I said, "When you two are finished with this game, I'd like to talk to you. Okay?"

My sons looked at each other. It was the kind of look that I had gotten used to from them, when they knew they had done something wrong. That made me feel sad. I wondered if there would ever be a time when we could simply sit and talk about the birds and the bees like normal people instead of them always expecting the worst.

"Would you two stop looking so pitiful," I told them. "You didn't do anything. I did."

They looked at each other again.

Jimmy asked, "What did you do?"

"That's what I'd like to find out," I answered.

They looked even more confused.

To clarify, I said, "Okay, here it is: I know that I haven't been a perfect mother to you guys, because I'm only human, and nobody can be perfect. So what I wanted to do was ask you what I've done lately that may have been wrong, or self-centered on my part. If I've hurt you in some way, either psychically or emotionally, then I want to apologize for it."

They gave each other one more look.

I added, "And I want you both to be honest with me."

Jimmy didn't speak up, but he did start to grin, and that told me that he definitely had something to say about it.

"Okay?" I asked him. "Be honest with me. What did I do?"

He said, "Well, I was just wondering why my dad can't come by and pick me up from the house. I mean, he told me what happened with him and all, but he wouldn't try nothing like what you're thinking."

I could tell Jimmy didn't want to get too specific around Walter. He was referring to his father's prison time for armed robbery and my reluctance to forgive him for it.

I nodded. I said, "Okay, you're right. That was wrong of me. I'll think it all over, call him up, and straighten that all out as soon as I can. Anything else." I didn't want to go too much into that topic, because it was more of a private discussion between Jimmy and me. I figured I would pick up the conversation about his father at another time, like after Walter went to bed, because the boy had a big damn mouth, and J.D.'s prison time wasn't everybody's business.

Before Jimmy could add anything, Walter spoke up and said, "My father asked me almost the same question last weekend. And then when I told him, he started crying and stuff."

Jimmy and I looked at each other.

"He started crying for what?" Jimmy asked his brother with a chuckle. I could never imagine J.D. crying for anything, and Jimmy was well aware of that himself. Jimmy wasn't the crying type either. I had never even thought of Walter Jr. crying, however. He seemed far too selfish for tears. His only tears would be for his own disappointments. Maybe Walter had cried when I told him I was pregnant with his child thirteen years ago. That was a real disappointment for him. So what could he be crying for now?

My son said, "He asked me if he was mean like my grandfather. And I said that he used to be, and that I didn't like being around him before, but now it's getting to be fun. And then he started crying and said that he wouldn't treat me or you mean ever again." Walter looked up into my eyes and was really excited about it.

Jimmy smiled really hard and started nodding his head. "Yup, you're starting to like him now," he teased.

Walter snapped, "So? You like *your* father."

"I mean, I'm not saying anything's wrong with it, I just remember when you used to say that you hated him all the time. I never hated my father," Jimmy responded to him.

"Because your father was always cool."

"Yeah, but he was never around as much as your father."

"Now he is."

Jimmy said, "I know. And he is cool. He got a night job now so he can see all of my games when the season starts."

"Well, my father told me that I should go out for the track team this year."

"Well, good for you."

"Would you come out and see me?"

Jimmy smiled and said, "If you win."

Walter sucked his teeth. "*You* don't win all the time. That's why your team lost the summer leagues."

"Yeah, but it wasn't *my* fault," Jimmy responded. "But I'll go to your track meets, man. Our track coach wants me to come out for the high jump. He said I got the hops and height to make it to the Olympics if I worked hard enough."

"He said that?" Walter asked in shock.

"Yeah."

They had pretty much forgotten about me. I said, "Okay, I'm glad that you two like your fathers. Now is there anything else that your *mother* could do better?"

They gave each other one last look.

Walter said, "Not really. I mean, you're a good mom. I'm sorry that nobody married you yet. Maybe Mr. Brock would want to marry you."

It felt like a hot dagger had poked me in my heart. I asked for honesty, and I had gotten it. I looked over to Jimmy, and he quickly ran his eyes away from me. That told me that he agreed with his brother. For the first time, I felt how my mother must have felt. My sons were pitying me like I pitied her. I wanted to tell them that I would be all right and that I didn't need a man, per se, to make my life complete. Yet they had been around me all of their lives, and just like I knew the truth about my mother, they knew the truth about me. I was too proud to beg, and too dignified to be told what I should or needed to do. However, deep down inside, I already knew the truth. I wanted a complete family like anybody else.

I was practically up all night, thinking about everything. I called my mother and apologized to her and Nikita. I called Camellia and apologized for not making the meeting. I called Brock and left him a message to have a safe trip on the road. Then I planned to settle with both of my sons' fathers and support them in any way I could in reestablishing themselves in their sons' lives, despite my own disappointments with them. I still had to deal with my feelings about the Perry family in Barrington, however. Maybe I needed to wait before I called Walter, so I could gather some calmer words for him. He was proving that he was the asshole I already suspected him of being. I still didn't want his family's money, but I did want to at least protect my son's future. He was a Perry whether they liked it or not, and I had the duty of raising him.

When I was finished with my phone calls, with setting out my plans, and with thinking over the events of the day, I closed my eyes and tried to imagine Walter Perry Jr. breaking into tears in front of his son. I thought about the last time that *I* had broken down and cried for anything. I had to think all the way back to my relationship with J.D., and his cowardice as a father. I cried on many of those sleepless, lonely nights when he had failed to come back to his mother's house to me and his son, deciding instead to stay out all night and run the Chicago streets with his gang-affiliated "friends."

I thought about those tears and how I was able to strengthen myself against the hurt and pain, not allowing them to fall so freely ever again. So that when I was pregnant with Walter, there were no more tears to cry. I simply dealt with my situation. And over the years, there had been plenty to cry about that I refused to. In the rejection of those tears, I had become something else, some different kind of woman, and a different kind of human. What kind of a woman could not cry? I even tried to force myself to cry again, and could not do it. I shed not one tear.

I found myself wanting to cry for not being able to cry. I needed to cleanse myself with tears. I needed to wash away all of the denial of hurt and disappointment, and start all over again. But how could I do that without becoming vulnerable? And if I did allow myself to become vulnerable again, how would I ever be able to climb back on my feet and continue being the *thing* that I had become? Or maybe, I did not need to be this *thing* at all. Maybe I needed to be connected to someone else for strength, so that my tears would never fall on empty pillows. In the Good Book, God's gifts to humans were the world and one another. Could it all be so simple . . . yet so hard to attain?

Role Models

I walked into Kim's place before she left for work to talk to her about a few things. I had to stop procrastinating and get a conversation going about what she really wanted from me. She had given me a key to her apartment, but she hadn't asked for any rent money yet, and her son was getting close enough to becoming at least a nephew to me. What was it all about, and where exactly were we headed? I had to get to the bottom line before things started to get hectic. I was getting too comfortable with the way things were.

J . D .

Jamal ran up to me for his usual jump on my legs, and tripped over his untied shoelaces.

"Would you stop running in the house!" his mother yelled at him. The boy was always falling around in the house. He needed to get out and have more space to run around in.

"Come here," I told him, leading him over to the living room couch. "You don't know how to tie your shoelaces yet?"

Kim stuck her nose out and said, "Nobody taught him."

I wanted to say, "Why couldn't *you* teach him?" but I let it slide. I was beginning to realize that silence was golden. The more you respond to everything a woman says, the more petty arguments you get into. So instead of going that route, I showed Jamal how to tie his shoelaces.

"You're working another half day?" I asked Kim.

"That's what it looks like. If I wasn't, I'd be gone already."

I stopped tying Jamal's Reeboks and looked up at his mother. She was really pushing it close to my breaking point. Years ago, I would have been out of there in a hurry, but I had to learn how to fight for something. I had to learn how to keep things together. It just didn't seem like Kim was up for helping me much.

I asked her, "You're about to take him to your mother's?" It was three twenty-five. Jamal was just getting in from school.

"Yeah," Kim answered.

"Doesn't he get tired of getting picked up so late from his grandmother's, and then having to get up early and go to school in the mornings? No wonder he has a hard time getting up." It just seemed like Jamal was being punished because of his mom's crazy work schedule, not to mention his grandmother. I had never met her, but I could imagine that she could use a break. Jamal was far from being your sit-still-and-read-a-book kind of kid. He was a real attention-getter.

Kim said, "That's what I usually do. I mean, why all of the questions all of a sudden?"

I was trying to decide if I would watch Jamal. Instead of him going over to his grandmother's so much, he could hang out with me. But I wasn't sure if I wanted to commit to the idea yet. I was trying to talk myself into it. Asking Kim questions was my way of exploring the idea.

"Are you going to be back here before eleven?"

Kim finally got the message. She looked at me and Jamal and grinned. "I *could* be back before eleven if I needed to be." She said, "Jay, if you want to watch Jamal today, I wouldn't mind. All I have to do is tell my mother."

Jamal got excited about it immediately. "Yeah, let J.D. watch me, Mom."

Once Kim figured out what I was beating around the bush about, it was too late to turn back, unless I came up with some lame, last-minute excuse. I figured the least I could do was to find out how hard it could be. I used to get Little Jay when he was younger, but I never had him for any long stretch of time. Neecy always monitored how long he stayed with me, as if spending too much time with me would have ruined her son, *our* son, for life. I guess I had gotten used to spending only a few hours with him. Kim, on the other hand, was willing to let Jamal stay with me for as long as I could have him. I felt concerned about that. Kim already had enough free time to herself. Her mother may as well have kept Jamal permanently.

I asked, "Did you tell your mother anything about me?" I was still stalling. Taking Jamal for a day would be a big step for me. Kim was the kind of woman who, if you gave her an inch . . . I realized that watching Jamal for a day would only be a tease.

"She knows about you. Are you gonna keep Jamal until I get off from work then?"

I was curious. "What did you tell your mother about me?" Did she include information about my prison time? I always thought about my prison history. Employers made it hard for me to ever forget.

"I told her that you were a hardworking black man. In fact, let me call her right now and tell her that you'll be watching Jamal tonight."

Jamal jumped up and down and celebrated. I had the feeling that Kim had buttered me up and cooled me off with her quick answers. I wanted to go into more detail about what she told her mother about me.

"And what did you mother say?" I asked.

Kim jumped on the phone and held up her index finger to quiet me down. I felt like I was her second son. I didn't like the vibes I was getting. Kim was already taking advantage of the situation, and I hadn't even addressed what I wanted to talk about between us.

"Yeah, Mom, you won't have to watch Jamal today. My friend Jay is gonna watch him," Kim told her mother. "They get along good together. I think Jamal needs a man in his life," she said, looking toward me with a grin.

Jamal was all over me. I was sitting there feeling like a turkey on Thanksgiving, ready to be carved the hell up!

"I like how you just ran with things like that," I told Kim after she hung up the phone. I didn't think the shit was cute, either! "But since I'll be watching Jamal," I said, "we could use this extra time that you have now to make it to work to talk about things."

Kim nodded her head like an eager Girl Scout. "Okay. Let's talk." She walked over and sat down next to me and her son. With all three of us sitting on the couch like that, I couldn't help noticing that we appeared to be like an average American family.

Suddenly, I had problems getting my words together. "Ah," I mumbled. "What I wanted to talk about is, um, you know, where we, ah, see ourselves."

Kim hunched her shoulders. "Like I said before, I can't force you to do anything."

"And that's exactly what I'm talking about," I responded. "I mean, what is it that you want me to do? What do you really want from me?"

Kim slowed down and looked right at me. "If I have to ask, then can I have what I want from you?" she questioned. She looked sexy as hell when she asked me that! I wanted to do her in a heartbeat, but her son was in the way. Besides, she had to be to work soon, and since I had been staying with her, I had gotten used to getting the long treatment instead of those wham-bam quickies expected by uncommitted visitor types.

I said, "That's what I'm still trying to ask you. What is it that you want? I mean, I'm already here as much as I can be. You know I still have other things to do."

"Yeah, but it just seems like I don't have your full attention when you're here. It's like a piece of you is always missing. I want to have *all* of you."

Kim was dead serious. In the past, whenever women talked about men not giving their all, I used to act as if it was an alien philosophy. In my immature years, maybe it was. But I had done a lot of growing up over the last couple of months of being with my son again, and I realized that women knew what the hell they were talking about. I *wasn't* giving my all. I wasn't quite ready for that last hurrah. I was still wondering if a wedge would come between Kim and me to make things unbearable for a long-standing relationship. I was holding on to my last boat of freedom, and at the same time, I realized that my ship was sinking. I was getting too old to keep playing them same old games. I was tired of feeling detached from shit, like how Neecy had me feeling toward my son. I was tired of feeling detached from a job, and counting down the days before I would be laid off or fired again. I knew exactly what Kim was saying, because I wanted the same thing. I wanted to feel that I was a part of something too, and not just a temporary component that wasn't always needed. I was tired of living that way.

I stepped up to the plate and asked, "So how are we gonna do this? Do we start all over and lay down the rules? I mean, there's just a whole lot that we need to discuss."

Kim said, "Well, we don't have to rush it. We have time."

I shook my head. "Time is just getting in the way. Now either we're gonna settle this or we're not. Because you're not *acting* like we have any more time, especially with the way you've been going off lately. You said it yourself, you don't know what to expect from me. So let's get to the bottom of it."

It occurred to me at that moment that Kim was just as paranoid as I was. When you're not used to having things go your way, you don't know how to have any faith in your future. Kim was actually giving me room to squirm my way out of anything serious, because she was afraid of things breaking down again. How many relationships had broken down on her before? It was the same predicament that made Neecy so tough to handle. They had a lack of confidence in others, particularly in black men, and I honestly couldn't blame them for that.

I realized just how difficult a situation single mothers were in. They couldn't just lock on to a guy, and since they couldn't, they had no confidence in continuing any relationship with a man. A steady man for Kim was like a dream where you always wake up just to find out that you've been bullshitted. I knew those dreams well. I had them when I was in prison. But after the first year inside, they just faded away from my consciousness. From then on, the only dreams I had were about protecting the pieces of myself that I had left. That only makes you skeptical of every situation you find yourself in while you're awake. It seemed as if someone was always after you, and you're forever feeling guilty about shit, while just waiting for things to fuck up again. It was an ugly way to live.

Kim and I were both silent for a minute. In fact, Jamal was doing the talking.

"Are you gonna take me to get a haircut?" he asked me.

I smiled and nodded to him. "Yeah, it does look like you need one." I ran my hand through his hair. Jamal had hair growing down his neck. "When was the last time you had a haircut?" I asked him.

"He got it cut three weeks ago," Kim answered.

I was surprised. "And it grew this much already?"

Jamal had really thick kinky hair. He could have grown a hell of an Afro! His baby pictures proved it. I guess I hadn't been noticing too many things in my detachment from him. A man who was planning on staying around would have noticed.

I gave my attention back to Jamal's mother. "Well, have you thought about it? How are we gonna work this out?"

Kim took a deep breath and stood up. She seemed more hesitant about the state of our relationship than I was. "Look, let's just talk about this later on. I mean, you just caught me off guard, and now is not the time for it. I have to be to work soon."

I began to smile. I had called her bluff, and Kim was backing down, but I wasn't bluffing anymore.

I said, "When is gonna be the right time to talk about this? I mean, you said you wanted all of me, right?"

"Yeah, but I don't want to force you to do nothin'."

She kept repeating that as if she really could *force me* to do anything. If that was the case, it would be a lot less single mothers walking around.

I said, "Trust me, Kim. You're not forcing me to do anything. I've been *forced* to do things before, and I *know* the difference."

She calmed down and asked, "Was it tough being in there?" She was referring to my prison time without using the word around her son.

I said, "Now, you know I don't have to answer that. We've talked about this a hundred times."

She looked at her son and said, "Well, could you make sure that he knows. I don't want him *ever* to go in a place like that."

When she mentioned that, I thought about my own mother. You had to be strong and consistent with your boys, leading by example, like Neecy was doing with both of her sons. You could never be passive while *sounding* like you're on the job. Kids always notice the inconsistencies. Maybe my mother's fussing while overprotecting her boys was not the right way to go, because in the end, she couldn't protect us, and all of her fussing fell on deaf ears.

I thought about Jamal, Little Jay, and Neecy's other son, Walter. "Oh, he won't be in there," I answered Kim. "Not if *I* have anything to say about it." And I meant that! It was too many black boys being sent away from society already. I guess that's because society didn't want to make room for them in the first place.

I went with a sudden urge to wrestle Jamal down to the couch, where I held him tightly. Of course, he thought I was only playing with him, so he wrestled me back. In actuality, I was telling him, as well as myself, that I would take on the job of trying to secure him a healthier future than the past that I had.

Kim smiled at us and said, "Well, I have to get ready to go. We'll talk about this over the weekend. Okay? I'm just really surprised right now, that's all. I have to get all of my thoughts in order."

I smiled back at her. I knew exactly how she felt. I had dodged many bullets the same way. I said, "All right, you do that then. That'll give me a chance to get my thoughts in order, too."

Kim looked at me and nodded. "Okay. So that's how we'll do it then. We'll both think it over."

After she walked out the door, it was just me and Jamal, face-to-face and all alone for the first time. I immediately thought about his future as a black man in America. Black men were not ready-made mules to the workforce like many women had become. It was in the average man's nature to have a say in his livelihood, and without it, most men went to self-destruction, like my father and his health, and Neecy's father with his drinking. Men have an innate desire to feel as if they are in control of something. In America, few black men had control over anything. So how in the hell could black boys survive without going to jail and joining in the madness of feeling caged? We felt caged whether we had freedom or not, because we had no control over anything. I thought about how difficult it would be to save Jamal from that terrible fate of powerlessness with no real power of my own. Yet I had to try anyway, and see if I could make a difference.

"So what do you want to do first, little man?" I asked him.

"Um, we can go get my haircut, and then we can go to the movies?"

"The movies? To see what?"

"I want to see that dinosaur movie again. I saw it with my mom. It was scary."

"*Jurassic Park?* That's not out anymore. We could see if they have it out on video."

"Okay. And then we could make some popcorn," he suggested.

I never liked popcorn. I hated it getting stuck in my teeth. "If we make popcorn, I'll let you eat it all by yourself."

Jamal was in love with that idea. "Oh, all right," he told me.

"So what barbershop does your mom take you to?"

"My grandmom takes me to one on Madison Street."

Madison Street ran straight through the West Side, and all the way out to the suburbs. There was plenty of activity going on, too, all night long on that street, and much of it was illegal. I knew that personally. I had been there. There had to be at least ten barbershops on Madison, but I had an idea of which one Jamal's grandmother took him to. Kim had mentioned the place to me before.

I nodded. Sometimes I had to remind myself that I was actually talking to a six-year-old. Jamal had seen a lot in his six years, and he seemed to know all of the answers. He spoke with a lot of clarity, too. When Little Jay was his age, I got a bunch of shoulder hunching and "I don't knows." Maybe Neecy was just as negligent with Little Jay in his earlier years as Kim was being with Jamal. It didn't help much that I wasn't there to do *my* part, or Jamal's father not there to do his. We were definitely negligent! Yet some kids were much harder to ignore than others. Jamal Levore was the hard-to-ignore type. I wondered if his father had ever spent any quality time with him.

"You ever go to the movies with your father?" I asked him. It seemed real easy to talk to him.

He said, "No. I don't like him. He's mean. And he don't buy me toys for Christmas, and for my birthday."

I chuckled. "Buying toys isn't the only thing that fathers do."

"I know, but he's just mean, and he always tells my mom that he don't want to watch me."

I felt like an iron crowbar had slapped me across my face. How could a kid talk so freely about his father's negative attitude toward him? Jamal seemed unaffected by it. But I knew that he *had* to be affected. There was no way he couldn't be. However, his willingness to talk about it would benefit him in the sense that someone could always reach him. All you had to do was ask and listen.

I thought about my own son and had to be honest with myself. With Little Jay's passiveness, it was a damn good thing that he grew so tall and mastered the art of basketball. Otherwise, he would have been a really hard kid to reach. Basketball was bringing a lot of attention to him, even my own.

I went out on a limb and asked Jamal if he liked me.

He looked up at me and smiled. "Yeah," he answered.

"Why?" I asked him.

"Because you're fun," he told me. He didn't miss a beat.

"What if I wasn't fun?"

He finally paused and gave me the hunched shoulders. "Then I wouldn't like you."

I laughed and stood up to get ready to go. "Well, I'll make sure that I'm fun so you'll always like me. But you have to listen to me when I tell you to do something, too. Is that a deal?"

He nodded, standing up beside me. "Yeah."

"All right then, let's shake on it," I told him. I extended my hand, and he shook it. "Now, let's go get this haircut."

As soon as I stepped outside with Jamal and rounded the corner for the bus stop, I spotted Barry, the weed man. He was cruising by in the passenger seat of a black Ford Explorer. He rolled down the window and smiled at us.

"I see you're becoming a family man. How you like it?"

I thought about it. "It's something we *all* need to get used to," I said.

Barry nodded. "Tell me about it. I got three of 'em myself."

"Do they know you?" I asked him. In the 1990s, it seemed like a sad but relevant question to ask a brother.

Barry said, "You damn right they know me." He seemed offended by it. But I didn't care about his feelings. Brothers had more ego than character sometimes. Not to say that *I* had made a full turnaround, but at least I could see the difference in the two words.

I asked Barry, "Do they *really* know you, like on an everyday basis?"

Barry smiled and shook his head. "Man, I ain't around them every day like that. I got business to take care of. But they *do* know me. I'll see you around. Aw'ight?" he said in a hurry. Then his young driver pulled off. Barry caught me at the wrong time and had jumped on the wrong subject. I knew damn well he didn't spend any time with his kids. The only reason he even mentioned them is because he saw me with Kim's son.

When Jamal and I caught the bus to Madison, I noticed how people treated me with a lot more compassion. They were all willing to give me a helping hand with him, and they were a lot more talkative than usual. I don't believe I paid much attention to that when I was with my own son years ago. I began to wish that I could do it all over again. Then I realized that I *was* doing it all over again with Jamal.

One woman even asked me, "He looks more like his mother?"

Jamal had them small eyes like his mom's, and a pretty-boy face. I nodded and said, "Yeah, he looks *just* like his mom."

That made me want to have another son who looked more like me. Little Jay didn't. He only had my brown skin and my height. Then again, Neecy's father was tall and dark brown, too, so that wasn't even something I could brag about.

I kept thinking, *This is just what I get. No passing down of my last name, no looks or nothing.* All I had was the first name Jimmy and the skill of basketball to relate to with my son. Hell, any kid could learn to play basketball. Nevertheless, Little Jay loved me. That brought a smile to my face. I figured if I hung around long enough, Jamal Levore would learn to love me too. That bought an even bigger smile. Imagine that, a kid who wasn't even your son growing to love you because of what you were willing to do for him, and the quality time that you spent with him. It was the same code that I had learned from being in the Gangster Disciples. The older guys looked out for the younger guys like real fathers should. However, once the love for money got to be too high of a priority, all kinds of loyalties began to be tested. As the saying goes, "Money changes everything."

I didn't even know most of the new guys coming through, nor did I *want* to know them. I was leading a totally different lifestyle. I was never a hard-core gang member anyway, I was simply misguided, like most of them are, desperately seeking something to belong to.

I got to the barbershop with Jamal, and a few of the barbers knew who he was already.

"Hey, Jamal. Where's your grandmother?"

"At home," he answered.

All eyes were on me, as if to say, "Who the hell is this guy that you're with?"

I asked Jamal, "Who's your favorite barber?" to break the ice.

Jamal looked around and spotted this short, young guy with low-cut hair. He had the look of a young slickster. He had gold rings on both of his pinky fingers and a gold chain around his neck.

"Hey, Short Dawg. You next. Aw'ight?" he said to Jamal.

The older barbers in the shop started grumbling about the youth connection.

"Man, we gon' have to fire him if he keep taking all our customers away. That boy ain't even got no mouths to feed yet?"

"I got one on the way," the slickster commented.

"Oh yeah? And what do you plan on doing about that?" another one of those older barbers asked him.

"I'm gon' take care of him."

"Who said it was a *him?*" somebody asked. We all started laughing. I don't think women will ever understand how men feel about boy babies. Even if you don't take care of them, brothers are always pressed to have those hardheaded boys.

"The doctor told me," he answered. "So you next in my chair, aw'ight, Short Dawg?" the slickster said to Jamal again. I didn't like that nickname that he kept using. Those nicknames were an easy way of being sucked right into the gang crowd. The wrong people start being attracted to you simply because of the name. In fact, that's one of the first things police ask you when you get booked for jail: "Do you have any other names or aliases that you go by?"

Jamal nodded his head and said, "Okay." He was obviously impressed with the young barber's coolness. I used to be impressed by those slicksters when I was young, too. So were my brothers. We all wanted to grow up and be slick ourselves one day. I learned my lesson the hard way about following those guys. A lot of them slicksters weren't the best examples to follow. I was wondering if that young barber had something going on outside of the barbershop, if you know what I mean. Maybe he had a little extra money action in illegal pharmaceuticals.

One of the older barbers was finished with a customer before the younger guy was, so I told Jamal to go ahead and get his haircut. It was perfect timing to get him away from a flashy influence. I wanted Jamal to learn how to honor and respect the hardworking older men who were not as concerned about flash and fast money.

Jamal pouted and said, "I want to wait for him," referring to the young guy again.

I got hip on him and said, "If we want to make the movies on time, then we have to be out of here as fast as we can."

Jamal cheered right up. "Okay."

Mission accomplished, I told the older guy to give him a close fade and a shape-up.

The younger barber gave me a look as if I was taking money out of his pocket. I said, "No offense to you, man, but we have to split."

He shook it off, just like a slickster would. "Oh, no problem. I'll just get 'em next time."

When we walked out of the barbershop twenty-five minutes later, Jamal asked, "So what movie are we gonna see?"

I had forgotten all about it. I thought fast and said, "Well, we can go down to the Navy Pier and see what they got playing. I think they have the Children's Museum down there, too."

He got real excited about that. I wanted to go to the Navy Pier on the waterfront for a while, I just hadn't gotten the opportunity to go. So I waved down a cab and got us a ride. Of course, once we got there, Jamal was more concerned about the Children's Museum. It was a good thing it was a Thursday night, too, because the museum usually closed at five o'clock, and we got down there closer to six. I had no idea. So by the time we finished looking around at all of the attractions inside the museum, it was too late to catch a movie. They all started at around eight o'clock. That meant that the movie wouldn't have ended until after ten, and we wouldn't have made it back home until close to eleven. That would have been cutting it too close for me to make it to work in time. Besides, I didn't think it was right to have a six-year-old out that late on a school night anyway.

"Let's get a video movie then," Jamal said while riding back to the apartment in a taxi.

Unfortunately, I had forgotten to get the video card from Kim that day. Then we happened to pass a toy store that was still open downtown.

"Hey," I told the taxi driver, "you can let us out right here." I figured we could catch a bus the rest of the way. There was no sense in wasting more money on another cab. The bus or train would do just fine.

We went inside the toy store, and I knew exactly what I wanted to buy him: a mini basketball hoop. We walked right in, found one that was sturdy, and bought it. Since we were right downtown, we ended up catching the train back home.

Jamal asked, "You're gonna teach me how to play basketball?"

I nodded. "*If* you do your homework," I told him.

"I do my homework," he responded.

"And you get straight A's?"

"Yeah."

I didn't even know if he got grades yet, but he sure believed that he could get straight A's. If he was serious about it, I'd help him on his way, if I could. I had no idea how rusty I would be in schoolwork after so many years of not having any. Living in capitalistic America, most grown folks knew how to count money, but beyond that, we could all use a touch-up here and there on a lot of things. It wasn't only me who was rusty. I guess that's why older folks love crossword puzzles so much, to keep their minds sharp. It wasn't as if I was a brainiac to begin with. Nevertheless, I was up for the challenge of helping Jamal.

We got back to the apartment and put the basketball hoop together. A lightweight plastic ball came with it. Jamal immediately started firing it up, and was making most of his shots.

"I thought you said you didn't know how to play?" I asked him. I was impressed. The boy had good form with his shot. He had his elbow aimed at the basket and shot with good rotation and everything.

He said, "I didn't say I couldn't play. I just wanted you to teach me to play better."

I couldn't believe my damn ears! The boy sounded like a perfectionist! They were the best kids to teach because they were never satisfied. *I* used to be like that a long time ago, until I could finally beat Marcus playing. Once that happened, I started to get a big head when I should have kept working to improve my game, *and* my study habits.

The next thing I knew, I started talking basketball and showing Jamal a few things. Kim walked in on us hours later. She looked at the basketball hoop, towering inside of the living room with all of her furniture pushed out of the way, and said, "What in the world?!" Then she looked at me and shook her head with half a smile. "So, y'all are in here just having a *good* time, tearing up my damn living room."

I laughed and asked her what time it was. I had taken my watch off once Jamal and I really got into things.

Kim looked at her watch and said, "Quarter after eleven."

I was shocked! "Damn, I gotta get on the move then." I had lost all track of time. Funny how it flies when you're having fun. "I thought you said you would be here before eleven," I complained.

"I got tied up."

"Yeah, I bet you did." I began rushing to get ready.

"Well, *I* wasn't the one who got all wrapped up in playing basketball," Kim responded to me.

Jamal asked, "We gon' practice again tomorrow?"

"After you do what?" I asked him.

"Um, my homework."

"And get what in your school grades?"

"A's and B's."

"But mostly A's, if you can get them," I told him.

Kim looked at me, and *she* was impressed. "Well, isn't *this* special," she told me. "I don't know what to say."

I said, "You save it for later, 'cause I gotta get out of here." I grabbed my things together for work and was ready to head out. Then I told Jamal, "It's time for bed, man. You're up later than you need to be."

"Okay," he responded to me.

I picked him up, squeezed him real good, and put him back down. Then I looked at his mother. She was all shocked, like she didn't know what to make of things.

"And you," I told her with a kiss, "I'll see you in the morning."

When I slipped out the door, Kim said, "I wish you could see me tonight, but I'll wait until the morning. You just make sure you come right back."

I ran down those apartment stairs feeling like a new teenager with a pocket full of money and no curfew. I knew that the transition I would be making with Kim and Jamal wouldn't be all peaches and damn cream, but at least it felt good when it was supposed to. Those good feelings are what get you through all the tough times, as long as you had enough of those good times in between.

I felt real good about my budding relationship with Jamal, though. I was getting a chance to start all over again as a father figure. And the best part was that I didn't have to change any late-night diapers.

Where Do We Go from Here?

I was in a game of emotional tug of war, and I needed time away from Denise to think again. The only thing was, I didn't have any long runs for the week and no one wanted to switch with me. It's hard to get any

B R O C K   swaps for the longer runs at the end of the year. Everyone wants that extra money pouring in before the holiday season. Longer runs, like anything else in America, meant longer pockets.

What made my situation worse was that Denise was constantly calling me up to chitchat. It seemed as if she was finally opening up to me. I was confused about that because I thought we were supposed to be slowing things down. I guess because of the problems she was having with her youngest son, Walter, we were heating up again.

I was thinking about Denise and her boys while loading my truck at the shipping docks. I had a short trip to make that day to Champaign, Illinois. I spotted Larry walking toward me. We hadn't been talking as much as usual. I had cut back on some on my longer runs to be more available to Denise, so Larry began to team up with other guys for the income. For whatever reason, he seemed eager to talk to me that morning.

"Hey, man, you got a minute?" He was looking around and speaking in a hushed tone, like a man who wanted some privacy.

I was apprehensive and curious at the same time, wondering what he wanted to talk to me about. Usually, we only talked about sports, the job, and women, and not necessarily in that order.

Larry asked, "How do you deal with seeing a woman who has some-one else's child?"

I immediately started to grin. "Why, you're seeing a woman with a kid now?"

He smiled back at me, still speaking quietly. "It's only been over a month, but I feel like she's sucking me into this thing. Her little girl is just starting to walk, as cute as she can be."

I didn't know we were talking about an infant. I said, "How old is she, nine, ten months?"

"Yeah."

I cracked up laughing and couldn't help it. I imagined rock-headed Larry holding a baby girl in his arms.

He said, "This shit ain't funny, man. I mean, this girl is *fine*. *Fine* fine! I'm just not ready to be somebody's daddy."

Larry was getting close to thirty himself, and I was about to reach the forty mark. How old did we need to be before we were *"ready"* to be-come fathers?

I immediately thought about Denise and *her* sons' fathers. I said, "You know what, Larry? I've been thinking about this for a while now. It seems to me that a lot of us black men need to grow the hell up. I mean, we come up with all kinds of stupid-ass excuses, even with '*fine*,' edu-cated, *good* women, to run like a damn ghost is after us when it comes to being a father.

"When is this shit gonna stop, man?" I asked him rhetorically. "Be-cause evidently, this sister wasn't '*fine' enough* for her baby's father not to leave, if *you're* in the picture so soon."

I was really worked up, thinking about all of the struggles that single mothers had to go through to raise kids without a steady man around to help them.

Larry just stood there and nodded his head to me. Then he looked at me and said, "He's dead, man."

I was confused. I asked, "Who's dead?"

"The baby's father. He got hit in the chest by a stray bullet during a drive-by shooting. He was visiting family in Gary, Indiana."

"Hmmph," I grunted. "That's another thing," I commented. "Some of these sisters have to stop choosing to be with these knuckleheads out here."

Larry shook his head at me. He said, "Naw. This guy was a straight college boy, working for a master's degree. They were making plans to get married when it happened."

I calmed myself down, feeling like a fool for jumping to conclusions. "I guess I owe the brother an apology then," I said. "So, how do *you* feel about all of this?"

Larry gave me a blank stare. "What do you think I'm talking to you for? I mean, I've met her family and *everything* now. It looks like I'm stepping right in as the good brother who takes over the family. But I feel like I need to slam on the brakes for a minute. You know what I'm sayin'?"

I began to smile again. I said, "Trust me, brother, all kinds of things are gonna run through your mind before it's all over with. It damn sure has with me."

He said, "Yeah, this sister told me she's never been without a boyfriend since she was fourteen."

"How old is she now?"

"Twenty-four?"

"And she's been with this guy for ten years?"

Larry frowned and responded, "Naw, man. She's just fine enough to pick right up where she left off," he answered with a chuckle. Then he got serious again. "She was with this last guy for three years. He didn't even get to see his daughter's birth. And I'm the first guy that she's dated since."

I thought about all of the different emotions involved in Larry's situation. All I could do was shake my head and mumble, "Damn!"

Larry nodded. "That's what I'm talking about."

I said, "And you still got involved, *knowing* all of this?" It didn't seem like the Larry that *I* knew.

He said, "Honestly, the shit just happened. I was on a panty chase like the next man, and then *wham*, she just laid it all out on me."

"She didn't tell you up front?" It was getting more interesting by the minute, and both of us had to be going.

"She basically needed some companionship, if you know what I mean. But she didn't want just anybody, so I guess I said all the right things to her."

I couldn't imagine that. Larry was no Casanova. I guess the girl was just in the cards for him to handle. "So she went from a master's degree to a truck driver, hunh?" I asked, teasing him. Larry had rode me enough about the oil-and-water thing. I felt it was ironic that he was finding himself in the same situation.

He smiled and said, "Naw, she's just a nice girl from a nice family. She's not into all of those degrees and whatnot. She liked this guy *before* he decided to do all of that. She just wants a nice, caring man."

I nodded with an even bigger grin. "And she considers *you* 'a nice, *caring* man'?" I asked.

"I guess so."

I said, "Yeah, you're in trouble now, brother. It's time to grow up, *for real!* This is a sign from God."

"Yeah, you're telling me," he said. "But we *all* got that good man in us. It just takes a while for him to come out. So maybe this *is* my sign. And if it is, then I got to thank God for giving me a *fine* one!"

I shook my head. I asked, "How come you're so stuck on this *fine* thing?"

Larry looked at me as if I was crazy. He said, "Wait a minute. Now your woman is fine, right?"

I saw where he was going with it and cut him off. "Yeah, but that's beside the point. I got into her because of her knowledge, her inner strength, maturity, and everything else about her."

"But *initially*, you were attracted to her *physically*. Am I right? Remember, I was there when you met her," he reminded me.

I started to smile. A vision of Denise's fine self in her charcoal suit at the McCormick Center flashed in my mind.

Larry said, "Shit, man, women talk that stuff all the time: 'Why I gotta be all of that? *You* ain't all of that?' It's simple to me, because when you finally make that decision to settle down, you want to make sure that you got all you need in the looks department *at home*. Otherwise, you'll be thinking about every fine woman who passes you by in the street. And that shit is torture."

"Larry, that's maturity again," I told him. "Because no matter how fine you *think* this girl is, there's *always* gonna be somebody finer!"

Larry smiled. "Yeah, I understand that," he responded, "as long as I don't have to see a finer woman every day. Because if *that* ends up being the case, then I gots to come home and tell my lady to get *her* act together! You know what I'm sayin', Brock?"

I shook my head and grinned. I just didn't know what to do with Larry. But we both had to get back to our trucks and hit the road.

I said, "Hey, man, we need to have a part two of this. Maybe even a part three. So if you need to talk to me some more, you just let me know."

Larry said, "Oh, I will. You can count on that."

We said our good-byes and climbed into our trucks. Larry had given me a hell of a lot to think about. I felt like a woman watching a soap opera. I couldn't wait to hear his next episode. It seemed like the older you got, the more drama there was. And to think that *teenagers* thought *they* knew everything. Shit, they had a *long* way to go!

I headed for Interstate 57 South to Champaign, and had an urge to call Denise on my cell phone before I could travel thirty miles. She decided not to sue Walter's junior high school, and to settle things out of court. I couldn't blame her. Many people hear about dramatic money cases in the beginning proceedings, but rarely do they ever hear reports on what happened years later, and they were *not* all happy endings.

Denise was looking out for the integrity of her family's future, and I respected her for that. She wanted both of her boys to appreciate succeeding because of their hard work and not by default. Many irresponsible people would have simply run with the money, despite the long-term harm it could have caused to their family. Lifestyles can be easily complicated with an unexpected boost of wealth, and much of that new money can be taken for granted, especially if you never learned how to earn it. Denise made perfect sense. Then again, I figured her career in finance would have made her the perfect recipient of any extra monies. I couldn't imagine her wasting anything.

Before I knew it, I found myself on the phone with her. "Are you extra busy right now?"

"Yes, but I can call you back on my lunch hour."

"One o'clock?"

"One o'clock."

"All right, then. I'll make sure to get myself ready by twelve fifty-five," I told her.

"Yeah, you do that."

I hung up and felt an urge to call her right back and tell her that I loved her. Larry got me thinking about my own level of commitment, and I came to the conclusion that I actually *did* love Denise. I loved her not only in a man-to-woman way, but in a spiritual, purposeful way, where no lust was involved. She was just a great person, trying to fight and win the battle of life. So I got right back on that phone.

"Denise, it's me again."

"Okay, I can see that," she answered with a chuckle. "Did you, ah, forget something?" she asked me.

Perfect, I thought to myself. "Yeah, I forgot something," I told her. "I forgot to tell you that I love you."

Right after I said it, I started feeling anxious, as if I shouldn't have. *Was I pushing the buttons too fast again?* That was exactly what I was concerned about *not* doing. Immediately, I started trying to explain myself:

"And what I mean by that is—"

Denise cut me off and said, "You don't have to explain it. I understand. And I feel the same way."

I was surprised when she said that. "About everything?" I asked, just to make sure that we were on the same page.

"About everything," she answered. "But we'll talk about it at lunchtime. Okay?"

I said, "Okay, yeah, 'cause you have business to take care of. I'm sorry. I lost my head for a second."

"*I* don't think so," Denise responded. "I think that you've found it, and I've found mine. So one o'clock."

"One o'clock," I repeated.

I hung up the phone and didn't know what to do with myself. I needed a damn drink to calm my nerves. *What the hell did I just do?* I asked myself. I felt good about telling Denise I loved her, but also confused. Did she tell me that she loved me in code simply because she had someone in her office and she didn't really want to discuss it? Was she going to tell me that she loved me again when I talked to her at one o'clock? Were we finally going to decide on where we were heading in our hold-tightly-and-release-again relationship? I was a nervous wreck! I asked myself, *What the hell happened to all of the confidence I once thought I had with this woman?*

Suddenly, I began to smile. It was a beautiful and sunny day outside, the end of September. I had just told my young friend, Larry, that black men needed to grow up and smell the coffee in regards to committed relationships and fatherhood. And I assumed that I would be taken to the test when Denise called me later on that day. But I felt as if I was ready. I was ready to go to that next step, to be a happily committed man *and* a father, whether they were my kids or not.

As fate would have it, when it came time for my important phone call, I was in the middle of a traffic jam. I needed to radio Dispatch to inform them of the situation and to find another route to take if I needed to. Sometimes it took three and four conversations to straighten everything out. I didn't need that in the middle of my talk with Denise. But that's life for you. Not much comes by easily.

"What's going on?" Denise asked me. She heard the racket in the background as soon as I answered the phone.

"There was a three-car accident that they're trying to clear up on 57 South," I told her. Fortunately, it wasn't as bad as I thought it would be, so I didn't expect too many interruptions. I was only running thirty minutes behind schedule.

"So, you feel the same way that I feel about you?" I asked her. I tried to sound as lighthearted about it as I could, while still getting down to business.

"I feel *exactly* how you do," she answered. "I've had to do a lot of thinking lately, and I can't lie to myself anymore about what I want."

"And what is it that you want?" I was cool, calm, and collected, sitting high in my Volvo White tractor in the middle of traffic on 57 South.

Denise said, "I want someone to share my love, my struggles, my good times *and* my bad times with without feeling guilty about it. I want to be able to live my life without apologizing for wanting to be with a man. And I no longer want to lie to myself by saying that I *don't* need one. We *all* need each other in different ways to make our lives complete whether we like it or not, and I'm just now coming to grips with that reality.

"The question is, 'Are *you* willing to deal with the realities that I have?' "

"No, the real question is, 'Are *you* willing to allow me that opportunity?' Because *I've* been ready for that for a while. I understand that you have two sons, and they have living fathers, but up to *this* point you were not willing to allow me a chance to integrate myself into the pot."

"But I did do that," she responded. "If I hadn't, you would have never gotten so close to my sons. I mean, you've eaten dinner with us *plenty* of times!"

"Yeah, but that was all under the guise of your 'friend.' Now am I right or am I wrong?"

"Well, what else was I going to call you?" she asked.

She had a point, and I had no answer. We both went silent while I was caught up in traffic.

"How do things look on the road now?" Denise asked, as if reading my mind.

"It doesn't look much better. I got another mile or so before I reach the accident."

We were casually getting away from the subject. There was no easy way of closing out the conversation without coming to some conclusion, I just didn't know what that conclusion would be.

I spoke up first, like the traditional man had been trained to do. "So, now that we have all of this out in the open, what's next?"

Denise said, "Well, I believe I need to reintroduce you to my sons as my companion, and more than just my friend."

"Do you feel comfortable with doing that?"

"Well, it's not as if they didn't already have their assumptions about it. We've talked about it."

"You've *talked* about it?" I was curious. "And what was said?" I asked.

"I found out that both of my sons had already told their fathers about you, and of course, both of their fathers were already painting pictures in their minds as to what was going on between us."

I started to chuckle. "Yeah, I can imagine. That's normal for a man to do, whether he's still involved with a woman or not. It's like a lifelong code of male competition."

"So, anyway," Denise continued, "this Thanksgiving, maybe I can have you over for a family dinner. And that will *definitely* be a test, because my mother and sister will get a chance to meet you."

"Have you told them much about me?"

It's amazing how American relationships have become so private and fragmented. There were times where, if you went out with a guy for a year, the entire *extended* family had been around him, and most likely, you were well on your way to being married. Engagements were nothing but a preliminary hearing back then. Some couples would be engaged for a month or two before getting married. Engagements in the nineties, however, could last up to a year or two, which was plenty of time to change your mind. No wonder family units were falling apart.

So there we were, two grown adults who had been dating for a year, and didn't know the first thing about each other's families.

I said, "How about that? You haven't met any of my family members either. I have a couple of wicked uncles. One of them even led me into this truck-driving business."

Denise laughed and said, "That sounds like a good place to start to me. Let's get the tough ones out of the way first."

I joked and said, "I'll call them up tonight."

"You do that."

We made some more small talk before Denise had to run for a bite to eat, and I had to get back to my driving. I was hungry my-damn-self, but

I had a schedule to make. However, my hunger for food could wait. My deeper hunger for love was more important to me, and for the time being, it had been satisfied. That made my driving with an empty stomach a lot easier to handle. Denise Stewart loved me, and she was no longer in denial. I felt like a man with a winning lottery ticket. And before I could blink, I had cleared the accident and traffic was moving full tilt again. Hallelujah!

November/December 1997

Basketball Season

I was rushing with Jamal to make it to Little Jay's first home basketball game at four-thirty. He scored 11 points and had five rebounds and two blocks in only sixteen minutes of their first away game. They won in a close one, 55–53. Little Jay scored some crucial baskets, and already the coach was willing to give my son, the freshman, more playing time. It was hard to keep a guy out at the high school level when he was 6'5" and could play. That would have been like committing athletic suicide. Natural height was a hard thing to come by and very tough to make up for. Either a kid had the size and the ability to play against tough competition, or he didn't. My son had what it took, physically *and* mentally.

I paid six dollars for both of us to get in. Jamal and I slid through the gym doors and marched up into the stands to find ourselves some good seats at half-court. We had only missed the tip-off, and no one had scored yet.

"Which one is Little Jay?" Jamal asked me. With me talking about my son so much, Jamal was as eager to see him play as I was. It would be the first time that the two boys would meet each other since I had taken on the role of becoming Jamal's guardian, so to speak. I promised to take him to every home game with me.

"He's number forty-four in white," I answered.

Jamal looked around and said, "I don't see number forty-four."

Damn, this kid is sharp! I thought to myself. I smiled and said, "He didn't get in yet. He's on the bench right now."

"Oh. So, when does he get in?" Jamal was about to start up with his million and one questions. I didn't mind it though. At least he would make good company.

I said, "As soon as his team starts losing."

This older white guy who was sitting in front of us turned and looked at me with a grin. "You're talking about Jimmy Stewart?" he asked me.

"Yeah, that's my son," I told him. I was the proudest man in the gym!

He nodded. "Your kid has a game. I saw him play in the summer leagues. If he keeps his grades in order, he'll be going Division 1 in four years."

I chuckled, but I didn't like the sound of that. It was as if that white man was expecting my son to have academic problems. I spoke up and said, "Yeah, he'll be ready. He's right at a three point oh grade point average now."

The white man nodded his head again. "If he can maintain that or do better, and score over nine hundred on his boards, he'll be raring to go. I figure by his senior year, he can put up twenty-four points, grab fifteen boards, and get five blocks a game. And this is a good school to do it in. It's well respected in the college circles academically."

I started wondering if that guy was a college scout. He made everything sound so mechanical, as if we were talking about experimental machinery or race cars. I hated when guys talked about high school sports like that. Those damned newspaper and magazine writers were the worst! They used to write nothing but negative stuff about me. *"He needs better footwork and ball handling. He doesn't really have a shot, he's more of a scorer than a shooter."* I averaged 18 points, seven rebounds, and three steals a game, but I guess that wasn't good enough to get any respect from those guys. And the thing that got me was that none of *them* could play. However, that was how the system looked at these kids, as names, numbers, and future projects. That white guy had definitely taken my mind off the game. I started drifting off again, thinking about my own years of high school ball and how I had messed up my opportunity to be a name and number.

I snapped out of it when Jamal finally shouted, "Little Jay is getting in! Dag, he don't look little to me!"

I started to smile and got my head back into the game. My son's team was down 18–7 at the start of the second quarter. As soon as Jay got in, he blocked a shot, ran the floor, and got an alley-oop dunk at the other end. The fans went wild! But I hoped my son wouldn't become a dumb jock. He was already behind in school a year.

It was weird, sitting there at my son's second high school game and thinking so negatively about his future. All of a sudden, all I could think about was his grades. I never thought that way before. Not seriously. When I talked about grades, I was basically going through the motions, even with Jamal. Most people would ask about school grades as if it was the weather, and then go right back to talking basketball. So none of us took academics seriously until it was too late.

After it was all said and done, Little Jay played twenty-two minutes off the bench, scored 16 points, pulled down eight rebounds, and blocked three shots while forcing a couple of steals. His team won another close one, 62–59. Their shooting guard, a 6'3" senior, was the lead scorer with 21 points. He had 23 in their first game.

The white man sitting in front of me stood up and smiled. "A three point oh and a nine hundred on the SATs, and he's *definitely* in."

I was tempted to say a few harsh words to that guy for telling the truth so bluntly, but I thought against it. The truth needed to be faced and swallowed raw. I had done time in jail and had been away from my son for not dealing with the truth. The truth was that we all had responsibilities to take care of in order to make it in life, no matter what. I had to realize that every action in the world has a reaction, and every non-action has a consequence.

As fans began to flow out of the stands and made their way to the exits, Jamal and I waited for Little Jay inside of the gym while the teams changed back into their street clothes.

Jamal looked up at the basket and said, "I hope I can dunk the ball when *I* get big."

I looked at him and said, "You have to work at it, just like anything else in life. The shorter you are, the harder you have to work." That was like everything else in life, too. Nothing was fair and nothing was equal. I found myself in a real cynical state of mind that day, nevertheless, the facts were the facts.

Little Jay walked out of the locker room with a few of his teammates. Even though his high school was mostly white, there were only four white boys on the basketball team, and only one of them started. I guess that showed who was working the hardest at playing basketball. Most of those NCAA Division 1 colleges were white, but you wouldn't know that by looking at their basketball teams. I used to swear up and down that Georgetown University in Washington, D.C., was a black university. They had an entire black basketball team, *and* a black coach, way back when I played ball. I even dreamed of going there.

I shook my son's hand and said, "Good game, Jay. You'll be a starter before the season is over with."

He said, "Next game I'll be starting."

I smiled. "That's pretty ambitious thinking."

He said, "Naw, the coach told me already."

When I thought about that, I was *really* pressed about his grades. He needed to get on the ball immediately if he was going to be a starter. A freshman starter would attract college scouts like a starting gun at a track meet.

Jamal asked him, "Can you teach me how to dunk when I get big?"

Little Jay looked over at him. "It depends on how tall you get."

I corrected him and said, "It depends on how strong your legs are. I'm sure a lot of these short track and gymnastic guys can dunk. A lot of football running backs can dunk, too, and they're not the tallest guys in the world. They just have a lot of leg power to get up in the air."

Jay nodded his head and agreed with me. "I got a white guy in my gym class who's five-ten and can dunk with two hands. He's not too good at basketball though. He plays soccer."

I smiled. "See that? But we think that white boys can't jump. They could jump if they worked at it." I guess I was really getting into work ethics. That white man had done a job on me. But again, it was the oldest truth in the book: hard work pays.

I said, "So how are your grades looking, Jay?" I was so focused on talking to my son about his grades that I forgot to introduce him to Jamal. "Oh, yeah, this is my little man, Jamal Levore. I've been staying with him and his mother. This boy has skills already. And he's smart."

Little Jay said, "Oh yeah. He looks like a point guard."

Jamal said, "That's the guy who dribbles the ball, right, and passes inside? I can do that." He was already picking up on what I had taught him, and studying the game well at only six years old.

Little Jay started laughing. "Yeah, he *is* smart."

"So how are your grades looking?" I asked my son again.

"I'm trying to get a three point oh this semester," he answered. We began to walk toward the exits.

"Aim for a three point five or something," I advised him. "You always aim for the best. That way, if you don't achieve your ultimate goal, you'll still have something to be proud of. But if you get used to aiming low, you'll be satisfied with too little, and start talking that 'I got lucky' stuff whenever you do better than you expected. You have to *expect* to do well. Ain't that right, Jamal?"

"Yup. I'm gonna get straight A's." So far, he only had two B's out of six grades. Yet, I took it for granted that Jamal would do well in school. It's funny how that works. Once a kid shows a parent potential, they never let the child live it down. Yet, kids who need an extra push were always being carried along to the next grade without being challenged to do their best. That attitude in education circles needed to be changed from the parents *and* from the school system. *All* kids should be challenged to do their best. It was a sad situation that they were not.

It was also funny how *my* mind was changing. I was thinking like a damn nerd. But since I was no longer a kid playing the game of basketball, my understanding of academics was five times clearer. As the saying goes, *If I knew then what I know now . . .*

Once we made it out of the exit door, their star shooting guard hollered, "Aw'ight, Jay! I'll catch you later, man!"

"Aw'ight, Speed!" Jay yelled back at him.

I got curious. I asked, "Is he going to college next year?"

"Yeah, he signed at Illinois already," Jay answered excitedly.

"So his grades are good to go then."

Jay said, "Yeah, his mom had him taking college courses during the summertime."

I grinned. "Good idea. Maybe we need to do that with you." Suddenly I had new respect for their star shooter, *and* for his parents. They had him on the ball.

I wanted copies of Little Jay's report card, but I wasn't going to ask him about it. I was planning on waiting to ask his mother. I couldn't let the same thing that happened to me happen to my son, even if he had to sit out a year to focus on what he needed to do in the classroom. I'd rather him hate me early and love me later on than to be all lovey-dovey while he screwed up his grades and ended up not being eligible for college in four years.

Of course, Little Jay and Jamal were still talking about the game while we were on our way to the bus stop. All I could think about was the future and academics. It was beating in my head like a drum. I almost wished that I could trade places with my son and do the work for him. It's amazing how hard some people can work when they mature and are given a second chance. Most young folks don't understand how long this so-called short life can be if you make all the wrong decisions. Funny how times flies when you're having fun, but when you make the wrong decisions, time just stands still. Too bad I had to go to jail before I realized it.

When we got to the bus stop, I looked to my son and asked, "Your mom told you what happened to *my* basketball career, right?" I had already told Jamal my sad story. But I didn't want either one of them to pity me. I wanted them both to learn from my mistake and not make the same in their lives.

"Yeah," my son answered. "She was just talking about it again last night."

I nodded to him. "Good. Because neither one of us wants to see that same thing happen to you. You hear me? Neither one of wants to see that."

Little Jay looked me in the eye like a man and responded, "Yeah, me either."

I said, "All right then. You make sure that it don't. Because this is *your* life, right?"

He nodded. "Yeah."

I reached out to shake his hand again. "Okay then, son. That's all I'm gonna say to you about it."

I knew damn well that I was lying! That wasn't all I was going to say to him. I planned to ride his talented ass for four years if I had to. I wanted to watch my son play ball in the NCAA tournament on a big-screen TV. Damn I wish he had my last name! Anyway, that wasn't just *my* dream. To play in the sixty-four-team tournament was something I'm sure that my son wanted more than anyone. And after four years of playing college ball, if he made it to the pros, we would *both* be making it.

I had changed my mind about young guys going pro right out of high school. A lot of them needed the maturity of going through four years of college, not to mention learning the academic and life skills that they would need later on in their lives, even if they *did* go pro. I was tired of hearing about star dummies with money, and I damn sure didn't want my boy to become one. Nor did I want him walking away from the game talking that coulda, woulda, shoulda garbage. There were a million guys walking around, talking that "I could have" shit. I know that for a fact, because *I* was one of them. So if my son loved the game of basketball like I thought he did, then I wanted him to be ready to do whatever he had to do to make sure he was able to play the game for as long as he wanted to play. For the guys who made it, I realized that it had *more* to do with attitude, and less to do with their talent. Because every baby out of the womb comes into this world with some kind of talent, yet it's only those who take the extra steps they need to take to succeed who strike the gold.

When I got back to Kim's place with Jamal, it was eight o'clock. To my surprise, Kim was stretched out on the living room couch watching television.

I looked at her and asked, "What happened at work?"

"I had a headache, so I came home early."

"You took some Tylenol?"

"Yup."

"How long you been here?"

"About twenty-five minutes."

I took my jacket off and smiled. "So I guess we're all here for the night," I commented. It seemed like Kim and I were always running around doing our own separate things. I guess that's how most working couples are. I didn't know, because I had rarely been in a relationship long enough to find out. I had been like a revolving door with women, *and* with jobs.

Jamal ran over and grabbed his miniature basketball and tried to dunk it on the refrigerator.

"What the hell is wrong with you, boy?!" his mother yelled at him. Then she looked at me and said, "See, *you're* the one who got him all crazy about this basketball. That's probably why I have a headache now."

I said, "Jamal, calm down and get something to drink."

"I'm not thirsty."

"Well, get *me* something to drink then, and pour it in a big glass."

I made room and sat down next to Kim on the couch, where I began to massage her feet.

She got into it and moaned, "Mmm, that feels good."

I looked at her and smiled. I whispered, "Too bad the boy's still up and I have to be to work soon, hunh?"

Kim said, "Tell me about it. I've been wanting you to change that damn night shift for a while now."

That was news to me. Jamal brought me my drink, cherry Kool-Aid, filled to the rim. Then he spilled some of it while handing it to me.

"Watch what you're doing, boy!" Kim yelled at him again.

I took a sip to level the drink off and shook my head. "Why do you have to holler at him so much," I asked her.

"Because he's hardheaded."

"He listens to *me* without hollering."

Kim looked at me and grinned. "That's exactly why these hardheaded boys need their fathers around."

I couldn't argue with that. Jamal definitely listened to me more than he did his mom. If she learned how to control her emotions, he would have respected her as much as he respected me. It was the same way with *my* mother. I believe that had my father been around and healthy, my two brothers would still be alive. A lot of women wasted too much energy when trying to reprimand their sons with shouting and nickel-and-diming, which only showed their boys how powerless and frustrated they were. Since I was a boy once, I understood that the dramatic approach rarely worked. In fact, the less you said, the more they listened, as long as you were consistent about what you wanted from them. Fathers who overdid it found their sons ignoring them like they would a woman. I was going to make sure that would never be the case with me. I wasn't going to stand for that shit! I had been through far too much in my life to be ignored. And I *knew* how to get a kid's attention if I had to, but I didn't want to take things to that harsh physical end. I wanted to use my mind and life experiences.

I felt more connected to Jamal by the minute. It made me feel good inside to be looked up to and respected so much without having to break somebody's face in half. I figured it was a stronger example of a *real* man, one who could get respect *without* violence.

Kim noticed my thoughtful mood and asked, "What are you thinking about?"

I paused for a minute to finish my thoughts. I said, "I'm just thinking about the difference in how men raise kids as compared to women. I mean, you know how that saying goes, 'Mothers love their sons, and raise their daughters.' "

Kim responded, "Well, I don't have any daughters, so I couldn't tell you."

"How did your mother treat you?" I met Kim's mother, and she seemed like a pretty nice woman. She never did say anything about my jail time. Maybe Kim never mentioned it to her. Why should she? I guess I had to stop thinking about it so much myself.

Kim sighed. "She got on my damn nerves," she answered me. "She was always comparing us and shit. 'Why don't you do your homework like your sister? Why you gotta hang out so late? Gelencia doesn't.' And I was just tired of that shit."

Kim had a younger sister who lived in Cleveland. She was single with no kids and had a nice job with the gas company. She looked damned good, too, all the way around, face, hair, *and* body! Sometimes I found myself staring at the pictures that sat around the house whenever Kim wasn't at home.

I asked, "How come your sister ain't married or something?"

Kim gave me the evil eye. "Why, you want to buy her a ring?"

I started to chuckle. "Naw."

"Well, she ain't married for the same reason I ain't married. Everybody wants to sleep around and leave," Kim answered me. "I remember when she first got her virginity taken," she commented. "She swore up and down that she was gonna be with this one guy forever. And I said, 'Gelencia, just because you gave him some doesn't mean that he's gonna marry you.' But she was just so damn naive! A damn *nerd!* She should have kept her legs closed."

I smiled and asked, "And what about you?"

"What about me?"

"Should you have kept your legs closed?" I asked in low tones. Jamal was still in the room shooting hoops.

Kim said, "No. And I'm not ashamed of nothing I've done either. You live and you die."

I thought about that. *You live and you die.* "Damn! Is that all we do?" I asked her.

She hunched her shoulders at me and said, "Eat . . . drink . . . shit . . . fuck . . . work—"

I cut her off and said, "Watch your mouth around your boy. You just say *anything* around him."

She smiled and responded, "Aren't you just a saint," mocking me.

"Can you go a day without cussing?" I asked her.

"Can you go a day without talking about basketball?"

Right as she asked me, Jamal's ball bounced off of his plastic rim and knocked my glass from the coffee table and onto the floor. It was a good thing I had finished my Kool-Aid.

Kim said, "See? He's 'bout to give me *another* damn headache!"

I said, "Jamal, give me that ball." He looked at me and slowly handed it over. "You've played enough for tonight. All right? We'll play again to-morrow," I told him.

He looked around like he didn't know what to do with himself. I said, "Go bring me your homework so we can look it over again with your mother."

Kim looked at me and frowned. I was waiting for her to say something negative, but she didn't. I was looking forward to reprimanding her if she did. You should always want to go over a kid's homework, especially when they're young. Hell, that's when it's the easiest! Because by the time Jamal made it to high school, we probably wouldn't be able to help him. It was smart to get him off to a positive start.

Jamal was still hesitant.

I said, "You want to go down to the gym tomorrow, right?"

He nodded his head. "Yes."

"Well, go get your homework then."

As soon as he ran into his room to get his black-and-white notebook, Kim smiled and said, "Now you're gonna bribe my son."

"So what? It worked, didn't it? Kids need to be rewarded for doing their homework anyway."

"Oh, so you're gonna reward him with basketball?"

"Yeah. What's wrong with that?"

Kim shook her head as Jamal came back out with his book. She said, "What's this thing with men and basketball anyway? It's like a damn re-ligion or something."

I snapped, "Oh, don't tell me you wasn't jumping up and down when Flo-Jo was smoking people in the hundred-yard dash years ago. So what about that? And women and this ice skating stuff, what about that?"

"That's different," she said with a grin.

I nodded. "That's what I thought," I told her. I said, "It's just amazing to me how women will complain about men and sports, as if we're sup-posed to be doing something else. I mean, what are we supposed to do, go clothes shoppin' and read boring-ass books on relationships? It just makes sense to me that the more women get into sports, the more they'll be able to relate to their men. So take a note or two on that."

"Yeah, whatever. They still don't wanna marry you," Kim responded. "They just want to hang out, eat your food, take your kid to a few ball games, and start pulling on your clothes whenever they want some."

"Yeah, and they also pay half of the rent, look out for the kids, lay some mean wood when they need to, and make damn good company!" I snapped back at her. We had only been in our new arrangement for a couple of months, and already she was talking the "M" word. I wondered how long I was going to have to put up with that. But it *was* my fault. I was the dummy who started talking about it by asking about her sister.

We both chuckled at our humor. Then I took Jamal's notebook. I held his basketball up in the air with my left hand and his book in my right.

I said, "What hand do you shoot the ball with?"

Jamal held his hands up and did a demonstration. He looked confused for a minute. He said, "I shoot with both hands."

Kim started laughing. I guess my approach was going to take more than I thought to get my point across.

I said, "Okay, which hand do you *push* the ball with?"

He held his hands up and demonstrated again. "Oh, with *this* hand," he said, excited.

"That's your right hand," I told him. Then I put his book in his right hand and the ball in his left. "Now which hand comes first?" I asked him.

He paused. "My right hand," he answered correctly.

I said, "That's right. Because you're right-handed. Now which hand comes second?"

"My left hand."

"That's right. And in your *right* hand, your *first* hand, is what?"

He looked and said, "My schoolbook."

"And in your *left* hand, your *second* hand, is what?"

"My basketball."

"That's right. Because your *books* come first, and that *basketball* comes second. So if you want to play ball, then *first*, you have to take care of them *books*. You hear me?"

Kim cut us off and said, "Your *mother* comes first." That just messed up my entire groove. I was on a roll for a minute there.

I backed up and said, "Okay, she's right. Listening to your mother comes first. Then the books. And then me. Because if you want to play ball, then you have to talk to somebody who knows the game. And I know it well," I told him with a smile. He was getting a kick out of all that attention. That's why he liked me so much in the first place. A woman could never take the place of the attention that a man gives a boy. It's impossible to do. And if it didn't make a difference, then men and women wouldn't be from different planets.

Kim threw another monkey wrench in my program. "What about his grandmother?" she asked with a grin. She was getting a kick out of it too.

I started laughing. I said, "Okay. First you listen to your mother. Then your grandmother. Then your books. Then me—"

"How is he gonna listen to his books?" Kim asked.

I said, "Would you just leave me alone. I mean, I'm trying to set up a program here, and you're just talkin' to be talkin'. See? That's why women can't raise no boys," I told her. "Y'all talk too damn much, and that just gets boys confused. You got *me* confused now. I was making some good points. Now just leave me and Jamal alone."

We all broke out laughing and enjoyed the moment. I admit, Kim was far from being perfect, but so was I. Nevertheless, I was learning to feel connected to her and her son. Whether he was my boy or not, we had a lot of fun together, meaningful fun. That was what family was about, feeling comfortable with one another, needing one another and being able to laugh and suck in the good moments as well as deal with the bad whenever they came around. It wasn't an overnight process for me, but all of a sudden, I was becoming a complete father. Nevertheless, Kim was right, I still wasn't ready for that "M" word. So I hoped she wasn't planning on pushing it.

Thanksgiving

M O M , would you just relax, please. This is *my* Thanksgiving and you're a *guest*. Okay? Now just sit down, relax, and *be* a guest," I commented to my mother. She insisted on hovering around the kitchen while I worked on dinner. I wanted her to just enjoy herself and rest for a change. She had been working hard for us most of her life

She took a quick look behind herself and whispered, "I just wanted to say that he seems like a very nice man."

I smiled. That's why my mother was forcing herself into the kitchen. She wanted to say something about Brock while he used the bathroom. You know how mothers are, they just can't wait to say what's on their minds. I wondered if I would be that way with my sons, and I already knew the answer. Of course I would. I guess it's all a part of having mother's instincts. Waiting to discuss things would seem like forever, especially when it involved your kids and dating. You want them to have the best situations and not make any mistakes that you can help them *not* to make. But they go right ahead and make those mistakes anyway, just like I did, and probably like my mother did before me. The sad thing is, families in my mother's era seemed to know how to hold things together longer. Especially the men. My father may have hit the booze a little too often, but while he was alive, he was always there when we needed him. Maybe that's why my mother couldn't bring herself to love another man. She was loyal to the grave. And maybe my sister needed more of him. Nikita was only eight when my father died. Hell, I wondered how *my* life may have been different had he been alive through my high school years, and beyond.

I looked at my mother and responded, "Thank you. And did you tell him that?" I asked, referring to Brock.

"No, not yet," she answered. "I just said a few things to him here and there. But I'll tell him when I'm ready to tell him."

We shared another mother/daughter smile before she made her way back into the family room with Nikita, Cheron, and my two sons. Nikita and I had made up as usual, and she reluctantly decided to come over for Thanksgiving. I knew that she would. She was never a grudge holder, and once she arrived, she quickly got herself involved with playing video games with her nephews. Sometimes I wished that my sister *could* hold grudges. That way she could stop going out with so many poor excuses for men, because you *are* who you date.

Brock came out of the bathroom with clean and dried hands, and asked me what he could do next in the kitchen. He was being great about things, and had been there since nine in the morning to help get everything ready.

I looked at him and snuck in a quick kiss. "We're almost finished now," I told him.

He smiled and said, "Yeah, well, that kiss is gonna get me started on something else that we ain't even begun yet."

I gave him an evil eye. "Behave. Okay?" You give a man an inch and even the good ones are capable of trying to sneak a mile. I guess it's in their genes. God most have spoken extremely loud when he told them to be fruitful, because they surely never forgot. And like I said, many black men were not even familiar with Genesis.

Camellia had asked me before to invite Brock out to church with the family. Maybe that needed to be my next move. In the past, I made sure to restrict Sunday service as a close-knit family affair. Brock had been right all along. I *was* being exclusive. Then again, he had never asked to join us at church either.

"Brock, do you believe in God?" I asked him. Had I asked him before? Amazingly, no. I guess I was also separating church from dates. What in the world was I thinking?! Once I had agreed to let the chips fall as they may, they seemed to be falling all over the place.

Brock frowned and looked at me as if I were a Martian. "Of course I believe in God."

"So why haven't you asked to go to church with us?"

"Because that was your private space, and I understood that. So unless we just happened to go to the same church, inviting people out to service is a big deal."

"Is that so?"

"Yes it is," he answered. "Unless you're a Jehovah's Witness. They invite everybody out."

We started to laugh. But it wasn't right. I said, "Why do people have such a problem with Jehovah's Witnesses?"

"Because they don't allow you a chance to praise your God in peace. Personal religion should never be competitive. But they're always out trying to solicit to people. That just doesn't seem right to me."

"*All* churches solicit to people," I reminded him. I took out the ten-pound turkey, basted it, and slid it back in the oven. Brock opened the can of cranberry sauce and slid it out on a serving plate.

"Yeah, but most of them only do it once you've decided to show up for a service. They don't go out and knock on your door to recruit you."

"That's right," my mother said, walking right in on our discussion. "And they're always passing out those funny papers and carrying on. The Bible is the *only* thing you need to read about God. Who are *they* to say what you need to do with your life? The Bible says, 'Thou shall not judge.' "

"Amen," Brock told her with a smile.

I looked at him and grinned.

Mom asked him, "So what church did your family go to?"

"Faith Tabernacle on Stony Island on the South Side," he told her.

"Oh, I know that church," my mother responded. She was really excited about it. "They had that real good youth choir."

"Still do," he told her. "I even wanted to play the piano because of it."

"Oh, you play?"

"A little bit, but I'm no Herbie Hancock or anything. I can't jam on it."

"And you still go to Faith now?"

"Not like I used to. No, ma'am."

My mother nodded at him. "Nobody goes to church like they used to. Maybe we all need to start going back again, and the world would be a better place to live. But the Bible said that these last days would come in the Book of Revelations. Do you still read the Good Book?" she asked him.

I hadn't heard my mother so enthused about church in a long time. Brock was definitely getting her full attention. I knew I wouldn't hear the last of it when the night was over. I was beginning to fear for my own privacy. My mother hadn't tried to be my matchmaker in a long time either. Nevertheless, if she kept going like she was with Brock, she would try and tattoo his name on my forehead.

"Oh, yeah, I still read the Good Book," he answered her. " 'And I looked, and behold a pale horse: and his name that sat on him was Death, and Hell followed with him. And power was given unto them over the fourth part of the earth, to kill with sword, and with hunger, and with death, and with the beasts of the earth,' " Brock quoted. That caught my mother off guard, and me too.

"Oh, yeah," she commented hesitantly. I don't think my mother had read the Good Book herself in a while.

Brock eased her obvious embarrassment and said, "Don't worry, that was just my favorite passage. I probably can't quote anything else like that," he commented with a chuckle.

My mother said, "Well, we all need to start going again," and made her way back into the family room.

I looked at Brock and smiled. "She wasn't expecting that," I told him.

He said, "I know. But I figured I'd quote something before *she* started to."

I frowned. I told him, "My mother hasn't quoted anything from the Bible in ten years."

"Yeah, well, just in case she did, I wanted to be ready for her."

We laughed in hushed tones like two teenagers sitting in the back of a classroom.

It was nearly two o'clock in the afternoon by the time we were finished making dinner. Camellia, Monica, and Levonne were expected to arrive at any minute. They were involved in a Thanksgiving Day food drive in Chicago's Rockwell Gardens, one of the worst areas on the West Side. Since I was throwing dinner at my house, I couldn't make it. However, I still should have sent my two sons. They'd definitely be going the next time. They needed to show some kind of responsibility to the African-American community. The more I thought about it, the angrier I got with myself for not sending them.

Anyway, Camellia had met Brock before, but her two kids had not. I was curious as to what they thought about their mother not having a man in *her* life. I just didn't know how Camellia did it, and I was afraid

to ask. Or maybe, I just didn't want to know. I guess she was your typical, hardworking, single mother. She kept herself extra busy to cut
down on any long periods of loneliness. Not to say that we didn't enjoy
being busy and making a living for ourselves and for our kids, I just
wondered how many of us were honest enough to admit that we would
also enjoy relaxing with a gentle man, or that we at least thought about
the idea.

By the time Camellia and her kids arrived at my house at two-thirty,
we were all anxious to rock and roll with our soul food.

Camellia announced, "Let the soul food party begin."

I nudged her and said, "That's exactly what I was thinking."

She said, "That movie did a lot for Chicago and black families, child.
Because we *need* to get back to good old-fashioned home-cooked meals
and family."

"Mmm hmm," Brock mumbled with his mouth full at the table. "I
agree with that," he said.

"I bet you do," I told him. Since I didn't have an old-fashioned-sized
house like in the movie, we had to eat our food in two rooms. The kids
all ate in the family room, with Nikita and Cheron, while the rest of us
ate in the dining room.

"Your sister didn't want to eat with us?" Brock asked me. We still had
two empty chairs at the table.

"I guess not," I told him.

"So how have things been with you, Mother Stewart?" Camellia
asked my mother. She got a kick out of Camellia calling her that.

"Denise is going to send me to Florida for Christmas. Did she tell
you?" my mother said with a smile. She was bragging. And to think that
I had to talk her into going.

"Florida?" Camellia responded. "No, she didn't tell me," she answered, giving me an evil look.

"I needed to wait and make sure she didn't change her mind on me
like she does so much," I told my good friend.

"Well, Florida's exactly where *I* need to go," Camellia told us. "Somewhere hot and humid. That way I can lose another ten pounds," she
commented with her rumbling laughter.

"Congratulations," my mother said with a nod. "I thought you looked
a little thinner."

I looked at my mother and shook my head. "Now, Mom—"

"No, no, Denise. She's right," Camellia said, cutting me off. "I lost fifteen pounds. And I'm working on losing fifteen more. Then I can slip on a skirt and go out and find a good, strong man like Brock."

Brock looked like he choked on his food to get out a nervous laugh. Camellia had caught us all off guard. I guess that's what holidays are for, family and friend embarrassment.

Brock said, "If you feel good about *you*, then the weight doesn't really matter."

Camellia said, "I'm a grown woman, okay? Now don't you sit here and lie to me. I know good and well what men want; a woman they can wrap their arms around."

I hadn't heard Camellia talk like that since I'd known her. I was really beginning to be concerned about her. I knew she had been on a diet lately, but I never really took it seriously. Since she was so busy in the community, I guess I never sat down and thought about what Camellia thought of herself. She had always been the one to inspire others. Maybe the superwoman, single mom thing was finally catching up with her like it had done with me.

I looked over at my friend and said, "Now you know that's not true. *Definitely* not with *black* men. Maybe you need to stop looking in these white women magazines for a while."

Camellia looked at me and frowned. "You know good and well I don't read white women's magazines like that, Denise. What are you talking about?"

I was reaching for anything to lighten the discussion about her weight. Suddenly I had lost my appetite. We all had. All but my mother.

"I weigh two hundred twelve pounds, Denise. Now Brock, how much do you weigh?"

I cut him off before he could answer. I said, "I don't believe we're even talking about this."

"Well, at least you're tall with your weight," my mother commented.

"Yeah, it would be even worse if I was only five foot two or something," Camellia responded. She was five-seven and a half, slightly taller than my five-seven even.

I was just about ready to jump up from that table and go to war with her. How long had Camellia been feeling so bad about her weight? I calmed myself down and asked her about it. "How long have you been feeling this way?"

"Girl, you know I always talked about my weight. You just never wanted to listen to it."

She was right. I ignored her weight discussions, and she ignored my discussions about being a single mother with money. What are friends for?

"Well, why did you pick today to talk about it?" I asked her.

"Because it's time that I stop being passive about it and do something. It's the same thing I told the people in the homeless shelter we visited today. 'If you know it ain't right, then don't just sit there, *do* something about it!' "

"Well, who said that having a little weight isn't right?"

"Let's see: dietary advisors, exercise trainers, cardiologists, and even funeral parlors, because they have to order extra-large coffins for us."

Brock looked at me and began to smile.

I said, "It's *not* funny, Dennis."

Camellia said, "No, it *is* funny. Because see, I don't want to have a problem when I talk about it anymore. I don't want people saying that it's okay, unless it really *is* okay. That means that *I* have to feel that it's okay, and *not* somebody else."

"That's right," my mother said, instigating again.

I was glad that Nikita wasn't sitting at that table with us. Camellia was on a subject for mature adults only. Nikita would have had something childish to say about it.

Camellia said, "Denise, just like it's not healthy for women to have to raise their kids on their own, it's not healthy for me to keep gaining weight. And I have to be honest about that."

"Some people are meant to carry more weight than others," Brock said. "Look at Luther Vandross. He never looked right as a skinny man. And could you imagine Barry White with no weight? I'm no stringbean myself."

"Yeah, well, you're not falling over the sides of your chair either."

My mother started to laugh. I guess she was comfortable with her added weight.

"Stop, Camellia. Now I don't like this," I protested. "I don't like this at all. Especially not on Thanksgiving."

"Oh, well, I'm gonna eat tonight, so don't even worry about it. I'm not out to starve myself. I just won't be taking any leftovers home. Not even for my kids."

I paused and thought about that. "Levonne could use some extra weight."

Camellia looked at me and asked, "Did you look at him today?"

"No, not really," I answered. "He had his coat on when I saw him. Jimmy took his coat."

"Well, Levonne is *gaining* weight. You go in there and look at him. He has gained about twenty-five pounds since the summer."

"Well, that's good," I told her.

"Not when you have big genes, it's not. I don't know if he's gonna stop or keep right on going."

"Get him involved in playing football," Brock suggested. "The activity of playing a sport would level his weight off so that he would reach a set point."

Since Levonne had always been prone to getting sick, Camellia had always babied him. More than I had with Walter. I doubted if she wanted him to play any sports.

"Maybe that's what I'll have to do then," she responded, to my surprise.

Camellia had sure enough dropped an unexpected bomb on me! I was speechless. What was I supposed to say? What I needed to have was a private conversation with her, and not during a Thanksgiving dinner. So when the phone rang I was more than thrilled to answer it.

"Hello?"

A gruff voice asked, "Yeah, can I speak to Nikita?"

I grimaced. I just *knew* that my sister couldn't be giving people my phone number! I asked, "Who may I say is calling?"

Nikita jumped on the other phone before he could answer. "Hello? Is it for me?"

"Yeah, it's me," he said to her.

"Well, who is *me?*" I asked him again.

"It's my friend, Denise. God!" Nikita fussed at me.

"Well, let your friend announce who he is. Especially if he's calling *my* house."

"I just paged him. I didn't give him—"

"Look, I don't care what you did. When people call my house, I want to know who they are. Period!" I ranted, cutting my sister off.

Her "friend" on the other end began to laugh, as if it were all a joke to him. "It sounds like y'all got problems," he commented.

"No, *you* have the problem," I told him. "When you call somebody's house, you should have the common courtesy to identify yourself."

"I was about to do that, but I didn't get a chance to."

"Can I speak to my friend for a minute, please?" Nikita asked me harshly.

By that time, Camellia and Brock were staring at me from the table. My mother went right on with picking through her food. She knew her second daughter, and the drama was nothing new to her.

I hung up the phone and went back to the table, pissed! If I had said anything else, I may have been forced to wring Nikita's damn neck!

"What was that all about?" Camellia asked.

I shook my head, not wanting to talk about it. But in light of what Camellia was going through, I felt a need to reach out and share my thoughts with her anyway.

"You know who went and paged somebody on my damn phone. And then wouldn't let him identify himself."

Brock shook his head with a grin. He had heard enough stories about my sister before he even met her to understand the constant turmoil she was able to drive me through.

The next thing I knew, Nikita was in the dining room with us, wearing her coat and a colorful ski hat. "Mom, are you gonna be here for a while?"

"Where are you going, Nikita? This is a family event," Camellia asked before anyone else could.

"I'm just going out for a second. I'll be back."

I didn't even have the energy to try and argue with her anymore. If she wanted to throw her damn life in the streets, then I was finally ready to let her do it. But what would happen with my niece, Cheron? A crazy mother would no doubt affect the mental state of a child in the long run. In fact, it was already affecting my niece. She wasn't learning as fast as she should. She was nowhere near being potty trained. And she cried far too easily to have any confidence in herself. I had some thinking to do about that, because my mother was in no condition to raise a child. With my niece in my mother's care, she was allowing Cheron to become just as underdeveloped as Nikita had become. I just couldn't understand what happened to my mother's spirit. It just seemed lost somewhere.

Camellia stood up to talk Nikita out of it. She could see that *I* wasn't going to.

"If you have someone you want to share Thanksgiving Day with, then invite him over here. We would all love to meet him," she said.

I looked up at Camellia as if she had lost her mind.

Nikita looked back at me and said, "*Denise* doesn't want to meet him."

"You got that right," I told her. "And I *damn* sure don't want him coming over here."

"Yeah, because *you're* too good for him. *You're* too good for every-body," she snapped. Then she looked at Brock and said, "You must be the best man in the world. Congratulations!"

I looked at my mother who was beginning to shake her head. She didn't even look up from her plate. Her food had gotten cold twenty minutes ago.

"Mommy," Cheron's mousy voice called through the commotion. Camellia's daughter Monica was holding her hand, and Cheron had spilled fruit juice all over her yellow skirt.

"Dammit, girl! What did you do?" Nikita yelled at her.

"What does it *look* like she did?" I snapped back to my sister.

Camellia looked and shook her head. "You see that, Nikita. That's a sign for you to stay and spend more time with your daughter. You're not even supposed to leave here today. Your daughter needs more of your attention. That juice on her skirt is a message from God."

Nikita sucked her teeth and said, "I don't even have a change of clothes for you." She all but ignored Camellia.

"Mmm hmm," I grumbled. "I don't know why not. The girl's far from being grown," I commented. Luckily, I had three outfits in my closet for Cheron, just for awkward occasions. Actually, I had bought my niece a few outfits in case the family had some formal affair to attend, or even a church affair. Instead of listening to Nikita run around and complain about not having the money or the time to buy her daughter anything to wear, I had stocked my closet with three such outfits that were slightly different sizes.

"I have something for her to wear," I said, excusing myself from the table.

Nikita was still itching to leave. "So, are you gonna be here for a while, Mom?"

My mother finally lifted up her head and answered, "I'm not watching her today. This is my day to rest."

I stopped in my tracks for a minute to see what Nikita's response would be.

Nikita looked at Monica. I read her mind before she could open her mouth, and I'm sure that Camellia was doing the same.

"Well, could you watch my daughter for a couple of hours, Monica? I'll pay you for it."

"No, she cannot," Camellia stated. "Cheron is *not* Monica's responsibility, Nikita. She's *your* responsibility. She's *your* daughter."

"I know whose daughter she is," Nikita snapped. She had found herself between a rock and a hard place.

Monica said, "I could watch her for a couple of hours, Mom."

Camellia said, "I know you *could,* but you're *not.* And I mean it!"

"Why can't she?" Nikita asked desperately. She was just plain sickening!

"Nikita, I just told you that God was trying to tell you something," Camellia repeated.

My sister let out a long sigh and said, "Fine. If nobody wants to watch her, then she's going with me."

"Going with you where?" I asked, sticking my nose into things. She still never said where she was going.

Brock sat there embarrassed by it all. I felt sorry for him, but on the other hand, he needed to experience just how hectic things could become if he wanted to be a part of my personal life and space.

"Where I'm going is *my* business!" my sister snapped at me.

"Oh, no it's not, either," Camellia responded to her. "Especially if you're asking *my* girl to watch your daughter. She needs to know a name, an address, a phone number, a time, *and* an emergency number in case something happens."

Frustration was written all over my sister's face. "Well, she don't have to know none of that because I'm taking my daughter with me." Then Nikita looked back to me. "Now do you have a change of clothes for her?"

I said, "Do I? *You're* making all the rules here. So maybe *you* have a change of clothes."

I wanted to see just how irrational my sister was going to get, and in front of everyone so that I could prove to myself, and to everyone else, that it wasn't *me* who had the problem. And Nikita went there.

"Well, shit, I don't need your damn clothes then!" she shouted, yanking her daughter's hand away from Monica.

Tears came streaming down Cheron's tiny face. "NOOOO!" she screamed. "I don't wanna go!" She yanked her arm away and ran into my legs, holding on to me for dear life. And there was no way in hell I was letting her leave with her insane mother!

"WELL, FINE! YOU STAY YOUR ASS HERE THEN!" Nikita shouted at her daughter.

Camellia was staring in bewilderment. Brock was horrified. And even the boys had come out of the family room to see what in the world was going on.

"What is wrong with you?" Camellia asked my sister. "You can't scream at a child like that."

Nikita turned and made her way for the door and slammed it when she left. Everyone in the room was silent, even Cheron. I wiped her tears and soothed her in my arms.

Finally, Camellia shook her head. "I've never seen anything like that in my life. At least not in *real* life. I thought that kind of stuff only happened on TV."

I grunted. "Hmmph, you know better than that. We've been around a *few* off-the-wall mothers. You're usually just too positive to notice them."

Camellia nodded and said, "Yeah, I guess I am."

That was the longest Thanksgiving Day dinner of my life! Brock called me up as soon as he got home, after eleven. He helped clean, wash the dishes, and straighten everything up before he left. My mother and my niece were staying the night.

"Well, you got to see us all up close and personal. Do you still want to be with me?" I asked him lightheartedly.

"Of course I do. Have you forgotten already? You had to *force* me to leave."

I smiled. He was really hanging tough, I had to admit it. "So what makes you want to deal with all of this? I'm just curious."

He said, "Denise, let me ask you something."

"Go right ahead."

"Do you believe in perfect families?"

I started to laugh. "Once upon a time," I answered him.

"Exactly. Because a perfect family would mean that there are perfect people involved. And from what I know, the only person who was *ever* perfect was Jesus Christ. Am I right or am I wrong?"

"You're right."

"So no matter what family you associate yourself with, there's gonna be hurdles to get over and land mines to dodge," he said with a chuckle.

"Land mines, hunh?"

"Yeah. Sometimes it gets that deep."

"Is that how it was tonight?"

"Well, no. But if your sister would have grabbed a knife and tried to stab somebody, that would have been another story."

I chuckled. "She better not. I'd really have to kill her then."

I thought about Brock's sister in Arizona. "How do you and your sister get along?"

"We were real competitive, and then I just stopped competing with her altogether," he answered. "But we rarely hung out or anything. And we definitely never had any drama like you have with your sister," he commented.

"But that's something that's interesting to me, because I've never had to struggle through much," he said. "Even when I was married, it was like I was just going through the motions. But while I'm involved with you and your family, I can't be that way. I either have to be all the way with it, or back away. And I like that, because it finally solidifies my intentions. I mean, I *want* to be there. And I *want* to be with you. I love you."

I felt all warm inside like a little girl. After that Thanksgiving dinner, there was no way that Brock could be lying, unless he was as crazy as Nikita was.

I said, "You know what, I have to stop calling my sister crazy. I just realized that. But she *does* need some help. Don't you agree?"

"Yeah, I agree," he answered. "But I don't want to talk about her right now. I want to talk about you. Were you embarrassed tonight?"

"Oh, not at all," I told him. "I've been dealing with my family for too long to be embarrassed, but I could tell that *you* were."

"What about when your girlfriend started talking about her weight problems?"

I calmed down and answered, "Oh, yeah. I *was* embarrassed by that. I'm gonna have to talk to her. I never knew she felt that way. She just seems like nothing gets to her."

He said, "Some people could assume the same thing about you, that you don't worry about your public imagery because you're a successful businesswoman, but you do."

"Of course I do. My imagery is very important to me."

"Yeah, well, I'm just glad that you finally see that it's only imagery, and that you don't have to hold up to being this super black woman, because that can really mislead you."

"Don't I know it," I told him. "Too many of us get caught up in that stuff. And a lot of us don't know how to get out until it's too late."

"Well, it's not too late for you. I'm here to tell you that."

"Well, thank you. I'll remember that."

"Now tell me that you love me so I can go to sleep with a smile on my face."

I grinned. "Just like that?"

"Yeah, just say it like I do."

"Ah . . ." I didn't know that I could actually struggle with that. I hadn't said I loved him before, I just hinted at it. Nevertheless, Brock was patient with me. He didn't say another word. And the words finally slipped out of my mouth. I said, "I love you, Dennis, for all the—"

"Wait a minute," he said, cutting me off. "You don't need to explain it, because I understand already. Okay?"

I laughed out loud, remembering when I said the same thing to him.

"Now let's just hang up, call it a night, and go to sleep with smiles on our faces and talk again tomorrow. Tomorrow's a new day."

"Okay. I can agree to that."

"All right then. *Ciao*, baby."

"*Ciao*," I told him with a grin. When he hung up, I actually didn't expect him to. I wanted more, and he left me hanging. And while I was hanging, I realized that I was becoming attached to him like I hadn't been with a man in a long, long time. I felt that I was a part of him, and he was a part of me. And I was no longer afraid of that feeling. So I rolled over in bed, with everything done, and fell asleep. How many times had I fallen asleep that easily over the last fifteen years? Rarely! But before I could enjoy it, the telephone rang and woke me back up anyway.

"Hello."

"It's me. Mom and Cheron are still over there?" Nikita asked me from a pay phone.

"Where are you?" I could hear the street noise in the background.

"I'm safe. I just wanted to know where they were," she answered, still protective.

"You actually care?" I asked rhetorically.

She sighed. "Whatever. Just tell Mom I'll see her tomorrow."

"And what do I tell Cheron, your daughter?"

There was a long pause. "Tell her Mommy said she's sorry. Tell her Mommy still loves her."

I felt a touch of pity. Maybe because Brock had brought it out of me. I said, "She loves you too. And so do I."

We lingered on the phone for a minute, and I could tell what Nikita was saying in her silence. She was apologizing, and telling me that she still loved me. I knew her. She was my little sister.

I said, "I'm still angry at you, Nikita. And we *do* need to talk about this. But you go ahead and think to yourself tonight while you're out on your own. And then we'll talk again when we get a chance to."

"Okay. We'll talk. I gotta go now," she told me.

I hung up with my sister and couldn't go back to sleep. She had no idea how much pain she caused me because I loved her so much. I just didn't know what to do about her. It just seemed to be no way to reach her. But as long as she was alive, I had to keep trying. And maybe God would help me find a way.

A Long Time Coming

O N Thanksgiving Day, I was all worked up to give my father a verbal lashing for all of the years of mental abuse he had put me through, and had attempted to pass on to my son. No wonder I was so screwed up and selfish. In spite of fighting everything my father ever wanted of me, I had been fast becoming a spitting image of him, until I was forced to see his, and many of my own, imperfections with clearer vision. However, as we got the house ready for my parents' visit that evening, Beverly insisted on trying to talk me out of it.

"This isn't the time to do that, Walter," she advised me.

Her kin were all going to visit her older sister Elaine for dinner, but I needed to sit down and talk with *my* family, so we decided to join her family again for Christmas. Beverly was a much-in-demand guest with her pregnancy and all. I was unaware of how much attention expectant mothers could receive from family and friends. Even people in the street seemed to take on a whole different approach to expectant mothers. It was really something else. All the while, I felt guilty all over again for not being supportive when Denise was pregnant with Walter.

I said, "Honey, I understand that you would like this to be a peaceful evening and all, but my father and I need to stop putting this thing off. We need to talk. Tonight!"

"Well, just make sure that you don't do it at the table. Okay? Because I don't need to be upset," she snapped.

She sounded upset already. I looked down at her rounding stomach and thought about the emotional stress that could be passed on to the baby. "Yeah, I guess you're right," I told her.

Nevertheless, I planned on dealing with my father one way or the other, even if we had to take a long drive out in the cold. We were right around the corner from December, wintertime.

"Don't you think we need to settle our differences?" I asked my wife about my father and me. "I'm thirty-two years old now. I'm not a child anymore. This is absurd. I should have gotten this out of the way a long time ago."

"Well, it won't look like you've learned anything if you present yourself with a temper tantrum."

I faced Beverly and asked, "Is that what you think this is, a temper tantrum? I think it's a grown son demanding that his manhood be respected, and that extends to respect for my son, *and* for us. Whenever he disrespects me, you, or Walter, he needs to be dealt with on a level of adulthood. But here *you are* speaking as if we're kids, asking for *permission* to be adults."

Beverly sighed. "That's not what I'm saying at all. I just think that you don't need a big buildup like this, that's all. You need to be more level-headed."

I calmed myself down and thought about all of the great advice Beverly had given me. She was a very mature, respectable, supportive, and thoughtful woman. I was fortunate to have her on my side. And she was having my child in May.

I smiled and walked over to rub her belly. Then I kissed her on the cheek.

"What was that all about?" she asked me.

"I just remembered why I love you so much."

"I didn't know that you had forgotten."

"I never have, and I never will. Not as long as you keep being you."

"And what if I change?"

I stood there cradling my wife and my unborn child. I said, "Then I'll cry my eyes out and pray to have the woman that I married back again."

She chuckled and broke away from me. "Let's finish what we're doing, okay?"

"What do you mean? We *are* finished." I looked at my watch and added, "It's only eleven-thirty. My parents won't be here until two."

"I thought they said they'd be here by one?" Beverly asked me, confused.

I nodded with a smile. "Exactly. And that means two. They're going to be *leaving* around one."

She smiled and agreed with me. "Yeah, I guess you're right. You think we'll ever be like that?"

"I hope not. But you never know. When this baby comes along, things will get a lot more complicated," I answered. "Just look at how long it takes for your sisters to get ready. It takes them an hour or so to leave, so you can imagine how long it takes for them to get ready."

Beverly broke out laughing. "Oh, that *won't* be me. I was *always* the first one ready to go, *and* to leave in our family." She was the third child of four daughters.

"Yeah, well, we'll see when it happens," I told her.

"Are you planning on helping me?" she asked.

I frowned and said, "Of course I am. What kind of question is that?"

"I'm just making sure that you realize it's not going to be all on *my* shoulders. The more you help, the easier it'll be. Look at your brothers-in-law," she told me. "Randy is very helpful, and Greg is not, and you can see the difference that it makes."

Beverly was referring to her sisters' husbands, and she definitely had a point. A strong helping hand got immediate results.

"I'll try my best to remember that," I promised my wife.

By the time my parents arrived, at exactly two o'clock, I was good and leveled. I don't know if that was a good thing or a bad thing. Sometimes when you cool off too much, you forget many of the points that you wanted to make while you were heated.

My mother gave Beverly and me a hug and a peck on the cheek like some political dignitary. Then my father followed up with some rather weak handshakes and shaky eye contact. He was already starting the day off wrong. It almost seemed as if my mother had forced him to accompany her against his will. That brought all of the points that I wanted to make with him back to the front of my mind.

"You need any help with the food?" my mother asked Beverly. She looked around at our empty house and added, "Where is everyone?"

I had already told my mother it would be only us. Nevertheless, she loved being dramatic. Beverly and my mother were like night and day. Whatever happened to the saying "Sons grow up to marry women like their mothers?" That was far from the case for me. My mother and Beverly were both the third child in their families, but the similarities stopped there.

I said, "Mom, this is a private affair between us."

My father sat down at the dining room table and looked up at a new picture that Beverly and I had purchased only a week before. "Is that new?" he asked.

"Yes, it's new. It's from John Ashford. He's out of the Maryland/D.C. area."

My father nodded. The print of the spectacular oil painting was of a naked black child with dreadlocks, who was playfully running through the bushes from his mother after just getting a bath. Ashford called it *Innocence*. Each of his pictures came with a short summary and a certificate that explained them to you. Beverly and I bought it as a positive reminder of our expected child.

"Is it an original?" my father asked me.

I grinned. It was his typical question, and the more I noticed myself in him, the more I realized that I wanted to make a change.

"No, it's not. But I don't think that takes away from the message. It's still an excellent painting whether it's an original or not," I responded to him.

Beverly swiftly jumped in and said, "You can't come here and sit down. Everyone has to help set the table. You have a pregnant woman on the premises." She always knew how to handle my father just right. In fact, Beverly was the social match of anyone. She was simply gifted in that way.

We all set out the turkey, string beans, potatoes, wild rice, stuffing, gravy, buttered biscuits, and cranberry sauce.

"You didn't fix all of this on your own, did you?" my mother questioned Beverly.

"Not at all. Walter helped me every step of the way."

"Well, you're going to need some help around here when the baby comes. Have you two started thinking about a maid or a nanny?"

In the light of a recent child neglect/murder case involving a nanny from Britain, Beverly and I were terrified of the thought, but it *had* crossed our minds. We had had a long discussion about it.

"We've decided that it will be a long and grueling process of selection, so we've started looking at different avenues to go in already," I explained.

"You can never be too careful about that kind of thing," my father warned.

I never liked any of the day-care providers that I had as a kid. I could not remember far enough to recall any nanny in my life. And I had never asked.

"Did you have a nanny for Walter?" Beverly asked on cue.

I looked at her, smiled, and shook my head. My wife was simply mystical sometimes.

She said, "What, I wasn't supposed to ask that question?"

"No, it's not that. It's just that you were reading my mind as usual, that's all."

"Oh," she responded.

My mother answered, "Walter didn't get a nanny until after I stopped breast-feeding him around eight or nine months."

I was embarrassed. "Look, ah, can we talk about this *after* we eat," I complained.

"Aww, what's wrong, sweetie? Breast-feeding is natural," my mother teased me.

"Mother, I'm trying to concentrate on eating right now," I responded. I always wondered why my parents never had another child. When I asked them as a kid, they used to talk about how expensive children were. Then for years, they told me they were considering adopting a little sister, but that never happened. I was tempted to ask about it again, but I changed my mind. It was far too late to change anything. Beverly and I planned to have at least two kids. We both agreed that a child should have someone to share its young experiences with, and Beverly had a great upbringing with her sisters. I just hoped and prayed that we didn't have all girls like her parents had. But if that *were* to happen, then at least I still had Walter.

We wasted no time digging into our food. We said a family prayer and began to pass the wild rice and turkey.

"Is this Uncle Ben's rice?" my mother asked.

Beverly nodded. "Mmm-hmm. Yes, it is."

One of the reasons why my parents considered child-rearing so expensive was because they were reckless, name-brand consumers. I never had a piece of Kmart or Sears clothing in my life. Everything was from the high-grade department stores. Everything had to be "the best." However, buying a child "the best" of everything didn't necessarily guarantee him a healthier childhood. Love, happiness, and sharing good, clean fun with children went a long way, producing confident and progressive adults, who were not hung up on supposed quality.

I thought again about having a good, long conversation with my father while we all ate. He was there physically, but his mind was somewhere else. I hadn't talked to him about business in a while. Mom told me a few years ago that he was getting involved in real estate again, and I wondered how that was going. My father had talked to me back then about making another killing off white families who wanted to move *back* into the city. It was supposedly a national trend to regain the cities from black residents who were perceived as running them into the ground. According to my father, the process had already started and was heating up at a rapid pace across the country. He said that I would have known that had I worked in the real estate department at the bank. And he was right, because plenty of bank loans were being secured for new or renovated housing in urban areas. He called it "re-urbanization," and he wanted to hire some new young white faces to do his handiwork.

"Are you still thinking about re-urbanization?" I decided to ask him. I was curious about it myself, especially if my father may have been thinking of cutting me off, which I strongly doubted. Nevertheless, I did think about it, and with my growing interest to break into some form of entrepreneurship, compounded by my boredom at work, I could use something new to get me going again.

My father nodded. "I'm looking at a few properties. Yeah," he answered. He looked alive and inside of the room again. "Why, are you getting interested now?"

I had never told him that I wasn't interested, he just *assumed* that I wasn't because I had previously spent so much time trying to establish my own interests. At the time, I didn't want to commit to the idea either. If I *did* get interested, I wanted to try things on my own.

"You still think that you need the right color faces to do it?" I asked him.

He said, "Not in some areas. We have some well-to-do black families buying up urban housing, too." Then he looked at Beverly and added, "You all are going to need a house soon."

"Yes, we probably will need a bigger house," Beverly said. She knew I was about to hit the ceiling, but it was too late.

My father's comment was true, of course, but I didn't like how he said it. He made it sound as if we didn't have a house. I always felt that nothing I did was quite good enough for him.

I snapped, "I can't seem to get your support or respect on *anything* I ever say or do!"

"Walter, we respected and supported you on plenty of things. How could you say such a thing?" my mother cut in.

"He's been saying stuff like that his entire life. He's never been appreciative of what we've given him," my father added.

"That's because you've been holding it over my head like some kind of *ode* to my parents!" I shouted. "You've done what any parents should do; provide for your child. Yet you think you should be awarded for it. And that's not the way to go about receiving love from a son," I told them.

"That's like every time I buy Beverly some flowers or a bracelet, I turn around and say, 'See how much I love you' and expect her to be excited about that. You can't buy love, you have to share it and make it surround yourself and your children."

"Walter, we did surround you with love," my mother refuted. "What are you talking about?"

"No, you surrounded me with *things*. So I was always *searching* for love; love for myself, as well as love from others."

My father stopped eating and wiped his mouth. I knew what that meant; it was time to go to war!

He said, "I know one thing, if he still doesn't see all that we've tried to do for him, then we need to stop trying to force ourselves on him. And it's a shame that kids are growing up to disrespect their parents like they're doing nowadays. I guess the last days are really here."

Beverly held my arm at the table before I jumped up and hit the roof. My father was pulling himself from his chair. I said, "Good, let's take a drive and get this thing settled."

He looked startled. I guess I had never stood up to him before. My mother was always in the way somehow.

"It's cold outside," she complained, interjecting again. "You don't need to be out there. We had to warm the car up for twenty minutes before we drove out here today."

I said, "We have coats. And we're men."

My father nodded. "All right. Let's talk then."

"Talk about what?" my mother insisted. "We can talk about whatever we need to talk about right here."

Beverly said, "It's not a 'we' kind of talk, Mrs. Perry. It's a father-and-son kind of thing."

My mother looked at her pregnant daughter-in-law, ready to respond, but thought better of it. My father and I then grabbed our coats and headed for the front door.

"Well, how long are you going to be out there?" she asked.

I looked at my father and answered, "As long as it takes."

My father looked at his watch and responded, "We'll be back before six."

I didn't look at my watch to see how much time that would give us because I didn't care. I planned on driving my car, and I wasn't letting my father out until I said everything I wanted to say to him.

"Well, make sure you drive carefully. Okay?" my mother asked of us.

"I will," I told her. Then I gave Beverly a hug and a kiss. She gave me a quick stare. I said, "Okay. I remember." She was telling me to keep my composure.

As soon as I walked out the door and down into the garage with my father, he began to head for his car.

I said, "We're going to take my car."

"No, we're not."

"Why aren't we? I'm the one who decided to take this ride. Not you. So we should be using my car."

He looked over at my gray Lincoln and submitted without a word. I clicked the door open with the remote system so he could climb in, and walked over to the driver's side.

"Do you have temperature controlled seats?" he asked, rubbing his hands.

"Yes, I do," I answered.

"Well, put it on."

"It is on. It has to warm up first." *The same way* you *have to warm up,* I thought of commenting. My father had been like a statue for as long as I can remember. He rarely smiled, laughed, or seemed to enjoy himself. His life seemed to just drag along, with each new day presenting a new problem to solve.

"What is it with you?" I asked him. "You're a successful man, so what makes you so damn angry?" I thought of the conversation I had with my son at the Titan Hotel.

"I'm not angry," my father answered. "I'm just disappointed."

"Disappointed in what? In me?"

He looked me in my eyes and said, "You should be disappointed in yourself."

"Well, I got news for you. I'm *not* disappointed," I responded. "I think every day about finding new ways to enjoy my life. You need to learn how to do the same."

My father nodded. "Yeah, I see. You're going to become like all the rest of them; laughing, drinking, and wasting their damn lives. I knew it all along. That's just how you wanted to be, no matter what I tried to teach you. You went right out and got some damn girl pregnant."

"And I *love* my son," I told him. It didn't even bother me anymore. The reality of my son was *his* problem, not mine. I had done enough alienating, and I wasn't planning on doing it anymore. My entire life had been about alienation, from my parents, from the black community, from women I was attracted to, and from the world in general. I just never felt a part of anything. And I didn't want to feel that way anymore.

"These illegitimate kids are the main ones out here doing crime, going to jail, and just screwing up the image of hardworking, *good* black folks," my father snapped.

I said, "And that's exactly what I don't want my son to add to. That's why it's so important for him to be loved and accepted by his father *and* his grandfather, instead of being frowned on and shunned."

My father looked away, feeling guilty. He knew that he was wrong. "And what about his mother? What kind of woman is she?" he asked me.

"She's a hardworking, successful businesswoman who cares very much about her sons. But you never gave her a human chance. You wrote her off without ever even meeting her."

He looked at me and asked, "She has two of them, and both are out of wedlock, right?"

He knew the answer already, so I ignored the question. "The point is, she *hasn't* and *will not* give up on the struggle to raise her kids correctly, no matter *how* they got here. Nevertheless, she needs support from the men who helped create her children, just like black people need support from the greater white society who created their situation of underclass poverty."

"Junior, these nonworking, shiftless welfare folks created their *own* poverty by not sacrificing time and effort to get educated and dig themselves out of the pits of the ghetto," my father responded. "Plenty of these poor white folks did it. And many of them were in the same situations that we were. Especially here in Chicago. Who do you think was the underclass when the stock markets crashed? Black folks didn't have millions of dollars in it.

"Jean Baptiste Pointe DuSable, a *black man, founded* Chicago, but now *we're* the underclass!" he snapped. "It's because we've stopped working hard and got used to somebody *giving* us something instead of going out and *earning* it. Now this woman laid down and spread her legs. You didn't rape her, did you?"

My father was as good at dramatic performances as my mother was. I said, "I may as well have raped her. I got her pregnant and walked away. That could be considered a rape; a rape of humanity, bringing a child into this world without the balance of the two people who created him.

"That's why it was so important for me to attend the Million Man March when I did. I needed to atone for the things I've done in *my* life. And I still do."

My father grunted. "Is that how you really feel?" he asked me.

"Yes, it is."

"Well, how come you didn't marry this girl then?"

"For the same reason that white folks won't marry us. Plain ignorance," I answered. "I was raised not to associate with her *type*, whatever that means, and so my involvement with her was only temporary, which wasn't right."

My father looked away again. We drove in silence for a couple of miles. I always drove the same route when I needed to think to myself, along Lake Shore Drive, down and back again. It always soothed my mind.

"You know, we never did talk much," I commented. "It just seemed like you were telling me what or what not to do half of the time."

"That's a father's job, to give his son guidance. Isn't that what you're trying to do with *your* son?" he asked me.

I nodded. "But at the same time, I'm just trying to be there for him when he needs me, to let him know that he's not alone in the world, and that he can count on me to help him," I answered. "I want to be able to talk about anything he needs to discuss with me. And it just doesn't seem that you and I ever had that same type of relationship."

"That's because you spent so much of your time trying to do the *opposite* of what I told you."

"Well, did you ever stop to think about supporting something that *I* wanted to do?"

"I supported you all of your life," he snapped at me.

I got angry and snapped right back at him. "I'm not speaking about monetary support, what I mean is *moral* support! The kind of support where you sit down and say, 'Look, son, whatever it is that you want to do, I'm behind you all the way. So I want you to put forth your best effort.' "

I turned and glanced at him, awaiting a response. He smiled and nodded his head. He said, "I remember when I was about fourteen years old. My father asked me what I wanted to do with my life, and I said that I wanted to go into politics and become the mayor. I thought it was a pretty good idea. And he said, 'That's a profession for beggars. If you want some *real* power, then you start up a strong industry, buy some property, build influence in your community, and then you'll find that the *mayor* will work for *you.*' "

That small reflection said a lot about my father, *and* about a grandfather whom I had never met. He had died of a heart attack the year before I was born. He was sixty-two years old.

I said, "So you're still trying to find a way to control the mayor, and I guess you've found out that it's not going to happen."

My father didn't say a word. In a way, I felt sorry for him. However, maybe he was finally ready to understand my point of view. So I used the opportunity.

"I don't ever want to hold such an uncontrollable goal over my son's head," I told him. "All that can do is break a person's spirit, or have them kill themselves trying to reach it."

"So what do you think, that you should settle for less?" he asked me.

"Not necessarily for less, but for whatever will ultimately make you secure. Even if it's an eight-dollar-an-hour job."

My father grunted. Maybe I should have said eleven dollars.

He said, "That's the reason why so many black people are in poverty now."

"No, we're in poverty because we've been denied so many opportunities at higher-paying jobs, because of our color, that many of our kids have stopped reaching for higher goals as a reality. I mean, *you* even used white faces to meet and greet for your real estate business."

He saw my point and backed down a bit. "Even if they won't give you an opportunity, you can still *create* your own method of making a better living. DuSable was a fur trader."

I nodded. "Yeah, and unfortunately, many black men have started to do exactly that with drug selling," I responded. "Just like the Kennedys built their empire off bootlegging. But they didn't end up in jail for it. And what I'm saying is that we're going to have to find a way to make integrity count a lot more than salary."

"Hmmph. Good luck on that," my father commented. "An honest man can still be a dirt-poor man."

I shook my head and frowned. There was a lot of baggage there between us, and so much to consider in regards to my misguided education about the world. Money and the drive toward power had always influenced my decision making, but after being reunited with my son, I wanted to be able to enjoy many of the smaller things in life, like playing miniature golf, tennis, and video games while sharing quality time with my son, my wife, and other loved ones.

I said, "With the way things have been going between us, I've just come to the conclusion that we're probably never going to agree on much. However, that does not give you grounds to disrespect the things I do or the people who I love. And as long as you respect that, that's all I can ask from you. Because I'm a grown and responsible man just like you are. And if that means that you'd rather not be involved with my son, then I'll keep you two away from each other.

"But I'll tell you this," I added, "whether I have your support or not, my son is going to have an opportunity to succeed at whatever he wants to do, and I *will* be there to support him in it."

My father looked at me and asked, "Are you planning on attaching him to your estate?"

I was surprised that he was asking. I answered, "Well, he *is* my son, isn't he?" While we were on the subject, I asked, "Am I *your* son? Am I still attached to *your* estate?"

My father nodded. "Of course you are." He didn't look at me when he said it, because he hated to admit that he needed me to continue the Perry legacy. I was his only child, and it became ironic to me how so many wealthy people of history had only a few, if *any*, heirs. Therefore, their wealth was either lost or separated between extended family members, which in my father's case, weighed more heavily on my mother's side of the family, who were not Perrys at all.

"He seems like a smart boy," he commented in reference to my son. "Maybe he *could* become something special."

I said, "He already is, and he always *will* be something special."

"What makes you so sure?"

"Because his mother and I won't have it any other way."

My father gave me another nod. "Maybe I can get used to him." My son and I were all that he had, and he was painfully realizing it. My father needed to face the music and dance to it whether he liked the song or not.

"Maybe you *need* to get used to him," I told him, to nail the point home. "But from now on, it'll be on *his* terms and not on yours. So if you want to relate to my son and get to know him, you'll have to do so by participating in things that *he* likes to do."

"What does he like to do?" my father answered me.

I leveled with him and said, "I've just begun to find that out myself. And that's sad."

I didn't have much to say after that. My father didn't either. Nevertheless, I was pretty satisfied with the outcome of our talk. He realized that I was my own man, and that I was going to support my son whether he liked it or not, and since he grudgingly admitted that my son *was* indeed his grandson, I could finally come clean about Walter's share of the Perry estate without so many insecurities about it. Then again, I could not help thinking that it would have been more *manly*, so to speak, to make my own way for myself and for my son without my father's wealth. So despite my want and need to establish respect and independence, I was still playing the role of a legitimate "Junior."

"So how did things go?" Beverly asked me later on that evening. We were in bed again.

"I'd say it was an eight out of ten," I told her with a smile.

"What would have made it perfect?"

"Well, nothing is perfect," I answered her. "It went a lot better than I expected it to go, actually. I expected a *three* out of ten."

"Mmm hmm," Beverly hummed. She seemed preoccupied with something.

"Is everything okay with you?" I asked her. I leaned over and rubbed her belly.

"Ah, yeah, I'm okay." Her hesitation meant that she wasn't.

"Now, I *know* that *you know* that I know you a lot better than that. Now what's on your mind?" I teased.

"Ah, I really don't want to talk about it right now." If it was bothering Beverly as much as it seemed, she was going to talk about it anyway. She had always been low-key in her response to things. Nevertheless, she always aired her concerns. So I sat and waited for the inevitable.

"Your mother told me that your father had an affair once. She said he probably had more than one, but she's not certain. How do you feel about that?"

I was speechless. I knew that it was true, I just never allowed myself a chance to think about it too often. "What do you want me to say?" I asked my wife. "It was something that happened, and I don't try to dwell on it."

"So how can he act like he's so perfect?" she asked me. Beverly seemed really hurt by it, as if she had lost a ton of respect for my father. I began to wish that my mother had kept the information to herself. I guess she was attempting to prepare Beverly for the many struggles of marriage. However, I do not believe that the love-and-keep-your-family-at-all-costs approach of my mother's generation works at all on the wives of the nineties. She had only made things more difficult.

"Because he still provided for his family and did the things that he was supposed to do."

Beverly responded, "That's the same thing your mother said. But what about his vow to his wife and family?"

The conversation was going nowhere. "What was supposed to happen, Beverly? You think that my mother should have gotten a divorce? You think that would have made everything perfect again? What was done was done."

Beverly turned away from me. All I could do was become frustrated. I said, "Why are you angry at *me*? *I* didn't have an affair."

"Yeah, but you still have the same nonchalant attitude about it. 'What was done was done,'" she repeated.

I said, "Okay, I'm sorry I said that."

"But you meant what you said though."

"Look, am I being punished for what my father did years ago? Because if I am, then this is ridiculous. And please don't bring up Denise again. I thought we had gotten over all of that."

Beverly gave me the silent treatment. I was just about ready to get up and sleep in the guest room. I didn't need that extra stress. I had just won a major battle with my father that day, and I felt that I deserved an opportunity to enjoy it.

Beverly pulled my hand back to her stomach. "I'm sorry," she said. "It must be the extra hormones."

I smiled. "Yeah, people told me about that," I said.

"But it's still wrong," my wife added.

"I know it is." I really wanted to continue the conversation, but I figured it would be of no use, especially while Beverly was still pregnant. I felt that most divorces failed to settle anything. It was a false illusion that legal separation would somehow lead to something better. Unfortunately, in many cases it didn't. Divorces only seemed to lead to more divorces, family problems, and insecurities.

"My father had an affair once, too," Beverly admitted. The wall was tumbling down. She said, "And the family was never the same after that. Sometimes I wished they *did* get a divorce."

I could only imagine what was coming next. I was being sucked in for the kill.

Beverly said, "It just makes me think that *all* men are suspect."

I wanted to pull my hand away and couldn't. I said, "You know that's not true."

"So what makes it happen then? Why do so many men do it?"

I felt like it was her hormones talking again, and honestly, I didn't want to answer her question. "I'm sure you can come up with plenty of answers to that yourself," I responded.

"But I want *you* to answer my question." To make matters worse, she turned and faced me.

I couldn't even look at her. I felt guilty for *all* men. *Men cheat because sex, to them, is as natural as breathing. And it has absolutely nothing to do with love and commitment.* But I couldn't tell my wife that. She knew that anyway. Most mature women knew it. Yet they would fight it until they entered the grave. Nevertheless, all men were not cheaters. And many of them were committed wholeheartedly to their wives and families.

I wish that I was innocent enough to look into my wife's desperate eyes and tell her that the average man never even thought about another woman, but I couldn't. I wasn't the man to answer that question. I had too many strikes against me, and as crazy as it sounds, I didn't want to put a hex on myself by saying that I would never cheat. It just seemed like too much pressure to live with. But what the hell, I had taken a woman to the altar and said "I do." That was pressure enough. I had already *made* the commitment. I guess that was why so many men considered marriage the ball and chain. They had to ask themselves the question, *Can I actually deal with not having any other woman for the rest of my life?* And many of them were responding, "Hell no!" That was the truth, and nothing but the truth; a truth that most women didn't want to hear.

"You really want an answer for that?" I asked my wife, stalling.

"Yes, I really do."

I nodded. I said, "Men and women have different biological functions. You do understand that, right?" I was attempting to figure out an answer as I went along.

Beverly just stared at me. She wasn't going to help me out at all.

I added, "Most young women desire long-lasting love affairs from the beginning of their interest in boys. For boys, on the other hand, much of their early dating boils down to experimentation, confidence, and practice. And once a lot of these young guys get any kind of consistency going with women, they are just really reluctant to give that up. Therefore, it takes a lot more maturity for a man to bring to a close his free-roaming sex life. As for young women, they are more interested in trying to *keep* a man, so marriage makes more sense to them.

"Am I making any sense to you?" I asked my wife.

"So once a man decides that he *is* mature enough to get married, and then he turns around and cheats, what happens then?"

I paused. "He breaks his vow, and he pays the cost for it whether he's caught or not, because he feels ashamed of what he's done. And if he *doesn't* feel ashamed, then all of his morality has been lost."

I hoped and prayed that Beverly would be satisfied with that, because I honestly had nothing else to add to the discussion. A man spreading his human seed across the land was a very natural thing. Polygynous marriage would then solidify a dominant man's genetic placement and family. And at one time, that marriage arrangement was the natural way of colored peoples who still make up the overwhelming majority of the world's population. So maybe monogamous marriage, a European philosophy, which has never been without prostitution, slaves, and mistresses, was what was unnatural and unrealistic. Nevertheless, there was no way in the world I could have a sane conversation on such a thing with my wife, a 100 percent American. She would only believe that I was thinking with my wrong head again, a battle that women would never have to fight.

My wife squeezed my hand and pulled me closer to her for a kiss. "I wouldn't be able to take it," she told me. "I mean it."

I know she did. And I couldn't wait for her to go to sleep. Because as long as she was awake, I couldn't sleep. I would have been up all night trying to soothe her insecurities, and I didn't know if I had the energy or the words to do so. So when Beverly fell asleep in my arms, I thanked God and asked him to give me strength to hold up my vow to her.

One-on-One

T

BROCK

H E R E were so many things going on in my mind that I didn't know where to start. It was Friday night, and Denise was coming over to visit. I don't know why I always waited until the last minute, but I was hurrying to finish my spaghetti dinner and corn while I straightened up my two-bedroom apartment. I had a nice place in an okay area on South Eighty-first Street, but every time Denise would visit, I thought for some reason that I should have had more. I did own a small house with my ex-wife, but during the divorce settlement, it got too complicated to keep. Luckily for me, we didn't have any children, or I may have been forced to keep up the payments on the house to support a separated family.

Anyway, a few of the things on my mind concerning Denise and me included where we would live if we ever decided to shack up. Would I move into Oak Park with her and her sons? I didn't think so. Would we buy a new house together? Maybe. And how would her sons and their fathers respond to that? There were plenty of questions to ask and answer that I always pushed to the back of my mind. Nevertheless, they were serious issues that *needed* to be discussed between us. I thought about those issues more intensely every time Denise would visit me.

She arrived at my two-story redbrick building around eight-thirty, wearing a mint green velour dress that stopped right above the knees. And boy did she look *good!*

"Wow! I'm speechless," I told her.

I was wearing a pair of plain black slacks, black shoes, and a colorful, Bill Cosby–like sweater from his old "Huxtable" days.

"Thank you," Denise responded, handing me her coat. "I see you waxed your hardwood floors again," she walked in and commented.

"Yeah, I always want them to look nice for company," I said with a grin.

"Hardwood floors always make a place look so spacious."

"Yeah, it does, doesn't it? Here, have a seat and I'll put on some music. Is there anything you'd like to hear?" I asked her courteously. She sat back and relaxed on my black leather sofa. My pad was all bachelor, but it had gotten boring to me, to tell the truth. I wanted a change in scenery.

"No, not really. As long as it's mellow," Denise responded.

I walked over to my stereo system in the corner of my living room and put on LSG: Gerald Levert, Keith Sweat, and Johnny Gill. Denise recognized the CD immediately, and began to nod.

"They have some good music on here," she said.

"Yeah, they do. So how long are your kids staying over at Camellia's?" I asked.

"Until Sunday morning."

"That means you can stay over for *two* nightcaps then," I teased.

Denise smiled and said, "If I want to, yes," teasing me right back.

I walked over and sat on the leather sofa beside her. "So, we've come a long way. Don't you think? I remember when you first came over to visit me, and you started to walk around like you were interested in renting the place."

She broke out laughing. "Yeah, because Camellia and I couldn't afford a place just like this one years ago. It just brought back memories of all of our struggles and successes."

I said, "Did you ever get a chance to talk to her about her weight concerns?"

"No. Not like I wanted to. She just kind of blew the whole thing off, as if she didn't want to remember. I'll catch up to her about it."

I nodded. I said, "You know, when we first starting seeing each other, a few guys at my job figured that you would have turned me down because you were considered a white-collar woman."

Denise frowned and shook her head. "I never got into that kind of thing. I've had all that I could stand with that from Walter's father. He kind of reminds me never to be that way."

"So he was heavily into class systems?"

"*Was he?* He still *is*, but he's coming around. He's been hanging out with his son a lot lately. He got inspired after the Million Man March. I was surprised that he even wanted to go, as selfish as he is."

I smiled. I never participated in the march. I had a run to Arizona that week, and I stopped over to visit my sister in Tucson. I thought it was a good idea and everything, I just didn't go.

I thought about Denise and her sons, and asked, "Whatever made you name both of your sons after their fathers? I always wanted to ask you about that." We had never gone into detail about her past relationships. I had never pressed the issue either. I figured it would all come out in time, I just never realized how much time it would take.

She hunched her shoulders and answered, "I don't know. I guess I just didn't think about too many names. Name giving is usually something that a mother *and* a father participate in."

"Their fathers didn't participate at all?"

"Jimmy's father was very pleased with it. He was just upset about not having Jimmy spelled the same way as his."

"How does he spell his?"

"With an *i-e* at the end."

I frowned. "The *i*'s are generally how women spell their names. Like Toni with an *i* as opposed to Tony with a *y*."

Denise smiled. "Yeah, I know. But he didn't care. And Walter Perry didn't want me to name his son after him at all, especially not the last name. I did it anyway," she told me. "And it's sad, because I was vengeful at the time. I named Walter after his father in spite, just to let the man know that he could never forget about his son."

I smiled and shook my head. "How do you feel about them now?"

"I don't. I'm just happy that they both decided to come back into their sons' lives. That's about all that I can ask from them. I wish that it wasn't because of basketball and pigheadedness, but I'll take it any way that I can get it."

I nodded. "You know, you're unique in that way. It seems like a lot of mothers only want to deal with their children's fathers on *their* terms."

Denise disagreed with a strong head shake. "That's not the case. Many mothers just don't feel like putting out the extra effort that it takes to get the fathers involved. I mean, these deadbeat dads have to *want* to do it. So all of the blame shouldn't be put on the women. And you have to remember as well that in a lot of these single-parent households, the fathers were the ones who walked out to begin with. Or else they forced the women to leave because of the man's terrible behavior."

I thought about it. "Yeah, I guess that's right."

"It *is* right. But it's also wrong. I just wish that more of these brothers could learn to love themselves and others and stop being such cowards about it. Sometimes it's just about sharing time."

"So what's a mother supposed to do for money?" I asked her.

Denise sighed. "It's not an easy situation to even talk about. I just don't know what's going to happen when they do away with welfare," she said. "At our SMO meetings, we discussed the idea of the government figuring out a way to train uneducated and unskilled men who have children, so that they can offer them quality jobs to support their kids, and use that in place of the present welfare system that seems to reward poor women for having more children with absentee fathers. And then allow these mothers to find jobs, too."

I laughed at the idea. "Then what happens to the jobs for these guys and girls who busted their asses in college? Hmmph." I grunted. "That jobs-for-everybody idea only happens in socialistic countries, not in America."

"We're going to have to find a way somehow," she told me.

I responded, "Well, I figure that even when these fathers *don't* have the jobs or the income, the time that they *do* spend with their kids is time where the mothers don't have to pay for child care, especially if these fathers aren't doing anything else with their lives."

"Exactly," Denise agreed. "I've never been the type of mother to keep my kids away from their fathers, so they don't have a lot of the negative baggage that some of these kids have. But Walter used to have a real problem being with his father. They've been getting along a lot better lately. And it's just like I said, I'm very fortunate that they've both decided it's better late than never to spend time with their sons, despite how I feel about them, or how they feel about me."

After that, I asked Denise if she ever thought about moving into a larger house.

She smiled, catching on to my gigantic hint. "I guess I would have to think about that if I were going to include someone in the family."

I backed down and said, "I was just asking, you know."

"Yeah, I know," she responded. I guess she could tell that I was still a little gun-shy.

Then I got restless and asked her if she was hungry.

"I've been hungry ever since I walked in that door," she answered.

"Well, the food should be nice and ready to eat by now. Let's walk on over to the kitchen then. Shall we?"

Denise extended her hand and said, "You lead the way."

I helped her up and escorted her to the chair at my kitchen table. I rarely used the dining room unless I was having more than one or two people over to eat. I usually ate inside of the kitchen or in front of the tube.

"What kind of place did you and your wife live in again?" Denise asked me as we packed our plates with spaghetti, meatballs, corn, and buttered biscuits.

"A three-bedroom bungalow. It was nice, but very small," I told her. "In fact, this apartment has much more open space."

Denise nodded and said, "Yeah, some of those bungalows are nothing but a bunch of walls."

"Don't I know it."

We said a quick prayer and began to munch down our spaghetti.

Denise started to smile and then laugh.

"What's so funny?"

"I'm just remembering the face my mother had when you quoted from the Bible."

"Yeah, I wanted her to know that I was a God-fearing man."

"Are you really?"

"Yeah. Nobody wants to die without being saved by the Lord."

"Is that your translation of what it means to fear God, a fear of dying without being saved?"

"Yes, indeed," I answered.

"Well, if that's the case, then *everybody's* God-fearing, because I have *yet* to meet someone who doesn't want to be saved before they leave here."

"Oh, trust me, Denise, there's plenty of psychos who *really* don't care," I told her.

"I'm talking about people who we *know*, not Charles Manson types."

"Hell, I think even crazy Charles is scared of Him by now. He's had a long time to think about it."

Denise began to smile again. "Is God a Him?"

I smiled back at her, as we talked between mouthfuls of food.

"I guess that's just what people are used to calling Him." I shook my head at my goof. "See that, I've done it again."

"It doesn't bother me. Women actually refer to God as Him more than men do," Denise suggested.

"That's because women speak about God more than the men do in general. You can hardly get the average man to go to church, unless it's a funeral."

Denise laughed and had to stop to finish her food. "Why is that?" she asked me.

"That's easy. Most men are egotistical enough to believe that they control their own destiny."

"Don't we though?"

I swallowed my food before answering. "To a certain degree. But I guess men believe that they have a lot more control over the world than women do."

Denise nodded, still eating. "Mmm hmm," she mumbled. "And they do, just not as much as we *allow* them to have."

"That's true, too. People *allow* others to control."

Denise agreed. "It's changing though. More and more women are beginning to understand their own power."

I paused for a second. I had a thought on the power issue, but I wasn't sure if I wanted to bring it up or not. After thinking it over, I decided that I would.

"Do you think that this realization of women's power has been good for black people or bad? I mean, I can say that it's *definitely* been good for the sisters, but how has it affected the black community as a whole?" I really wanted an answer to that question. Because it seemed that the more black women amassed their own wealth and power, the less qualified black men were becoming, which led to more broken unions that could have been healthy families. I was still afraid to even ask my sister, "D. Brockenborough," if she had started dating white men in Tucson.

Denise nodded and raised an index finger as she finished her mouthful. "Camellia and I thought about that a lot, especially after starting up the Single Mothers' Organization. We kept hearing sisters say that brothers were intimidated by their success and willpower. Now, what are we supposed to do, act meek and giddy for these brothers? Fuck that! We have children to raise."

I broke out laughing. "That's the same thing I told Larry when *he* complained about it," I responded. "But that still doesn't answer the question of what happens to our community at the outset of all of these broken unions?"

Denise gave me a long stare. She said, "I see where you're going with this, and it ain't gonna work. I'm not going to tell sisters to stop moving forward and doing what they need to do because these brothers have ego problems. That's on them.

"What they *need* to do is shove their damn pride in their back pockets and learn how to stick it out with a sister who will support them," she said. "But *no!* All I hear are brothers talking about how the white man has his foot on their neck and how they can't get a break, and all that other bullshit, as if *we've* had it easy as black women.

"Now, we never talk about it much, because I'm not really into the class and money thing, but I make a little more than you do right now, and I'm a strong sister with two growing sons, and yet you're not intimidated by me. So what are your thoughts on your *own* situation? How come *you* were able to stick it out?"

I nodded. "Good question," I said. My answer to that was simple. "I look past all of that other stuff because I am really into you. So, I guess that would be my reason. I love you as a person too much to care about everything else."

Denise smiled and held my hand across the table. "Well, maybe that's the answer then. Maybe more brothers need to learn how to care more about the women they love and less about everything else that gets in the way."

"Hmmph," I grunted. "That's *much* easier said than done."

"Well, *you've* done it. And it's paid off. So you need to go out and spread the word about it."

I thought about that and started to laugh again. I was thinking about Larry on the job. "You know, Larry fell for a sister who has a newborn daughter, and he asked *me* for some advice on it. Can you believe that?"

I had talked to Denise about Larry a few times before.

"So, what did you tell him?"

"I told him to hang on in there and see what happens. And that's what he's been doing. So if *Larry* can make an about-face, then maybe that approach can work. Then again, brothers are gonna have to pick the right sisters to be into like that, because it won't work if something crazy happens. I mean, you're asking brothers to put an awful lot of trust in a sister."

"And what do you think brothers ask us to do? 'Have some faith in me, baby. Support your man. Trust me. Look out for me. Give me what I need when I need it. Don't give up on me, baby.' What's all of that about?" she asked me.

I laughed. Denise knew brothers too well. I said, "Okay, you've made your point. I can't argue with that."

"Trust goes both ways," she added. "Too many brothers take us for granted, and that's gonna have to stop. They're going to have to get motivated and start taking us seriously, because we don't have *time* to play. And more of these immature brothers need to wake up and stop complaining so much and try and take some control over their lives with a little responsibility.

"That's what I'm trying to teach my sons now," she said. "My little sister, too. You get what you work for in life. But too many of us are out here looking for freebies."

"Amen to that," I told her. By that point, I was stuffed. "You got any room left for ice cream? I know I sure don't."

Denise smiled. "Yeah, I could eat some ice cream. What kind do you have?"

"I have some Breyers strawberry, chocolate and vanilla, butter pecan, and coffee. *And* I have Klondike bars."

"Sounds like you have a lot," she commented with a laugh.

"Yeah, ice cream is my thing. I never was into cake and sweets."

"You could have fooled me," Denise joked.

"Watch out now," I warned her. "So, what is it gonna be?"

"Ah, give me a Klondike bar, I haven't had one of those in a while."

I stood up and began putting the food away. Then I pulled out two Klondike bars from the freezer.

"I thought you said you were too full for ice cream," I was reminded.

"Yeah, but not for a Klondike bar. I could eat five of them, and it wouldn't ruffle a feather."

"I see. Well, maybe you need to give me three then."

I broke out laughing. "You're serious?"

"Yeah, I'm serious. I'm still hungry," she told me with a grin.

"For food?"

"For whatever," she teased.

"Watch out now," I warned her again. I went back to the freezer to see how many Klondike bars I had left.

Denise said, "I don't need three of those things. Just give me one."

"Are you sure? Because I don't want you to go home thinking that I starved you."

"No, you didn't *starve* me, you just took my plate away too early."

Denise was on a roll that night. I said, "You're having a good time with this, hunh? Do you want some more spaghetti?"

"No, I'm just teasing, Dennis. But I *do* want a Klondike bar," she said with her hand out. She had her hand too low to be asking for ice cream. I started giggling like a kid who had a secret.

"Come on, now, give it to me," Denise insisted.

I said, "I'll give it to you all right."

We were both having some good and fresh fun.

"I hope I won't be hungry anymore after this," she said.

"Oh, you won't be. Not after I give you this Klondike bar." I set it in her hand gently, as if it could break.

She smiled and said, "Are you trying to send me a subliminal message with that?"

"Maybe I am."

"Well, it's working."

We shared another laugh as we worked on our Klondike bars and stared at each other hungrily.

"Would you like to dance when your food settles?" I asked her.

She frowned. "Where, at a club or something?"

I said, "No. I'm talking about right here on my waxed hardwood floors."

"Oh. I thought you were talking about going to a club or something. Because, shit, I ain't been to a club in years. What dances are they doing now anyway?"

"Beats me. The Butterfly was the last one that I knew about."

Denise looked at me and said, "Now, you know good and well we're too old to be out there opening and closing our legs on some sweaty dance floor."

"Age is just a number, baby."

"Yeah, but stiff bones ain't. And I haven't used mine like that in a good while."

"It's never too late," I told her.

"Oh, yes it is. When it comes to my body it is."

"You're not out of shape," I told her. "Your body looks damned good! And I *mean* that!"

"Hmmph," she grunted. "Don't let these curves fool you."

"It's already too late for that," I responded.

When we finished our chocolate-covered ice cream bars, I pulled Denise over to dance in my living room against her will.

"Dennis, you're gonna make me hurt something," she whined.

"Aww, don't tell me that the superwoman is afraid to dance. Please, don't tell me that," I teased.

"Okay, okay," she cried, finally giving in.

I went back over to my CD player and put in five seventies classic collections.

"Oh my God, you done lost your mind!" she hollered at me.

"Naw, now, the seventies had the best music! It's *Dance Fever* time, Momma."

She laughed and said, "Okay, Daddy-O. Whatever you say."

Denise turned out to have more energy than I thought she would. We must have danced through two CDs. I hadn't had that much fun in a while! But by the time we got to the third one, the slow songs just took over.

"If I didn't know any better, I would think that you were trying to seduce me," Denise commented. I was beginning to kiss her neck and fiddle with her earlobes.

"I guess you don't know any better then, because that's exactly what I'm doing."

The next thing I knew, Denise was squeezing my ass and smiling at me.

"Now what do you call that?" I asked her.

"I figured I'd give you some of your own medicine."

"We're seducing each other now? Is that it?"

"I guess so."

"Love T.K.O.," the classic from Teddy Pendergrass, came on, and Denise and I proceeded to wrestle tongues.

I paused for a second and looked into her eyes. "I'm not letting you go," I told her.

She smiled and said, "Well, don't." Then we went back to wrestling tongues and added the squeezing of hips.

I whispered, "Will you let me do what I want tonight?"

"It depends on what that is."

"Everything you could imagine."

"Everything? Hmmph. Not hardly," she doubted.

"You have some extras moves then. Is that it?"

"I may have a thing or two extra," she answered with a kiss.

"So, you've been holding back on me. When am I gonna get the full package?"

Denise burst out laughing. "The *full* package?"

"That's what I said." I slid a hand right up the side of her dress like a cobra reacting to a flute.

"I think something's on my thigh," she teased. "And now it's on my ass."

"Does that something feel good to you?"

"Maybe it does."

"So, what are you gonna do about it?"

She smiled. "Imagine what it's going to do next."

I slid my hand inside of her panty line. "What's it doing now?" I asked with a grin.

"Invading my privacy."

I laughed. "Is that so? Are you about to call the cops for trespassing?"

She shook her head. "No. I'm about to give this trespasser the scare of a lifetime."

Denise reached down and grabbed my crotch.

I said, "Oh. That seems more like the *thrill* of a lifetime."

"Not if he doesn't know what I'm going to do with it."

I started to smile and back out of range. "Say what?"

"Mmm hmm," Denise hummed. "See how easily I can scare him?"

"Yeah, well, you got that right," I told her.

Then she pulled my face to hers and kissed me with all tongue. Suddenly my ears stopped working. I could only taste, see, touch, and smell. And Denise tasted as good as she looked, felt, and smelled. It was all beautiful; two adults with the time, place, and peace of mind to fully enjoy each other's company. We stripped each other naked right there in the middle of the living room. Then we traveled to the bedroom, hand in hand, like a contemporary Adam and Eve, giggling at our naturalness, and were ready to enjoy what the Creator had given us to share.

Christmas Presents

I was riding the train in from work after eight in the morning on a cold day in December. I didn't mean to, but I happened to eavesdrop on a fat black man talking to a friend about buying Christmas presents for his five kids, and for his nieces and nephews.

"It's that time of the year, man. So every new year in January, I start off broke. I mean, you're looking at the real Santa Claus over here. And most of them damn toys are lost, broke, or forgotten about by summertime."

His tall, thin friend shook his head, pitying him. "I'd just stop doing it if I was you."

"I can't. Everybody's gotten used to it. I've been doing this for three years now."

"Yeah, well, they'd have to get *unused to it* if it was me," his friend responded.

My stop arrived, and I stood up to exit with Christmas presents on my mind. My first thought on the subject was that I would only buy things that would last for a while, or things that would definitely be used. I could thank my friend, "Mr. Real Santa Claus," for that. I didn't have any money to waste, and I was tired of being broke. It hadn't been just in the month of January for me, so I had to watch my money a lot more carefully, especially since I had begun splitting the rent money and grocery bills with Kim. Not to mention all of the intangible money that I was spending on entertaining Jamal and getting his hair cut. I was spending more money on him than I did on my own son.

Anyway, when I got back to the apartment, Kim was out taking Jamal to school. I looked around at the place and asked myself what might be a good house present to buy her. Or better yet, knowing Kim, she'd probably want a more personal item like a piece of jewelry or something. She didn't seem to wear much of it, and that was a good thing because I wouldn't have to think too hard about what to get her. So I planned on taking a trip to a jewelry store and pricing a few things. I didn't know what I would buy for Jamal. Maybe I'd ask him what he wanted first and pick the things that made the most sense. I planned to spend the most on my son. He deserved it. I hadn't been taking care of him in years. Maybe I'd buy him a nice sweatsuit and a pair of basketball shoes. The only thing was, with his school colors being green and gold, there weren't that many pairs of basketball shoes that would coordinate. I wanted him to use my shoes in his games without his colors clashing.

A pair of black-on-white Jordans would work, but those things cost a hundred and thirty dollars, *on sale!* But what the hell, I hadn't bought my son anything worthwhile for years. If I included a nice sweatsuit, we were talking well over two hundred dollars. Then I had to think about getting my mother something. She had put up with my irresponsibility for a long time and had never stopped supporting me. I guess that's what mothers are for. I *had* to buy my mother something. Then I thought about Little Jay's brother, Walter. Could I grab him a book bag or something, just so he won't feel left out? Then again, *his* father had plenty of money. Would he buy *my* son anything? So I changed my mind. And what about Neecy's truck-driver friend, would he be buying anything for her sons?

I got so wired up about the Christmas present thing that I could hardly sleep. It was weird, too, because I hadn't been into the spirit of Christmas since I was still a kid! Besides having a job to be able to *afford* Christmas, I guess you really have to care about other people in your life to give a shit. Christmas was about sharing. The way the Bible tells it, God shared his only son, and then Jesus laid down his life on the cross for all of humanity. However, for many years, I had only shared bad times and bad news. So I forced myself to write a Christmas list to work from when I woke up that afternoon.

• • •

When I woke up after three, Kim was getting ready for work, and smiling at me.

"What's so funny?" I asked her.

"Nothin'." She was still smiling when she said it.

I looked over at my Christmas list on the nightstand and figured it out. I said, "Kim, have you ever heard of the rules of Santa Claus?"

"The what?" she asked me.

"The rules of Santa Claus."

"No. What are they?" She started to grin.

"Rule number one says that you should never look at Santa Claus's list, otherwise, you don't get shit."

Kim started to laugh. She knew she had been busted. "So what's rule number two?"

"Rule number two says that you never open your present before Christmas."

She was tickled by the idea. I was just making the shit up as I went along. It all made sense though.

"And what's rule number three?"

"Rule number three says that you should never break your presents, lose them, or give them away. Because if you do, you don't get any for next Christmas."

"So you get a one-Christmas suspension?"

"That's right. And another rule is that you don't tell people what Santa's gonna get for them. So don't say anything to Jamal about it." I looked over at the clock. Jamal would be getting home soon. A neighbor's kid sometimes walked him in from school when Kim and I couldn't pick him up. Before I came into the picture, Kim's mother often arranged his pickup to her house. No wonder the woman didn't have a problem with me, I was lightening her load. She still watched Jamal on occasions, so it wasn't as if I was taking her grandchild away from her completely.

"I know what he wants already," Kim told me.

As soon as she finished her sentence, there was a knock on the door.

"That's him right now," I assumed. "Don't tell me what he wants. Let me ask him," I told his mother.

She went out and let him in. I climbed out of bed and made a trip to the bathroom. The Christmas idea was getting me excited. Imagine that. To buy all of the things that I planned on, it would take nearly a full paycheck. Somebody must have smacked me over the head with a baseball bat.

When I returned from the bathroom, Kim was still grinning away.

"You didn't do what I told you *not* to do, did you?" I was referring to Jamal and the Christmas list.

"No I didn't," Kim snapped at me.

"Good," I told her.

"Well, I'll see you two later on," she said, walking out the door.

It was just me and Jamal again. It had been that way for a couple of months. I was actually a full-time guardian. A father every day.

I said, "Jamal, I'm about to take a shower, and I want you to do your homework while I'm in there, because we have some runs to make today." I planned on visiting my mother, who was off work for the day, and then buying all the presents I needed, outside of Jamal's and his mother's. I would get those when Jamal wasn't with me.

"Do you want something to eat or drink before I take my shower?"

He nodded. "Yeah."

"All right. Come on then." I led him into the kitchen and made him a peanut butter and jelly sandwich and poured him some juice. "Now eat your sandwich, drink your juice, and do your homework," I told him.

"Where are we going?" he asked.

"You'll find out when we get there," I told him. Then I got out a change of underwear and a towel.

When I finished getting ready, I went over Jamal's homework to make sure he did everything. Once I got used to doing it, it got easier to remember. And at six years old, Jamal's homework was a breeze.

I nodded my head and said, "Good job. You just got one thing wrong." I pointed out his mistake to him.

He looked at it and said, "Oh," before making the correction with his pencil.

"When you take your test, you take your time, okay? Don't rush anything. That's when you make mistakes. And the more you rush, the more mistakes you can make."

I listened to myself talk and said, "Damn, that's a lesson for life."

Jamal looked at me and smiled. He knew what he wasn't supposed to say. I apologized to him anyway. His mother wasn't the only one who slipped with the language.

I called my mother and told her that Jamal and I were on our way. I had taken him over there a few times, so she was familiar with him. And she liked him.

"Are you two hungry?" she asked me.

I looked at Jamal and figured that a peanut butter and jelly sandwich wouldn't hold him long. I already knew that *I* was hungry. "Yeah, we're hungry," I answered.

"Okay, I'll have something ready when you get here."

"Thanks, Mom," I told her.

"And make sure you dress him properly."

I smiled. Once a mother always a mother. "I will, Mom. I'll make sure that I'm bundled up, too. See you soon."

As soon as we walked out the door and were on our way to the bus stop, I asked Jamal what he wanted for Christmas.

"A Sony Playstation," he answered excitedly.

I didn't know exactly what that was, but anything with Sony in front of it sounded expensive. "Is that a video game or something?"

"Yeah, it's a lot of them." Then he started naming things that I couldn't even repeat.

"Do they have basketball and football cartridges?"

"Um, I think so," he answered. He didn't seem too sure about it.

I remembered when my brothers and I had a video game called Intellivision. Intellivision had the best sports games ever! You could control nearly everything, and it had an infinite number of plays to choose from, not just a dozen or so like the new games that were out.

"Well, we'll see what Santa Claus can do," I told Jamal.

He smiled and said, "There's no such thing as Santa Claus."

People waiting at the bus stop with us began to laugh.

"Who told you that?" I asked him. "And if there's no Santa Claus, then where do all the toys come from." I was just asking to see how much he knew.

"Those toys come from the store."

"So they make them at the store? Or do the elves make them at the North Pole, and then ship them to the stores at nighttime with Rudolf and the rest of the reindeer?"

"Unt unh. There's no such thing as Rudolf. And reindeer don't fly," he told me.

"How do they get around then?"

"They run."

I was having a good time with him as the bus pulled up.

He said, "If reindeer could fly, then I would want to get one. Then we wouldn't have to ride buses."

People were really amused at how sharp he was. I was too, but I was getting used to it. Most kids were bright until people stopped challenging them. Then they would fall into a dark stage of destruction. I knew, because I was one of those kids. My dark stage didn't come until much later.

"He's really smart, isn't he?" an older woman asked me.

"All kids are," I told her. I wanted to think positive.

An older man nodded and agreed with me. "Mmm hmm," he mumbled. "They can use them smarts in the streets, *or* in the books. But most of them choose to use it out in the streets."

"Yeah, well, *this one* won't," I told the older man. I noticed that most people were more negative than positive when talking about a kid's future. It was almost as if we *expected* black kids to fuck up. That attitude was pissing me off! I wished someone would have told me that I could do anything when *I* was young. Even make the NBA if I wanted to. But most people thought of me as just a good high school player, and I fell right into their game.

By the time we made it over to my mother's, Jamal had fallen asleep. He usually took naps in the late afternoon because of the crazy schedule he was used to with his mother. As long as he didn't doze off in the classroom, I didn't have a problem with it. Kids needed more rest than adults anyway. A nap was good for him.

Jamal yawned as soon as he spoke to my mother.

"Oh, so you're tired, are you?" she said to him. "You can take a nap then. Take your shoes off and lay down on the couch. You can get something to eat when you're good and ready. Okay?"

It seemed like Mom treated Jamal better than she treated me. He took her suggestion, and stretched out on the comfortable couch.

I smiled at her and whispered while we entered the kitchen. "I don't know, Mom, it seems like you like him."

"I *do* like him. He's a nice, respectable boy. And I'm so glad that you're looking after him like you are. Him *and* Jimmy."

"Yeah, it just took me a long time to realize it, Mom. I can't start all over, but I can pick up where I left off, and that was basically nowhere. So I guess I have a whole lot of catching up to do."

"Well, at least you're *trying* to catch up. Some of these fathers are not even trying. It's just sad. Don't they know that their kids need them in their lives? What is wrong with these young fathers today?"

I felt guilty. Just a year ago, I was one of those young fathers, but I always cared about my son. I said, "It just takes some deep thinking and a lot of courage, Mom. A good job helps too," I added.

"Well, most of them don't even want to *look* for a job. A good job is not going to walk up and smack you in the face. You have to go out and *find* one."

I sat down at the small kitchen table as my mother fixed me some chicken and dumplings. She was a chicken and dumplings expert. Trust me! My eyes lit up. Jamal didn't know what he was missing.

When my mother sat down to join me, I noticed how everything had been scaled down. We used to have a big kitchen table when my brothers and father were still living. Suddenly, my meal didn't taste as good as it should have to me. Nevertheless, I tried to think of brighter things.

"So, Mom, what do you want for Christmas?" I asked, trying to get my mother as excited about it as I was.

She seemed to be in a daze for a moment. "I don't need anything for Christmas," she told me. "Besides," she added, "what *I* would want I can't possibly have."

Then it hit me that my mother was thinking about the absence of my brothers and father, too. Maybe that was why she was so happy to see me with Jimmy and Jamal. It served as a new beginning of bonding between a black man and his sons.

I looked into her eyes and decided to ask her the question I had been thinking about for months. "Hey, Mom . . . have you ever felt that we would all still be here if Dad was alive and healthy?"

My mother began to nod and rock back and forth in her chair. She said, "Every time things were going right, something would just go wrong. And every time your father would have the best job, he would get sick or injured. I always wondered what he had done to deserve so much bad luck. I ended up putting a lot of pressure on your older brother to help out, and we all just let *you* play basketball."

I thought back and remembered the arguments that my mother used to have with Marcus. They always seemed to calm down when I was around, and I always wondered what was going on. Maybe I was Mr. Special Son all along, because of my basketball skills and my father's enjoyment in watching me play.

"Boys need their fathers or somebody to look up to," my mother told me. "You remember how hurt you were when your father died?"

I nodded. "Yeah, I remember. I still do hurt. For *all* of us."

"But you had that extra eye from your father that your brothers never got. They didn't feel as hurt when he died. But you, it just changed your whole attitude about life. I saw the changes happening, but I was too busy trying to hold on to *all* of you to do anything about it. I couldn't give that special attention that your father gave you. And poor Neecy couldn't either."

She said, "I remember when your high school basketball coach called me. He was so concerned that you were losing your focus. You remember that?"

She was bringing up a lot of things that I wanted to forget. My high school coach had basically begged me to go to a junior college to gain a sense of maturity in the hopes of making it to the Division 1 level, but I looked at junior college as an admission of failure and didn't want to go.

"Yeah, I remember that, too," I told my mother, painfully.

"That's why I am so excited that you're sharing with these boys, because they're gonna need it. And not just for a couple of years, but until they are old enough to stand up on their own, as good men. You hear me? Boys *need* fathers! *All* of them! And I don't care if you're with their mothers or not!"

I raised a brow, and my mother went on to correct herself.

"It would be *nice* if you all were strong enough to make a decision about a girl and stick to it," she said. "But I can't *make* you do it. And just because you can't get along with the woman does not mean that you can't love the son. He's *your* flesh and blood. So I would *never* allow Denise to keep Jimmy away from you, no matter *how* wrong you were, because you still have the ability to do right.

"So if you want me to tell you what kind of Christmas present that *I* want, then here it is: you keep doing what you're doing with these boys. And you love them just the same, whether they can play basketball or not. So that when they get older, they can know what it means to be a responsible man who loves, cares, works hard, and tries his best to do what's right.

"You hear me, Jimmie? So let *that* be my Christmas present. For as long as I live."

I looked into the glassy brown eyes of my mother and nodded to her. "Okay," I told her. "I'll do that."

She nodded back to me and said, "Good, because that's all that I want."

I left my mother's house with Jamal, close to eight o'clock at night. By the time we would have made it to a store to buy anything, it would have been closing time.

I said, "Hey, Jamal, do you want to rent a movie?"

Of course he did. He said, "Yeah, *Alien Resurrection.*"

I smiled. "We can't rent that one yet. That just came out in the theaters."

"So when can we rent it?"

"Probably next summer. We can see it at the theater though. But not tonight. We'll go see it this weekend. All right? And maybe your mother will want to go. So pick another movie."

"Umm . . ."

I said, "I'll tell you what, we'll get to the video store *first* and let you pick what you want. But I don't know if I want you watching horror movies. You pick a comedy or something."

When we got to the video store, Jamal and I picked *Toy Story* together. I wanted to see that movie myself, because of the different kind of animation that they were using. We got back to the apartment after nine. Then I went and called my son.

"Hi, Denise. How's everything going?"

"Fine. And how are things going with you?"

"You won't hear me complainin'," I told her.

"That's good to hear. Complaining rarely leads to positive results anyway."

"Ain't that the truth," I told her. "Is my son around?"

"Of course he is."

"Can I talk to him?"

"Hold on," she told me. It was sad that I couldn't talk more to my son's mother, but that's just the way that things were. Neecy had become less worried about me visiting my son at her house, but I still didn't feel comfortable over there, so I chose not to. I figured it was best for us to keep a respectable distance.

Little Jay jumped on the phone and said, "What's up, Dad?"

"You tell me. I see your school plays Lewis Academy tomorrow. They have a pretty good team this year."

"Yeah, I know," he answered.

"What do you think y'all will do?"

"Well, we're gonna play to win. We haven't lost yet."

I smiled and nodded. My son's high school team was 6-0. "That's a good attitude to have," I told him. "So, what was your last test grade?"

"An eighty-four."

"In what subject?"

"Algebra."

"Did you find out how you went wrong?"

"Yeah, I could have gotten a ninety-two. I messed around and rushed a couple of problems."

I grinned. It's funny how right you can be once you start to use your head. I asked, "Were you running out of time when you answered them?"

"Naw, I just thought I knew it, and it turned out that I left out some things."

"Well, you know what you need to do on the next one then. If you get a ninety-six, it'll bring that eighty-four up to an A. That's how it works, right?"

"Yup."

"So how is school otherwise?"

"It's all right. I can't complain."

"Good. You got any girls chasing after you yet?"

He laughed and seemed hesitant to respond. We had talked about girls with no problem before, so I realized that something was up.

"Your mother's sitting right next to you?" I asked him.

"Yeah, sort of," he answered with another laugh.

I laughed with him. My mother was right. There were some things where fathers were able to relate to their sons, where mothers couldn't. Talking about girls was one of them. My mother was also right about choosing to be with a girl, and being strong enough to stick it out with her. That was a lesson I had to learn, among many others.

"All right, well, I'll see you after the game tomorrow," I told my son. "We'll talk about it then."

"All right then, Dad. I'll see you tomorrow."

Before I could hang up with him, I got curious. I asked, "Have you went all the way with a girl yet? All you have to answer is yes or no, and we'll go into detail about it tomorrow."

He answered, "Naw."

"Have you gotten close?"

"Not really."

"Have you *thought* about it?"

He laughed again. "Umm, yeah."

"Well, you know, take your time, man. And whatever you do, don't listen to those other guys, because a lot of them will lie about it. I've been through that stage myself. If a guy says he's had six girls, he's probably only had two," I told him with a chuckle.

Little Jay said, "I don't know about that." He sounded like he doubted my logic.

I smiled, and knew exactly who he was talking about. "That guy Speed is a senior. So don't try to compete with him. You hear me? Just play your game and do your scoring in basketball. Because if you hold out long enough, and don't get tied down, by the time you get in your twenties, you'll have the pick of the litter with women. Especially if you go pro. Oh, man!"

Little Jay burst out laughing again.

I started to envy the boy. I asked, "Has your mom started bugging you about it?"

"Of course."

"Did you tell her anything?"

"Yeah, but you know . . ."

I smiled. "You didn't have anything to tell her and you felt uncomfortable about it anyway," I said, filling in for him.

"Yup. That's it," he answered.

I could imagine. I was a young guy, too, once. The last thing you want to do is talk about girls with your mother until you're old enough to handle the embarrassment.

"Well, look, I'll see you tomorrow then. And hey, I love you, man," I told him.

"I love you, too."

When I hung up, I noticed that Jamal was eavesdropping on the conversation.

I said, "Come here, man."

He walked over to me. Then I grabbed him and spun him upside down. "I love you too, little man. You hear me?"

"*Yes*," he squealed through his giggles.

"You're my new little homey. And you leave them little girls alone, too. They'll be around for as long as you're living. Probably longer. They live longer than we do anyway."

He broke out laughing, trying to free himself. I let him go and sat him down on the couch next to me. I said, "Okay, let's shake on it."

Jamal extended his hand. I took it and pulled him into a bear hug. He broke out laughing again. Damn it felt good! I just wished that I was able to feel that fatherly love a long time ago. I wanted to stand up on a tall building and share it with the world. FATHERS, LEARN TO LOVE YOUR BOYS, AND YOUR DAUGHTERS! And the love that they'll give you back will be unconditional!

Bulls Tickets

I

BROCK

was giving Denise, myself, and her two sons an early Christmas present by taking us all out to the Chicago Bulls and Indiana Pacers game at the United Center. The tickets were an arm and a leg to get, but I figured they were well worth the price, especially with Larry Bird coaching the Pacers. Indiana, a longtime Chicago rival, would be fighting for the lead in the central division of the NBA, for home-court advantage in the play-offs. That meant more games for the United Center and Bulls fans, as well as national exposure and business opportunities for the city of Chicago. So I talked to a few contacts on the job and got in touch with a bookie/ticket salesman for a five-ticket package. They were some good seats, too, right at half-court! It doesn't get any better unless you're sitting at courtside. I invited my uncle William, my father's youngest brother, along with us.

Denise and her sons had already met my parents. Things went fairly well with them. My parents could see that Denise was a decent, hard-working woman, and that both of her sons were well cared for and respectful. Then Debra talked to Denise long-distance from Arizona. They clicked immediately. I was pleasantly surprised. My sister rarely had much to say to the women I'd dated in the past. She never considered any of them intelligent or independent enough, especially my ex-wife. I guess my sister *would* click with Denise. Actually, I expected as much. Denise was a real go-getter. My uncle William, however, was another story.

Mr. William Brockenborough never let my sister and me call him "Bill" or "Willie." It was always "Uncle William." He had aged well physically, but underneath his youthful energy, expression, and truth-telling speckles of gray hair, he was a cranky old man with a biting sense of humor. He also had five children, my first cousins, by three different women. He married and divorced two of them, and was still with the third, with no plans of getting married a third time. "I got too much life still left in me for another marriage," he liked to tell me. Maybe he wasn't the best example to have around Denise and her sons. Nevertheless, he was my family, just like Nikita was *her* family.

"Light 'em up!" my uncle hollered as soon as Michael Jordan got his first touch of the ball. He sat on the far right, next to Jimmy. Walter sat in the middle, and Denise and I were at the other end.

I had no idea how things were going to play themselves out. But I *did* know that my uncle William was a Jordan fan, like the rest of the sports world, while Denise seemed to despise Jordan because of his lack of interest in black community–related affairs. She felt that Jordan represented all that was wrong with blacks in sports in the nineties. Too many of them were shopping around for unlimited sponsorship and more money than they knew what to do with. Then they would spend the money recklessly, and only a few of them felt any responsibility to their communities.

I couldn't really argue with her about that, but I was still a supporter of sports. Maybe I did need to be a bit more concerned about black athletes. After all, they *were* children of the black community *before* college and *before* the pros. Denise had a damned good point!

"Shit!" my uncle commented. "That damn Reggie Miller shoots that ball like a machine gun! A damned Uzi!"

Jimmy and Walter were getting a kick out of him already. Most guys did. Women, for the most part, would much rather stay away from him. They never knew when he was about to say something inexcusable.

"This is one of the uncles you were telling me about?" Denise asked me on the sly.

"In the flesh," I told her with a smile.

She looked at me and frowned. "In the *mouth* would be more like it," she responded with a chuckle.

I laughed myself. Then I overheard my uncle asking Jimmy if he wanted to be like Mike.

"Naw, I'd rather be like me," Jimmy answered.

That brought a smile to his mother's face. "That's right. He doesn't have to '*be like Mike*' to play well. He can be *better* than Mike," Denise spoke up for her son.

I looked at her fearing that she had fallen into a more familiar man's game of trash talking.

"Better than Jordan, hunh?" my uncle responded with a nod. "So you want to be like Kobe Bryant then; that young blood who plays for the Lakers?"

"No, he said he wants to be like himself," Denise repeated.

I don't know what it was, but Uncle William always seemed to bring out the fire in women. I guess he just wasn't built for the new sisters of the nineties who had plenty to say and were not holding anything back.

"These young black men need to stop *following* other people anyway. Especially *Mr. Jordan*," Denise added. She was paying my uncle more attention than she was the game. That was to be expected though. Denise only agreed to go because she considered it a "family outing." I felt that she should try and make more of Jimmy's games in the future if she had the chance. I know I planned to, whether his biological father was there at the game or not. Why shouldn't I have an opportunity to see the boy play just because of his relationship with his father? I wasn't there to intervene. I just wanted to support him and enjoy his talents like anyone else.

Uncle William started looking around and responded, "You better stop talking about Jordan like that. These white folks'll mess around and kill you for that nigga. And I'm *not* just talking about the ones in Chicago.

"Some of these white folks'll let Jordan's sons marry their daughters," he said. Then he changed his mind. "Then again, I can't take it that far. You know how these white folks are. They don't even want *supernigga* blood in their genes."

I was embarrassed. Things were just about to get out of hand. I could feel it! Denise was already beginning to tense up. *Why did he have to go and use the "N" word in reference to Jordan in front of the same fanatic fans who he suggested would kill for the man?* I asked myself. But that was my uncle for you. He was full of nasty surprises.

I stood up and said, "Let's take a walk to the bathroom, Uncle William. You gotta take a smoke or something?" I wasn't sure if you could smoke inside the United Center, I was just saying anything that would work.

"Hell naw, I ain't going to no damn bathroom!" he snapped at me. "The game just started. I'll catch a smoke at halftime with the rest of the nicotine fiends."

I sat back down and shook my head. I could have forced my uncle to leave with me, but I didn't want to cause an even bigger scene.

Denise looked at me and smiled. "We all have 'em and it seems that we can't do anything about them," she told me. She was right about that, too. At least she found some humor in it. I guess the joke was on me this time.

I tried my best to ignore my uncle for the rest of the first half, praying for halftime to come so I could get him somewhere alone. I wanted to let him know that he couldn't always be so inconsiderate of others. I *did* offer him the ticket to join us at the game. I wanted to remind him of that.

"So, what position you think you'll play in the pros?" he asked Jimmy. "Small forward, like Scottie Pippen?"

Jimmy nodded. "Probably. It depends on how much more I grow, if I make it."

"If you *make it?*" Uncle William asked him. He said it as if it was the wrong attitude to have.

"That's what he said," Denise interjected. "Maybe he'll want to do something else with his life, like become a schoolteacher and *coach* basketball. That way, he'll have more commitment to the kids in his community."

Uncle William frowned at her. He said, "Shit, with the way these boys been getting paid to play basketball lately, he'll be able to *buy* a community, and then come back and coach high school basketball when he's done playing. Most coaches are over forty anyway. How long do you think his career is gonna last? Until he's *my* age?

"Shit, Kevin Garnett can barely drink a beer legally, and he signed for a hundred and twenty-six million dollars for seven years," he argued. "He ain't stepped *a foot* on a college campus! Now you're gonna tell me you'd rather your son teach at a high school! What kind of medicine are you on?!"

I jumped in and said, "That's enough, man."

Walter sat there in the middle of things and laughed at it all. He could see that tempers were beginning to fly. He considered it all to be quite humorous. Jimmy, on the other hand, didn't look so amused by it.

"Can you knock down the three pointer?" my uncle asked him.

"Not all the time," Jimmy answered grudgingly. He didn't bother to face him when he answered. I don't think he liked his mother being disrespected.

"Well, shit, nobody knocks 'em down all the time. But can you make 'em?"

Jimmy faced my uncle and said, "Yeah, I can make 'em." He looked two seconds away from telling him off. It was a good thing Jimmy was such an easygoing kid.

My uncle didn't even get the hint. "Good," he responded. "Because that's what you're gonna have to do to make the pros. Everybody who is somebody can shoot the three. Unless you get as big as Shaquille O'Neal," he commented.

He leaned forward in his seat to talk to Denise again. "How tall is his daddy?"

"Not tall enough for him to be seven foot," Denise snapped.

"Well, neither was Shaq's daddy. So how tall is he?"

"Shorter than his son."

Finally, Jimmy cut in and said, "I hate to be rude and all, but can we all watch the game."

"Exactly," I agreed with him.

"I am watching the game," my uncle commented. "I ain't missed nothing yet. I can do two things at once."

Jimmy began to shake his head. If he was less respectful, I'm sure he would have let my uncle have it, which was exactly what *I* was planning to do.

At halftime, the Indiana Pacers were up 47–43. Reggie Miller had 17 points for Indiana, and Michael Jordan had 17 points for Chicago. Scottie Pippen was on the bench in dress clothes, still out until further notice, while recovering from a foot injury he suffered during last season's finals.

I caught up to my uncle in the crowded hallway and pulled him aside before he could find a place to smoke. "Are you trying to make this difficult on purpose?" I asked him. "Why can't you just enjoy the game?"

He looked at me and said, "You watch who you're talking to like that. I know you're younger and stronger than me, but—"

"Would you just stop the bullshit for a minute?" I asked him sternly. "I invited you out here because I love you, man. And now you come out here and make a fool out of me in front of my lady and her sons. For what?"

He leaned back and smiled. He said, "You and your sister always got embarrassed too easily."

"This ain't about *embarrassment,* this is about *respect,*" I told him.

He asked, "Are you planning on marrying this girl?"

"What if I am?"

"Then we can talk about respect *after* your wedding."

"*No,* we're gonna talk about respect *right now.* Because that 'Poppa was a rollin' stone' shit ain't happening here. And disrespecting women so you can leave and make some new babies somewhere else is a sorry-ass way to live. That's why 'Poppa' left nothin' when he died."

I didn't mean to say all of that. Lord knows I didn't. But it came out of my mouth anyway, so it must have been meant to be said.

Uncle William looked me in the eye and asked, "So is that how you think of me?"

I wanted to back down and let him off the hook but I couldn't. Somebody needed to tell him about himself. I guess it had to be me.

"That's how I feel about you right now, yes," I answered him. "I love you, but you can't keep treating people like you do. It just ain't gonna work."

He nodded and stuck out his hand for me. I took it in mine.

He said, "Thanks for coming at me like a man about it, Dennis. You're a much better *man* than your father. He always went behind my back to say shit. But not you. You say it to my face, you *and* your sister. Now let me go catch a smoke before halftime is over."

I didn't know if he had just given me a compliment, or an insult to my father, or both. I was just happy that it was over with.

"All right then," I told him. "I'll see you back in the stands."

Denise and the boys had their laps filled with refreshments when I returned; pizza, hot dogs, sodas, chips. All I managed to come away with was some peanuts and a cup of beer. The lines were shorter.

"How did you get back so soon with food?" I asked them.

Walter said, "They opened up a new line as soon as we walked up."

"Shucks! I should have followed y'all then."

"Do you want some of this pizza?" Denise asked me. She had a giant slice of mushroom.

I said, "Naw, I'll try and get something on the way out." I never did like sharing food. It always seemed like a tease.

"Are you sure?" Her eyes had such genuine concern in them. A lot of brothers really read career-oriented sisters wrong. They just have to be less intimidated by them and give it a little time to see what was inside: a woman who wanted to be held and loved like any other. Nevertheless, I shook my head and turned her down.

Then she turned ice cold, the cold shoulder that simpleminded, impatient brothers got to see. "Suit yourself," she told me.

I laughed. *How can men stand themselves?* I wondered. We could be some of the coldest creatures on the planet, yet would cry like babies whenever we got some of our own medicine.

Denise noticed my permanent grin and asked me what I was thinking about.

"The difference between men and women."

She looked at me, wiped the pizza sauce from her lips, and said, "Oh." She didn't need to say any more than that. I wondered how couples did it myself sometimes. How exactly did men and women make it work with so many obvious differences?

Walter broke my train of thought when he asked, "Where's your uncle William?"

It was halfway through the third quarter by then. Denise and Jimmy seemed to be enjoying themselves a lot more without him. Walter had been enjoying his raw sense of humor, and his absence had totally slipped my mind.

"Oh, he's out catching a smoke," I said. Then I joked, "Maybe the smoke police arrested him."

We all shared a laugh. The no-smoking-in-public-places law was really taking America by storm. However, by the fourth quarter, I began to get worried. The Pacers were up by one, 67–66. The Bulls were on the move and the crowd could feel a comeback. The Bulls were a fourth-quarter team up against rookie coach Larry Bird. The United Center was really starting to rock.

Denise said, "That sure is a long smoke he's taking. He's missing the best part of the game."

I said, "You just read my mind." I wanted to go looking for him, but I didn't want to miss any of the big plays in the fourth quarter. "Maybe he's watching from somewhere else," I commented.

Denise smiled. I didn't have to wonder too hard about what she was thinking. Uncle William not being there to bother her and her son was a good thing. Nevertheless, when the game got down to the last three minutes, and there was still no sign of him, I began to worry. What if he really didn't like what I said to him and had left? Uncle William was known for leaving places he didn't feel comfortable in.

The Indiana Pacers were still holding on to a three-point lead. Reggie Miller had 27 points. Michael Jordan had 36 and was calling for the ball on every play.

I got really anxious and stood up from my seat. "This is ridiculous," I commented about my uncle's absence. I had spent some good money on those seats. "I'm gonna try and look for him," I told Denise.

She nodded. "We'll wait right here for you then," she told me.

As soon as I began to walk out of the arena, "Your Airness" hit a three-point shot to tie the game. Coach Larry Bird was shaking his head, and the Pacers called a time-out to regroup. I used the time to sprint out into the hallway to try and find my lost uncle during the break in the action.

The United Center was so huge that it was like trying to find a needle in a haystack. I watched the game on the television sets in the hallway as I walked and looked in vain. When it was all said and done, Michael Jordan scored 41 points and brought the Bulls back to defeat Larry Bird, like he couldn't do for most of his years in the 1980s, when Bird played for the powerful Boston Celtics. Reggie Miller, the lightning-quick, rail-thin jump shooter, scored 29 points in the 98–94 loss. The Bulls were able to squeak out the home victory, but overall, they weren't looking too good.

"They need Scottie Pippen back," Jimmy said as we walked to the car without my uncle.

"When is he coming back?" Walter asked his older brother.

"I don't know. They keep changing it," Jimmy answered. "One week he's almost ready, then the next week they're saying it'll be two to four *more* games. So I don't know *when* he's coming back."

"Yeah, foot and ankle injuries are hard to determine because they support all of your body's weight when standing, running, or jumping," I responded. "A busted knee or a sore back can do you in as well. But you rarely hear about upper-body injures keeping guys out too long. As soon as an arm, wrist, or shoulder heals, you're basically right back in the game."

"So, where do you think he is?" Denise asked me, referring to my uncle again.

I was trying my best to remain calm about it. Uncle William wasn't suicidal or anything. Maybe he just decided to ditch us and find more agreeable company, which was part of his problem. He could always find someone who would put up with all of his bull-s-h-i-t.

I said, "Well, he knows where the car is. We'll wait around for a few more minutes and see what happens."

We all climbed into the car and immediately turned the heat on. Walter sat in the middle of the backseat so that my uncle and Jimmy could stretch out their longer legs. Jimmy, of course, had to sit behind his mother on the passenger side, where she could push her bucket seat forward.

"Did you say something to him at halftime?" Denise finally asked me.

I nodded, feeling guilty about it. "Yeah, I did. And maybe he didn't take it too lightly."

"Oh," she responded again with a nod.

After waiting another ten minutes or so, we took one last drive through the parking lot, in search of my uncle, and came up empty.

"Are you okay?" Denise asked me at the end of the night. I dropped her and her sons off after grabbing a late bite to eat. I was just about to head for home.

"Yeah, I'm just going to find out what happened to him. Then I'll be all right."

"Okay. Well, call me if you need to talk about it."

"I sure will."

We gave each other a kiss and I headed on my way to Uncle William's. He knew his way home, so that was the first place I went, over to South Sixty-third Street. But when I got there, no one answered the door. I must have knocked on it five separate times and waited for twenty minutes. I just didn't want to give up.

When I got back to my apartment, I immediately called my father and told him what happened. He was in bed and had to climb out to talk to me. My mother didn't even want to hear it. Anything concerning Uncle William was the same old news.

My father said, "Son, listen here. William went back out and found himself a good time. Trust me. I've known him a lot longer than you have, and I've tried every which way to turn him around, but I finally had to realize that despite the fact he's my brother, some people were just born to be confused about life. And he's one of them.

"Now I'm going back to sleep," he told me. "And you can find your uncle at the same place and same time tomorrow. You hear me? Now go on and get some rest. It's after midnight."

I hung up with my father and told him that I would, but I was lying. I was about to sit up and think long and hard about my uncle. What had I said to him that was so hard to take, and that would drive him away from my company? He was a "rolling stone." He sang that Temptations song ever since I was a young teenager. However, my grandfather wasn't a "rolling stone," so where did *he* get that idea? I thought the Temptations were singing about how *not* to be. I guess my father was right about his baby brother; he was just meant to be confused.

Then I thought about my own life. *I* didn't want to be a "rolling stone." But what did I have to show for myself? I was damn-near forty, and I had no kids, no wife, and no future outside of trucking. So who would be at *my* funeral when *I* died, outside of my parents and my sister?

The concept of "family" was about establishing lifelong bonds with other families through the union of love, marriage, and children who shared that love, commitment, and loyalty to one another.

I couldn't lie and tell myself that the sharing of genetic information didn't make that love, commitment, and loyalty a little stronger, but love was love, commitment was commitment, and loyalty was loyalty. Like old high school friends, you never lose the feelings that you have for someone who was there for you throughout the years, even if he was a stepfather.

Hell, I hadn't even thought of that word much. Maybe because I never thought as strongly before about what I was about to question. *Why not ask Denise to marry me?* I had everything to gain: a woman who made her own money, two talented and respectful sons, and a family that could possibly love me as strongly as I loved them.

Sure, I knew that their fathers were back in the picture, for the meantime at least. But I was willing to be there full time and love their mother like she needed to be loved: unconditionally. You don't have a child with a woman then walk away. I could never understand that mentality from brothers. I guess that was because too many of them were sleeping around with women who they knew they would never marry. Or, they were simply being "rolling stones" themselves. At the end of their lives, many of these men would be loved by no one but their mothers and their confused, so-called friends, who lived the same empty lifestyles.

If you sleep on a moving bed too long, eventually you'll fall off and bust your ass. Any self-respecting family man would tell you to get where you were supposed to be in the first place, on a strong, stable bed.

So I was going to lead by example, stop thinking about it, and take action. I was going to go out, find myself a beautiful ring, take Denise out for a nice dinner, and ask her to marry me. My uncle William's running out on me that night was a blessing in disguise. He reminded me of the kind of man that I did *not* want to become: a "rolling stone."

Reconciliation

 ENISE was apprehensive about me calling to invite her out for lunch. Nevertheless, I felt I had to. It was nothing too fancy, just a bite to eat at whatever nearby cafeteria would suit her. With both of us working in the downtown Chicago vicinity, I figured it would be a snap to arrange.

Denise had already decided not to take Walter's junior high school to court over the incident inside of the schoolyard in September, and I agreed that it was the right decision to make. He didn't need that kind of a black eye on his school records nor on his character profile. He also didn't need the money, which was part of what I wanted to finally discuss with his mother.

I wanted to talk about our past relationship as well as our future as co-parents. Since my attorney, John Ford, had explained to me that gaining full custody of my son would be a risky campaign that would require a lot of patience, I felt it was imperative, in the meantime, that I reestablish a respectful relationship with his mother. In the past, I hadn't exactly been a respectful man to Denise, so Beverly and I both agreed that it was the right thing to do.

"And where would you want to meet?" Denise asked me.

It was slightly after ten on a Monday morning, two weeks before Christmas.

"It doesn't matter," I answered. "We could meet at any cafeteria downtown."

"How about at the Presidential Tower?"

"Okay, that sounds fine with me," I responded.

The Presidential Tower was at a central location downtown. I would have liked to have met her some place more private, where we could really talk, but I had no time for a tug-of-war, so I agreed to meet Denise at the cafeteria at one-thirty, and planned to take a longer lunch.

When I met Denise inside of the cafeteria at the Presidential Tower that afternoon, I actually had butterflies in my stomach. She was wearing a yellow suit, of all things. Since she worked for herself, I guess she had more freedom to wear what was really expressive of her. Her curves hadn't simmered off in more than ten years, and I hadn't once met her alone during that time. I had even sent her checks for my son through the mail, to avoid her as much as I could. I just couldn't believe how immature I had been. Yet there I was, years later, still feeling nervous about the emotions involved in meeting her alone.

As soon as we sat down at a table with our food, Denise smiled at me. "Let's handle ourselves like the two grown adults that we are," she told me. I guess she could sense my tension. Believe it or not, some of it was actually sexual.

I took a deep breath and said, "Denise, I want to start off by saying that I'm sorry for all of the terrible and insensitive years that I dragged you through with my son.

"I was an extremely selfish and immature man, and I want to apologize for that. It just wasn't right," I told her. "And I would like to start over again as a respectful man to you and a committed father to my son."

For the moment, I stopped there, and Denise just stared at me and nodded. She had selected a large cup of soup. I ordered a turkey salad that I probably wouldn't eat. I wasn't even hungry. My stomach was as tight as a coiled spring. I expected to have an all-out conversation with her, but maybe she didn't have that same idea in mind.

"Well, you have nothing to say?" I asked her.

Her cool demeanor was making it worse on me. "I accept your apology," she said. Then she sipped her water.

For whatever reason, I wasn't satisfied with her response. "That's it? You have nothing else to say about it?" I asked, pressing her for more conversation.

She smiled again and took a sip of her soup. She had this overwhelmingly smug attitude, as if everything in her life was going just fine. Better than fine. Splendid! And payback was a bitch!

When she spoke again, she was asking me how things were going with my wife.

"We're fine. How about you?" I began to taste-test my salad for the hell of it.

She nodded. "I'm fine, too."

The conversation was going absolutely nowhere. I got the feeling that Denise wanted it that way. She was in total control of the situation, and there was nothing I could do about it.

"Walter tells me that you're going to be having a baby soon. Congratulations. I'm happy for you."

When she said that, I didn't even want to look at her. I just felt so damn guilty. I forgot I wasn't hungry and began to eat more of my salad.

I nodded my head and mumbled, "Mmm hmm," with a mouthful of food.

"Don't choke yourself, Walter. That new baby will need you."

By that time, I was beginning to get a little peeved. I looked up and finished my mouthful. Then I asked her, "Why are you doing this? I came here to apologize to you, and now you're riding me into the dirt."

She didn't respond. She just stared at me again. It was the worst kind of torture that I could have gone through. At least a fired-up argument can get your juices flowing. With the way that Denise was acting, I didn't know whether to swing for my life or put my bat away completely. It was plain nerve-racking.

I finally smiled and shook my head. I asked, "Are we here to play a game of charades, or are we really going to talk about things?" I wasn't planning on having so much small talk. I was still waiting for us to pick up the pace of our conversation.

Denise took another sip of her soup and nodded to me. When she finished her spoonful, she said, "You invited me out to lunch, so what do you want to talk about? I'm listening."

Either she was fishing for something specific, or she was being a plain smart-ass. Either way, I was fed up and ready to leave! "You know what, I don't have to take this," I told her. I wiped my mouth and stood up from my chair. If she didn't want to talk, then I was definitely not planning on forcing her.

Denise shook her head and said, "Same old Walter."

I was stuck in my tracks. She was proving to me that I was still a selfish man who had to have everything his way, even when apologizing. I immediately realized it, but I still wanted to leave. I had to force myself to stay, and Denise wasn't going to make it easy for me.

"You can go ahead and leave if you want to," she told me. "I can enjoy my lunch alone. I've *been* doing it."

She was eating me alive! I sat back down and pleaded with her. "Why are you doing this to me? I'm trying my best to start over with you, Denise. Why are you making this so difficult?"

The more I said, the more she dug her claws in me.

"Oh, I'm sorry, Walter. I forgot that things come so easy for you. They can be very hard for the rest of us in the world, but we all find a way, somehow, to make do."

I asked, "Did you have this in mind when I told you I wanted to meet you for lunch today?"

She leveled with me. "Actually, no," she answered. "But after you apologized, I had to stop and think about how much I've been through. And a simple-ass apology can't even *begin* to express all of the pain that I've had to go through. So if you're *really* sorry, then you deal with how I *respond* to your apology."

She had a point, so I calmed down and conceded. Then she asked, "How are your parents doing?"

I immediately thought of my inheritance, and of Walter's stake in my estate. How exactly was I planning to break the news to Denise? I also thought of my father's nasty comments to my son at the house in Barrington. Maybe Walter had told his mother about the incident. Why wouldn't he tell her? It was quite a traumatic experience for him, and she was his mother.

"They're doing fine," I answered. Then I took another deep breath and added, "There's a lot that I never told you concerning my family. That's part of what I wanted to talk to you about."

She said, "I know. There's *plenty* you haven't told me. I was just trying to wait and see how long it would take you."

She *was* fishing for something. *She knows!* I told myself. "Okay, so tell me what you know then," I responded.

She took another sip of her water. "I know enough to make sure that I never have to pay for Walter's college tuition. And if something were to happen to me, I've made sure that he'll be set for the rest of his life."

I was offended by her insinuation. "You think I wouldn't continue to provide for my son? How *dare* you say that to me? I've been supporting him ever since he was born. You've *never* had to worry about Walter!"

"That still doesn't mean that you've done the right thing. Because, see, I didn't *need* your damn money for myself. But it's just sad that you would try and hide shit from me, as if the truth would never come out."

"Look, I didn't know what you wanted from me," I snapped. "It could have all been a setup from the very beginning."

Denise gave me another intense stare and didn't say a word. She was allowing me a chance to reflect on my own venom. I didn't mean to say that to her. I shook my head and apologized again. "I'm sorry I said that," I told her.

She nodded and said, "Mmm hmm, I understand. You didn't want no black woman and child to get in your way. So now you're all grown up and ready to start your *real* family, while you leave us on the side. And that kind of bullshit has *never* changed!" she snapped. "It's just like the white man not wanting to pay for slavery, so he leaves his illegitimate black babies all over the country to find their own way. Then he puts the mothers and children on welfare and *acts* as if that's a solution."

I said, "Well, if you feel that way, Denise, then why don't you give my son to me to raise?"

"Don't even think about it," she responded tartly. "I know that's what you've been *plotting* lately. *I know you!* That's why you took Walter back up to your parents' house in Barrington. But it's not going to work. Walter's not that young of a child anymore. He can see what's going on. And he knows where he belongs, too. And it's *not* with people who want to use him as some kind of damn chess pawn!"

Suddenly, I looked around and was embarrassed. We were two black professionals talking loud about our personal business in a crowded public place. I had to calm myself down again.

I said, "Denise, whether you want to believe me or not, I truly love my son. And *yes*, I would like to be with him more than I'm able to now . . ."

"*Why?*" she cut me off and asked. "Why all of a sudden?"

I wanted to answer her, but I stopped myself. I wanted Walter because it would make me feel like more of a father if I could raise him every day, like Denise had gotten a chance to do. However, I realized that would have been a selfish answer. Everything was still for my own benefit, and I didn't want to admit to it. The truth was, I couldn't stand to have her in my way, second-guessing my every move with him. I wanted to be the sole parent.

Denise looked at me and said, "That's exactly what I thought. You're the *same* old damn Walter."

I took a deep breath and was ready to leave again. I couldn't stand that she could read me so well, and I was disappointed in myself for being so obvious.

"Is there anything else you want to talk about?" Denise asked me, rubbing salt into my wounds.

"My son will get all that he deserves," I told her as I stood up from my chair. Then I added, "Maybe you need to be *more* concerned about Jimmy's father."

"Why, because you feel that you're better than him? You've always felt that way, haven't you? But at least J.D. didn't have to go to the Million Man March before he started to care."

I said, "Yeah, he just went to a couple of basketball games instead. My son told me all about it."

I walked out of that cafeteria feeling more concerned about my future with my son than when I walked in. Denise seemed to be able to draw out my worst behavior. We could not even have a ten-minute conversation without fireworks of some sort. I headed back to my office and couldn't concentrate for the rest of the day. I must have called my wife at least four times, and left two messages at her office to call me. She finally got back to me around four-thirty.

"So how did things go?" she asked me. "I'm sorry I couldn't call you back earlier, but I've had a real busy day today. These students are always waiting until the last minute to do things. I mean, they wait right up until Christmas Day, practically, to pay their darn bills. And a lot of them are *seniors!*"

Immediately, I had to be thoughtful. If I dismissed how Beverly's workday went to talk about my own rough day, then I would be proving Denise right again. So instead of falling into that trap, I joked and asked, "Is our baby still all right? Maybe we'll have an action kid for sure with all of this activity he or she's been getting."

"*She* or he's getting," Beverly said, correcting me. "I told you, it's a good thing for mothers to keep working. You wouldn't want to come home after I've been sitting around the house all day anyway."

"Oh, I believe you there," I responded. "You don't have to convince me of that."

"Okay, so tell me. How did things go with you and Denise?"

I sighed. "Not too well. She's more bitter than I thought she would be."

Beverly paused. "Oh," she said.

I wanted more of a response. I said, "What do you think about that?"

"Well, I'm not in her shoes, so I really can't say. She didn't accept your apology at all?"

"Yeah, she accepted it. Then she went on to beat me over the head about how hard it's been for her. It couldn't have been that hard. She still ended up becoming a successful woman."

I shouldn't have said that, but it was too late.

Beverly grunted. "Mmm. I hope you didn't take that kind of attitude to lunch with you."

Unfortunately, I guess that I had. I let out another long sigh. How much more did I have to learn about myself before I could become a man who really cared?

"Is there some kind of class I can take for male insensitivity?" I asked my wife.

"I can check around for you."

She sounded serious, so I asked her about it. "Are you serious? I was only kidding."

Beverly said, "Yes, I'm serious. They have counseling for a lot of different things. All you have to do is look them up."

Suddenly I felt like a nutcase. I tried to laugh it off. I said, "You don't really believe that I need some kind of counseling, do you? Am I *that* close to my father? I thought I was getting better. What about some kind of counseling for angry single moms. Do they have any of those?"

"Isn't Denise a member of a single mothers' club or something?" Beverly asked me.

I had forgotten all about it. "Yeah, well, I don't see what she's learning there," I responded. "I don't think they're trained professionals anyway."

Suddenly, my wife went silent on me. I couldn't seem to help myself. All I had to do was listen to my own words. How did Beverly even put up with me? Denise was right again. *How in the hell was I doing with my wife? Really?*

I said, "Beverly, I'm willing to do whatever I have to do to become a better man. So if you think that counseling will help me, then get me signed up."

She said, "Stop sounding so down about it. I bet when you get into a program, you'll find out that a lot of men felt the exact same way that you do about things. And it'll be filled with men who really want to make a change. You should be *proud* of that."

I sure didn't feel proud. I felt imperfect, as if I had a nagging disease that only professional help could cure. I was checking myself in for selfish manhood.

After her futile attempts to cheer me up, I hung up the phone with my wife and began to gather my things. I wondered if my white counterparts at the bank ever took counseling on how to treat black people, or if such a thing even existed. Sexism, racism, and classism seemed to be three unbreakable chains, not only in America, but around the world. So even if I did succeed in becoming more sensitive, I wondered how that would play itself out in the long run, and if it could change my productivity at the job, for better or for worse. In arenas that called for limited amounts of mercy, too much sensitivity could ultimately lead to a man's failure.

I sat back in my office chair on the seventeenth floor of the building and thought about my career while staring out at the Sears Tower again. I rarely even thought about my work. It was a blind drive, and I never really enjoyed it.

"Like father like son," I mumbled to myself. And it was the truth, so what else could I say?

Girl Talk

DENISE, I meant to call you last night, but I just got all caught up in the moment," Camellia was telling me. She was talking fast and excitedly. "Girl, my daughter finally went out and did it," she said. It was a quarter to eleven, Tuesday morning.

"Did what?" I asked. I still hadn't found the time to talk about Camellia's weight problem. She wouldn't slow down long enough for us to discuss it. Her feelings about her weight sure didn't stop her from being active. Or maybe some of her overactivity was about running away from her weight concerns.

She said, "Monica went out and had sex, despite everything I've been telling her."

I tried to stay levelheaded about it. I asked, "How do you know? Did she confess?"

"Yes, she did confess. And if she *didn't*, I would have been ready to *drag* it out of her."

"How did you find out? You didn't catch her in the act, did you?" Now *that* would have been a story to tell.

"Oh, Lord, no!" Camellia responded. "I wouldn't have been able to stomach that. Just knowing that she's *active* is heartache enough. Walking in on the act would have been like signing my death certificate."

"Well, did you ask if she protected herself?" I was prepared to take the discussion step-by-step, and I was already thinking about Jimmy.

Camellia said, "That's *besides* the point. And you would *never* guess who she did it with."

I started thinking crazy thoughts and had to stop myself. *Do I really want to know all of this?* Monica's partner didn't seem like any of my business, unless Jimmy was involved! I stopped breathing for a second. My mood was no longer even-tempered.

"Reverend Gray's son, Reuben," Camellia filled in.

I exhaled, but my heart was still racing. "Well, at least she picked a decent boy," I joked, once I knew that it wasn't *my* boy.

"How would you feel if Jimmy did it with one of the girls in the choir?" Camellia asked me.

"Which one?" I responded harshly.

We stopped and burst out laughing. I sounded just like a mother, a tough matchmaker. I felt sorry in advance for the first girl that Jimmy would bring to the house.

"Girl, this isn't funny," Camellia reminded me. "I'm bringing Monica to the meeting tomorrow night, and I hope that Selena shows up. Monica *needs* to meet her."

Poor Selena was nineteen with two kids, but I didn't see Monica fitting in *her* shoes. "I can't see Monica going down that road," I commented.

"Well, *I* couldn't see Monica losing her virginity at sixteen, but she did it."

I looked at my clock again. I had my third client of the day at eleven. A phoner. "We'll talk about it, but I have to get back to work now," I said.

"Okay, we'll talk," Camellia agreed.

"Lunch?"

"You name the place."

"Brenda's."

"One o'clock?"

"One o'clock it is."

"All right, I'll see you then."

I hung up the phone with my good friend and planned to talk to her about everything, including how she felt about men. We hadn't had a good girl talk in ages. Everything was about our children, parenting, educational programs, single-parent issues, etc. What it all boiled down to was that Camellia wasn't leaving any time to think about herself. However, I wanted to make sure I eased her into things instead of taking her right there. I didn't want to scare her away and force her to change the subject on me like she had done so many times in the past. So I met her at Brenda's Cafe under the downtown Loop at one, and began to talk about my own problems. Otherwise, Camellia would have controlled the entire conversation.

"You know I had lunch with Walter yesterday. We met over at the Presidential Tower for a half a minute," I said.

Camellia looked surprised. It totally threw her off. "Over at the Presidential Tower?" she asked. "What was up with that?"

"He wanted to apologize for all of the changes he's taken me through with our son."

"Mmm," Camellia grunted. The mission was accomplished. "So what did you say?"

"Well, after I started adding things up, he couldn't take it."

Camellia grinned and nodded. "That's always the truth. I guess they figure that just saying sorry is supposed to make our day and change a rainstorm to bright sunshine. But it doesn't quite work that way."

"So anyway," I continued, "he went ahead and did his usual thing and left early in a hissy fit."

Camellia just stared at me for a moment. "Well ain't that something. And he just asked you to go to lunch with him out of the blue?"

"Out of the blue," I told her. "What, Samuel has never—"

Camellia cut me off and said, "That man ain't even thinking about us."

I shook my head. In all of the years that we had known each other, and through all of the meetings we had organized for single mothers, Camellia still refused to talk about her high school sweetheart and the father of her two children, Samuel Woodson. It was as if he no longer existed. Nevertheless, the man still lived and breathed in Chicago!

"So, you've never even thought about calling him?"

Camellia was already shaking her head. She held out her hand and said, "Denise, we've been there and done that already. Now I have my own life to live, just like the rest of us single mothers."

"Well, I've never heard you tell the women who come out to our meetings that they should never hunt down the fathers. In fact, I've heard you tell a few people to go out and *make* those calls," I reminded her.

"And not *once* did I tell them to expect a miracle," she responded.

When our food arrived, I immediately thought about the weight problem again. Camellia was having a grilled chicken salad. I had a greasy cheeseburger with everything on it.

"I didn't know you thought so much about your weight," I commented. I tried my best to make it sound like the weather.

Camellia said, "I don't." She had forgotten all about filling me in on the details about her daughter's escapade with the preacher's son. That made me realize that it was the best time I'd probably have to get some answers from her. She was usually always focused on talking about *something*. Suddenly, *I* had the floor, and my plan was working better than expected.

I said, "You know, Camellia, I have never pressed you into talking about what went down, because I was there for a little bit of it, but it just seems like you're running away from a lot of things in your head, while claiming to be helping others. I mean, what about helping *you* for a change?"

"Help me to do what, Denise? Find a man?" she snapped. "I mean, I'm happy for you and Brock, but we already know that it's just not going to happen for all of us."

I nodded my head in agreement. "Okay, but does that mean that you just cut off the sensations in that part of your body? I mean," I leaned over the table to whisper, "don't you ever feel like you need one, or you *want* one? *Ever?*"

Camellia leaned back and started laughing. "Girl, you crazy!"

"Answer the question," I told her. It wasn't funny to me. I couldn't imagine not even *thinking* about sex, no matter *how* busy you were.

"Okay, of course I do. Is that what you want to hear?"

"I want to hear the truth," I said. I took a wild-ass guess and said, "Do you feel like no man is going to want you because of your kids and your weight?"

Camellia started eating her salad. Her silence was answer enough.

"You shouldn't feel that way," I told her.

She stopped and looked at me. "Denise, I can get a man into *bed* if I wanted to, but I just think that a relationship should be more than that."

"Well, you still have to seek them out to see. I mean, you're not going to attract anyone by closing yourself off."

"Denise, when the Lord feels the time is right, it'll happen. Okay? In the meantime, I have a sixteen-year-old daughter, who *doesn't* need to be there, no matter *who* it is that's there waiting for her."

That was it. Camellia had rediscovered her train of thought.

I thought fast and said, "If this were the nineteen forties or fifties, you'd be jumping for joy, saying that Monica was marrying a good man."

"But this is the nineties and I'm *not* jumping for joy."

"So whatever happened to getting married right away when you found out you loved someone?"

"It got old like the convertible Cadillac," Camellia answered without skipping a beat.

We fell out laughing.

I said, "Some people are still in love with those cars. Have you seen any of these California videos lately?"

"Yeah, I've seen those wannabe Mack Daddies a thousand times."

"You ever have those dreams where you saw yourself in a big family, and the lady of the house?" I asked her.

"Yeah, when I was eight. Every little girl has that dream," she told me with a chuckle. At least I got her away from talking about her daughter again, and I wanted to keep it going in that direction, *away* from Monica. Not that she didn't need to be discussed, but like I said, Camellia needed to talk about *Camellia*.

"You think that these young girls growing up in the nineties have those dreams?"

She stopped and thought about it. "I don't know," she said. "Maybe we need to ask some of them. Black History Month is right around the corner. Maybe we could go to a few schools this year and ask the little girls what they think about love."

Shit! I snapped to myself. If I knew Camellia, she was ready to brainstorm for the rest of our lunch hour concerning asking little black girls about love.

I said, "What do *you* think about love?" I was trying to see if my magic could work again.

"I think that love has become too easily given, and therefore, it's too easily taken away. And that's exactly what I need to tell my daughter. Because that high school sweetheart stuff doesn't happen anymore."

"It doesn't?" I questioned. "That's funny, because I hear a high school sweetheart story every day."

"And those people are exceptions, that's why we even talk about them. In the forties and fifties, as you've already said, it wouldn't have been anything special. But now we tend to celebrate the high school sweetheart stories, because we realize that it's hard to come by nowadays."

"We're still having *babies* by our high school sweethearts," I said with a laugh. It was sad but true.

."Yeah, and these guys are a lot less likely to have jobs, or houses, family support, or any of the strong foundations that we *used* to have."

"So what happened to those strong foundations?" I asked.

Camellia frowned at me and snapped, "Do I look like I know the answer to that? They stopped going to church. They stopped trying to get ahead. They stopped looking out for each other in the streets. And then they started watching these videos, and listening to this crazy music, and watching these hoochie mamas, and now they all want to go to Hollywood to be pimps and gangsters or play basketball or football to sign these hundred-million-dollar contracts with sneaker deals and everything else. And most of them don't understand that they *can't* all be millionaires, *especially* when *half* of them don't have any valuable skills for employment and many of them can barely read or write. So now they're walking around feeling sorry for themselves and don't want to commit to anything that takes any hard work, and then every time their little *pee-pees* get *hard*, they *expect* to be able to stick it somewhere warm and wet, and then jump up, pull up their little pants, and leave, whether there's a baby coming out or not, and then get *attitudes* about it as if that's *supposed* to be normal behavior!"

When Camellia finished with all of that, we looked at each other and laughed.

I said, "I guess you *do* know the answer then."

Camellia caught her breath and sipped her glass of water. "Well, we *all* know the answer as to *why*. The hard thing, though, is figuring out *what* we can do to change things for the better.

"I mean, we *all* know the numbers," she said. "More than *half* of the children being raised in the black community today are born to single-parent households. And that's just plain *treacherous!*"

All I could do was finish my food. Camellia had a lot more on her mind than I could have imagined. I felt that asking about her weight was petty after that. Her weight didn't mean a damn thing! This woman's *mind* was powerful, and if brothers were unattracted to that, then to hell with them!

After a while, though, I did come up with another question. "What kind of man do you think Levonne is going to be?" My sons had always been able to have at least a limited presence with their fathers. Levonne, however, wasn't that fortunate.

Camellia sighed. "You know, the whole sickle cell thing made me a bit overprotective with him. He's just now starting to assert himself more and come out of his shell, and Brock made a good suggestion about him being involved in sports. I think I might have to take him up on that. I never allowed him to play many sports because I was always so afraid of him getting hurt or something. But I'm going to have to get over that."

I said, "You know, this whole sports thing for boys is just really overrated. *Walter* even started talking about running track because his father talked to him about it."

"So, are you going to let him go out?"

"If he can keep his grades up. Yeah."

Camellia smiled at me. I knew exactly what she was thinking before she opened her mouth.

"They are *two* different boys," I told her. "Jimmy would fall apart if I took basketball from him. I mean, he gets his entire personality through his ability to play that game. And if he stopped playing, I don't know *what* would happen. I mean, yeah, it's sad, but it's the truth."

"So, with that attitude, you're actually adding to the cycle," Camellia argued.

I disagreed. "Not necessarily. Look at it this way," I said. "Let's say Jimmy gets a scholarship to college to play basketball. We can't assume what type of changes he'll go through. He's going through changes right now. Believe it or not, *his* father is starting to ask him about his grades, and Jimmy is actually paying attention. He's doing the best in his schoolwork right now that he's *ever* done. And I was really concerned about how he would do at this school because the pace is a little faster than most schools in Chicago, and Jimmy wasn't doing too well *there*."

Camellia smiled. She said, "I thought sports was overrated. It doesn't sound like it to me."

I smiled back. I guess I had gotten so tired of sports talk with my basketball phenom of a son that I was turned off by the entire fanatic atmosphere of it all. Nevertheless, I realized that sports were a vital part of my son's life and a source of motivation for young black boys whether we liked it or not.

I said, "On second thought, maybe you *should* let Levonne go out for a team. You just make sure you tell him that academics comes first."

Camellia grimaced. "Who do you think you're talking to, an amateur over here? No grades means no play. And I don't care *how* good he is. But my son is not good at anything yet, so I don't have to even worry about that. He'll just be playing for the fun of it."

I nodded and grinned. "Right up until he scores that first touchdown.

And after that, you'll have five and six girls calling your house a night: 'Can I speak to Levonne?' "

We laughed. Then Camellia asked me how many phone calls Jimmy received from girls.

"You know what, I don't think he's giving his number out, because I have *yet* to answer a phone call from a girl. Isn't that weird? I'm going to have to ask him about that. But you know what? I bet his father knows. And that shit eats me up! I do all the work for all these years, and he'll still go and tell his father things that he won't tell me."

"Boys will be boys," Camellia said with a smile.

I just wondered who was going to be a *man* for *her* boy. I had to admit, I was getting a much-needed hand from both of my sons' fathers, and from Brock. Despite all that I could do, and had done for my sons as a mother, there was just no substitute for the attention of a man.

Before heading to another SMO meeting at the library that night, I stopped by my mother's to see if I could talk Nikita into going again. I felt like I just couldn't afford to give up on her. However, when I got there, my mother told me that Nikita had a new job. I was skeptical to say the least. She hadn't said anything to me about it, but she had never told me much anyway.

"So she has you here watching Cheron again?" I asked my mother rhetorically.

"I don't mind. Cheron is good company."

My niece smiled up at me and said, "Hi." She was sitting in between my mother's legs, getting her hair greased and combed. She was very calm, too. I hated getting my hair greased and combed when I was young, and I'm talking about a lot older than three.

"Well, hi to you," I told her.

My mother would often read to my niece and even do her hair when she was in an active mood. I guess it was one of those nights.

I said, "Well, you fly to Florida next week, Mom. Are you looking forward to it?"

"I wanted to ask you about that," she said. "Are you going to be able to watch Cheron while I'm away?"

I felt offended. I don't know why. I didn't mind watching my niece, but my mother made it sound as if Cheron was *her* responsibility.

"I'll have to work that out with Nikita, since she has this new job and all," I answered sarcastically. I couldn't believe my mother was falling for it. Nikita was one lie after the other. Not just the men were acting up in the nineties, some of the women were losing their marbles, too. My little sister was living proof of that.

Since I had the extra time on my hands, I said, "Mom, when you're finished with Cheron's hair, we need to talk." Then I went and called my boys from the kitchen phone. "Jimmy didn't get home yet?" I asked Walter. It was close to six o'clock. Jimmy usually got home from basketball practice at five-thirty.

"Here he comes now," Walter answered.

"Put him on the phone."

"Hey, Mom."

"Hey. How are things going?"

"As far as what?"

"As far as school, homework, your life, anything. How is it going?"

"Oh. Fine."

I shook my head. "What's wrong, you can't talk to your mother anymore?"

"I didn't say that."

"Yes, you did. You say it every time you give me those one- and two-word answers."

"My fault. My life is doing fine, Mom. I love my life, and I love you, too."

"Watch yourself, boy," I warned him. "I know when I'm being buttered up, but it's still good to hear it," I told him with a smile. I wish they thought of telling me they loved me more often. I said, "I love you, too. And order some pizza with the money I left on my dresser. Okay?"

"All right."

"Okay, put Walter back on the phone."

"Walter!" Jimmy called. "Mom wants you."

"Yes," Walter answered.

"I've decided to let you run track this year, but only if you keep your grades up."

"When have my grades been down?" he asked me.

"You watch who you're talking to, boy," I warned him. I could see that both of them still needed my strong tongue-lashing every once in a while. I couldn't ever afford to let my sons slip away from my authority, whether their fathers were back in the picture or not. You respect your mother *first*, and then everything else will fall in line.

By the time I hung up the phone with my sons, my mother was finished with Cheron's hair.

"Are you ready to talk now?" I asked her.

She looked at me and grimaced as if I was bothering her. Cheron climbed onto the sofa to watch television. Mom stretched and stood up.

"Would you like some herbal tea?" she asked me, heading for the kitchen.

"Sure, I'll take some," I told her. I was getting ready for the "I'm so tired" speech that my mother often gave me whenever she didn't want to talk about something. She was as evasive as Camellia. I smiled at that. However, my mother always found time to watch Cheron.

I said, "Mom, are you absolutely *sure* that Nikita has a night job?" I had a hunch that my mother knew that my sister was lying, and she went along with it anyway. I needed to be able to understand why. Why did she keep doing it? Why did she keep letting Nikita get away with murder?

My mother ignored me while she put some water on for tea. Instead of answering my question, she asked me one of her own. "Have I ever told you about your two brothers?"

I gave her a long stare. "My what?"

"Your two brothers. Or at least, that's what your father called them."

My mother was throwing me for a loop. I said, "Mom, what are you talking about?"

She sat down at the kitchen table. I sat there with her.

"Have you ever wondered why Nikita was so much younger than you?"

I was six years Nikita's senior. I said, "I figured that it was odd, whenever I stopped to think about it, yeah." I had never bothered to ask, however. A little sister was a little sister. I did wonder about having brothers though. I think most sisters do, and vice versa.

"So what are you telling me, Mom, that I had two brothers in between?" I was just shooting from the hip, trying to find out what my mother was talking about.

"That's what your father thought," she answered me.

"Well, did I or didn't I? Why do you keep saying that's what my father thought? You had miscarriages?" I almost whispered it. I was so unprepared for that discussion. Where was my mother coming from with it?

She nodded to me and said, "Your father was so hurt. I had two miscarriages in a row. I think the second one was due to plain stress. Your father was just so hurt by the first one that he drank himself through the second one. And then Nikita came. By that time, your father was drinking nearly every day, believing that he was being punished for something."

"Just because you didn't have any boys?"

She didn't answer me. She just sat there at the kitchen table in silence until the teakettle blew.

I didn't know what to say. I wasn't too happy with my father, that was for sure. And I had never known about it.

"So, you're telling me that our father drank himself to death because he didn't have any male children? What if they were all girls? How did he know for sure that they were boys?" It just didn't make any sense to me.

My mother was busy preparing the tea. "It didn't matter what they were, that's just what your father thought."

"And how did you feel about that? Because I would have been pissed!" I told her. "I would have told him to get a damn grip!"

"I know you would have." She said it as if I was very different from her. And I was. My mother was a traditional, stand-by-your-man woman. I started off that way, but once my man didn't stand by me, that was all that I could take. I had been standing on my own ever since.

I said, "I can't believe you're telling me this." I was so frustrated that I didn't know what to do. I felt like cursing my father's grave. "So is that why you've been so sad all these years?" I asked my mother.

She said, "I just kept asking myself if there was something more that I could do to have a boy. I even asked the doctor about it."

"And what did he say?" I was curious.

"He said it was all a matter of chance."

"Well, the man carries the chromosomes for boys, right?" That part I *did* know.

"Yeah, that's what they told me," she said.

"It was something that *he* needed to do, not you, Mom!" I couldn't believe we were even having that discussion. Was I in a bad dream or what? It was just so unreal and unexpected.

My mother got angry at me and nearly spilled the tea. "Well, it didn't matter whose fault it was or who was supposed to do what, I'm just telling you what happened!" she snapped at me.

I calmed myself down and thought about it. I just felt so sad about it. I wished she hadn't told me. "So why are you telling me this now?" My voice was actually cracking. For years I had been trying to figure out what my mother's problem was. But to find out that my father had turned into an alcoholic because of miscarriages, and had devastated my mother for the rest of her life, was not the kind of answer that I was seeking. I was beginning to think that *all* men were terrible, no matter *what* era they were from.

"I wanted to tell you and your sister . . . I just didn't know how." My mother took a sip of her tea and passed me mine. I didn't even want it anymore. I didn't want anything. I just sat there thinking, and was crushed by my mother's revelation to me.

"So is that why you baby Nikita so much? You just gave up on her? Is that it? Because she wasn't a boy?" My eyes hadn't felt that heavy in years. They were flooded. I was actually crying, and I didn't realize it until the tears rolled from my face and dripped into my tea.

My mother just stared into empty space.

I wanted to say more, but I was so angry and hurt that I lost my voice for the moment. I believe I was more hurt than angry though. If I was angry, I wouldn't have cried. In fact, had it been *me*, I wouldn't have cried. I was crying for my mother, my sister, and for my father, wishing that they could have all been as strong as I had become. Then I was just overcome with grief, and started to cry harder. Imagine not crying for fourteen years and having it all pour out of you at once. Once I started, I wasn't able to stop the downpour of tears.

When I finally lifted my head again, my mother was comforting me as if *I* was the one who needed a helping hand.

"What's 'da matter?" my niece was asking me.

She looked as if she was ready to cry, and Cheron could cry at the drop of a hat.

I wiped my face and told her, "I'm okay. Aunt Neecy's okay. All right?" I found myself saying anything. It was no use though. Cheron was already starting to tear up, so I sat her on my lap and squeezed her like there was no tomorrow. As for my mother, I guess she didn't have any tears left. Who knows for how many days and nights she cried?

I don't remember how I managed to make it back home that night, but I had to, so I did. I was a virtual zombie for the entire SMO meeting. I just wanted to get back home to my sons. I didn't even have many words for Camellia and Monica that evening. I had to see my sons. I had to hug them. And I had to ask them if they loved me. That was all that I could think about.

"What's wrong, Mom?" Jimmy asked, defensively. He was at the age where he was ready to protect.

"Just hold me," I told him. I still hadn't regained my usual level of strength yet.

Walter asked, "What happened?"

I held both of them together. "Nothing happened."

"Something happened," Jimmy said. I could feel him tensing up in my arms. "Did somebody rob you or something, Mom?"

"No," I told him forcibly. "Nobody robbed me. I just—"

I lost my voice again, so I just shook my head.

Jimmy looked even more confused. "You just did what, Mom?"

"Jimmy, I'm okay," I told him.

"So why was you crying then?" Walter asked. I guess I didn't do such a good job of cleaning up my face that night. Since I wasn't used to wiping my own tears, maybe I didn't know how to. My sons were definitely not used to seeing me that way. It was scary for me, too.

"Do you two love your mother?" I asked them.

"Yeah," they told me.

"Well, just hold me then."

My sons held me, and I squeezed them into me, kissing their foreheads and rubbing their faces. Then I closed my eyes and said a silent prayer: *Dear God, I know there's no guarantees in life, but if I could have just one thing, just* one, *it would be that these two boys grow up to love black women the way they need to be loved. Is that so hard to do, God? Is that so hard to wish for? Because I don't know what else I can do. It's all in your hands. I give it up to you. All I can do is my best. And I'm going to make sure I keep trying until the day I die.*

February 1998

A Long Journey Home

T H E first game of the play-offs was in February. Little Jay's high school team had a record of 17-3, and they were seeded number six in a sixteen-team championship tournament. I was so excited for my son that I could hardly sleep that week. I could have put in sixteen straight hours of overtime at work without missing a beat. That's just how wired I was.

J . D .

"Come on, Jamal, let's go! We're running late!"

I was in a rush to get to the game, while Jamal was busy tying his shoelaces. I had bought him some new boots and a hooded coat during the after-Christmas sales. I didn't have much to offer when Little Jay was young. I was struggling just to clothe myself, get a bite to eat, and buy a dime bag of weed to ease my nerves. My son didn't need much with his mother's success as a businesswoman though, so I was giving a helping hand however I could.

The gym was jam-packed when Jamal and I arrived. We could hardly find a seat, and the first two minutes of the game had already gone by. Those suburban leagues don't play. They start the games on time, every time.

"Who scored for Belmont Creek?" I asked a high school–aged spectator.

"Ah, number forty-four scored twice," he told me. "Two of them were from the foul line. It's a pretty tough defensive game so far. They're trying to shut our shooter, Marc 'Speed' Wilkins, down."

I looked at the young guy again. Everybody sounded like scouts at them damn games! Whatever happened to watching the game for the fun of it?

"Who do they play next?" Jamal asked me.

"They have to win *this* game first," I told him. "Then we'll have to wait and see who else wins."

"What if they *don't* win?"

I smiled. "Then the season's over with."

"And they don't play no more games until next year?"

"That's right."

Jamal grimaced. He said, "Dag. So they *gotta* win." Then he asked, "How many games do they have to play to win the trophy?"

"Four."

"Do everybody on the team get trophies?"

"Wait a minute," I told him. I was trying to pay attention to the game. "Okay, what did you ask me?"

"I asked if everybody on the team get trophies if they win?"

I rubbed my chin and thought about it. "I think they get jackets and letters in high school, and the school gets the trophy. Players get trophies during the summer leagues."

"Can *I* play in the summer league?"

I turned and looked into Jamal's face. He was excited. "You wanna play in the summer league?" I asked him.

He nodded. "Yeah."

I nodded back to him. "All right then. We'll ask your mother about it when she gets home from work tonight."

The final score was 69–58. Little Jay scored 21 points and had plenty of rebounds and blocked shots. I didn't get all of his stats, I was just satisfied with the win and his strong contribution. Marc "Speed" Wilkins added 18 points and a couple of key steals on defense.

"Hi, Mr. J.D.," someone said. I looked around and faced Walter. He had been to a few of the games before, so I was used to seeing him there, but not with a bodyguard.

"Hey, Walter," I said to him with a hand on his shoulder. Then I nodded to his large friend. "You must be Brock," I assumed. Denise had told me he was no small man. He wasn't as tall as I was, but he did have size to him.

He held out his hand and smiled at me. "How are you doing, brother? That's a hell of a game your son has there."

I shook his hand and said, "Yeah, he worked hard on it, just like he worked hard this semester to get his grades up." Little Jay had a 3.1 GPA for the second semester, and I was making sure that everyone knew it, especially my boss, Roger Collinski. I don't know if he was doing it on purpose, but whenever I told him how well my son was doing in the league as a freshman, he would talk about his boy's excellence in academics *as well as* in sports. It got to the point where it seemed like we were competing against each other.

"Yeah, I heard," Denise's new friend responded.

"I hear you drive eighteen-wheelers." It just jumped out of my mouth. I didn't even think about it.

"That's what I do," he answered.

I backed down and said, "Yeah, I hear you, man. I move tons of paper around at night. As long as it pays the bills, right?"

"Actually, I've gotten a chance to travel quite a bit. You know, trucking takes you all around the country."

"Yeah, I bet it does."

He looked over to Jamal and asked me, "Is this your other son?"

I started to answer, then I stopped to think about it. I figured, *Why not ask Jamal?* I said, "Jamal, are you my son?"

I caught the little guy off guard. I almost wished that I could take that question back, but Jamal smiled and nodded his head anyway. "Yeah," he said. He reminded me of a little girl who had just agreed to having her first boyfriend.

I looked at Denise's new friend and said, "Yup, this is my other boy then." I was about to ask if Walter was his boy, but I knew better than that. The brother seemed pretty likable. There was no sense in making an enemy out of a guy who was just trying to be a part of Denise's life. I wouldn't feel too happy about Jamal's father sticking his nose into my business with Kim. In fact, I'd probably want to kick his ass if he had something smart to say to me. And in regards to his son, I *know* that Jamal liked me, but he never even talked about his real father. On the other hand, Little Jay always had a connection to me, so no man could have come in and established himself as a father figure with my boy, and that included Mr. Truck Driver. Nevertheless, I had nothing against the guy.

He said, "You think these guys can go all the way?"

He was talking basketball again. I guess he had the right idea. Basketball was safe common ground between us. Anything else could lead to embarrassment for either one of us. I didn't want him talking about his relationship with Denise any more than he wanted me talking about my son, or his lack of a son. Then again, I didn't know if he had kids or not.

I said, "Well, we'll see. You planning on being here?"

"If I can make it," he answered.

I didn't see the harm in it. The more support Little Jay could get in the stands, the better. Although, I didn't think he would need any extra support, because the students at Belmont Creek were already in his corner. They could clearly see that he was a rising star, and he was theirs for another three years.

Little Jay came out from the locker room and looked shocked to see me and his mother's friend together. I could tell right then that Mr. Truck Driver had simply popped up at the game. If Little Jay had been expecting him, he wouldn't have looked so surprised. Again, I didn't see any harm in it.

I made sure that I was the first to speak to my son, however. "Good game, man," I told him. "But it won't get any easier. The play-offs are step-up time."

Mr. Truck Driver nodded and remained in the background.

"Yeah, they couldn't handle our zone defense," Little Jay responded to me. Then he looked to Mr. Truck Driver and said, "Dad, this is Mr. Dennis Brockenborough, my mom's friend," as if we hadn't been standing there talking to each other.

I smiled. "Yeah, I just met him. He's an all-right guy. He wants to know if your team has what it takes to go all the way."

Little Jay smiled back. "I guess we'll see," he said.

I nodded and grinned. *Like father like son*, I thought to myself. "Yeah," I said, "that's exactly what I told him."

Jamal asked, "Little Jay, can I get trophies in the summer league?"

My son looked surprised. First he said, "It's *Big* Jay to you." Then he answered, "Yeah, you can get a lot of trophies in the summer leagues."

"Or, if your grades aren't right, you could end up in *summer school*," I added.

Walter overheard it and smiled. "I never been to summer school," he bragged.

"That's good," I told him. I really wanted to say, "So what?" Like father like son with him, too. That never-been-to-summer-school stuff sounded like something *his* father would say. Then again, what was so wrong with being proud of your schoolwork? I was sure proud of Little

Jay's grades, *and* Jamal's. I just wished I could have realized how important schoolwork was when I was their age.

Brock said, "Well, we'll see you later on, Jimmy."

Jamal looked confused. "Your real name is Jimmy?" he asked my son.

Little Jay nodded. "Yeah."

"Do they call you J.D., too?"

Sometimes kids can kill you with their innocence. They just don't realize what they're saying sometimes.

Little Jay looked at me and shook his head, but he never answered the question. He would have been a J.S., and that didn't even sound right.

"I'll see you at home, Little Jay," Walter said, teasing his older brother. Then he and his new bodyguard started heading out the door.

"You like him?" I asked my son, referring to Brock. It was obvious that Brock was around them enough.

Little Jay nodded. "Yeah, he's all right. What do *you* think?"

I smiled. My son didn't know how pleased I was for him to ask me my opinion. He really looked as if he cared, too. I loved it!

I said, "First of all, how does he treat your mother?"

"*Real* good," he answered.

I nodded. Jamal went and grabbed someone's ball and starting heaving it at the nearest basket. Little Jay began to laugh. I was standing there daydreaming. I thought about how it could have been if I had done right with his mother. I hated when I thought about that, because it was nothing that I could do to change things. I had even made an oath to call her Denise for my New Year's resolution, and so far I was doing a damn good job at it.

"Dag, he making them," my son told me, still watching Jamal.

I looked over at Jamal and watched him shooting and dribbling as others watched and marveled. He was not even seven, and he could shoot the ball over his head like a teenager. Many teenagers lacked the form that he had.

I shook my head and felt guilty again. What would have happened if Little Jay couldn't play basketball? Would I have cared as much as I did about him? Would I have been as involved? Denise had asked a good question.

I said, "Jay, have you ever felt that I was using you with this basketball thing?"

He looked at me as if I were drunk. "*Using me?* How?"

"You know, with my excitement for you playing basketball and all."

He smiled. "Naw. I mean, I'm not making any money off it, and I don't know if I will," he said. "If I don't make the pros, then I'm not going overseas to play. I'll just find something else to do."

I looked at my son and laughed. I was laughing because I was proud of him. He had a realistic perspective on things, and realism always helped people to focus.

I joked and said, "That's your mom talking, ain't it?"

"It's the truth though," he told me. "I got a long way to go before I start thinking about that. Right now I'm just thinking about the play-offs and school."

I said, "What about girls?"

"Oh, yeah," he said with a sly grin, "I meant to tell you; remember that girl I told you who was in my algebra class."

We had gotten a chance to talk more in detail about his social life. "The one who runs cross-country track?" I asked. She was the only girl he had mentioned.

Little Jay said, "Yeah."

I thought about my own relationship with Kim, but Kim was a sprinter. "What about her?" I asked him. I thought he was ready to tell me that he made it to home base with her. I had mixed emotions about that. On the one hand, as a guy, I thought it would have been nice to hear that my boy had scored, but as a father who had been through it all, I was terrified of my son getting some girl pregnant before he even graduated from high school. He *definitely* didn't need to go there. So I prepared myself for a detailed discussion about protection, traps, sexual responsibility, and everything else that I could think of.

"She wants to go see a movie with me this weekend."

I was relieved, so relieved that I broke out laughing. I said, "A movie, hunh? Well, you remember what I told you. You take your time. This is just a high school thing, so don't get too serious."

"Yeah, I know. My mom wants to meet her, too," he told me.

I smiled, imagining how Denise would act while I watched Jamal steal the basketball from another kid. "He's quick, ain't he?" I asked my son.

"Yeah, he looks like he got game already, especially for his age. He would probably make the six-year-old all-star team," Little Jay said with a laugh.

I jumped in with the fun. "Yeah, he probably has junior high school scouts watching him right now."

We shared another laugh. Then I got back to business. I said, "Taking this girl home to meet your mother is a good idea. I know you don't want to, but mothers are good judges of character. They can see things that we tend to take for granted, or just plain miss, especially if the girl looks good.

"Is this girl a winner or a beginner?" I asked him. "Winners are good to go, but beginners still need some work in the looks or in the attitude department."

Little Jay laughed and answered, "Oh, she's a winner. She's *definitely* a winner! I was surprised she even liked me."

"Why?"

He slowed down and thought about it. "Well, she's kind of smart. Her father's a doctor, and her mom's a dentist. I was thinking that she might just look at me as a basketball player and wouldn't want to talk to me.

"But once we started talking and all, I told her that I don't really walk around thinking about basketball all the time. You know, when I'm off the court, I'm just a regular guy. And she said that she could tell that I was humble. Then I told her that my mom wouldn't let me get a big head anyway."

"Yeah, your mom hasn't come to *any* of the games this year either," I mentioned.

"That's because she knows that you're gonna be here," he told me.

I said, "Damn. So, she don't even want to see me." My feelings were hurt.

Little Jay tried to explain himself. "Naw, I don't mean it like that, I'm just saying that she knows that you'll be here to cheer me on, that's all. She's not trying to avoid you or anything."

I felt a little better, but not all the way. I said, "Well, how do you feel about that? Don't you want your mom to come out to your games?"

He got quiet for a second. He said, "I think about it sometimes. But Mom is so busy doing so many things that a lot of times I just don't feel like bothering her about it."

"*Bothering her?* Shit, man, you're her *son*," I told him. Then I thought about my own neglect. "I oughta smack myself upside the head for not doing what *I* was supposed to do, but just because I'm back in the picture now, that doesn't mean that your mother shouldn't come out to see you at all. What the hell happened to her team spirit?"

Little Jay said, "She got burned out from having to lead by herself for too long."

I was shocked. I was surprised that he actually had an answer. I guess that he *would* have one since he had lived through it with her.

I broke down and said, "I'm sorry, man. If I could just—"

Little Jay shook it off and said, "Don't even worry about it. I'm doing all right. Especially now."

I said, "You think I had anything to do with that?"

"Oh, yeah. Definitely! Even my mom said it."

"She said what?" I asked. I wanted to know Denise Stewart's exact words. She didn't have many good things to say about *me*.

"She told me, 'I'm glad that you're able to reconnect with your father, because whether it's with basketball or not, you just have had a whole different attitude about things lately, and I'm actually jealous.'

"Then I kissed her forehead and said, 'Don't be jealous, Mom, you know I'll always love you. And if I ever get on TV, I'll do the same thing every other guy does: 'I love you, Mom!' Then she said, 'No you're not, because I'm gonna be in the stands.' And I told her that I was gonna say it anyway."

I smiled. Before my eyes, Little Jay was growing up, *fast!* He had more confidence about himself, he talked more, he carried himself with more authority, and he was very logical. I was just awed by him. Did I have anything to do with all of that? I still wasn't sure. Maybe I needed more confidence myself. When I looked at Jamal again, knocking down his final shot from nearly the foul line, I had my answer. I was a new man on a mission, and the rewards from dedicating myself to fatherhood were already paying off.

Marc "Speed" Wilkins walked over and shook my son's hand on his way out. "Good game, man. You're gonna have to do it again on Friday. It's gonna get tougher and tougher for me to score. Everybody's gonna be trying to shut me down, so you'll have to keep steppin' up. All right, freshman?"

Little Jay smiled. "Yeah, all right."

Then Speed nodded to me before he headed to the door.

A few other teammates and spectators spoke to my son on their way out. Then the head coach walked up to us.

"How are you doing, Mr. Daniels?" Coach Melecio was an old white guy in his fifties with plenty of gray hair and a trimmed mustache. He was Italian, with lots of youth and fire still in him.

I shook his hand and said, "Three more years, Coach. You think you'll get a state title before he graduates?"

The coach nodded. "It depends on the point guard situation," he told me. "We have another shooter who's a sophomore right now who's got more range than Speed, but our point guard play needs help." Then he looked at Little Jay. "But your son will definitely do *his* part."

"I know he will," I said.

Little Jay just smiled.

"And if he keeps his grades together, he's guaranteed a Division 1 free ride."

I nodded, but I hated those words "free ride." I'd rather use "scholarship," it sounded more established. That "free ride" shit sounded cheap. There wasn't a damn thing free about a scholarship! Those Division 1 colleges made you work your ass off to get them, *and* to keep them.

"Yeah, well, he's taking it one semester at a time," I told the coach. If I had my way, I'd have my son attend a school where the coach was a strong black man, like John Thompson at Georgetown, or John Chaney at Temple. There were a few other good black coaches out there, but Chaney and Thompson had been doing their thing for years. And it wasn't that I was particularly prejudiced, I just liked the connection that older black men had with younger black men, like fathers and sons or nephews and uncles. The world was about more than just basketball, and I felt that black men could relate to one another's strengths and struggles a lot more readily. Then again, there were plenty of older black men who I didn't relate to or learn anything from, while my boss and I got along just fine and talked about everything. He was an older white guy, and Polish, so maybe it didn't make a damn difference what color they were, just as long as they were men who were willing to care. My high school coach cared a lot about me, and he was a white guy, too.

Coach Melecio nodded. "Well, keep doing what you're doing, because this kid is seriously talented," he said with a hand on my son's shoulder.

I smiled and said, "Yeah, we figured that out already. It takes more than just talent to be the best, it takes a lot of hard work and a lot of practice. You hear me, Jamal?"

Jamal had rejoined us once the basketball was gone. He smiled and nodded.

The coach looked at him and asked, "So is he the next one?"

I responded, "Yeah, the next doctor, lawyer, or whatever he wants to be."

Coach said, "That's the right attitude to have. *My* son's a lawyer. My other son works in the movie industry out in Hollywood."

"Is that so?" I asked him. White folks always had something extra going on. I wanted to create that type of extra talent with my kids. We didn't have to necessarily play basketball or football. There were plenty of things young black men could learn how to do and be successful at.

I usually talked to my son in the gym until we were literally kicked out of the place, because it was cold outside. Sometimes I wished I had a car instead of having to catch trains, buses, and cabs, and whatnot, then we could just ride around and talk inside the car.

We all started walking toward the exit door.

Coach Melecio said, "I heard you played basketball for West Side in the early eighties."

I nodded. "Yeah, we lost a close one in the state tournament. I was heartbroken."

"Not everybody gets a chance to win the big game. It's just twelve kids out of hundreds, year after year."

I said, "You got that right." We walked out of the building and were smacked in the face by cold weather. I shook the coach's hand again and Little Jay, Jamal, and I headed on our way to the bus stop.

"I'm gonna have to get me a damn car," I told my boys. At the time, I didn't even have a valid driver's license. I hadn't had one for years. I just never took the time to go to the license offices to get one. I guess it was too many policemen around for comfort, but I would have to get over that to get myself a car.

We all got on the bus for a short ride. Little Jay was getting off after just five minutes. We would have walked him home if it was warmer out. Jamal and I had to ride to the blue line train, a twenty-five-minute ride.

I shook my son's hand and hugged him before he got off. "We'll see you Friday," I told him.

"Yeah," Jamal added.

"And tell your mom I said hi. Okay?"

"All right, I'll tell her."

I thought about my son, Jamal, and their futures for the rest of the ride home. I was very satisfied with the role that I was playing in their lives. If I went to church regularly, I would have testified on it. Being a father to a child was a good thing to be.

• • •

Jamal was so worn out from shooting baskets that night that he fell asleep on the train, and I had to carry him off. He went back to sleep as soon as we made it in. I laid him down in his room and immediately thought of calling Denise. I wanted to thank her again for letting me be a part of my son's life. She didn't have to do it, especially since I wasn't able to help out economically. I guess she realized that money wasn't all that fathers were there for.

"Hi, I heard they won their first play-off game today," she said to me. She actually sounded excited by it.

"Yeah, are you gonna be at the next one?" I asked her. I figured it was a long shot, but what the hell?

"Yeah, I'll be there. They all talked me into it."

I thought about her being there with Brock and Walter. I probably would have liked the idea more if she came alone. Then again, I wouldn't be alone, because Jamal would be with me. So I guess it was all a fantasy, a fantasy that I needed to forget about.

Denise asked, "You called to talk to Jimmy? He just started doing his homework."

I wanted to ask her if Brock had eaten with them, and if he was still there, but it was none of my business. "Actually, I called to talk to you," I told her.

"Oh," she said. There was a long silence on the phone, as if she wanted to ask me what I wanted to talk to her about, and she didn't have the heart to do it, which would have been rare.

I said, "I just wanted to thank you for not pushing me away from my son after all of these years. I mean, I know that you've done most of the work."

"*Most* of it?" she asked.

"Okay, *all* of it," I told her. She was still a tough-as-nails woman.

To my surprise, though, she chuckled. "No, I can't take all of the credit. Over these last few months, you've helped out a lot. I have to be honest about it. I kept thinking, *When is he gonna slack off?* but you never did."

"Yeah, at least not until basketball season is over with," I joked with her.

"Well, if that's the case," she said, "then you won't ever stop because that boy plays basketball all year round. And if he makes it to college with it, that'll be four more years, after the three that he has left in high school. And if you guys spend seven years together through all of those basketball seasons, then I really can't complain."

I had to slow her down for a second. I said, "Denise, it's not all about basketball. I've really had a chance to learn about my son's likes, dislikes, and tendencies as a teenager."

"I know," she told me. "I was just talking about that the other day. His work habits are really improving. He's just more focused and confident now."

"Exactly," I told her. "And I wanted to thank you again for allowing this to happen. I know I haven't been no saint, but no man *or* family is perfect, so we all have to find out a way to make it work."

"Amen to that," she told me. Then she caught me off guard. She asked, "What do you think would have happened if you and I had a daughter instead of a son?"

I had never even thought about that, or at least not for fifteen years. Once I had my son, that was it, and there was nothing to think about.

I thought fast and smiled. "Girls play basketball now too."

"Yeah, and I've noticed that a lot more mothers and little sisters are at those games as opposed to fathers and brothers."

"That's not true," I told her. "Their fathers are there right next to the mothers in the stands. How do you think a lot of these girls started playing ball?"

"Because they were interested in it. Jimmy didn't start playing basketball because of you."

She had a point there. I wasn't around Little Jay for most of the development in his game. In fact, he could teach *me* a few things.

I said, "Okay, you got me there. But I don't know what I would have done if we had a daughter."

"Mmm hmm," she grunted.

"What made you ask me that?"

"I was just curious about it," she said.

"Oh, there *is* a difference, if you want to know," I told her.

"Why? A child is a child."

"Yeah, well you tell that to China." I had watched a program on television where they talked about the Chinese literally killing girl babies to make room for boys in the families because girls were traditionally given away in marriages. In other words, if you had two daughters and both daughters were married off, then you'd end up without any kids. But if you had two sons, you would be gaining numbers.

Denise said, "This is *not* China."

I started to laugh. I said, "Well, you ask another man that question, and see what he says. Ask Brock. I met him at the game today," I told her.

"Yeah, I heard," she said, "and he feels the same way. But I guess it's normal for a man to relate to a boy, as long as he doesn't take things overboard."

"Well, again, I just wanted to say thanks," I told her. I didn't want to wear out my welcome, and it was better for my ego if *I* ended the conversation. I didn't expect to talk to her for that long anyway.

"How many times are you going to thank me?" she asked. "A son *should* be able to spend time with his father. I never stopped you from seeing him, you stopped yourself."

I nodded with the phone in hand. "Yeah, you're right," I told her.

"So stop making it seem like I did you a favor, because I didn't. I'm not that kind of mother. If I was, I would have taken your behind to court."

I chuckled, but the shit wasn't funny. "I guess that's what I'm thanking you for then."

"Well, if that's the case, then you *need* to thank me, because I can't sit here and say that I've never *thought* about it. I just knew you didn't have any money. But still, that was no excuse for you not to at least *try* to provide for your child, if we're going to talk about it. That's why single mothers are the lowest-income families today, not only because some of them are on welfare, but because it takes *two* incomes to survive in America."

"Not in your case," I told her.

"That's because I only have two children, and one has been taken care of since birth. Economically speaking, I only had to worry about one child."

Damn! I felt like crawling under a rock somewhere. But what was I supposed to do? "So how do we solve this problem, you know, of fathers who are broke?"

"Well, first of all, they're gonna have to stop getting in trouble with the law, because you can't get a job with a jail record."

"I know that's right," I agreed. "It took me *years* to find a stable one."

"They have to stop sleeping, unprotected, with women who they *don't* love and can't see themselves having children with," she added. "And then, they have to get motivated to be the so-called *man* of the house, and that does *not* mean just with attitude. If they want to complain so much about women doing what *they* have to do, then they need to start doing *more* so that they can still hold their heads up high without acting like assholes about who is doing what and making what."

I couldn't agree with her more. I had been thinking all of those same thoughts for the last five or six months. I had stepped up to the plate, and was no longer running away, complaining about my strikes like so many other brothers were doing. You just keep swinging until you start getting some good hits, but too many brothers were quitting altogether.

"I agree with you," I told Denise. What else could I say? It was the truth.

I don't know if she was expecting my agreement, because we suddenly had a long pause on the phone.

"I hear you've been raising another son," she finally said to me.

I smiled. I'm sure she knew that for a while. I never told Little Jay not to tell her, but after Brock popped up at the game, spotted me with Jamal, and posed the father question, I knew it would get right back to her.

I said, "Yeah, after getting back involved with raising Jimmy and liking it, I guess I got over my fear of raising kids."

"Is this Kim's son? His name is Jamal, right?"

I took a deep breath. Denise knew about Kim for a long time. She *used* to think that Kim's son was mine, but he wasn't.

"I remember you used to swear up and down that he was my kid," I reminded her.

"She *wanted* to have your kid," Denise reminded me.

"Yeah, she did, didn't she?"

"I always wondered how you were able to avoid that."

"It just wasn't meant to happen, I guess," I told her. "I mean, when things are meant to be, they're meant to be. And when they're not, they're not."

Denise sighed and said, "Yeah, that's just a bunch a B-S. I'm getting sick of people talking that stuff. That's why we have so many broken families now. 'It wasn't meant to be.' That's plain bullshit."

I chuckled. She was giving it to me straighter than an arrow. She was right again. I could have had a family with her. We could have *made it happen,* but I punked out, not because it wasn't meant to be, but because I didn't hold up my end of the bargain.

"It seems like a long, long time ago since we were together," I said to her. "The time just flew by."

"It didn't fly by fast *enough* for me."

I thought about Kim and Jamal before I moved in to live with them.

Things were a lot smoother with me there. "Yeah, I guess not," I told Denise.

"So, how are you liking this newfound father thing? Is it something you think you would promote?" she asked me.

She was reading my mind. I responded, "Definitely. I tell people about my two boys as much as I can now. My boss and I are having bragging competitions at work," I joked.

"What about *before* you came back into Jimmy's life?"

I grinned and shook my head. All I used to say beforehand was that I *had* a son. I really couldn't say too much about him then, because I didn't know much about him.

"I guess there wasn't much I could say back then," I answered.

"Well, I didn't give Jimmy enough attention myself when he was younger. That's why I was so fortunate that he liked playing basketball, because if he needed more personal attention like Walter did, I don't know *what* I would have done. Walter was a handful, and he still is. But he's starting to come around."

"How do he and his father get along?" I asked.

"They're doing much better than they used to, but it seems as if I have a harder time having a normal conversation with his father. I keep wanting to size him up when I talk to him. And I know it's wrong, but I can't help it."

I smiled. I thought that I was the only one she lambasted. I said, "I know exactly what he's feeling. Trust me."

"Well, do either one of you know how *I* feel, or how *I* felt? No, nor do you think about it. That's what makes my attitude about this entire thing worse, you two can't even see my point of view."

"What about *our* point of view?"

"What about it?"

"We have a story to tell in this thing, too. Nobody wants to listen to *our* story."

"Because the shit is weak, J.D.! Now don't get me started on that, okay? Because if you *really* want to let your story be told, then you come out to our next single mothers' meeting and tell *them*."

I could imagine the horror of that scene. It would have been a lynch mob. I started to laugh.

"Oh, don't laugh, because I don't see a damn thing funny about it! The only thing funny about this is that you would even *attempt* to think that your story held any kind of weight. You men just up and walk away from things. If it was a case where I had tried to trap you into something and take you to court for a bundle of money, that would be different, but that is *far* from the case here. So I don't want to hear *nothing* that you have to say. All I care about is that you are back in your son's life now, and on that note, I think it's time for me to go before my temperature gets too high."

I said, "Okay. Well, thanks for listening as long as you did."

"Don't mention it," she snapped at me.

I had worn out my welcome anyway, but right before I hung up the phone with her, I said, "One more question, and you don't have to answer it if you don't want to, but what do you think about your relationship with Brock?" I was still curious about that.

"That's none of your business," she told me.

"You asked me about Kim."

"No I did not. I only asked if you were involved with raising her son."

"Oh, yeah," I said, backing off. "Well, that must mean that your relationship with him is not perfect, because if it was, you would probably want to brag about it." I just couldn't leave it alone.

Denise said, "Try that reverse psychology stuff somewhere else, okay. I get enough of that from Walter's father."

"I'm not like him," I told her.

"No, but you *are* a man, a *black man*, who had a son with a supportive black woman, and you *didn't* try to marry her and make a family."

Shit! I thought to myself. I don't know why I kept trying to get to her. I guess only my mother could do it. Denise ripped me to pieces every time. All of a sudden, the name "Neecy" didn't even fit her anymore.

"Well, it's been nice talking to you, but I have things to do. Okay? I'll tell your son that you called."

When she hung up, I just held the phone in my hand and shook my head. I remember when Denise would worship the ground that I walked on. I was her first and only love for nearly five years, then it all just faded away. From an outside point of view, someone would wonder how I was able to get with her in the first place. She seemed light-years ahead of me. Nevertheless, she was dating a truck driver and couldn't stand Walter Perry, Mr. Money Banks. I guess it really didn't matter what a brother had, but more so how he treated her. Then again, with some sisters it was the exact opposite.

Little Jay said that Brock treated his mother *"real* good." I guess he was telling the truth, because Brock had the keys to her castle.

I walked around the apartment and looked at all of Kim's photos. She was a good-looking sister. She could look even better if she applied herself. Maybe I could buy her a few things and freshen up her wardrobe and appearance. She was a beginner that I could easily take to winner status, and she had been in my face for a straight half a year, bad breath in the morning and all. I sat there and laughed about it. But before I could work on her, I wanted to save up to buy a car.

I walked into Jamal's room and gave him another look. He was balled up like a snail. He wasn't my biological son, but I sure felt close to him. I realized that he could make me really proud one day.

I walked back out into the living room and took a seat on the couch. It was just after nine, and the University of Illinois was playing Cincinnati on ESPN. I sat there and watched the game while thinking about myself, Kim, and Jamal.

What if I did marry Kim? I thought. Then I shook it off. "Naw, she'd probably get too happy, and then shit would start changing too much around here," I told myself. Women get married and start expecting the world. I liked things just the way they were. But what about having another kid? A daughter. We didn't necessarily have to get married, as long as we were a family.

I called Kim at work just to ask her about it. What can I say, I felt hyper that night.

"What's wrong?" she picked up the phone and asked me.

"Why you always think something's wrong?"

"Well, it's almost time for me to get off, so if you couldn't wait, then it must be an emergency."

"Well, you're wrong."

She said, "You just called to tell me you love me then?"

I grinned and decided to humor her. "Yeah, that's it," I told her.

"You do?"

She was taking it seriously. I grunted, "Hunh?" as if I didn't know what she was talking about.

"You really love me, or do you just love my son?"

"Why can't I love both of y'all? It shouldn't be a competition thing. I don't see it that way."

"So you really love me then?" she asked again.

She was, as they say, fixated on the word. I asked her, "How many times are you gonna say that? You never told me that you loved me."

"Of course I do," she told me. She said it as if she had been waiting to tell me for ages.

"I didn't ask you, I was just stating the fact."

"Well, I do love you. And I know you haven't asked me to marry you or anything, but I love what you've done with my son, and I love how you've given purpose to his life, and to *my* life." Because of me, Kim's New Year's resolution was to stop smoking weed. She said that I could help her out with it by keeping her stress level down. That was going to be a real challenge. Kim got stressed about everything.

I said, "Wait a minute, slow down with all that. You're supposed to give purpose to your *own* life."

"Why don't you take off from work tonight?" she asked, ignoring me.

She had asked me that before, and I had turned her down. I actually liked going to work, and hadn't missed one night in seven months.

"Why?" I asked her.

"Well, I'm at work right now, and we really need to talk about things. You know we didn't do much for Valentine's Day."

I smiled. "Yeah, what about it?" You can send a woman hearts and flowers any day. Valentine's Day was a pain in the ass if you asked me. It was three times worse than Christmas. All that buildup and red shit for one day. At least Christmas was an entire season. But some women went as far as to break off entire relationships for Valentine's Day expectations and disappointments. That didn't make much sense at all.

"I just wanted to come home and hold you and my son tonight. Is that too much to ask?"

"And what about if you start wanting to do this *every* night?"

"Come on now, I know better than that. Besides, you haven't taken off *any* days from work. Don't you get vacation time or something?"

I hadn't been on one job long enough to even think about a vacation. My vacations had been getting laid off and fired. I said, "Yeah, you got a point there. Other guys are taking vacations. The boss even took one with his family in January."

"Yeah, so he shouldn't be mad at you for taking off *one night.*"

"But I still have to let him know in advance," I told her.

"Do you get any sick days or anything?"

I thought about my father. "Sick days to me are like a curse. I ain't sick, and I never want to be sick."

"A lot of other people aren't either, but if you're going to get paid for it, then take advantage of it."

Kim was talking about starting a lot of bad habits.

She said, "Well, I gotta get back to work. Just think about it, okay?"

I hadn't even gotten a chance to ask her what I had called for. "Damn, do you even want to know what I called for?" I snapped at her.

"Oh, what, besides to say that you love me?"

"I called to ask you what you thought about having a little girl or something."

"You mean like a baby?" Her voice elevated into a squeal. I was nervous to repeat it but I did it anyway.

"Yeah, like a baby girl," I told her.

"Oh my God! You're gonna make me get hollered at."

"Well, tell them this is an emergency like you said."

She whispered and said, "You know my tubes are tied."

"You can get them *untied*, right?" I asked her.

She said, "I don't believe that you're asking me this. And why a girl?"

"I just figured it would be something different from raising boys, you know."

"Now see, we *definitely* have to talk tonight! Call your job right now!"

"We can talk about this in the morning."

"No we can't either. If you wanted to talk about this in the morning, then you should have waited until the morning to ask me. But no, you called me on the job, so it must have been on your mind."

I had gotten myself in trouble. I said, "You know what, you get back to work and I'll see what I can do."

"Don't be lying to me, because I'm gonna be *real* disappointed if you do. Don't get me all worked up for nothing. You told me you don't want me to smoke anymore, right?"

"All right, well, let me make this call then," I told her.

"You promise?"

I shook my head and smiled. I really pushed Kim's excitement button that night. She was showing how much she felt for me. I guess single mothers *can* open up when they feel like it. I wondered how it was with Denise and Brock. Did she get that excited for him? I had to get her off my damn mind!

I said, "Kim, I promise. Okay? Now let me call the man."

"Okay, well, I'll see you in another hour then."

I hung up the phone and wondered what I had just gotten myself into. It was nearly ten o'clock. How was I going to call off just two hours before work? I didn't want to start any bad habits, but I had promised Kim that I would see, so I called Roger at his home anyway. Hopefully, he hadn't left yet.

"Hello," he answered. His voice was direct and distinctive.

"Hey, Roger, it's Jimmie Daniels. I may need a favor from you."

"What's that?" he asked.

I figured I'd take the honest route. I said, "You know I haven't asked for a night off in seven months, and I know this is short notice and all, but I have some pressing family issues that came up tonight that I may need to straighten out right away."

"It's not anything with your son, is it? He didn't get in any trouble, did he?" He sounded really concerned. At the same time, he was expecting the worst like so many others expected.

I was proud to say, "No, it doesn't have anything to do with him, I'm talking about the immediate family that I live with. We want to talk about our future together without always putting things off, because she works during the day, and then we work during the night. And you know, it's in the heat of the moment and all, so I understand if you can't—"

"Go ahead and take it," he said, cutting me off. "You're right, you haven't taken any days off yet. And it is short notice, but I'll let it slide this time. I like the fact that you're being honest with me instead of making up something. I know when guys are making up stories. I've been a manager for a long time, and I've heard them all. But during the first few months of the new year, a lot of young families have to rethink things. So this sounds like a legitimate concern. A man with family concerns that are not taken care of will eventually become a stressful worker who can't perform well on the job.

"So you go ahead and take off tonight and I'll see you tomorrow."

I didn't know what to say. I was shocked! I said, "Thanks, Roger. Thanks a lot!"

"Don't mention it, just stay on track with your family," he told me. "The family is the cornerstone of America. You make sure you remember that. A man's family comes first not just some of the time, but *all* of the time."

"Well, I'll see you tomorrow then. Eleven-thirty sharp."

"Don't be late," he joked.

"No sir," I responded.

When I hung up the phone, I sat back and relaxed like there was no tomorrow. After working for a straight seven months of night shifts, I had no idea how much a simple night off was needed. But I didn't plan on overdoing it. I'd be right back at work tomorrow, and the next day, and the next day. I was getting too old to fuck up again. I would be turning thirty-five on March second, and I planned to enjoy it like a grown man with a secure future.

I called Kim back and told her the good news.

She whispered, "Baby, we're gonna have a *lonnng* night tonight. You hear me? I can't *wait* to get home."

Jamal was back up and wiping out his eyes. I gave him the phone to cool his mother off.

He said, "Hi, Mom. They won the game again. And J.D. said I could play in the summer leagues."

He listened for a second and gave the phone back to me.

"He just woke up?" she asked me.

"You can tell?"

"Yeah, I can tell. What's this summer league about?"

"Basketball."

"They start that early? He's only turning seven."

"Yeah," I told her. I wasn't even sure, I just figured that they would.

"Mmm hmm. So *if* we have a daughter, I guess you're gonna be basketball crazy with her too, right?"

"Naw," I answered with a smile. "She'll probably run track."

Kim chuckled and said, "I have to get back to work. I'll see you two when I get in tonight."

"All right then."

I hung up the phone and started thinking about fixing Jamal something to eat. I asked, "How would you like to have a little sister?"

He smiled and hunched his shoulders. "I don't know."

I said, "Would you rather have a little brother?"

"Yeah." He was much more excited about that.

I asked him why.

"Because, I can play with him rough and stuff."

"Well, who said that girls weren't rough?"

He grimaced.

"You don't have to play rough all the time anyway. I used to be rough all the time, and sometimes it doesn't pay to be rough. Sometimes being rough can get you in trouble and send you to terrible places.

"Do you know what jail is?"

He nodded his head. "That's when they lock you up in bars and slide your food through a window."

I started laughing but it was no joking matter. I asked, "Do you ever want to go there?"

He grimaced again and shook his head like crazy. "No!"

"Good," I told him. "So stop thinking about being rough all the time.

A little sister would be good for you. Do you see me acting rough with your mother?"

"No."

"That's right. A good man *talks* to a woman; he doesn't rough her up. You hear me?"

He nodded his head again.

"Good. Now what do you want to eat tonight?"

"Cereal."

I smiled at him and shook my head. "Naw, man, you don't get any cereal at night, you eat that in the morning. Now your mom has some ravioli in here in the cabinet. You want some of that?"

"Yeah, ravioli!" he shouted. I used to love ravioli, too, when I was a kid.

I opened up the can and pulled out a small pot to cook it in. Then I burst out laughing again. I had been through so many changes in life that it was plain comical to me. I could have never imagined living the life that I was leading ten years ago, or even five years ago. I had been living day to day with no real plans or visions for years.

Jamal asked, "What's funny?"

I said, "Little man, life is a long journey. You hear me? So if you *ever* hear anybody talking that life-is-short stuff, you tell them, 'No it ain't! Life is *long!* Because you never know what's gonna happen with it.' "

I said, "I've come a long way with my life, Jamal. I just hope that I live long enough to see you go through your journey."

Jamal jumped on my legs like he did when I first started seeing his mother again. He yelled, "Yeah, me too! Then you can come to *my* basketball games in high school."

I smiled and shook my head again. I told him, "You know what, I think I've just created a basketball monster."

Jamal didn't care though. He just kept smiling and talking about how he couldn't wait to be on a team. And I couldn't wait to watch him either. In the meantime, though, I was more focused on raising him, like any good father should be.

To Be or Not to Be

SO, what did Monica say?" I asked Camellia. She made her daughter have a sit-down discussion with Reuben Gray about what they meant to each other. I was only asking for details because Camellia would not stop **DENISE** talking about it. It had been nearly two months since the teenagers had been intimate, and I don't believe they had a chance to do anything again. Camellia had Monica on a tight schedule with an after-school job to keep her busy. If Monica and Reuben ever indulged again, and Camellia had found out about it, she planned to take the matter to Reverend Gray himself.

"She said that Reuben is beginning to back away from her."

"I bet he would, as busy as you've made her," I commented. "He probably thinks she's too young for him now, like she needs an escort or something."

"Well, he's graduating from high school this year," Camellia argued.

"And Monica's graduating next year," I responded. "Will you at least let her go to the prom with him?"

"For what, so they can get a hotel room and go at it all night long?"

"Not if you hire the limousine and have him take them right back home." I really thought that my friend was being ridiculous, but what did I know, it wasn't my problem.

"Girl, I don't have any money for no limousine. You just wait until Jimmy starts dating," Camellia warned me.

"Oh, trust me, I'm already worried. I think he has a girl calling him now. Hold on for a minute." I clicked over to my other line and it was Brock.

"You almost ready?" he asked me. It was Friday night and he was taking me out for dinner.

"Yeah, I'm just finishing up my conversation with Camellia."

"Okay, well, I'll be over there in forty-five minutes. Tell Camellia I said hi."

"Okay. I'll see you soon."

I clicked back over to Camellia.

"Is it for Jimmy?" she asked a little too eagerly. Right before my eyes, Camellia was turning into a classic case of a parent living her life through her kids.

I said, "No, it was for me. Brock was calling to check up on me. He says hi. We're going out tonight. Maybe you should try it. You might like it."

"There you go with that again," she snapped. "So where are you going this time? Have you ever thought of just eating at home?"

"We do eat at home, but it's good to go out every once in a while. You should really try it."

"So where are you going?" she asked again.

"He won't tell me for some reason."

"Does he usually surprise you?"

"Well, he usually tells me where we're going."

"Oh, so this must be something special then," Camellia said, searching.

"Maybe," I answered her.

"So, anyway, do you think I'm going overboard with Monica?" She was getting right back to her daughter again.

"Yeah, sometimes I do, but since I'm not in your shoes, it makes it really hard for me to determine," I responded. "Like you said, I have to wait for Jimmy to start dating. Then we can talk.

"So how has Levonne been doing?" I asked to change the subject. Monica was getting far too much of our attention. That happened in a lot of families, the kid who goes astray ends up controlling the household.

"He's fine. I'm trying to find him a job for the summertime."

"So are you going to let him start playing football?" I asked her. I just wanted to round out the conversation before I hung up.

"Yeah, if he's any good at it."

"Some guys are late bloomers," I told her. "Look how he gained weight all of a sudden."

"Yeah, well, I guess you're right. Anyway, fill me in on the details when you get back in tomorrow."

"*Tomorrow?*" I asked.

"Well, you're not going to call me back tonight are you?"

I didn't even have to think about that. "Hell no," I told her.

"Well, that's why I said tomorrow. And don't forget, we have a lecture on Monday at Fletcher Elementary."

"I know, I know, the Black History Month thing," I said with a pout. I didn't see why we were only invited to schools during Black History Month or when something special was going on.

"At least we *have* a month," Camellia responded. "They didn't have to give us *that!*"

"Well, like the saying goes, 'He who gives can also take away.' That's why I say we need to create our own celebrations and holidays."

"We did. Carter G. Woodson came up with Negro History Week in the early nineteen hundreds, then it was expanded into Black History Month years later when the rest of the country caught on."

"So it went from a progressive idea into commercialism, just like they're trying to do now with Kwanzaa."

"Well, so what?" Camellia argued. "I guess you'd rather have a black holiday that nobody knows about so it can be considered authentic, like a rare painting or something, hunh?"

I laughed and said, "I guess so."

Camellia said, "You just make sure you show up on time on Monday. Nine-thirty sharp. Now do I need to drive you over there?"

"Look, girl, I'll *be* there, okay. I said that I would do it, and that's what I'm gonna do," I snapped with a grin.

I hung up the phone with Camellia and went to check up on my boys in the family room. They were playing video basketball. Since they both had good grades in school, I didn't mind. But I was still turning off them damn videos. BET needed to find something else to put on. My God!

"Haven't you had enough of basketball for one day?" Jimmy had just won his second play-off game earlier that evening. We were all there to see him, including Brock. He had the entire week off from work, and he spent most of his time with us. I was pleasantly surprised to see how well he got along with J.D. That shocked me. But I figured Brock and J.D. would have a lot more in common than Brock and Walter would. If

Brock and Walter could hit it off, then I would *really* be shocked. Not that I actually cared; however, it would just be something interesting to see.

Walter said, "I can beat him in this," referring to the video game.

Jimmy just smiled. "I figured I'd let him beat me in something, Mom," he commented.

"Aww, you don't *let* me beat you. I beat you fair and square."

I said, "Walter, do you have all of your things packed to stay with your father this weekend?" His father was picking him up that Saturday morning.

"Yeah, I'm packed, but not all the way," he answered.

Jimmy looked at me and started laughing.

"Did you hear what your brother just said?" I asked him with a grin.

"He don't make no sense sometimes," he said.

"I *am* packed," Walter repeated. "I just didn't put my clothes in my bag yet."

I let out a long sigh. "Don't let anybody in the house. You have my pager number, and you have Grandmom's number."

"And the police is 9-1-1," Jimmy added sarcastically.

Then Walter started to laugh.

I said, "You're not too big to be burglarized, Jimmy. You hear me? You're still only fifteen years old until June."

"Yeah, but I can hold mine," he bragged with his arms up. He had been doing push-ups to beef up his upper body. And it was working.

I said, "Burglars *do* carry guns. Okay?"

Walter asked, "When are *we* getting a gun?"

Jimmy sucked his teeth. "Why, so you can shoot me with it by acci-dent?" he said. "We probably already have one, but you'd be the last to know about it."

"No we *don't* have one, either," I responded. "But he *would* be the last one to know about it if we did. That would be a disaster waiting to hap-pen."

Walter dropped his head. Whatever his father *thought* he was teach-ing him didn't seem to be working, because he still said the silliest things.

"Have you learned *anything* this school year?" I asked him. He should have, with all of the drama we had been through.

He dropped his head even farther. "Yeah," he answered in a whisper.

"Well, act like it then," I told him. "You're going to be a teenager this year. It's time to stop acting so naive and silly. Silly boys don't do well in high school. They get turned into punks, class clowns, and start following the wrong crowds."

I hated to be so rough on Walter, but someone had to do it. I was getting fed up with his immaturity, especially with how Jimmy was developing. I guess I wanted both of them to develop at the same rate, which was unfair. I even felt like apologizing to Walter, but I couldn't bring myself to do it. He needed to be toughened up a bit. I couldn't wait until outdoor track season to get started. I wanted to see if Walter could actually take the practice schedule. I wanted to see him put his money where his mouth was. And I didn't consider myself a cruel mother, just a mother who was forced to raise two young black boys in inner-city Chicago. Whether we still lived there or not was besides the point. Chicago was my measuring stick of mental toughness, the toughness that young black men would need to survive in America.

By the time Brock pulled up to the house, I was ready to go. I was so ready that I was waiting for him at the front door. He was nearly a half hour late.

"What took you so long?" I asked him. He looked damned good, wearing a beige London Fog coat, a pinstriped black suit, and a black silk tie, with a fresh haircut and a shave. I had on a snazzy black dress under my long leather coat myself, and some new curls in my head. I didn't mean for us to be matching, but what could I say. I guess we were both in a classic mood. Black.

"There was an accident on the way here. A pickup truck hit a taxi, and smashed the whole back end. Are the boys all right?" he asked me.

I was still staring at his outfit. "Ah, yeah, they're in there playing them video games."

"Well, it's better than hanging out in the street," he responded. "Let me run in and say hi to them."

I followed him back into the house, thinking that Camellia may have been on to something.

When he walked back out after speaking briefly to the boys, I pressed him. "So, how come I can't know where we're going?" I asked again. I was getting extremely curious.

He let me in the car and asked, "Have you ever been to the Shark Bar?"

"I've heard of it, but I've never been there. No."

"Well, that's where we're going."

Maybe he shouldn't have told me so quickly. I started thinking, *Is this place all that fabulous?* "Have *you* eaten there before?" I asked him. I hoped that he wasn't taking me to one of his old stomping grounds.

He said, "No, but I did check the place out before making reservations."

"What kind of place is it? It sounds like some kind of gangster hangout in a mobster movie. The Shark Bar."

Brock broke out laughing. "Naw, it's a nice place, very low-key, and plenty of black people there."

"Is it black-owned?"

Brock grimaced. "Actually, I'm not sure. You know how some of these places are. You have black faces everywhere, but that doesn't mean that we're the majority owners. I hear that that's the case with everything that has Michael Jordan's name on it. And he can afford to be the *sole* owner."

I smiled. I guess my Michael Jordan beefs were starting to rub off on him.

"You know, I heard he recently said he's gonna start promoting a cheaper brand of shoes," I commented.

Brock nodded. "Yeah, he finally realized that these young poor kids were killing themselves to buy his hundred and fifty dollar shoes, as if he didn't know how much they cost all these years."

"Well, he's had a lot of things on his mind lately. We can't expect him to be informed on everything. And at least he's a good family man. You never hear about him getting into any kind of trouble."

Brock looked at me and frowned. Then he broke into another laugh. "Ain't this something," he said. "Now it sounds like *you're* defending him, and I'm ranting about him."

I laughed at the irony myself. "Well, I just thought about it, you know. Sometimes it takes us time to realize things. I mean, Jordan came into the league very young and worked very hard at what he was doing, and he's just now starting to pay attention to other things around him. It just took him a while to open his eyes to the real X's and O's and it's *not* basketball."

"Yeah, I guess everybody can't be like Isiah Thomas," Brock said.

I nodded. "You got that right. Because Isiah Thomas is ready to take care of business. Basketball ownership! That's what *I'm* talking about! And he'll get his chance, too. To hell with Canada!"

Brock chuckled. "Sounds like you've been watching the ESPN channel."

"Yeah, well, if Jimmy's going to be in line to get a basketball scholarship in three years, then I figured I'd better start paying attention to what's going on."

When we pulled up to the restaurant near downtown Chicago, Brock paid for valet parking.

"You were right, this place is low-key," I told him. The Shark Bar had a space all to itself, like a warehouse property. "I would have never been able to find this place," I commented.

We walked in, and Brock gave the receptionist his name.

"Okay, right this way." The sister led us to our quarter moon–shaped booth. It wasn't much of a fancy place, just very relaxing. It had an organic feel to it, with plenty of earth tones, space, and a brick wall background. I guess it *was* a warehouse, and they had done a heck of a job renovating the place into a restaurant. Before I knew it, I melted into my seat and felt totally at home.

"You know what? I think I like this place. It just feels *good* in here," I commented.

Brock smiled at me. "Yeah, it has that laid-back, relaxed feeling, right?"

"Exactly. Because some of these restaurants try to be extra fancy and end up overdoing things."

I looked over the menu to order a drink, and noticed that every employee there was black. I was tempted to ask somebody if it was black owned, but I just decided to enjoy it.

"I'll have a martini," I told our waitress.

Brock grinned. "Give me one of those, too."

"Okay, that's two martinis, and I'll be right back with your salads."

Even the waitresses had an organic mood to them. They were good-looking sisters who were too mellow to be snobbish, and too professional to be ghetto.

"You seem to be really enjoying yourself," Brock commented.

"Oh, I am."

"I'm glad you like it," he told me. "So how has Nikita been doing lately?" he asked.

I stopped and thought about it. Then I shook my head. "Do you have to ruin my mood with that?" I asked with a smile. I was serious though. I didn't need to think about Nikita. I had to check up on her and Cheron the whole time my mother was vacationing in Florida. Then I ended up watching Cheron for three days out of the nine that my mother was gone. And Nikita did have a nighttime job, but I didn't want to think about that either. The hours they had her working were plain ridiculous.

Brock said, "I'm sorry. I guess that was the wrong question to ask. I just figured I'd stop you from thinking about the restaurant so we can just enjoy each other. I mean, I like the place too, but damn!"

"So, I can't get excited about something?"

"Oh, no, I'm not saying that. Trust me, I *love* when you get excited. I'd just rather have your excitement be about me."

I broke out laughing. "I don't believe that you're jealous of a restaurant. And you're the one who brought me here."

"Well, I wouldn't take it that far."

I started rubbing the seat and the tablecloth, real seductively.

Brock was tickled by it. He snapped, "You cut it out right now, woman, or I'm leaving."

We shared another laugh as our salads and drinks arrived.

"Are you ready to order yet?" our waitress asked us.

Time flew by, and we talked about everything under the full moon while we devoured our food. Then Brock asked me, "So, how do you see the rest of your life filling out?"

What kind of a question is that? I thought. It just seemed so open-ended. I tried to answer it anyway. I said, "Well, I see both of my sons going to college and—"

"No, I'm talking about *your* life," Brock responded, cutting me off.

I smiled and thought about Camellia. I guess a single mother really couldn't separate her life from those of her kids. So much of our own lives were so intricately connected to theirs. It was like doing algebra, where the value of X depended on that of Y.

I thought about myself and said, "Well, I've been thinking about getting a bigger office space. My file cabinets are really starting to get crowded, and I want to make an extra set of backup files for all of my clients."

Brock just shook his head. "You're doing exactly what I thought you would do, talking about your sons and your work. I'm talking about *you*."

"Well, what about me? My sons and my work aren't a part of me?" I asked him. I figured out where he wanted to go. He wanted to talk about my social life, and that was as open-ended as his initial question.

"Have you ever thought about what happens when your sons *do* go away to college?" he asked me. "The years can fly past before you know it."

"I guess it'll be just me and you then," I answered. I knew that Brock wasn't expecting that.

He nodded and said, "Exactly." Then he went inside of his suit jacket. "Denise, I've been thinking about this moment for months now, and I'm tired of putting it off."

Oh my God! I panicked. My hands started to shake as I took a sip of my water. Brock had totally caught me off guard. I was ready to tell him that I had to use the bathroom before he opened that black ring case he was holding. Ironically, I really did have to go, but I didn't want to ruin his moment. Brock looked like a brown prince in shining armor who was offering a hand to the damsel in distress. How would I look telling him right then and there that I had to use the bathroom? And there I was drinking more water out of pure nervousness and shock. I was just pulling his leg when I said that we would be together after my boys went off to college. I wasn't serious! It would have been nice, but—

"Denise, will you marry me?"

The ring was right there in my face, a full carat. It had three circles with the two outside circles twisting diagonally into the middle circle which held the diamond. It was beautiful! Absolutely beautiful!

Oh my God, I'm going to pee on myself inside of this restaurant! I climbed up out of my seat and said, "I'll be right back," to run off to the bathroom. That's when I noticed people peeking in our direction. *Oh my God!* I told myself again. I prayed that I could make it to the bathroom before I injured something. The Lord showed me the way, and boy did it feel good. But when I was finished, I had to face Brock and everyone else who saw that ring being offered to me. Suddenly I wished that the Shark Bar was darker, and crowded, and noisy, and everything else that I could possibly hide in.

Brock had really done it to me! I knew I couldn't leave him out there for too long. I'm sure that he was dying from the suspense.

"*Oh*, I wasn't ready for this!" I hollered at the mirror. "I just wasn't ready for this!"

A sister walked in and looked at me as if I were crazy.

"Oh, don't mind me," I told her. "I *am* crazy." I would say anything to release some of the anxiety I was feeling. However, with the sister in the bathroom with me, I knew I couldn't stand there and mumble to myself like I wanted to, so I slowly walked out, thinking a mile a minute.

Everything was in slow motion as I walked back up the steps from the rest room area.

Oh my God! I didn't know what else to tell myself. I was walking on eggshells.

Dammit, I am turning thirty-five years old! I told myself. Suddenly, I found the strength to march up them steps and handle my business like a grown woman. I strutted through that place like I owned it, and sat back down at my booth with Brock. He sat there and smiled at me, confident, looking good and smelling good, with that one carat open on the table. I got nervous all over again.

Oh my God! I wanted to go back to the bathroom.

"Do you have to go to the bathroom now?" I asked him. I felt like a damn giddy teenager!

Brock stopped smiling. He said, "I understand how awkward this is for *both* of us, but I can't keep holding this off. The sooner we get it out in the open, the better. I want us to be a part of each other *for real*, and I'm ready and willing to deal with whatever I have to deal with. Do you hear me, Denise? What*ever* I have to deal with."

I didn't know what else to say. I finished my glass of water and looked for the waitress for a refill. "Ah, excuse me, can I have some more water, please. Thank you very much."

Brock sat there and pushed that ring at me again. "Denise, the question is still standing."

I looked away and tried to think. I needed time to think. *Just give me some time to think! Okay?* But I couldn't say the damn words!

"Denise?"

I tried to act as if I were dreaming. Maybe Brock was calling me to wake me up. But when I turned my head to look at him, that ring was still in my face.

I dropped my face into my hands to hide myself from the attention. People were staring. *Dammit, Brock!* I just wasn't prepared to answer a marriage proposal. Then he put his hand on my shoulder. The man couldn't take a hint!

I took a deep breath, raised up my head, and said, "I am really . . . surprised." Then I dropped my head back into my hands. I was as embarrassed as I ever could be. What happened to all of my strength? I felt like Samson with his hair cut off.

"I understand that," Brock was saying, "but we're not getting any younger."

His hand was still on my shoulder. It felt like it weighed a ton. I was extra sensitive to touch, sound, taste, *everything*. I was just a wreck on the side of the road, waiting for the tow truck to come and get me. However, Brock wanted me to start up again and move on my own. I just couldn't. I was in shock. Literally!

"Denise, what I want you to do is think about things over the next few days, even a week if you have to, and I won't bother you until you come up with a decision. In the meantime, I want you to keep the ring, because if you don't, I won't know what to do with myself. Okay? Can you at least do that for me?"

I looked at him and nodded without a sound, as he pressed the ring case into my palms. Talk about your waiting to exhale, I was waiting to be born again! I didn't have much left to say for the rest of that night, as that ring case burned a hole in my hand all the way back to my house. By then it was close to midnight.

Brock walked me back to the front door and kissed me on the lips. "I have a three-day trip starting on Monday morning to Texas and Louisiana. You think you'll need more time than that?"

I said, "We'll see. I just need some time."

Brock smiled and said, "I know exactly what you mean. You're just a little nervous about it."

"What about you?" I asked him.

"Well, once you get it out in the open, you calm down a bit."

"So, that means you're still nervous then, a little." I didn't want to be the only one.

"Big decisions are always difficult to come up with, Denise. But we have to get through nervousness. Otherwise, we would never make any big decisions. And trust me, I know plenty of brothers who are scared to death of that word 'marriage,' because they know that the word implies *wed-lock*. The *wed* part ain't so bad, it's the *lock* that kills them. Brothers hear that word *lock* and start running like slaves from a plantation."

I smiled and said, "Yeah, but then they always want to come back for free milk and cotton."

Brock laughed. "That's true, too," he agreed. "I can't even lie about it. But not with all men. Because some men leave, and you never will see them again."

"What about sisters?" I asked. I figured, that as a woman, I should have been jumping for joy, or at least that's what society *told* us we should do. Marriage was a woman's ultimate validation.

Brock thought about the question. "It used to be that sisters had to be married to feel like they achieved anything in life, but nowadays, a large percentage of women don't even expect it. And I don't know if that's just with black women, or with women in the nineties in general. But it just makes me wonder what will happen to the institution of marriage by the year two thousand."

I wondered about that too. "That's a good question," I responded.

"Well, you just think about how the word applies to us. And I promise I won't bother you about it. As long as I know something by next week," he told me with a grin.

"What if you don't know?" I was dead serious. I had to really think about it.

Brock was startled by the question. I guess he really felt that I was going to say yes.

"Well, like I said, give yourself some time to think about it, and that's all that I can really ask. But from this day on, you can never say that you haven't had a good man ask for your hand in marriage, because I *am* a good man. I love and I care about you and your sons, I'm employed, I'm intelligent, mature, and I *am* asking you to marry me. So you don't have any excuses.

"Life is about taking chances, and neither one of us can sit here and predict what *could* or what *will* happen between us, because we don't know. All that we can do is give it a try and see."

I walked into both of my sons' rooms and watched them as they slept. I wondered what they would think about their mother getting married at thirty-five. Maybe it would set a positive example for them that marriage was all right, so that they could expect to do the same when they were of age. Children do follow the example of their parents.

Then I thought about *my* mother and father. My image of them had been shattered. I saw the futility of the many bragged-about thirty- and forty-year marriages from the 1950s and '60s. I felt like they were filled with lies and cover-ups of cheating, hiding secrets, and plenty of emotional stress and endured pain. Yet many marriages had somehow survived it all. I couldn't understand how they were able to do it, and I was reluctant to even try. Maybe if society had as many open windows for divorces in the past as it does in the present, few of our parents would have remained married. Or if marriage was the broken institution that it had become in the nineties, maybe few of our parents would have married in the first place. That was a heavy thought to go to bed with that night. It was so heavy that I couldn't sleep. So I called my mother after two o'-clock in the morning, knowing that she was easy to wake up. How many years had she slept lightly, with the weight of the world always on her mind?

"Mom, what are you doing up so late?" I asked her. She was wide awake. I expected to be the one to awaken her.

"Cheron has a cold. I have to make sure she doesn't get too congested."

"Does Nikita know?"

"Yeah, she knows."

And what did she do about it? I wanted to ask, but that wasn't what I was calling for.

I asked, "Mom, can we talk for a minute?"

She said, "At two o'clock in the morning, that's about all that we can do."

"I'm sorry, Mom, I just couldn't sleep."

"Well, thanks for not telling your sister what I told you," she said. She had thanked me at least three times before.

I said, "Mom, the last thing Nikita needs to know is that Dad didn't want her."

"I never said he didn't want her. I never said that. I just said that he wanted a boy."

"Okay, okay, I'm sorry, Mom." I was snappy and impatient. I wanted to get right to the point of my call without all of the small talk. It was too late at night for small talk.

I cut to the chase and asked, "Mom, what do you think about marriage?"

"Did Brock ask you?" She sounded excited. I guess Mom knew how to cut to the chase herself.

"No, but I am thinking about it," I lied. I didn't need my mother's excitement, I needed her honest opinion.

She said, "Brock is a good man, a *God-fearing man.*"

Since when has God-fearing *become a criterion?* I wanted to ask. My mother only talked about religion when she wanted to, and she only went to church when she felt like it.

I said, "So it's an individual man-and-woman thing instead of an institution?" I asked her.

"It's both," she told me. "And I hope you told Brock yes."

I ignored her. I wasn't going to lie twice. Once you start lying repetitively, you lose sight of what the truth is, and for the sake of Brock's goodness, I didn't want to do that. After all, he *did* ask me to marry him.

"So, you weren't pressured to marry Dad at all? It was your idea to marry him, 100 percent? Is that what you're telling me?"

"Nobody got pressured into marrying unless the girl got pregnant. And if she was pregnant, then she made the decision to open up her legs in the first place, so she must have liked the boy. But now girls open up their legs for anybody, even guys who they don't like. We had names for those kind of girls when I grew up."

I was getting irritated. I said, "Mom, are you saying that everything is the woman's fault? Guys got pressured into getting married too, didn't they? *Especially* if the girl was pregnant. That seems like it was *his* fault, too. So let's stop making this thing a one-way show.

"It just seems that everybody lets the man off the hook," I argued. "We let them off the hook when they cheat and treat us badly. Then we let them come back to us and do *more* damage. And after all of that, we continue to blame ourselves."

I don't know how many different conversations Camellia, myself, and plenty of other single mothers had in our monthly meetings over the years, but in all that we discussed, the cycle of broken families continued to do damage to the emotional, economic, and cultural needs of mothers and children in every town in America. Maybe J.D. was right, we *did* need to hear the men's side of the argument because all *we* seemed to be doing was spinning around in circles.

My mother repeated, "Brock is a good man."

She didn't seem to get it. It wasn't that simple. Or was it? Maybe *I* had it all wrong. Maybe it *was* that simple. Brock was a good man who had asked to marry me, so I should accept his proposal and see how long he could be good. Or maybe he couldn't be good all the time. Then how would I deal with the change? That's what I was afraid of. Or how would he deal with my change? In either case, I had too many thoughts on my mind to carry on a sane conversation with my mother after two o'clock in the morning.

I said, "Mom, I'm sorry I bothered you so late at night. I guess I'll try and go on back to bed now."

"If you could, you would have already been asleep," she said. And she was right, but I didn't know what else to say to her without sparking an argument.

"Do you think that women have changed that much from when you were growing up?" I asked her.

"Yes, they've changed. Women are more concerned about what a man can do for them instead of what they can do for a man. When I married your father, I wanted to make a good home."

I stopped her and said, "Mom, was it really that simple? Because I can't see you living just to make a good home for a man."

"I guess you don't need me to answer your question then," she snapped. "You have your own answers. So what is it that you want? You women sure don't seem to be getting it. I hear more women complaining now than I *ever* did when I was a young woman."

"That's because you kept it all bottled up inside of yourself, Mom. I mean, you just told me what you went through with Dad, two months ago."

"But I didn't tell the world and get up here and start fussin' and fightin' with him on some talk show!" My mother was raising her voice.

I just couldn't do it. I said, "Mom, I'm gonna have to hang up, because women who are on these talk shows have some serious problems that need to be worked out."

"You think *we* didn't have any problems?" she asked me. "You ain't seen nothin' *yet*. You ain't even *lived* long enough to see it. If you want to hear some stories, I'll tell you some stories. That's what's wrong with so many of these girls now, they think they're the only ones who go through anything. Then they want to talk about what they do, and how much they make, and how they don't need nobody. Well, it sure doesn't sound like they're happy. Even that Oprah Winfrey couldn't get that skinny, long-headed man of hers to marry her. And I've heard some things about his family too. So who is perfect? Who can throw the first stone? You tell me!" she shouted.

"We were *much* stronger than *this* generation because *we* understood what was more important—our families. And we wouldn't throw that away for some whore out there on the street that ain't got a family to spit on. So don't *tell me* what I don't know, because I know *plenty!*"

Cheron woke up and started crying. That was my final cue to hang up the phone. And when I did, I still didn't get any sleep.

When I hung up, I said to myself, "They didn't have AIDS back then, men took care of their responsibility, houses were easier to buy . . ." and on and on. My mother and I could have argued all night long on the subject, and at the end of the conversation, I still had a broken family, and she still had a dysfunctional family with pain that had extended to the grandchildren.

I just didn't know where to turn. I clicked on my light and looked at that three-circled ring again. Boy was it beautiful! I was just concerned about it being forbidden fruit. I didn't want to rush into anything that I would regret. Maybe it was just my own selfishness, but I had gotten so used to my own space and my own set of responsibilities that I was terrified of having to share. I felt as if I would lose myself and become dependent upon someone else, and I could not afford that, so I resisted long-term arrangements. I knew that I could always count on myself, but I needed to learn how to count on others. I just had to convince myself that it was a reasonable thing to do.

After thinking over that long weekend, I was more than halfway there to giving Brock an answer to his pressing question. However, when Camellia and I met at Fletcher Elementary School for Black History Month that Monday morning, my answer became solidified.

I was in the wrong state of mind to lecture any schoolkids, so I planned on letting Camellia take the lead. She was used to leading discussions anyway. She had been hounding me all that weekend to find out what had happened between Brock and me on Friday night. It was as if she could sense that something extra had occurred. But I blew the conversation off until she finally left me alone about it. I wasn't ready to reveal anything until I had a definite answer.

The teachers introduced us to several classes of fourth- and fifth-grade girls inside of their auditorium. The first thing I thought was, *Where are the boys?*

Fletcher Elementary was a predominantly black school in the heart of the South Side. It wasn't a school filled with poor kids, because many of the students were middle class. Fletcher was chosen as one of the experimental schools in Chicago where they had magnet programs for accelerated youth. I sat and stared out at the many shades of brown, with ponytails, braids, and cornrows. Some of them looked as confused as I was, while others looked as excited as Camellia. I began to smile. I was thinking that it was funny how life continues on with the same types of personalities over and over again.

"Class, I would like to introduce our two guests this morning and talk about the continued legacy of strong black women in the African-American community," the teacher leading the event began. She was a lighter-brown sister with light eyes wearing African garb. I wondered if she dressed like that every day. It wasn't a judgment call, I was just curious.

She went on to introduce Camellia and me as two longtime friends and successful single mothers, who had both received college degrees and went on to form the Single Mothers' Organization to help others in their struggle for moral support, education, family, and economics.

After our introductions, Camellia began to talk about her job as a social worker for the city government, then I explained what I did as an insurance saleswoman and financial planner. Next, Camellia began to ask some of the girls what they wanted to do, and they were eager to raise their hands.

"I want to be a lawyer."

"I want to be a schoolteacher."

"I want to make movies and dance in plays and stuff."

"I want to be a basketball player, because I can beat my brother in basketball now. They have a girls' team that I'm going out for this summer."

I smiled at that one. Professional women's basketball had just started a few years ago, and the idea of professional women's sports was definitely taking off.

Camellia asked, "Okay, now do any of you know what you have to do to *succeed* at what you would like to become?"

That's when things really got interesting.

"Do your homework."

"Get all A's and B's."

"Don't do drugs."

"And don't have no babies."

The entire auditorium began to burst out laughing after that last comment. I hated being judgmental, but the little girl who said it looked like a prime suspect for early pregnancy. She was a hyper child who was quick to get an attitude when she wasn't immediately called on for her input. Everyone couldn't be called at the same time. Before she was called on, I stood there and watched her huff and puff like a miniature dragon. She was the kind of hardheaded, smart-mouthed girl who was quick to run right into trouble. In fact, the little girl's attitude reminded me of my sister.

I broke in and asked her, "And what would you like to become when *you* get older?"

"A police officer," she answered, "because I want to lock up all these boys that be out here causing trouble all the time. Like this boy named Damen, he lives on my block, and he *needs* to be locked up."

The auditorium broke out laughing again, but the scene wasn't funny to me. This little girl was also a class clown, and slightly overweight. I began to wonder about her family background. I could already see it. She had a young, single mother, had been around plenty of terrible men, probably had brothers and sisters from different fathers, and her mother was just as trifling as she was. Damn, I hated being judgmental, but I had been around her type far too long not to know!

I looked at Camellia, and she read my mind. Then I let her take control of the discussion before I got too excited in there.

"Okay, how else do we get ahead?" Camellia asked them.

"Education."

"And what does an education do for us?"

A well-behaved girl with a long ponytail was *dying* to answer. She was all up on her toes with her hand up high. When she was called on, she stood up and said, "You get a better job and make a lot of money, and then you don't have to have a husband to give you anything, and you don't stay at home and wait for him to come from work."

I sat there, shook my head, and read her, too. Her mother was a middle-class, single mom who was educated with only one child. Her mother was also pissed at her daughter's father for not doing what he was supposed to do. I'm sorry, but stereotyping was a way of life. There was just no way of getting around it.

I was tempted to break in again and ask the teachers why the boys were not included, because I could see the direction in which the discussion was headed.

Camellia struck the match when she went on to ask, "Why do you think it's important for women to have their own incomes?"

"Because boys are stingy," one of the girls yelled.

All of a sudden, they all started yelling out before they were called on.

"I don't want to ask them for anything anyway."

"They give you babies and then they don't want to pay for it."

"They don't buy the babies milk or anything."

"And then they always in your face, asking you for stuff."

The class clown screamed out, "And they always want to do it to you," for another laugh.

The head teacher broke in and said, "Wait a minute, young lady! You *watch* what you say!"

The girl's classroom teacher led her out of the auditorium. I wondered how long the girl would last in that school before they politely sent her somewhere else. I looked at Camellia to see how she was going to respond to all of that. I could tell that the head teacher didn't like it. I read her too, and something told me that she was happily married. She had a certain levelheadedness about her that was dominant in sisters who had either a balanced social life or no children. Because once you have children and mix it with an unbalanced social life, your emotions easily run hot and cold from one day to the next.

I forced myself to remember the teacher's name, *Mrs.* Debra Clarke. Since I was not focused that morning, I was only halfway listening when she introduced herself to us.

"I'm sorry about that," she apologized to Camellia and me. Once the girls quieted down, Camellia started up again.

"The reason it's important for women to have their own incomes," she stated—I was interested in her answer myself—"is so that we can be productive members of a household. In some situations, women are *forced* to work, but it should *not* be in opposition to our men. *Specifically*, in the African-American culture, the women have *always* worked, because we couldn't *afford* not to. Therefore, we are *used* to working and not just being housewives."

Mrs. Clarke nodded her head and could not hide her agreement. "That's right," she said. In fact, she said it twice to make sure the girls heard her. "That's right."

Camellia added, "It is very hard for *anyone* to raise a family in present-day America with only one income. And even if the second member of the family *does* stay at home, at least the family doesn't have to pay extra money for day care.

"Statistics say, in the African-American community, that even with success stories like myself and Denise's, the average single mother is forced to live below the poverty line.

"Because of a lack of education, African-American women earn the *lowest* income while having the *highest* percentage of working mothers in the country, with *no* or little help from their children's fathers," she added.

"Furthermore, the children do *not* receive the proper emotional balance that they *should* receive from a mother *and* a father."

I looked over to see if Camellia was okay. She seemed to be getting emotional in her discussion. That was unusual for her. Mrs. Clarke looked a bit concerned herself. Camellia was emitting more raw energy than she needed to.

As far as the percentage of working mothers was concerned, I do believe that Asian mothers had us beat, with Latina mothers not far behind. However, Asian *fathers* were definitely there to help out, where Latina mothers were not much better off than we were, with plenty of absentee fathers. I knew or met enough of them through my secretary Elmira to know.

I stood up to take over before my good friend suffered a stroke or a heart attack. I said, "It seems that we need to begin doing *more* to educate our young men *and* our young women on how to keep a productive *family* together. It's obviously no longer feasible for us to think as individuals. And so, although it's important that we as women *do* get our educations, and *don't* have kids before we are ready, and *do* earn an income that works for our specific needs, I reiterate what was said earlier, in that we *do not* do this in opposition to our men, because ultimately, it takes at least two adults to make a family. Since the men are definitely a part of making babies, they should also be a part of raising them *and/or* providing for them."

When we closed out the discussion that morning, Camellia was still in an emotional haze.

"Are you okay, sister?" Mrs. Clarke asked her.

Camellia nodded. "Yeah, I'm okay. I didn't get a chance to eat this morning. This diet thing can get to you sometimes."

I looked at Camellia and knew that we had to talk. She wasn't going to put me off anymore. And I wasn't going to blow her off about my marriage proposal either.

"Well, I want to thank you sisters for coming out again, and I also think you're right; we *do* need to start including the boys in these discussions," she said specifically to me.

I said, "Yeah, because I had *two* boys for men, and both of them have a story to tell." It was no use in me being hush-hush about it. The truth was the truth, and I had been dealing with it for close to sixteen years.

"If you don't mind me asking, how is your marriage?" I asked her. I just had to know.

"Oh, we're making it. And I don't mind talking about it at all."

"Do you have any children?"

"A boy and a girl; six and four."

Mrs. Clarke looked around our age. "Are you around thirty-three?" I asked her. I took two years off.

She smiled. "I turn thirty-two in November."

I smiled back. "I turn thirty-five in April. My sons are turning sixteen and thirteen."

"Mmm," she grunted.

Camellia added, "I turn thirty-six in July. My girl and boy are turning seventeen and fourteen."

We exchanged more small talk about children and motherhood before Camellia and I said our good-byes and headed out the door to our cars. I followed Camellia to hers. She had gotten a better spot because she arrived earlier.

"My car is right around the corner," I told her. "You mind giving me a ride?" I really wanted to talk to her.

She took a deep breath and said, "No problem."

I didn't ask Camellia much until we made it inside of her car. Chicago wasn't the kind of city to talk outside in February. I wanted to warm up inside of her car first.

Camellia turned on the ignition and heat and rubbed her hands together in front of the wheel.

"You really went off in there," I commented with a smile. I wanted to ease into things.

"You think we're making any ground with SMO?" she suddenly asked me. "It started off as a good idea, but now it seems like a welfare program. We just get more and more women who put themselves in worse situations than they were already in. I'm starting to feel the same way *you* used to feel. I mean, after we've discussed everything that we need to discuss, what's the use if we're still going to be single mothers? It's just like welfare, a continuous cycle."

I just let her talk. She seemed ready for it.

She said, "I thought about calling my kids' father this weekend, just to see what he had to say for himself."

I couldn't let that opportunity pass me by. I asked, "Why didn't you?"

Camellia nodded and answered, "I am. I'm planning on tracking his ass down if I have to. But if he's so screwed up that he can't offer any help, and I'm not talking about the money, because he doesn't have any, just his input and concern, then I'm gonna have to find some other way for a man's presence.

"I mean, this thing is just not working," she told me. "Monica and Levonne have been suffering for years with all the things that I've been running and doing. That's probably why everyone has become so separated in society now; we're all doing too damn much and not taking care of the most important things. I *can't* be in a million places, and I *can't* be a million different things."

I smiled and put my hand on my friend's shoulder. "I got your back, girl," I told her. "This has been very hard, for all six of us," I said, including our children. "I came to that same conclusion. We have to stop acting like these superwomen they have us cracked up to be, because we're getting broken down from every angle."

Camellia took another deep breath and shook her head. "So where do we go from here, Denise? Is this something we need to look forward to from all of our families now? Can we change the damn world somehow? I mean, what do we do? How do we change the cycle?"

I thought about it. I said, "Brock asked me to marry him Friday night."

Camellia nodded and smiled at me. "I knew. I could feel it. You just didn't want to talk about it."

"I didn't have an answer yet."

"Do you have one now?"

"Hmmph, I have the only answer," I responded. "My mother told me, 'Brock is a good man.' "

"I knew it was gonna happen after the Thanksgiving dinner," Camellia commented. "Once a man accepts your family, no matter how crazy they are, then he's ready for that next step. Because *none* of these families are perfect.

"So, anyway, when is the wedding? I'm the maid of honor, right?"

"Of course you are. And you'll be the first to know the date. But first I have to tell this *good man* that I *will* marry him, before he gets nervous and takes his ring back."

We sat there and laughed. Then I asked, "And what about you? What are you planning on doing with your social life?" I was dead serious.

Camellia smiled, showing the ray of hope that she used to preach. "I'm right behind you, girl. I got someone in church who's been asking me out for months, and I've been steady ignoring him. Well, I'm not gonna ignore him anymore. But I'm not rushing into anything either."

"You can't," I told her.

"One day at a time," she said.

"One day at a time," I repeated.

Camellia got excited and said, "And if Reuben Gray messes with my daughter again, we're going to have *two* weddings this year, because I'm sick and tired of these trifling young boys screwing and leaving. If they want to keep humping like a dog, then they're gonna learn how to *sit* and *stay* like a damn dog!"

I broke out laughing and said, "Amen to that, girl. Amen to that!"

That was the Camellia that I knew—she was always looking ahead and on the bright side.

Tranquillity

W H A T ' S that big old smile for, Brock?" Larry asked me at the shipping docks in Cicero. Since his involvement with the mother and daughter he was seeing, we talked more often. I say that he was seeing them both, **B R O C K** because once you get involved with a mother, you date her *and* her child. That's just the way it is, and if it's not, then you're not all that serious about the woman, or she's not all that serious about her child.

"I feel good," I responded to Larry. "What, I can't feel good about myself and the future?" It was six A.M. Monday morning, at the crack of daylight. We both had early runs to make.

"At six o'clock in the morning? Shit, whose bed were *you* in last night?"

"It's not *last* night that counts, it's *every* night. I see you still haven't learned that yet," I told him.

"Well, yeah, it takes some getting used to," he said. "I'm still talking to the same girl though."

"After buying her and her daughter those Christmas presents, I would hope so," I joked.

Larry said, "I told you she made me take them back. And you say it's because she doesn't want to feel like she's using me."

"That's what it is. She's a decent woman."

"So, when will she start accepting my gifts?"

It was a wonder that Larry was even thinking about gift giving. I guess the saying is true, *every man has his match*. I said, "That depends on you. The more you're around her, the more comfortable she'll become. But there's never any strict timetable on it. Each woman is different."

"Oh, yeah?" he responded with a nod. "So really, what has you so happy this morning?" he asked me again.

I smiled at him and walked to the front end of my truck. I climbed in and said, "It's time for me to check out, young blood. I'll tell you about it next time. I got a feeling something good is about to happen."

"Something good like what?"

"Have patience, Larry. Patience is a virtue."

"Aww, man, go 'head with your old-ass. When you turning forty again?"

"In two more years, on April twenty-ninth," I told him with a chuckle.

I started up my engine and got ready for another trip out of town. I felt damned good that morning! I had been waiting since Friday for Denise to give me an answer to my marriage proposal, but the way I figured, there was no way she could turn me down. We had been dating for nearly two years, and there was nothing more to discuss. Either we were going to do it and get married or we were not. We were too old to spend four and five years thinking about it like younger couples do. We were both adults who were already well within our careers, so there was no time to waste.

I pulled onto I-57 south and headed for Texas as happy as a new driver with a quarter-per-mile raise. I was thinking about saving up my money for a down payment on a new home in the same Oak Park neighborhood where Denise and her sons were already established. I didn't want to uproot the family, I just wanted all of us to start over again in a neutral home. I didn't feel right moving into the home that Denise had already established. Maybe we could keep that one and rent it out or something. That seemed to be a good idea. Maybe we could put both of our efforts together and start buying up property to rent throughout the Chicago area. Denise was always talking about expanding black wealth by investing.

I had so many things running through my mind that I reached the state of Missouri before I even realized it. As soon as I connected to I-55 south, a black Ford Probe came flying out from the right lane and jumped in front of me. It all happened in milliseconds. I tried to slam on the brakes and switch lanes to my left, but there were cars in the lane already. People started honking their horns like crazy and swerving out of the way.

Luckily, I only sideswiped the Probe before its driver could make it to safety. Nevertheless, even a sideswipe from an eighteen-wheeler on a tiny sports car was enough to damage the entire left end of the car. I was ahead of schedule before that accident happened. And since it wasn't my damn fault, I was good and ready to be pissed!

I pulled over to the side of the road to scan radio channels for the police. Hopefully, there was a Missouri trooper in the vicinity, so I wouldn't have to wait too long. At least we didn't jam up the rest of the traffic. That would have made the situation worse.

I jumped out of my truck with my license and insurance card ready.

This young black guy wearing sunshades stepped out of the car as pissed as I was. "You didn't see me switching lanes, man? I had my blinkers on."

I could tell already, it was going to be a stressful argument, and I didn't feel up to that shit!

I said, "Just get out your license and insurance. We'll let the insurance companies be the judge of this."

The guy looked at my front end and said, "Ain't nothin' happen to your shit. You the one that fucked my car all up."

"Are you gonna get your license and insurance or what?" I started to think that he didn't have any. He was stalling.

He said, "I'll be right the fuck back," and started heading for his car. I looked at his Illinois license plate and wondered if he was from East St. Louis. The car didn't look like it was in good shape, either. Suddenly, I didn't think that waiting for him to go inside his car was such a good idea. In the nineties, young guys were capable of anything, even out in the middle of the road. So I wisely headed back to my truck to wait for the police. While I waited, I wrote down the guy's license plate number. The next thing I knew, he began to pull off.

All I could do was honk my horn at him. It was no way in the world I was going to run down a Ford Probe. I sat there and smiled. I guess he *didn't* have any car insurance. I wondered if I should wait for the police to arrive or just let the incident go. Like the guy had said, he hadn't done any harm to my truck. It was *his* loss, but since I had radioed for the police, I felt it was my duty to at least report what had happened. I would have let the guy slide, but with *his* attitude, I figured he was heading for trouble somewhere else, *if* he wasn't already in trouble. Maybe it would have been a good idea to head him off. Not only that, but he could have turned the story around and lied to say that *I* hit *him* and ran, while faking all kinds of injuries for a big payday.

I scanned for the police again and reported a hit-and-run.

"What kind of vehicle?" I was asked.

"A black Ford Probe, with Illinois license plates." I gave the police the license plate number and asked if I could head on up the road while keeping an eye out for him. I had a schedule to keep.

"Ah, you sit tight until we can run this guy down, and then we'll let you know," I was told.

Shit! I thought to myself. I started thinking about ignoring those orders and getting back on the road anyway.

"Why did you let him drive off?" I was asked.

"I didn't think it was safe to sit out there and wait for him to go inside of his car for his insurance papers. The guy didn't seem too cooperative about it, so I returned to my truck to take down his license plate number, and that's when he took off."

"What kind of damage are we looking at?"

"Ah, he has a damaged left end."

I waited another two or three minutes before the trooper got back to me after he informed his superiors and radioed for backup. That seemed like forever. I was ready to go. I had too much energy to be held up that morning.

"Trailer, are you there?"

"Yeah, I'm here," I answered.

"We're gonna have a few cars on the lookout right up the road from you. You can pull up the road a few miles and pull over to the shoulder when you see our troopers flashing."

"All right then. Thanks." I restarted my engine and crawled back onto the road. All of a sudden, there was a lot more traffic. I had a nice pace going before that damn accident!

I listened in on the radio frequency until I heard the Missouri troopers in pursuit of the car. The guy wasn't even smart enough to get off the highway.

When I got about eight miles up the road, they had the young brother in custody, spread-eagle against the car. Suddenly, I felt sorry for him. They were searching his car for anything they could find.

"You want to help us file this report?" I was asked.

I answered all of their questions and asked if I could be on my way.

"Is this the correct address and phone number of your trucking company?"

"Yes, it is."

"All right, then, we'll be in touch."

The brother in custody gave me one last evil look without his sunshades. I climbed back into my truck and thought about the entire incident. If the young brother had been at least respectable and had explained to me that he didn't have any insurance, I could have let him go to fix his own damages. But with the way *he* acted, he didn't deserve a damn break! And I bet he was back there calling me every name he could think of because I had simply done what was right. He had messed up my entire damn mood! *Shit!*

Brothers were always trying to get over, and always blaming the damn white man for shit! The white man didn't have a damn thing to do with that accident! Nor did he have any responsibility in raising a black man's family. All I heard were young brothers complaining about not being able to find jobs while getting themselves in a world of trouble, and then bragging about the stupid shit they think and do on rap records. Denise was right about everything she had told me. That young motherfucker *needed* to be locked up, but yet *I* felt guilty!

Shit! Excuse my choice of words, but that shit just ruined my damn drive! I didn't need that shit no more than the president needed some young, sexy intern working in the White House.

I knew exactly what the problem was; we had too many damn "rolling stones" in our community, and no one was willing to tell these young, rock-headed punks to shape the hell up and start taking care of business in their families but Minister Louis Farrakhan! Hell, I felt like calling my uncle William and giving him a piece of my mind just for loving the song so much.

Marrying Denise was the right thing to do. Not only that, but I loved the woman. Brothers had to start finding a passion to do right for the people they loved and for the people who loved them. Every black mother I've ever seen on TV or read about in the newspapers was always crying her eyes out and telling anybody who would listen how good her boy was before they locked his ass up and drove him away. And we try and keep blaming America for that. It's not always America's fault. We had to stop passing the damn buck on to society. Somebody had to stand up and make an effort to do right, and *know* what doing right is all about!

I must have mumbled a million different thoughts about the black community on my way through Arkansas. The only thing that stopped my ranting was a call from Denise.

"Hey, baby," I cheered. It was good to hear from her. She had perfect timing, too. The way I was driving, with the many downfalls of the black community on my mind, I was likely to have another damn accident!

"You sound happy to hear from me," she said.

"Damn right," I told her. "It's been a rough-behind day for me. I was involved in a hit-and-run accident in Missouri."

"Oh my God! Are you all right? Those truck accidents are the worst kind. Did the truck flip over? Where are you now?"

I smiled. I liked all of her concern. Denise sounded like a woman in love.

"Naw, baby, you're overdoing things," I told her. "I'm all right. It was just a minor hit. My truck wasn't even scratched. I was more damaged mentally if anything."

"Oh. Well, what do you mean by that?"

"It's a long story, but basically, it boils down to another rock-headed black boy with a lack of a father figure."

"Is that so? And how did you arrive at that notion?" she asked me.

I said, "Denise, only a rock-head with no father around could treat me with no respect the way *this* punk did. He had *no* respect for his elder. And yet and still, when the police caught him and locked his ass up, I had a nerve to feel guilty about it."

"That's because you care," Denise told me. And she was right, I *did* care.

"Well, I just called to see how your trip was going so far," she told me. It was slightly after four o'clock in the afternoon.

"Yeah, it started off good, then it went into a slump, now it's picking up again, thanks to you," I responded.

"Oh, well, in that case, I'm glad I was able to help."

"Yeah, but I know you didn't call just to check up on me," I commented with a smile. "You got something else you want to tell me?"

"Oh, yeah, I guess that I *do* love you," she said with a chuckle.

"You *guess* you love me?"

She chuckled again. It's always a good sign when a couple can humor each other; joking couples seem to have longer-lasting relationships.

"Well, I do have a little something else I'd like to tell you," she said.

"Oh yeah, and what's that?" I was all ready for it, smiling from ear to ear.

"I tried on your ring today," she said. "In fact, I'm staring at it right now, and I'm wondering who helped you to pick it out."

"Woman, I have taste. I don't need anybody to hold my hand when I go shopping."

"I hope not," she said. "But it is nice to do sometimes, with the right person."

I grinned with sexy thoughts on my mind. "All right then, we can hit a Victoria's Secret together as soon as I get back to Chicago."

She laughed and said, "Men just get dirtier as they get older."

"And the women continue wanting to hear it," I responded.

"Oh, no we don't either."

We were both stalling before the inevitable.

"So, are you calling me just to run up my phone bill, or do you have something *serious* to tell me?" I asked again, with a strong hint.

"Running up *your* phone bill. I'm the one who's calling *you* long distance."

"At corporate rates from an office phone," I argued. "Meanwhile, *I'm* paying about a quarter a minute to talk on this cell phone."

"You want me to hang up and call you later at a truck stop or something?"

"Not before you tell me what you called for," I told her.

Denise laughed and still didn't tell me what I was dying to hear.

"How long is this going to take, Denise? The cat got your tongue or something?"

"I don't own a cat. I never liked them. They were always too independent for me. I was afraid of them as a child."

I thought about that comment and smiled. I said, "That's exactly what brothers are saying about you nineties sisters."

"Only the stray dogs are saying that, because the ones with a clean house and a healthy bone are still very much in demand."

I laughed and shook my head. I said, "I heard that! I must have me a healthy bone and a clean house then, hunh, sister?"

We broke out laughing together, but I was getting impatient. Denise was stringing things out a little longer than I expected.

I said, "I'm still waiting for that answer, woman. I've already been thinking about plans."

"What kind of plans?"

Shit! I knew I shouldn't have said that! I thought to myself. Everything I said was only making the conversation longer. Not that I didn't like talking to Denise, I just had something specific on my mind to talk about at the moment.

"We'll discuss all of that when I get back. *If*, that is, we have anything *important* to talk about. Do we?" I hinted to her again.

"Oh, we have plenty to talk about."

"And why is that?" I baited her.

She said, "Because we're getting married."

I was speechless. I held the phone to my face and grinned. "Is, ah, that so?" I finally asked her.

"That's what I said, unless you've changed your mind already. I can't force you to do something that you don't want to do."

"Now, why would I change my mind?" I asked her.

"I don't know. You may have found someone on the side of the road who you liked a little better."

I shook my head and said, "Naw, you got the wrong man, baby. I don't pick up no hitchhikers."

"Never?"

"Never in my life! I like to ride with people I know, people I've eaten and drank with, people like Denise Stewart and her two sons."

"It's good to hear that," she told me. "So, are you happy with my answer?"

"Does a dog's tail wag when he's happy?"

She broke out laughing again. "But I don't want a *dog*," she snapped at me, "I want a *man*; a *good* man!"

I got serious and said, "Denise, that's exactly what you're gonna get, for as long as we're together, and until *death* do us part. You hear me?"

She said, "I know, because you're all into me."

I laughed and said, "You got *that* right."

"I just hope this spell I have you under doesn't wear off too soon."

I said, "You kiddin' me. I'm a long-distance driver, baby. I don't get bored easily. So get ready to travel around the world for a hundred years. In fact, we'll be driving in space cars by the time I'm finished with you."

Denise asked, "Are you serious? We're going to travel around the world?" She was calling my bluff.

I backed off and said, "Well, for now, we'll do that in the mind and spirit, and then maybe later on, we'll do it with our actual bodies. Is that a deal?"

She laughed one more time and said, "It's a deal."

I told Denise I'd call her as soon as I got into Texas that night, and slowly hung up. We could have been talking for an hour if I didn't cut things short. I wanted to savor her acceptance of my marriage proposal anyway. I was back to feeling good! I was sky high! The next thing I knew, I started singing that same song I was having so many problems with, and couldn't even help myself, because I knew that the Temptations were *not* singing about me.

"Poppa was a rolll-lin' stone. Wherever he laid his hat was his home. . . ."

Why Me?

"WHAT event do you think you'd like to run?" I asked
my son. It was the third Saturday in February. We were
on our way to a sporting goods store at the Water Tower
Mall on the near North Side to buy running shoes and
WALTER   spikes. Outdoor track practice was starting that coming
Monday at his school. Everything had calmed down at Walter's school
since the stabbing incident in September. Denise settled things with the
school out of court, and Walter had worked his way up to straight A's
and one B, ironically in gym. He seemed really excited about going out
for the track team though.

He said, "I have to get my endurance up to run long distance. I'm not
fast enough yet for sprints. I'm too short for the high jump and long
jump, so I'll probably pick an event right in the middle; the quarter
mile. That's one time around the track, right? I can do that."

I broke out laughing. My son was naming about the most strenuous
event in track and field, the quarter-mile run. "Ah, are you absolutely
sure you want to run the quarter?" I asked. I don't believe he knew just
how tough that race was. "That's a serious event you're talking about," I
told him. "Olympic track star Michael Johnson runs the quarter mile.
You see how he's built, don't you? Those guys are usually tall and powerful, more powerful than your older brother."

"Well, I'm only a kid right now. Maybe I can work out."

I nodded to him and smiled. I said, "Yeah, maybe you can.

Everybody's not born with speed and muscle. Some people had to work hard at it. In fact, *most* athletes had to work out. You're absolutely right."

I had never been into athletics myself, so I didn't know. Yet whenever they interviewed top-notch athletes, they always talked about their work habits, just like businesspeople would talk about reading *The Wall Street Journal* and staying up on what was going on in the business world. To be the best, you have to work hard at what you do in any arena.

Walter asked, "Remember that part in the movie *Forrest Gump* when those metal rods came off his legs and he started running real fast? Maybe if I wear some real heavy shoes or something, I could run just like him," he joked with a smile.

I broke up laughing again. I don't know what his mother was talking about, but Walter was sure making progress from my end of things. When I used to get him on the weekends, he was nothing but attitude. I guess *my* attitude back then had a lot to do with that. Kids can tell when grown-ups aren't really giving their all to them. I could surely tell when my father was half stepping with me, so it was obvious that Walter knew when I was doing the same with him. However, I hoped he hadn't made a 180-degree turn and decided to be on his best behavior with me while acting up with his mother. I set my mind on investigating what was going on.

"How are you and your mother getting along?" I asked him.

He looked at me and frowned. "She was acting weird for a while, crying at night and stuff, but now she's acting better because she's getting married."

Jesus Christ! What a bomb! I thought to myself. "She's getting married?" I asked, to make sure I heard him right.

Walter sounded proud of her. "Yup."

I guess it was no big deal to him. *I* was married to someone else.

I decided to ask him about it. "And how do you feel about that?"

He hunched his shoulders and answered, "I'm happy for her. At least somebody wanted to marry her."

I said, "And how do you feel about Brock?"

"I like him," he answered. He had a healthy attitude about it.

I had run out of questions already. I was supposed to be asking my son how he was getting along with his mother, but after dropping his bomb of an answer, my whole state of mind had been rattled. I could only think about her marrying Brock.

"How does your brother feel about it?" I asked my son.

"He likes Brock, too. We all went to Jimmy's play-off game together."

I thought about it. Walter had told me before that Jimmy's father was back in the picture and that he had been going to all of his son's games. I asked, "Has Brock ever met Jimmy's father?"

My son nodded. "Yeah, they met. Mr. J.D. comes to *all* the games," he told me again. "My brother's team might make it to the state championship if they win two more games. They have a game on Tuesday. They're in the final eight."

Suddenly I felt like a huge outsider, and I wanted to change the subject immediately. I said, "Well, I'll try and make it out to as many of your track meets as I can. Okay?"

Walter nodded. No big deal again. "Okay," he told me.

Then I changed my mind. "In fact, I'll be at *all* of your track meets," I told him. There I was competing with everybody else, and I couldn't even help myself. I wondered if I would have felt the same way before attending the Million Man March. I had plenty of time to involve myself in Walter's life before then. I began to feel sorry for all of the fathers who paid child support or alimony with no personal involvement with their kids. I was fortunate that Denise and I never took that road. I guess she *had* been supportive of my involvement with Walter. I just wished she could get beyond her personal beef with *me*.

We made it to the sporting goods store inside of the mall, and all that Walter wanted to look at were Nikes.

I said, "Try on these New Balance. I hear that they're *excellent* track shoes."

Walter looked at them and grimaced. There were Nike Swooshes on everything in the store. I hadn't seen a New Balance advertisement in ages. Who says exposure doesn't pay? I wondered how much influence popular culture was having on my son. I knew he didn't wear oversized clothes, because his school wouldn't allow it, nor would his mother. But I wondered how many other things he could have been influenced by.

Nikes it was. The total came to over a hundred dollars. I remember when I could buy two pairs of shoes for *half* that amount. Then again, that was long before Walter was even born.

We walked through the mall and headed to the food court to get something to eat.

I asked Walter if he wanted to buy any tapes or anything while we were there.

"No, it's nothing all that good out," he said.

"What about this guy Mase from Puff Daddy's crew?"

My son looked at me and smiled at my attempt at being *"down."* "I'd rather have Tupac's new tape," he responded.

"Why, is that an East Coast/West Coast thing, and Tupac's more accepted on the West Coast? He was *born* on the East Coast, you know. And besides, Chicago is the Midwest anyway. We shouldn't even be taking sides."

Walter nodded and said, "I know."

"So do you like Allen Iverson or Kobe Bryant?" I asked him. I had been doing my youth culture homework just for him.

"I like Allen Iverson, but my brother likes Kobe Bryant," he answered.

I said, "I guess that's because he's closer to Kobe's size. Your brother might reach six foot eight before he finishes high school."

Walter shook his head. "I don't think so," he said.

"Well, we'll see what happens," I told him. "Does he know what college he'd like to go to yet?"

"Kansas," Walter responded. "He says he likes how they give the big men the ball."

"So he must be expecting to grow taller then."

"I guess so. I guess he can grow another inch or two. I wonder how tall I'll be."

I smiled. "Well, I'm only five foot nine. Even your mother is taller than me when she puts on high heels. Your grandfather on your mother's side was over six feet, and my father is five-ten. So you add that all up, and I'd say you have a good chance of being anywhere from five-eleven to six-one."

My son smiled and nodded his head. "I hope I reach at least six foot."

"Why, you want to play basketball, too?"

"No, not really. I just want to be tall."

"Five foot eleven isn't exactly short," I told him.

"It isn't six foot either."

I couldn't argue with that, and there was nothing I could do about it. I said, "It only matters how big your heart is, son. Only the strong survive, no matter how tall you are. You remember that, because there are plenty of six foot eight guys who are doing absolutely nothing with their lives. Some of these guys have weak hearts and weak character.

"Do you think you have a strong heart?" I asked him.

He nodded. It looked as if he was trying to talk himself into it. "Yeah," he answered.

We walked into the cafeteria section, found ourselves some seats, and both ordered slices of mushroom pizza.

"How come you didn't try any Chinese food?" he asked me.

I shook my head and grinned. "Beverly and I just had some Chinese food last night, General Tao's Chicken."

"Was it good?"

"Yeah, it was pretty good. I've had it before. What about you, you like Chinese food?" No matter how many weekends I spent with my son, it always felt like I was starting over again. I began to think that maybe I could at least keep him for a summer of serious bonding instead of going through the weekend thing. I wondered if Denise would agree to that.

"Yeah, I like *some* Chinese food," he told me, in between bites of pizza. "I like shrimp rolls with duck sauce."

"Yeah, that is a good snack," I agreed. I asked, "Are you planning on going to summer camp this year?"

He hunched his shoulders. "I don't know. Probably."

"Are those tennis rackets I bought you still in good shape?"

He perked up and said, "Yeah. I hardly get a chance to play with them though."

"How about if I got you in a tennis camp this summer? Would you like that?"

"Yeah, that would be fun."

"Have you ever heard of Venus Williams?" I asked him.

"Yeah, I've seen her play. She's *real* tall. Her and my brother would make some tall kids."

I almost choked on my pizza laughing. "Is that so? Does you brother like tall girls?"

"I don't know. But they can't be too short. He would have to bend all the way down to kiss them."

I laughed again and thought about our conversation. I don't remember my father asking me much about anything outside of my grades and my career goals, and I lived at home with him until I left for college at eighteen. I wondered how many fathers actually took time out to talk to their sons about what *they* were interested in. It didn't seem like many conversations were going on with the Generation X kids whether their fathers lived with them or not. I think more fathers were trying to tell their kids what *they* did rather than listening to what their kids wanted to do. Fathers were spending far too much time trying to make their kids understand them, instead of trying to understand their children. I wasn't saying that you let a kid do whatever he wanted to do, because that could lead to disaster. But maybe a different approach to parental communication was needed. Instead of saying, "Listen to me, young man," maybe we should have been saying, "Let's listen to you," and challenge more kids to make sense out of their own lives.

When we got back to the house after a full day of quality father-and-son time, I couldn't wait to tell my wife the news about Denise. By then, Walter and I had watched a new movie at the mall's theater, as well as rented an old one from the video store, because that's what *he* wanted to do, check out some movies he hadn't been able to see.

I didn't get a chance to talk to Beverly alone until eleven o'clock at night when Walter was in bed.

"Guess what?" I asked her. We were in bed ourselves, as usual. It seemed as if Beverly and I did most of our talking at night. We were both such active people during the day that bedtime was one of the few periods where we actually were calm enough to discuss anything in detail, especially when Walter was over.

"Do I really have to guess, or are you going to tell me on your own?"

Beverly was nearly seven months pregnant and really showing, but she refused to stay home from work. The spring semester at school was over in early May, and our child was due in mid-May, so she actually planned to work straight through the pregnancy, and there was nothing I could do to convince her not to. I guess that was the nineties woman for you. Beverly had read all kinds of new books and pamphlets that said it was good for her *and* the baby to keep a normal schedule of activity.

Anyway, I went ahead and told her the news. "Denise is getting married to Brock," I said. Neither one of us had ever met the man, but we had heard enough about him through my son to believe that he was at least a good guy.

Beverly turned and faced me. "Walter told you this?"

"Yes, he did."

She smiled. "I guess now Denise is going to know that *we* know."

I giggled. "I guess she will." Kids were not known for keeping grown-up people's business to themselves, or at least not *my* son.

Beverly thought about it and said, "I wonder if she would invite us to the wedding."

I said, "I wouldn't count on it. The way things are between us, we would probably get into an argument at her wedding."

"Not if you kept your mouth shut," my wife told me. "All you need to say is congratulations, and *nothing* else."

I smiled. "Denise could probably *look* at me and find something to argue about. We can't even stand in the same room together."

"Well, I don't believe she'll be like that if I'm there."

"We'll have the baby by then," I commented.

"You think they're going to have a big wedding?" my wife asked me.

I shook my head. "I doubt it. Unless *he* has a big family, because Denise doesn't. All she has is a sister, a mother, and a couple of girl-friends who she doesn't really have much time for."

"Don't be surprised. People tend to come out of the woods for a wedding ceremony," Beverly responded. "You find yourself sending out invitations to people you haven't seen in ten years. Look at how many people I had to invite to our wedding."

I said, "Yeah, and they were *all* your people."

"I can't help that you had a secluded family," she snapped. "That's why we have to work on your selfishness now. You know we have another session on Monday evening, right?"

Beverly and I had gone to three sensitivity classes, and we were scheduled for five more. She had signed us up for an eight-week program. After the first two sessions, I was ready to move on. I had made a lot of progress already. I wasn't *half* as bad as the rest of the husbands and boyfriends in the program. Beverly and I were the only black couple there. If you think *black* families have problems, sit in on a couple of white family discussions. I had a case of *minor* insensitivity compared to some white men. Black women would never let their men get away with the things that white women allowed. And I wasn't talking about something I had read, I heard it with my own ears.

"Yeah, I know," I mumbled.

"I know you think this program is extreme, Walter, but it's a start. Maybe if you can see how crazy these other guys can be to women and their wives, then you can begin to curb your own attitudes."

"Yeah, but my attitudes are not that bad."

"Nevertheless, we paid for eight sessions, and I expect us to finish them."

My mood was soured. I didn't feel like thinking about those damn sessions! They made you feel so awkward in those groups. I didn't even like how the guy talked to me: "Walter, what are some of the major concerns you have with women? Walter, explain to the group what your perfect relationship would be? Walter, do you have problems speaking to your wife about pressing issues without feeling surges of anger?" Those sessions made me more anxious than an argument with Denise or my wife ever did. Once you begin listening to that flimflam, you can start to believe that you really *are* crazy. White couples have been doing it for years. My only question was, did it really help to solve your problems, or did it only make you dependent upon more sessions before you ended up filing for a damn divorce? Plenty of couples who were married for thirty and forty years never had to put up with a shrink session, so why did I?

I sat there and wondered how Denise would do in one of those sessions. I could imagine her cursing the guy out and asking for a refund. I sat there in bed and grinned at the idea.

Beverly asked, "What is so funny?"

I said, "You don't want to know."

She responded, "You just make sure you remember to be home on time."

Another thing I noticed was that those sessions seemed to be giving Beverly a stronger voice of authority. Or maybe that was the pregnancy again. Whatever it was, I didn't like that so much either.

I was just about to finish up my day at work when Beverly called me at the office to remind me, for the third time, about our counseling session that Monday evening.

I said, "Actually, I was just finishing things up here."

"Okay, well, I'm making us a snack to eat while we're on the way," she responded.

I hung up the phone and shook my head. "She's about to drive me insane with this," I mumbled to myself.

One of my coworkers, Lawrence Isaacs, stopped by to see me before quitting time. He and his wife had just had their third child a few days after Christmas. Lawrence was an easygoing white guy in his early forties, who seemed to know how to turn his assertion off and on when he needed it. Maybe I could learn a thing or two from the guy so that I could last at work and at home without burning myself out.

"So how's your wife's pregnancy coming along?" he asked me.

I said, "I'm not sure. That's what I need to ask *you* about."

"Oh, yeah? Well, spit it out. Is she driving you crazy yet?"

"Exactly," I told him. "Is that normal?"

He broke out laughing. "Of course it's normal. You got a lot of different hormones going on down there, pal. But it really depends on each pregnancy. When my wife was first pregnant with our daughter, Anne, I thought for the life of me that I needed an exorcist. But while she was pregnant with my two sons, Larry Jr. and now Michael, it wasn't all that bad."

"You think it makes a difference between boys and girls?"

"I don't know, maybe it was just the first-child thing. You have a hundred different myths and old wives' tales about these things," he told me. "I'm a guy like you, man. What the hell do I know? I can barely change a damn diaper. I'll just take over when they're teenagers, you know, once the hard part is done," he said with a slap on my shoulder.

Lawrence just confirmed what I already knew: most men didn't think twice about being insensitive. That was just the way we were. I couldn't ask Lawrence about going to some damn shrink! The word could get around at the office, and I could lose the respect of my peers and end up being pushed out of my job.

I smiled and said, "Thanks, man. It's good to know that I'm not the first guy to go through this."

"Yeah, and you won't be the last guy either. You just hang in there, Walter. There's no joy greater than the joy of having a child. Trust me."

I drove my car back home as slowly as I could from work that day. I was trying to come up with the strongest excuse I could offer not to go to any more sensitivity sessions. Maybe what we could use, instead, was a trip out of the country. Spring break was coming up for Beverly at the school, and I had already coordinated it with my first vacation week to spend time with her. I thought about ordering two round-trip tickets to the islands, and calling the money I had spent for the sessions a simple sacrifice.

I had it all planned out by the time I made it home. All I had to do was phone the travel agency that Tuesday, but Beverly was waiting for me at the front door.

She kissed me on the cheek and marched right out the door, heading for the car in the garage.

I said, "Beverly, we need to talk. I've been doing some thinking."

"Okay, we can talk in the car. Come on, it's cold out here."

She was all wrapped up like an Eskimo.

I took a deep breath and let her inside the car. I didn't want her to catch cold. Maybe I should have called her on the cell phone to discuss things before I arrived.

"Okay, what do you want to talk about?"

Before I realized it, I had turned the ignition key and was driving toward Western Avenue to head north for Evanston where the sessions were held, far away from anyone I knew.

I said, "You know, I've been thinking, Beverly. And instead of going to these sessions, what I really need is a good vacation to the islands or something. Maybe even to Hawaii. We could go on vacation during your spring break."

To my surprise, she said, "Yeah, I thought about that myself. After we have the baby this summer, we may not be able to go on a vacation for a while. So that would be a good idea."

"That means you agree with me then?" I asked her.

"Not about canceling our Monday sessions. We'll just have to miss it that week."

Shit! I thought to myself. I finally said, "Look, honey, I'm sorry, but I don't feel comfortable with this thing anymore."

Beverly looked at me with an evil eye. I started thinking of an exorcist myself.

She said, "We have hardly finished *half* of the program. Need I remind you that this was *your* idea?"

"*My* idea? All I did was joke about it. You're the one who took it to the third degree and started calling around."

"You still initiated it with all of your past actions. This is actually something you needed to do a long time ago."

"So how come you didn't tell me *then*?" I was getting so worked up that I hadn't noticed the light was changing to red. I ran right into a busy intersection before I could try and hit the brakes. I should have swerved to my left, pulled back to the right, and kept speeding through, but I wasn't thinking clearly. I jammed the brakes and an overzealous driver, who was already committed to the green light, charged ahead. Instead of screaming, Beverly braced herself for the hit from our right side, the side she sat on.

BANG! The car ran right into us. The seat belt was the only thing that stopped my wife from being thrown into my lap. The first thing I did was try and get her loose. She was pregnant!

I unstrapped her seat belt and tried to slide her out, but Beverly wasn't helping me.

"Try and push yourself out," I told her.

When she faced me, all I saw was her tears and an excruciating look of pain on her face. "I can't!" she hollered at me.

Someone from behind said, "Her leg is stuck." I looked down and noticed that the car door had folded in on her right leg. The entire passenger-side door had been smashed in. If Beverly hadn't braced herself, it could have been much worse. As it was, she was still stuck.

"Someone call the fire department!" the same guy behind me yelled.

"*Fire department?* Call an *ambulance!*" I screamed, grabbing my cell phone.

"They're already on the way!" someone else yelled.

I looked into his face and said, "Thank you." Then I turned back to my wife. I held her hands and asked her, "How do you feel?"

She just shook her head and was unable to talk while crying in severe pain.

"OOHHH, SHIT!" I hollered, clenching my teeth. My emotions were starting to get the best of me.

"You need to stay calm, sir," the guy outside the car told me. "That's not going to do her any good. You have to keep her calm until help gets here."

Instead, I tried to position myself inside the car where I could try and push the door off Beverly's leg. I couldn't just sit there and *wait* for help! My wife was pregnant! The stress could have killed *her and* the baby!

"Sir, I wouldn't advise that. SIR!"

I yelled, "She's *pregnant!* I *need* to get her out!" and continued with what I was doing.

Beverly screamed and grabbed on to me. I knew it would hurt, but I just couldn't sit there and do nothing, so I began to push my right foot against the crushed door with everything I had.

"Try and pull your leg out," I told Beverly.

She shook her head at me.

"Please, Beverly, just try and pull your leg out as I push against the door!"

She grabbed me even harder and screamed, "AHHHH!" as she tried to pull herself free.

"JESUS CHRIST! WAIT FOR THE FIRE DEPARTMENT, SIR! YOU'LL KILL HER, MAN! THINK! THIS JUST ISN'T SMART!"

I ignored the guy, and Beverly was strong enough to pull her leg out. After that, however, her pain seemed to increase. I tried to comfort her but she wouldn't let me.

"NO, NO, NO!" she ranted, pushing me away.

The guy outside the car said, "Her leg might be broken."

There was plenty of blood running down her leg, but it looked as if it was cut more than broken. I took my suit jacket off and tied the sleeve around her leg to try and stop it from bleeding.

The fire department, the police, and the ambulance all arrived at the same time and went into action. It was a good thing we lived on the North Side. I don't know how long we would have been waiting if we lived somewhere else in the city.

I was immediately hauled out of the way.

"THAT'S MY WIFE!" I complained. "SHE'S PREGNANT!"

They wouldn't let me near her, but at least they took in the information. The guy who had helped me along just looked at me and shook his head. I guess he felt sorry for me. He also looked to be reprimanding me for being so defiant. I ignored him again and concerned myself with my pregnant wife as they led her to the ambulance on a stretcher.

"IS HER LEG BROKEN?! IS THE BABY ALL RIGHT?!" I asked them. I was in a state of panic. I didn't even realize that I was yelling.

One of the paramedics grabbed me. "Sir, if you don't calm down, I can't let you ride in the ambulance. Your wife needs you to be calm. Okay? Please."

I shut up and climbed into the ambulance and leaned forward to hold Beverly's hand.

The paramedics advised me not to even speak.

"Your husband is with you inside of the ambulance," they told her. "He's holding your hand."

Beverly squeezed my hand with her eyes closed. I had so many questions to ask, but the pressure from Beverly's hand left me immobile. Suddenly, I just wanted to hold her hand and cry. I broke down like a big baby.

The paramedic grabbed me again and whispered, "Sir, I know this is very difficult for you, but you have to remain calm. What's your wife's name?"

"Beverly," I told him.

"We're almost at the hospital, Beverly. You're gonna be just fine. Your husband is with you."

When Beverly squeezed my hand again, I was able to gain my composure. She seemed to be in full control of her senses. I think they might have numbed her or something to lessen the pain.

We arrived at the hospital emergency entrance, and my wife was immediately rolled into a room.

A doctor stopped me at the door. "Sir, I'm going to have to ask you to wait here. We'll let you know about your wife as soon as we can. She's in stable condition, we just have to run a few tests on her. So far, I've been informed that she's lost a lot of blood from a cut on her leg, and that she's going to need plenty of stitches. So what we need you to do is to remain calm."

I nodded my head and let him walk away. There was a chair right outside the emergency room, but I was too nerve racked to even think about sitting down. I couldn't remain calm either.

"Oohh, shit!" I mumbled to myself. I began to pace back and forth outside the emergency room like a predator. I kept thinking that maybe I should have just gone to the counseling session instead of whining about it. I should have gone if only to please my wife!

"SHIT!" I screamed at myself again. I ignored everyone inside that hallway.

A nurse asked me, "Sir, is there anything I can do for you?"

Why me? I thought to myself. *Why did I have to be this way? Why?*

"Sir?" the nurse asked me again. She put a soft hand on my shoulder. I was too weak to even respond to her. Before I realized it, she was able to sit me down in the chair. "Would you like me to get you some water?" she asked me.

I shook my head. I just wanted to be left alone.

I sunk my face into my hands and mumbled, "Why me, God? What did I do to deserve this?"

It seemed that nothing I ever did turned out right. *What if Beverly had lost the baby?* I thought to myself. *And what if I had killed* both *of them?*

I broke down and began to cry again, thinking of a more urgent question. Knowing that I had almost killed her and our child, I wondered, *Will Beverly still love me when she gets out of the hospital?* I could only hope and pray that she would.

May 1998

KIM and I were talking about moving into a bigger apartment on the South Side when the lease was up in June. The only problem was covering the distance we would have to travel to our jobs. I guess we would just have to leave for work earlier. I was asking Kim to look into finding a daytime gig, and I was poking around at the job myself to see if Roger could get me on line for a daytime position. I had proven that I was accountable. Most of my son's games were late anyway, so I wouldn't miss much. I wanted to be home at night instead of Kim and I alternating shifts and sleep until the weekend.

I had been living with Kim and her son for close to nine months, and it looked like I was going to be with them for a while, so I was thinking about expanding what we had. If we were going to add to the family, we would need more space. My mother was in love with the idea, so much so that she started talking about the "M" word. I guess it was no way around it. Mom kept saying, "If you *know* you're going to be with a woman, and raising children, then the *proper* thing to do is to marry her."

Denise was getting married to Brock, but I didn't have time to be jealous anymore. I had to move on with my own life with Kim. That's just the way it is. You can't keep holding out on sisters, thinking that you're going to luck up with some dream girl or some dream situation, because the shit is a long shot. I had to secure what I had. Kim was willing to hang in there for me, so I had to be willing to hang in there for her.

Little Jay's high school team lost in the semifinals to Fenwick, another school in Oak Park. Fenwick had one of the top high school recruits in the country, Corey Maggett. My son played him toe-to-toe for twenty-eight minutes. Little Jay scored 16 points, had eleven rebounds and four blocks, two of them on Maggett. Maggett still scored 27 points, but he was supposed to, he was a graduating senior. Marc "Speed" Wilkins scored 20 points for Belmont.

Belmont lost the game 67–60, but I was *damn* proud of Jimmy Stewart! I was also proud that he was still pulling up his GPA, past the 3.3 mark. If he kept that up, he would be right on schedule for a Division 1 scholarship. I just had to make sure he got a high enough score on the SATs. I was talking to Denise about summer prep courses. I told her that *I* would be paying for them. I knew it couldn't add up to all of the years of my absence, but it *was* a start, and it was much better than nothing.

As for Jamal, I had him ready to play in a nine-and-under summer camp. Even Kim was looking forward to it. I told her that her support made sense, because even if we had a daughter, she could expect to have sports all up in the place. I told her she might as well get used to it. Sports and manhood went together like women and Oprah Winfrey, and that was the case in more than just America. Men played some kind of sport everywhere around the world. Women, in fact, were starting to catch on with their own enthusiasm for sports. And since Kim had run track in high school herself, I didn't think she would have that much of a problem with it anyway.

J.D.

W E were counting down the days before having our first child. Fortunately, after the car crash Beverly and the baby were all right, but if I didn't get help on correcting my selfishness, my marriage was definitely in trouble. Beverly had suffered a sprained ankle and needed thirty-two stitches in her right leg. Talk about being fortunate; at the time of the accident, I thought it was *much* worse than that. Nevertheless, her sisters blamed me for careless driving, especially since Beverly was expecting. I couldn't argue with them, so I kept my mouth shut. Beverly had not told her sisters about our argument inside of the car just before the accident, and I was happy that she had forgiven me and decided to stick by my side. I knew, however, that I wouldn't have too many more chances to screw up with her. I had to make some serious changes in my attitude and my general approach to the world, which included finding a new field of work that would be more fulfilling to me. Beverly and I had both decided that a real estate venture with my father would not be one of them. We realized that it was necessary for my father and me to distance ourselves so that we could both grow apart, and by doing so, eventually be able to come closer together.

Denise, my son, his brother, Jimmy, and Brock all visited us at the hospital a few days after the accident. Brock was a nice guy. I congratulated them on their wedding plans, and they invited Beverly and me to the ceremony in August. Denise even agreed to let Walter spend the summer with us. In the meantime, I took a leave of absence from my job to spend time with my wife, realizing that I had to stop taking her for granted. I had to learn how to treat everyone with respect and fully appreciate the things that they do. That was obviously baggage that I had picked up from my father. It was a problem that we *both* would have to continue working hard to solve. I just wondered if it was too late to realistically change; too late for myself, and definitely too late for my father. I was just looking forward to having another child, and being a part of the entire experience the second time around. And maybe that would help to change me.

Walter

O U R wedding date was set for August 15, 1998, and the wedding band that Denise had picked out for me was dynamite! She told me she wanted me to make sure that people would notice it, just in case I went somewhere and forgot that I was married. There was no way in the world I was going to do that, because nothing in the world meant more to me than taking Denise up to that altar and saying "I do." I never thought that I would ever anticipate a wedding so much, especially after my divorce, but stranger things have happened.

As far as where we were going to live, Denise understood that it was a "man's thing" for me to want to start over on neutral ground instead of moving in with her. So we began to put our heads together and look at new homes, while planning to rent out the other, just like I had been thinking. Denise said that her mother, sister, and niece could even move into her home. That was fine with me, too, as long as I didn't have to live there. Don't get me wrong, I didn't mind Denise making more money than I did, but I *did mind* not feeling that I could pull my own weight. And you can call it a "man's thing" if you want, but that's the way things were going to be, and Denise understood how I felt without an argument. That's why I loved her so much, she was willing to work it all out with a brother. And besides that, she was simply a hell of a woman; brains, curves, and all.

Brock

I N less than one full year, a hundred different changes have happened; I was getting married in August, both of my sons' fathers were doing their jobs, J.D. had matured with steady employment, Walter Jr. was straightening up *his* act, Jimmy had good grades in high school, Walter III was doing well on his school's track team, Camellia was dating again, Monica had lost her virginity, Levonne was gaining weight, my mother was alive again, Cheron was doing better, and Nikita was still as *trifling* as she ever was. Not *everything* changes, but at least she had a damn job and was not asking me for money so much.

I guess perfection in *this* world is only what you can *hope* to have. Obviously, some people expect more than others. I expected a lot, but I was willing to compromise on some things too. Maybe I compromised too much in the earlier stages of my life, which led me not to give anything later on, not even tears or pity. That's a hard way to live, yet many single mothers are forced to live that reality: a reality of fear based on too much compromise that makes you weak, or no compromise at all that makes you almost inhuman.

Marrying Dennis Brockenborough was a chance, a chance to see if I could expect to have perfection while I was still alive. Most women would like to have a man, whether they want to admit it or not. And most women want a father for their children, yet many have learned and now *expect* to do without. Again, that's a hard way to live, even for someone as successful as myself and Camellia. Who knows when that breaking point will come when you find yourself slipping into darkness, while telling yourself that you're actually making it. Then you find out years later that your kids actually didn't get all that they needed to survive in this hard world they must live in. Not to mention the emptiness that you may have felt while living for years without a stable partner. I didn't want to live that way anymore, with so many questions concerning happiness, and outright lies for answers. So if I offend any superwomen, single mothers out there, then I'm sorry, but I no longer want to be one. And I don't find anything wrong with that. Whoever said that we were supposed to be single mothers in the first place?

Denise

like the sharks and the whales

belong to the ocean

the wind and the birds

belong to the sky

and the roots of the tallest trees

belong to the earth

all by design

and never by accident.

When I first held my son
Time <u>4:33 p.m.</u>, Date <u>May 31st, 1996</u>
I knew I'd never let him go
simply because he was mine
and so was his mother
they belonged to me
and I belonged to them
like the sharks and the whales
belong to the ocean
the wind and the birds
belong to the sky
and the roots of the tallest trees
belong to the earth
all by design
and never by accident.

THE NATURE OF THINGS

by Omar Tyree

Acknowledgments

First off, I want to thank all of the single mothers in the community who allowed me an opportunity to understand the importance of this issue. Single parenthood is definitely one that needs to have an all-out discussion. So let's not read this book as a "fictional" story, but as a spark plug to begin national forums on single motherhood, as well as responsible fatherhood. Without fathers, there would be no single moms because there would be no children. We are not speaking of test-tube babies and storks dropping kids on the doorsteps of thousands of homes in our communities. Therefore, we need to come to some concrete and realistic solutions that include men *and* women. I also would like to acknowledge the many single fathers in the community. I have not forgotten about you; however, I can only write one book at a time. So feel free to include your concerns.

In the process of getting this book completed, I would like to thank my agent, Denise Stinson, for pushing to have our new contract done and signed in time to continue my work. I am not a "hold-out" kind of guy. However, if we ever make that New York top twenty list, we can expect to up the stakes accordingly (smile). We'll just have to wait and see if the community of readers supports me enough to push me to that big-time level of American literature.

I want to thank my new editor, Marion Maneker, for your patience and psychological approach; "Omar, maybe for your next book, you want to think about sticking to fewer storylines and creating a definite plot. Then again, your books cover a lot of different issues with one story often following upon another." (These are not your exact words, but I did get the point, and I do agree.) So our next book, for the same time next year, will be *Sweet St. Louis*, a classic love story for the relationship-loving ladies, and the emotionally dieting men. Stay tuned out there for a real black love story! I also want to thank Marion for having the courage not to follow trends with our groundbreaking cover design. Fight the power of the copycat! Let's always do something challenging and new . . . that is, as long as it *works* (smile).

I want to thank Karintha and Ameer for putting up with Jekyll-and-Hyde Dad again, for four whole months this time. And Ms. Jewly and family for taking Ameer into your tight-knit clan of kids. Bless you! As you can see, the boy has as much energy and persistence as his dad (smile)! I wouldn't have been able to get anything done without you, Ms. Jewly. Thanks a million!

And then I want to thank all the individuals who helped me in the creative process of this book, as well as new friends who are actively pushing my career forward. My Chicago crew: attorney Randy Crumpton, Dawn Kelly, Beatrice Shoular, Jeff Roshell, DaTasha Harris, DeShong Perry, cousins Derek Hughes and Lee Gray, and authors La-Joyce Brookshire and E. Lynn Harris. My Philly crew: Pamela Artis, Vanesse j. Lloyd Sgambati, Uncle Joe, Larry Robin, Lecia and Joel Brickerstaff, Betty Jean, Kellie L. Dutton, Dawn Jones, Steve Satell, and Stephanie Renee. My New York soldiers: Yvette "Stay Busy" Hayward, Pam Crockett, Esq., Christene Saunders, Jackie Jacob, and Ed Lover and Dr. Dre for putting me on the mike up there. Peace & Love, brothers. Let's do it again like J. J. Walker, Bill Cosby, and Sidney Poitier in some seventies zoot suits (smile). My New Jersey connections: Evangelia Biddy, Sundiata and Shondalon, and Uncle George. My Florida soldier: author extraordinaire Lolita Files. My D.C./Maryland/Virginia peeps: Brother Simba and Brother Yao, Walter "Rap" Pearson, Kwame Alexander, Mercedes Allen, Georgianna Bodwin, Rashena Wilson, Gigi Roane and Willie Jennings, author Ralph Wiley, Derrick McGinty for putting me on the mike in D.C., and Kojo Nnamdi for putting me on the tube. My North Carolina crew: cousin Priscilla "The AKA" Tyree, Bruce Bridges, Byron Johnson, and Tekoa K. Hash. My Delawareans: Kendra Patterson and family, Teresa Knox, Haneef Shabazz and family, and Lynette Edwards and family. And plenty of new friends I've met along the way: author Denene Millner, Kay Burdy, Cathy Harrell, Tammie

Wright, Ann Hart and family, Rod Ambrose, Ebony Williams . . . And to everyone else, make sure I include you next time.

To all the readers who love my work, always stay tuned for my next one, because whatever it may be, it will always be thoughtful and will always say something to the community.

Peace & Love

Omar Tyree

About the Author

O M A R T Y R E E , a native of Philadelphia, is an author, jour-
nalist, lecturer, and poet. His books include *Flyy Girl, Capital
City, BattleZone, A Do Right Man,* and *Single Mom.* He lives in
New Castle, Delaware.

To learn more about Omar Tyree, view his Web site at
www.OmarTyree.com, send an e-mail to Omar8Tyree@aol.com,
or write to MARS Productions, P.O. Box 12814, Wilmington, DE
19850.

Look for Omar Tyree's New Hardcover in
October 1999 from Simon & Schuster

EVEN A STREET-SMART LOVE STORY CAN HAVE AN OLD-FASHIONED, HAPPY ENDING.

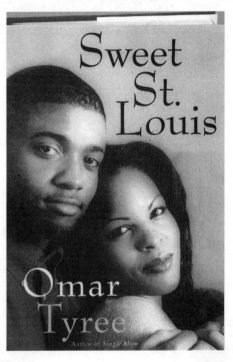

**Also available in
paperback by Omar Tyree**

To learn more about
Omar Tyree, visit his Web site
at www.OmarTyree.com